UNDER A

DESERT SKY

"Under a Desert Sky," by Loren Lockner. ISBN 1-58939-890-4.

Library of Congress Control Number on file with publisher.

Published 2006 by Virtualbookworm.com Publishing Inc., P.O. Box 9949, College Station, TX 77842, US. ©2006, Loren Lockner. All rights reserved. No part of this publication may be reproduced, stored in a retrieval system, or transmitted in any form or by any means, electronic, mechanical, recording or otherwise, without the prior written permission of Loren Lockner.

Manufactured in the United States of America.

UNDER A DESERT SKY

by Loren Lockner

Prologue

The finely boned, petite girl plunged breathlessly down the expensively carpeted mauve hallway before halting abruptly outside the double glass doors leading to the hotel director's office suite. Her tightly braided black hair, hanging halfway down her back, flung wildly from side to side as she searched for an avenue of escape. Elena froze suddenly, her pretty dark head tilted to one side, listening intently. Weren't those barely discernable muffled sounds the quiet even pad of approaching footsteps? The tiny, blue-uniformed maid desperately rattled the resort director's glass door, but it was securely locked and she had no time to search for the correct key hanging among the large bunch attached to her slim waist.

The young woman, called Lena by her friends, spotted the men's washroom only a few yards farther down the immaculate hall, just past a large potted palm. The small Latino girl bolted to the heavy oak paneled door, pulling the heavy brass latch downward, praying to the Holy Virgin that she hadn't automatically relocked the door after cleaning the expensively designed facility only one hour ago. Fortunately, the paneled door swung open silently, thanks to well-oiled hinges, and Elena darted quickly inside, easing the heavy door shut behind her. A short entrance hall decorated with full-length ornate mirrors edged in fancy gold designs depicting intertwining wine leaves gave way to the square facilities of the immaculate restroom. Shiny clean urinals lined the huge, tiled washroom's left-hand side, while porcelain sinks, surrounded by lovely stone gray tile, hung below huge gold-framed mirrors.

Hugging the back wall stood four spotless stalls and the lovely Hispanic woman hurried toward them. Which one, she debated, her dark eyes flitting between each of the four cubicles. Resolvedly, Lena picked the third stall, locking the gray metal door behind her before jumping onto the toilet seat, enabling her telltale feet to be tucked safely out of view. The terrified girl held her breath and listened intently. At first it appeared reassuringly still, but then she discerned a faint padding sound coming from the wide hall beyond the men's room. The prolonged strain and ensuing panic threatened to tumble Lena off her awkward perch as she realized they were indeed deliberately quiet steps. Worse yet, they were headed unrelentingly her way.

Under a Desert Sky

Striving for self-control, Elena willed herself to keep still, pressing both sweating palms firmly against the cold painted metal of the stall's sides. She leaned her damp forehead upon the closed door and listened intently. All the nagging doubts the young woman had bottled up inside over the past few weeks threatened to overwhelm her and Elena chided herself for her enormous stupidity. She'd made the fatal mistake of so many poor and uneducated women; the error of determining that a rich man could free her from the restrictive dead-end of poverty, sparing her the same fate that had befallen both her mother and grandmother. All those pretty things Lena had so desperately craved suddenly seemed grossly insignificant, and, if the truth could be told, might lead to her premature death.

The faint swish of the nearly silent outer door's methodical opening made her freeze anew. Her pursuer's steps were slow and precise. Breathlessly, she counted those measured paces, knowing it took less than five to turn the corner of the small hall that led into the large square men's room. The murderer, who only twenty-four hours previously had seemed the perfect lover, stopped abruptly, and Lena sensed him peering into the seemingly empty room. Unable to hold her breath any longer, Lena forced herself to breathe through her nose, hoping he couldn't hear the desperately controlled inhalations. Her pounding heart thudded so loudly inside her chest that the tiny woman, who had desired way too much, was positive the stalker could hear its traitorous sound. Finally, and unbelievably,

Elena discerned the soft shuffle of departing movements, and later the nearly silent hiss of the heavy outer door closing. Still, unconvinced, she waited, not trusting the rapidly burgeoning hope that he'd really and truly gone.

After two full minutes Lena finally relaxed and slowly placed first one black utility shoe and then the other upon the gleaming tiles she herself had scrubbed less than ninety minutes ago. Slim legs shaking and aching from the strain of balancing herself on the uncomfortable toilet seat Elena cautiously slid the metal latch left and swung open the door, simultaneously relieved and amazed at her escape.

There was no time to scream or pray. Elena's black eyes widened in mute recognition of her killer. His own dark eyes remained as cold as the knife that suddenly sliced unmercifully at her neck, even though Lena stretched her hand out in a hopeless plea, uttering his once-welcomed name. Oddly enough there was no initial pain, only a sudden gush of warmth at her throat. She felt herself falling as a strange horrifying numbness overtook her unresponsive limbs. When the shapely uniformed girl hit the hard cold tiles, Elena was oddly aware of tiny crimson droplets splattering his expensive dark leather shoes. The floor became increasingly icy to the dying girl until at last a huge wave of darkness mercifully took her last breath away.

The unrepentant man reached for a paper towel and slowly and deliberately wiped his knife clean, folding the switchblade deftly before removing his thin latex gloves and shoving them and the knife into a large black trash bag.

Under a Desert Sky

He shrugged off the long white lab coat he'd worn especially for the occasion and carefully bent and wiped the splattering of blood from his expensive Italian shoes with a clean sleeve of the coat and stepped away from the widening pool of blood, gazing for a moment at the small, still body that had given him so much physical pleasure.

The coat was soon carefully deposited in the garbage bag and the murderer stepped gingerly around the deepening red puddle to quietly move out of the men's room, pausing before the ornate mirror in the hall to adjust his silk blue tie and smooth back his damp hair. He cautiously turned off the light switch with the cuff of his still white shirtsleeve, which had miraculously avoided any encounter with blood. The killer glanced down at his gold Rolex and noted the time, which read just after one in the morning. A much-deserved rest was in order and this time the outer oaken door creaked shut with an awful finality.

Chapter 1

When Nicole Lewis walked through the swinging doors of the Palm Springs Police Department on this Monday morning, right after the fourth of July weekend, she nearly collided with Otto Presman, the department photographer. Her coffee sloshed and the bag holding Dusty's favorite jelly donuts hit the floor with a muffled thud.

"Sorry," Otto threw over his thin shoulder as he raced by. Amy, the plump redheaded desk officer and dispatcher, leaned over the high counter and flashed a sympathetic grin.

"I wouldn't be getting too comfortable Nicole, since it looks like you'll be heading out again in just a minute."

"Really?" asked Nicole picking up the crumpled sack and grimacing at the sad shape of the squashed donuts inside. Hopefully Dusty wouldn't notice the condition of the besmeared sweet bread.

"There's been a homicide at The Desert Sky Hotel and Golf Resort. Captain Hernandez is gathering the task force together as we speak," the busty redhead announced with relish.

Nicole frowned and hurried through the busy, over-worked department to her large gray metal desk. Laden with paperwork as usual, it appeared relatively neat considering the caseload she and Bud had taken on over the past few months. A recent photo of her brother's happy family smiled up at her, bright and cheerful in its Navajo print frame. Nicole smiled back, looking forward to seeing her little niece Carrie in a couple weeks while enjoying the damp coolness of San Diego. She squared her shoulders and scanned the busy squad room. The homicide and vice task force, of which she was a part, reminded her of a chaotic scene from one of her favorite reruns, *Hill Street Blues*, with its constant noise and harried personnel scurrying about the hectic department. Nicole placed the two hot coffees gingerly near her healthy philodendron and tossed the tan shoulder bag onto her gray desk chair while checking for Dusty Morant.

Dusty's cluttered desk was empty and Nicole frowned at the small pile of empty candy wrappers mixed among the piles of projects her colleague currently worked on. Although his computer hummed and an energetic Elvis screen-saver gyrated over the dark monitor, Dusty was nowhere to be found. Nicole finally pinpointed Dusty and the rest of her small unit massed in Captain Hernandez's too cramped office. She grabbed a pen and pad, and bringing the donuts and coffee with her, tapped on Jerry's door before entering.

"My donuts," chortled the portly Dusty, a wide grin spreading across his freckled face. Nicole smiled and tossed him the white paper sack, hoping once again that her overweight friend didn't mind squashed donuts, and placed the styrofoam cups on her superior's neat desk.

"Glad you could make it Nicole," stated her slim Captain without rancor, glancing at his watch. Jerry Hernandez always managed to look calm and under control, no matter what the situation, in his pressed white shirt and dark brown suit with its coordinated pale beige and gold silk tie. Jerry in turn assessed her slim form dressed professionally in an understated tan suit with a yellow chemise peeking underneath and nodded. Nicole's delicate oval face remained serious but her steady blue eyes indicated she already knew what was going down.

Captain Hernandez's special homicide and vice unit consisted of two uniformed officers; Nancy Williams, a trim, efficient blonde woman of twenty-nine, and her partner Lee Gianotti, a graying, gregarious career officer in his late fifties, who spent much of his free time teasing the younger members of the squad about their lack of experience compared to his thirty-odd years of service. The hefty Dusty's official title was Police Sergeant, but he spent the majority of his time ensconced in front of his computer squirreling out all the subtle information regarding people and events that everyone else seemed to miss. Occasionally, he complained to the captain that he didn't see enough action and Jerry would assign him to a few days with one of the two teams. Usually a couple days outside the station cured Dusty of his yearnings for several months. Nicole's partner, Bud, leaned against the wall as he sipped coffee and listened intently to his captain.

"I've just sent Otto out to take photos and help cordon off the area. The forensics team will meet us there. Hotel security has shut down the executive wing until we arrive." Jerry didn't notice Nicole's lifted eyebrows recollecting her sudden encounter with the department photographer, and continued. "Bud, you and Nicole lead on this. Nancy and Lee, hook up with the coroner and the hotel management at the scene. Dusty, I want all the information you can muster regarding the resort and its tenants and we'll meet back together at 9:30 a.m. and try to piece the details together. Mr. Zachary, the hotel's top executive, will meet us at the scene. I want quick action on this homicide since the Mayor has already called, wanting to know if this murder is somehow race related." The phone blared and as Captain Hernandez took the call Nicole's tall partner beckoned to her.

"Come on 'pard'," ordered Bud. A muscular Hispanic-looking man in his late forties; he had a penchant for rock and roll and motorcycle racing. She followed him out of the Captain's office and tweaked his thick ponytail.

"You understand what's happening?" he asked, poking at Dusty in front of him who turned and grinned, powdered sugar frosting his upper lip. Bud put his hands up as if to ask where his donut was and Dusty shrugged, pointing at Nicole accusingly who shook her short chestnut curls sadly.

"Sorry Bud, you know Maggie has strictly forbidden you to have any more of those greasy donuts and I don't want to get on her bad side. And, as for the case, it's a homicide at The Desert Sky. I got that tidbit from a *very* reliable source." Bud smiled at Nicole's reference to Amy, who invariably knew everything first, and gazed dejectedly at Dusty who placed the coffee and half-eaten donut on his desk out of Bud's reach.

"Who's the victim?" asked Nicole, hoping to distract him.

Bud checked his notes. "Female, Hispanic, late teens to early twenties and a housekeeper at the hotel. Not sure of much else except she was found in the executive men's room with her throat cut. She's probably an illegal, thus explaining our Mayor's justifiable concern after the Rodriquez incident."

The Rodriquez incident was a hate crime perpetuated by some teen-aged neo-Nazi types who had waylaid a young illegal citrus worker out in the desert and proceeded to hang him from a date palm. He and Nicole had broken the case less than two months ago and personally, Bud hoped this crime wasn't somehow related. The senseless act had affected both of them more than he cared to admit, so he watched Nicole's countenance carefully. Her pretty, calm face stared back at him, appearing far younger than her 31 years. A straight, slightly freckled nose rested below steady blue eyes and her shoulder-length thick tawny hair was styled in a practical, but attractive under-turned style, trying its best not to curl. Nicole carried herself straight-shouldered and proud, even though she measured a fairly tall 5'8" in her stocking feet. In deference to her job and height she wore low-heeled tan pumps that were also a great deal more comfortable than their dispatcher Amy's ankle-breakers. Soft-spoken and efficient, often head-strong and pugnacious, and totally, always unashamedly honest; Nicole still believed she and Bud could make a difference in the multi-cultural desert region she'd come to love so much. Bud adored her and those too-rigid shoulders, but he couldn't resist a light-hearted jab.

"A bit overdressed for the occasion," he added cheekily, hoping to get a rise from her, knowing full well she'd bought the smart tan suit only this weekend during the holiday sales.

"I thought I was going to be happily working all day on the Monroe investigation. The way things are going I'm going to have to take another holiday just to finish up all the paperwork!"

Chapter 2

Nicole had originally never felt that the stark beauty of the desert could ever appeal to her. Born and raised in Ventura County, near the ocean in the peaceful town of Ojai, she had thrived in the oak and avocado tree laden valleys of the region situated north of the dominating and bustling city of Los Angeles. Her mother and father had loved the small inland city, tucked miles away from the shore, where her father worked as a police officer patrolling the beautiful beach areas of Ventura his two children so loved to visit. As a child, Nicole vividly remembered the Saturday drives to Ventura and their subsequent strolls along the beach as she kicked up the sand and heard the shrieks of the seagulls overhead. She had body-surfed with her bother David, buried her cousins Mike and Shannon up to their necks in sand, and battled sunburn and freckles all her young life, her skin too fair to tan properly.

Police work had run in the Lewis family. Her mother had been a police dispatcher for over twenty-five years and her father had been a beat officer before retraining and transferring to the California Highway Patrol. Her older brother pursued a similar career with the FBI, much to his parent's approval and Nicole's undisguised envy. Within three years he was receiving justified accolades from his peers and had been promoted twice. So it seemed only natural that Nicole would follow in her family's footsteps and graduate from the Academy; beginning work in the Santa Barbara Police Department with the blessings of her family.

Nicole, at twenty-four, had for four wonderful years devoted all her time and energy to the University town with its beautiful mission, unspoiled beach, and interesting architecture. But the tight-knit family had spread out now, with David transferring to the San Diego area to work for the Bureau while raising a beautiful little daughter with his lawyer wife, Beth. Both her rambunctious cousins had married and moved to points east and north, and her beloved parents now rested side by side in the quiet Santa Barbara cemetery near the church they'd exchanged wedding vows in some thirty-five years earlier; her mother quietly following her husband in death only eighteen months after his tragic murder. Suddenly the entire Santa Barbara and Ventura area seemed sterile and empty without her family and vital support system and when a job offer beckoned her to the southern desert regions, Nicole had leapt at the chance.

Her breakup with Mark Leone, a fellow officer in Vice, had certainly been a motivation, but with her vulnerable heart aching but not broken, that hadn't been the only impetus. Mark had initially appeared in every aspect to support the ambitions and obvious police skills of Nicole, but when it came to making that final matrimonial commitment, both he and Nicole hesitated. Mark suddenly decided he wanted a wife in a less dangerous job, someone who was a helpmate, not a competitor in his own field.

"I need to know that my wife is home safe, not pinned to a wall dodging the knife of some zoned-out junkie or crackhead. You're the best and most dedicated officer I've ever had the pleasure to work with, but I need someone less ambitious to go home to. I want to be with someone who really doesn't understand my job as well as I do, or even want to." He had begged her understanding and Nicole had looked into his sad hazel eyes and nodded forlornly, a little piece of her dying in the process. It had been the piece that up until his concise and shattering statement, had really believed that two police officers could marry and have some sort of normal life as lovers, friends, and co-workers.

But Mark Leone had, after all these years, given her the opportunity to prove that she was not simply Sergeant Gerald Lewis's daughter or Special Agent David Lewis's sister, but Nicole Lewis, police detective; a separate entity dependant upon no one but herself, her successes and her failures her own to claim. If Nicole was not what another officer might desire as a dream mate, she was at least satisfied with herself, and secretly vowed to never date another man on the force again. Nicole resolutely took the offered detective training and three months after its completion transferred to a place where no one knew her family's reputation or how her father had died. It was a pleasure to finally get out of those too-restrictive police blues.

So Nicole admired the scenic landscape of Palm Springs as she and Bud headed east toward The Desert Sky Resort, which was located closer to Palm Desert than the ritzy town of Palm Springs. The San Jacinto Mountains towered above the city, promising each evening to deftly obliterate the strong rays of the scorching sun by casting the city into deep shadow. The cactus and sand would subsequently take on orange and purple hues, and in the winter a substantial chill would overtake the desert town, so carefully manicured and watered, lush in its man-made humidity.

Every weekend after her first hectic month in that Desert City of the Stars, Nicole had taken off in her trusty Toyota Corolla and headed east toward the desert. She'd climbed the steep road to Yucca Valley and hiked among the rarely blooming plants after which the high desert valley was named, or visited Indio, even attending the famed date festival. During the spring she broadened her explorations and observed the Ramona Pageant in Hemet and played at the dam in Lake Perris. The mountains above the emerald city became an escape when it got too hot and Nicole haunted the quaint shops of Idyllwild and swam in Lake Hemet, often camping with newfound friends from her local hiking club.

Her friend and accountant Sherri Matthews, a successful African American graduate of USC, constantly insisted that Nicole needed to meet someone and was notorious for setting her up with 'successful' eligible men. After the first few fiascos Nicole halted her overzealous friend's matchmaking and dated casually though infrequently, never finding anyone who possessed the quiet assurance and confidence Nicole had finally determined were the key qualities she was looking for in a mate. That and the heartfelt demand that a potential mate render total acceptance of her career choice and quest for personal independence, she added quietly to herself. Nicole determined finally, over the past couple of years, that she might never find that ideal man and thus threw herself into her work, never once dreading her next workday or worrying that at age 31 she was destined to become a spinster as her great-Aunt Elizabeth so predicted with a horrified face. Aunt Elizabeth had been married four times and had never yet found contentment from any of her trips down the aisle, so Nicole quietly tucked her aunt's advice deep into the remotest recesses of her mind, positive that marriage guaranteed no happiness if Elizabeth was any example.

So the desert region became her home and her future. It was here, Nicole determined, she would build her own reputation and friendships. She became an admirer of the stark land's purple hues and blowing sand. Nicole purchased a good camera with a powerful telephoto lens and began photographing the flora and fauna of the region. Her small apartment's walls were soon lined with enlarged snapshots of her new environment. Among them were photos of a Greater Roadrunner pausing near its nest in a clump of cactus and a Costa's Hummingbird with its violet hood hovering over the dry chaparral. Beside them, in startling crimson, perched the Vermilion Flycatcher, a native of distant Argentina that often haunted the oasis of Palm Springs and whom Nicole had personally stalked near a large golf course for over two grueling hours. The beautiful photograph now adorned her white-washed walls, intermixed with candid photos of her scattered family, including her favorite of her little niece Carrie straddled upon a giant tortoise at the San Diego Zoo's petting center.

Nicole could now point out Bob Hope's large mushroom shaped house on the hill, narrow down to several streets the places where vice was common outside the tourist community of central Palm Springs, and locate the spiciest enchiladas in the desert less than a mile from her apartment. So, as she and Bud pulled into the hectic Desert Sky's parking lot and maneuvered around the flashing lights of the police cruisers, Nicole braced herself for one of the more unfortunate aspects of her career, confident she could handle a young woman's brutal murder just like all the other traumatic events of her life.

Under a Desert Sky

The glaring florescent lights illuminating the crime scene made the posh tiled bathroom look surrealistic. The tiny Hispanic girl outstretched in a pool of her own blood was real enough and Nicole wanted to gasp, but she'd learned long ago not to show any emotion in the face of such brutality. A woman in her position could not be thought of as too emotional or soft. Her father had taught her well, instructing her early on that the cool, levelheaded woman who thought first and spoke later was deemed as effective as any man. It was tough enough being a detective under the best of circumstances, and for a woman in a predominately male field it was vital to remain professional at all costs. Nicole tore her saddened dark blue eyes away from the bloodstained girl and focused on what Captain Hernandez was saying.

He spoke in low tones to Otto Presman, whose beloved camera seemed permanently affixed to his shoulder, and another police officer who was unknown to her., Jerry, motioned for Bud and Nicole to join them.

"Nicole Lewis, Bud Ochoa, this is Officer Nelson. He was first on the scene this morning." Nicole and Bud solemnly shook hands with the middle-aged uniformed officer who looked tired and dejected and kept running a hand through his thinning, gray-streaked hair. He flipped through his hand-sized notepad, reading them the background facts of the homicide in a gravelly voice.

"The girl's name is Elena Gonzalez. She's a housekeeper at the resort and was identified by one Rosa Leon who discovered the body about an hour ago. Gonzalez

19

worked the late shift last night and this was apparently her floor. From the looks of it, Ms. Gonzalez wasn't cleaning the bathroom at the time of the murder even though it appears she was coming out of this stall." He motioned toward the third cubicle whose blood-splattered door stood halfway open.

Officer Nelson bent down and pointed at the girl's throat and Nicole bit her lip. "It was a clean cut, just one stroke. Poor kid didn't even have a chance." The world-weary officer shook his head grimly and mumbled, "Not much older than my girl at UC."

"What could she have been doing in the men's bath-room if she wasn't cleaning it?" muttered the Captain more to himself than anyone else.

Nicole was used to her slim Captain thinking out loud and answered. "Running away from someone perhaps?"

Jerry Hernandez nodded grimly in agreement. "Time frame?" he asked.

"I'd place the murder at sometime between midnight and four a.m.," answered Officer Nelson. "The blood is becoming dry at the edges. The housekeeper Rosa found her at..." he checked his notes, "exactly 7:50 this morning. It'll take forensics to narrow down the actual time any closer." The four moved away as Otto methodically snapped photos from every angle. Nicole noticed Otto's thin, freckled face appeared paler than usual.

Jerry motioned to Nicole. "Mr. Zachary, the Resort's Di-rector, just verified her identity. You might want to check with him first for any insight and later speak to the girl, Rosa. That'll give her a chance to calm down. She's outside with Nancy and was understandably too upset to get much out of earlier. See what you can do, and while you're at it send Nancy down here. I want her to check out the stairs and elevator as well as the staff locker room. Zachary seemed a little pale and may have hotfooted it to another men's room. You'll just have to check around." To the gathering police crew, armed in rubber gloves and emotionless expressions, Jerry ordered "Begin dusting and check all the other stalls. Bag anything and everything that looks even mildly suspicious."

Nicole stepped outside the claustrophobic men's room and took a deep steadying breath. Yellow police tape already sectioned off the area outside the restroom and uniformed officers scurried through the wide hallway. Nicole searched the corridor but saw no one resembling a hotel executive. Lee Gianotti stood jotting down some notes outside the taped perimeter.

"You seen Mr. Zachary, the head official here?" she asked of her colleague who glanced up and grinned, a smug expression on his lined face.

"Sure did. He hightailed it that-a-way, appearing a bit under the weather for all his good looks. You'll probably find him in the stairwell. He appeared as if he could use some air." Lee flipped a nonchalant finger in the direction of the emergency exit.

Nicole opened the fire door and headed down the echoing stairs. She welcomed the quiet coolness of the stairwell, the sight of the young girl lying in her own blood affecting her more than she cared to admit.

She turned the corner and found a slender man leaning against the gray walls, his forehead pressed against the cool paint, hands splayed against the concrete sides.

"Mr. Zachary?" asked Nicole tentatively.

The tall man turned and Nicole met his face with a shock. He proved to be exceptionally handsome, in a dark exotic way, with straight raven-black hair swept back over doe brown eyes, above a straight nose. His full lips, perfectly set in light olive skin, now held an unhealthy pallor. Tall and slim, his physique resembled that of a long-distance runner, though stylishly dressed in a beautifully tailored gray suit befitting his role as hotel executive. But it was none of his ample physical attributes that startled Nicole, it was the unshed tears in his dark brown eyes and the way his anguished breath hissed in short ragged spurts that reminded Nicole cruelly of the personal tragedy of the moment. A young woman had brutally died and the chief executive who'd observed the horrible reality of her senseless death was deeply affected by it.

"Yes, I'm Justin Zachary," he managed to whisper as a rebellious tear trickled down his lean face.

His desolation and grief were so overwhelming that Nicole felt a tremor course through her rigid body. Nicole immediately became aware that Justin Zachary was embarrassed at anyone witnessing the unveiled extent of his agony and now desperately tried to regain some semblance of control. Nicole fumbled in her tan handbag and removed a small package of tissues.

"Here, take these. I'll wait for you at the top of the stairs whenever you feel ready to speak to me. Please take your time, there's really no hurry."

She discreetly left him to battle his sorrow and quietly ascended the concrete steps to wait. Justin Zachary took a full five minutes before slowly climbing the wide steps of the stairwell. Having regained control he resolutely stood before her, his eyes still red from grief.

"You needed to talk to me?" he managed.

"Yes," she flipped out her badge. "I'm Detective Lewis and have been assigned to this case. I realize that now might not be the best time for you to speak to me, considering the graphic nature of the crime, and wondered if you could come down to the station later this morning for an interview?"

He hesitated for a moment, scanning her delicate oval face and frank blue eyes before answering.

"Thank you Detective. I never expected such discreet compassion from the police and want you to know that I appreciate your empathy. I do need some time to collect myself so I can guarantee I'll present an adequate face to those people who depend on my calm demeanor for strength and guidance." The words were gently self-mocking as if only he knew the façade necessary to calm his subordinates.

"The young woman met a terrible end and even to those of us who have witnessed this type of thing before, it still remains horrifying. I just wanted to let you know that one of my colleagues will be checking the stairwell any minute now and you might, um, want to find another place to..."

"Retreat?"

Nicole nodded in sympathy.

The young executive took a deep breath and held out the small package of Kleenex, now clearly missing several tissues. "I'll meet you at the station at half past nine."

Justin Zachary made no move to vacate the stairwell so she decided to leave him to the quiet confides of the sterile walls. As the swish of the swinging doors shut behind her, Nicole held his disturbing image in her mind, somehow more deeply moved by his emotion than his hauntingly handsome image.

Nancy Williams, appearing efficient and calm in her pressed blue uniform, spoke gently to a slim Hispanic girl farther down the hall who was crying softly. Nicole approached them slowly.

"Rosa," said Nicole softly. "I'm Detective Nicole Lewis. Could you come into the office here and we'll talk about what happened?" Nancy nodded sympathetically at the Latino girl and headed for the crime scene, joining up with her partner Lee, who motioned toward the exit stairs and distant elevators.

Nicole led the distraught young woman into the personnel office where several couches and chairs of muted gray and mauve hugged its expensively decorated decor. The personnel office bespoke of the same high standards of design the rest of the hotel and golf resort boasted. Nicole had only been to the five-star resort once before, attending a lecture by a prominent African American novelist who had written several biting mystery novels pleading for the empowerment of women and an end to racism. It seemed ironic that Nicole now sat with the pretty, dark-haired maid, who sagged so forlornly upon the couch weeping bitterly for another lost sister. She wished it were simply a mystery novel and not a real murder drama unfolding in glaring realism. Death was so final, with no way to rewrite the final chapter.

Nicole put her arm around the young woman's slim shoulders and tried to comfort her. The girl was pretty, boasting beautiful hands and oval black eyes overflowing in tears. A pleasant voice spoke softly behind them.

"Here's some tissue and water." An attractive blonde woman in her early thirties, dressed in a stunning lavender suit, held out a box of scented tissues and placed a glass of water in front of the trembling girl. Nicole removed a couple of white squares and handed them to the girl, trying desperately to regain control. "I'm Judith Chamberlain, director of Personnel here at The Desert Sky," said the attractive older woman politely at her side. "If there's anything I can do to help, just ask."

"Thanks. As a matter of fact, you can check your files for any information regarding the deceased young woman and make me a copy. The facts regarding her are sketchy at most. It would save a lot of time in the long run and I'd really appreciate it."

"Of course," Judith replied without hesitation, and hurried away, speaking briskly to a pretty, dark-haired secretary sitting slumped in her office chair. The young woman roused herself, and together she and her boss began opening filing cabinets.

Nicole returned her attention to the sniffling girl. "Can you talk now Rosa?"

"Si...I mean yes. I didn't know you detectives were women." She took the offered tissue and blew her nose loudly.

"Just your luck of the draw since my partner's a man. Could you tell me exactly what happened this morning as best you can remember?"

"You mean when I saw her?" whispered Rosa, and Nicole nodded. Rosa took a deep breath. "I arrived as usual. My shift starts at 7:30. I always get ready the offices for the day. You know, unlock the supply rooms, open the toilets, and turn on all the lights. Everyone comes in between eight to 8:30. Then I go down to the main lobby. That's part of my job, you know." Her Spanish accent was thick, but Nicole had no difficulty following her.

"Yes...?" soothed Nicole encouragingly.

"I opened the women's bathroom, but the men's, it was already unlocked. I think to myself that strange you know. The lights, they were off, so I turned them on. I know Elena. She always clean the bathrooms every night and lock them, so I think it strange. She is real good at her job, you know. And, and, there she was. So still, so much blood. I don't know what to do. I scream I think. Ms. Chamberlain and her secretary, Genny, they come. I don't remember much after that. I think they call the police. I'm not much sure." She placed a slim hand to her forehead and Nicole dug into her purse for some aspirin. Rosa swallowed the two tablets with a gulp of water.

"What time did you enter the men's room this morning?"

"Maybe 7:45, I don't know. Maybe later." She gestured vaguely. Nicole noticed Rosa was attired in the same light blue uniform the blood-soaked Elena wore.

"Maybe this will help," broke in Judith Chamberlain, handing Nicole a thin manila file. "I noted the time exactly when I called the police. 7:50 this morning. Here's the file on Elena Gonzalez. She'd only been with us about six months." Judith Chamberlain looked sad. "Just 19-years-old. Would you like some coffee, officer?"

Nicole had finished off her coffee and one of Dusty's doughnuts in Bud's old bronze Chevy, but needed the reassurance of more of the warm liquid. "Yes, if you please, with a little milk, no sugar." To the trembling younger woman she continued. "What were Elena's hours, Rosa?"

"She work from 5 p.m to 1 a.m.. I think it's called the swing shift. She say she like it when there is no noise. To me it's too quiet. Me, I like noise."

"Does anyone work between the time she's off to when you come in for your shift?"

"No, not being hotel rooms to clean, they don't need no one. This area is always locked up after six. Only Elena and Mrs. O'Toole have a key I think. She's our boss." Nicole made note of Mrs. O'Toole's name and continued.

"Was there anyone you know whom Elena might have been having a dispute with?"

"Dispute?" the girl repeated, looking puzzled.

"Fight or argument," Nicole translated.

Rosa's sad face exploded into anger. "So dumb! I told her. I say, never two boyfriends. Never!"

"Elena was seeing two different men at the same time?"

Rosa spat. "Both were dogs, dogs. Enrique give her nothing, except here." She showed her fist and Nicole understood grimly. "That other; the gringo she talk about. He only want one thing. She think he give her money and things. I tell her he just use her for the sex you know. Men, they no good. Better to be a Sister, si?"

Nicole smiled at the girl's vehemence. "So you think Enrique found out about the other man?"

"I think. I think Enrique finally kill her. He go with other women, but if his woman go with other man, then..." Her gesture was a sudden slice across the throat.

"Do you know this Enrique's last name?"

"Diaz, I think. Yes, it is Diaz."

Nicole jotted it down. "Does Elena have family here?"

Under a Desert Sky

"No, in El Cajon, her mama I think. You call her maybe?" Rosa's face was haunted.

"I'll see what I can do. Did she live with her boyfriend Enrique?"

"Sometimes, but she had a room at Carmen's."

Everyone in the department knew about Carmen. Carmen, though born in Mexico City, had immigrated to the United States when she was just a teen. She'd met Alvaro Salvador during Mass one day and lost her heart to the police officer twenty years her senior. Unable to have children of their own, she and Alvaro had made it their mission to look after many of the young Hispanic girls who came to the Palm Springs area anxious for work and a better life. She tutored the girls in English, fed them, and taught them how to manage their money. Her large rambling house in Cathedral City, inherited from her husband's family, became a boarding house and safe refuge for the lonely girls.

After her husband's Alvaro's death from a premature heart attack, Carmen continued her self-proclaimed mission of continuing to look after the young Hispanic women of the desert, many of whom came from poor families without legal papers. A heavy, middle-aged woman nearing fifty, up to fifteen girls lived in her rather run-down house during the week, though most went home to their families during weekends and holidays. Carmen cooked authentic Mexican food, gave lots of motherly advice, and required her girls to attend Mass and confession at least once a week. Nicole had met the compassionate woman twice, once at a shelter for unwed mothers where she'd been looking for a missing teen, and later at the station where Carmen had barged in and demanded that every police officer buy a raffle ticket to help support her girls. The local Women's Club had donated a weekend in Las Vegas to the persistent woman's cause. Nicole hadn't won the weekend on the Strip, but had proudly bought ten tickets. Carmen was a Godsend to the Latino community, and Nicole dreaded telling the wonderful woman that one of her "girls" hadn't made it.

"Did Elena ever tell you the name of the other man?"

"No," Rosa paused and chewed her lip. "I get so confused sometimes. Lena, she talk a lot you know, and she talk of two men besides Enrique, but I not sure which one she with, you know. One was her man, but the other was like her brother she say." She flung her arms wildly about, in exasperation. "She was always angry and wanting everything now. Always now! Lena say her new man take care of her and give her money to learn the computer and get a better job. But men, I think they nothing but trouble and they lie to get the sex you know. If Enrique found out . . ." she let the sentence dangle but Nicole understood clearly. "You gonna get that Enrique?" asked the girl, her dark eyes filled with hatred.

"We'll definitely check into her relationship with Enrique Diaz," assured Nicole. At Rosa's confused look, she amended. "We'll find Enrique and talk to him. Thanks for the help Rosa. You can go home now and we'll contact you if we need anything more. Do you have a contact number?"

"I stay with Carmen too, that's where I met Lena. Thank you. You help," she stated simply. "You watch out for that gringo," she added.

"Which gringo?" questioned Nicole, not sure if Rosa was talking about Elena's lover, or the brotherly friend.

"The boss man, the new one. I think maybe he's the other boyfriend. She said she knows things about him, but cannot tell because of the secret. Maybe he married or something."

"And she never mentioned a name?"

"I tell you she never told his name. And she only see him for a couple months maybe. But I tell you the new boss man... he look like us...but he's really a gringo. I know!"

Chapter 3

Nicole scribbled down a few more notes, trying to make sense of what Rosa had related while the pretty girl sniffed into her tissue. Nicole finally rose and led the much calmer Rosa outside the office where Nancy stood patiently conversing to her partner, Lee, who shook his head grimly. Nicole approached the pair with a brief smile.

"Could you see that Rosa gets home, Officer Williams? She's staying at Carmen's and I'm certain she'll need a ride." Nancy smiled, and taking the girl's arm gently led her away.

"I'll call you a taxi right away," reassured Nancy in her pleasant voice. She continued to chat quietly in Spanish with the dazed girl as she urged her down the hall and Nicole knew that if anyone could, Nancy would soothe and comfort her. Her fellow officer was one of the most efficient and warm women Nicole had ever known. Nicole turned to Lee who leaned against the wall biting his mercilessly chewed-down fingernails.

"Found anything Lee?"

"A smudge on the toilet handle and a slight smear on the towel dispenser. Nothing else. We're trying to contact the housekeeping manager so we can check out the girl's locker. I can't seem to get hold of anyone who knows the whereabouts of this Mrs. O'Toole. I wish we could get some cooperation here," he said loudly, clearly exasperated. A uniformed officer called to Lee who immediately scurried away. Nicole watched her colleague's tense back, noting that the harried Lee seemed to lose his temper more and more often these days. Unfortunately it was the nature of their occupation.

"Nicole, do you have a moment?" Captain Hernandez was speaking to a tall middle-aged man in a light gray suit who looked pale and visibly shaken. The balding, agitated man had a slight potbelly for all his thinness and plucked at his spotted maroon tie nervously.

"This is Richard Greaves and he's currently the budget manager at The Desert Sky Resort." Nicole politely shook the older man's hand, noting his wet, limp grip. "Richard's been employed at the resort for over seven years and can give you a general overview of the hotel, as well as a run-down of all the employees working this floor. Did you find anything out from the girl?"

"I'll meet you in my office," blurted Mr. Greaves, who clearly wanted to distance himself from the murder scene.

Under a Desert Sky

"Thank you Mr. Greaves, I'll be right there," assured Nicole and watched the older man bolt down the hall, keeping to the opposite side of the men's bathroom as if the horror within would reach out and grab him. Nicole couldn't say she blamed him. She consulted her notes before continuing. "Rosa indicated that Elena was seeing two different men. The first was named Enrique Diaz. All indications suggest he was a jealous sort of guy, though unfaithful himself. Rosa was also convinced that Elena was seeing a 'gringo.' She referred to a boss man who looked like them but was a gringo nevertheless. However, there seemed to be some confusion in her report, as Elena seemed to be friends with 'two' separate gringos. I couldn't ascertain the names of either from Rosa, and all in all her statement was pretty confusing."

Jerry shrugged his dark face pensively. He folded his arms and thought for a moment. "Greaves can probably help you with that. Justin Zachary is the new director at the resort. Perhaps she meant him. Did you get to talk to him?"

"Never got to discuss the case with him," modified Nicole without compunction.

"So," continued Jerry, "our first scenario is the jealous boyfriend entering the restricted area of the hotel and taking revenge on his unfaithful girlfriend. Highly implausible, but you and I both know stranger things than that have happened before."

Nicole mentally agreed and nodded. "I'd have someone check out Carmen's boarding house in the City. That's where Elena was staying."

Jerry smiled and pointed a finger directly at her, a vicious twinkle in his eyes. "That would be a great job for you and Bud this afternoon, since you're so eager to improve your Spanish."

Nicole grimaced slightly; her mispronunciation of Spanish words was a source of constant humor between Bud and the Captain. The sound of muffled wheels on carpet made both turn simultaneously.

"There's the coroner now. You go check with Greaves. You've met Ms. Chamberlain and her secretary. Crosscheck them, first with Greaves, then back, just to compare notes and personalities. Why do I get the feeling this is going to be a messy one? We'll meet back at the station at 9:30 sharp. Mr. Zachary, the new director, says he'll meet us there and bring along the Budget Director. He's been taking this time to phone all the employees of the floor and warn most of them not to come in today. Zachary sounded mighty cool for one who saw a body in that condition, though he seems very anxious to find out all the details."

Nicole remembered the anguished man in the stairwell and simply commented, "Appearances can be deceiving. I'll meet with Greaves now."

"Good, then let's get on with it. I'll find out who else has keys to this wing besides our dead girl."

"You might want to check with a Mrs. O'Toole; she's the housekeeping manager. Lee's been trying to contact her but is having little luck."

Under a Desert Sky

"I bet that's sweetening his disposition." He waved a hand and disappeared into the men's room again.

Nicole wandered down the hall, noting the different doors with their fancy names and titles engraved in gold letters outside them. She smiled, visualizing the tiny metal nameplate on her desk that simply spelled out *Detective N. Lewis* and wondered once again if she shouldn't have followed her mother's playful advice and become a highly paid corporate lawyer. Nicole passed the personnel office and stuck her head in.

"I'm going to speak with Mr. Greaves right now. May I have a moment with you after I'm finished?"

The secretary, Genny, glanced up from the pile of folders on her desk and nodded. "We'll be here." Her pretty face was drawn and worn, but she resolutely returned to her task.

The Financial Director's office was situated directly across the hall; it was tastefully decorated, yet clearly deserted. Nicole noted the name to the right of the door, stated in bold gold letters; Scott Adams, Finance Director, MBA, CPA. The adjacent office belonged to the director, Mr. Justin Zachary. No degrees or fancy lettering marked his name, whose title simply stated 'Executive Director'. Nicole paused, resisting the strange urge to touch the simple nameplate and forced herself to move on. To her left an open door led into the Chief Accountant's office, one Mr. Richard Greaves.

Nicole observed the haggard man hunched over his computer terminal, scanning columns of figures. His face appeared tired and thin under his receding hairline. He physically drooped, as if the life had been punched out of him. Nicole approached the office and tapped on the open glass door.

"Come in, come in," Richard beckoned, rising to usher her onto a red-cushioned seat directly across from him.

"Working, I see," she observed.

"Trying to work you mean. What a horrible thing to have happen. I should probably just go home, but I knew the police wanted to talk to me and the paperwork helps get my mind off that poor little girl's death. Excuse me if I appear to babble, but nothing like this has ever happened here before and it is quite disconcerting. What do you want to know Officer? I'm afraid I wasn't acquainted with the young lady, though I have to admit I've been here on several occasions when she began her rounds. A nice looking girl with beautiful long hair, though very young I'd say."

"Only nineteen I'm told, and those are pretty long hours you're putting in Mr. Greaves, since I believe Elena begins her shift after your normal working hours? And that's Detective Lewis, Mr. Greaves. Do try to relax," she added noting the tensing of his shoulders. "I'll be as brief as possible and after that I'm sure you can head home. We're interested in what you can relate to us about the employees who work on this floor." She crossed one slim leg over the other and opened her pad, pen poised.

The balding man cleared his throat before beginning. "Let's see, well, there's Judith Chamberlain of course. She's the personnel director. Been here about a year I believe." He stopped and Nicole could see him ticking off the time frame in his head, and determined that Richard Greaves was the consummate accountant who wanted his figures to be accurate. "About 14 months actually. She's a real go-getter. People like and respect her and Judith came in with a lot of new ideas that have proved to be quite progressive. She tightened up the hiring procedures and did a survey on how much other hotels in the Palm Springs area are paying their people. Judith took the figures, first to me and then to the old director, Robert Severns, informing us we should pay 1-2 percent more if we wanted to hire and retain the best people. Mr. Severns agreed and we raised beginning salaries across the board for all employees. Even that poor little girl would have started at more here than the hotel down the street."

"Is she married?"

"Ah, Judith? I don't think so. But I can tell you more than one fellow has wanted to walk her down the aisle. She's a workaholic though, kinda like me, and I don't believe she's with anybody right now, at least not that I know of." He grinned woodenly and Nicole wondered if he carried a torch for the attractive personnel director himself.

Nicole recorded the information and watched as Mr. Greaves pulled a battered pack of unfiltered cigarettes from his pocket, withdrawing one and then offering the pack to her. Nicole shook her head and watched his trembling hands shakily light the cigarette. He took a long pull and blew, seeming steadier.

"The resort's got very strict smoking regulations, but Mr. Severns said I could smoke in my office if I kept the door shut. The new director, Zachary, wants me to go outside with my smokes. Says there's danger of secondhand smoke. You won't tell him will you?"

"Of course not. Are you alright Mr. Greaves?" she asked, watching him wipe his wet forehead with a trembling hand.

"Yes, well kind of. I asked your Captain if I could see the body...that's the first dead body other than my parents I've ever seen." He was clearly trying to get a grip on his emotions and Nicole deftly changed the subject.

"And the secretary, Genny?" Nicole pushed her troublesome brown hair back from her face and listened closely. Richard took another deep pull on the cigarette.

"Genny Huff. She's a newlywed and I think is expecting her first child in a few months. Genny's worked here maybe eight months. Husband Jeff's a Honda car salesman down at the Auto Plaza and I know they just bought a house in Indian Wells."

"And Scott Adams?" She looked at her notes, "the Business Director?"

Nicole could see the man struggling with some intense emotion.

"He's my boss technically. Age thirty-two or so. Good looking and quick to laugh, though not everyone can see the joke. A real ladies man, I'd say, though you can't blame the women for preferring him considering his looks and charm.

Seems to know his stuff however, and is quite conscientious." He paused and puffed again. "Of course he should with an MBA from UCLA and all the right credentials. Been here around eighteen months and looking for another promotion I suspect."

Richard Greaves' tone sounded condescending and Nicole wondered at the barely hidden animosity. She could see he didn't have anything else to say about his much younger boss so she switched to Justin Zachary.

"Yeah, Zachary's the new resort director and only took over the past six weeks or so. I know he came highly recommended. I believe he worked up in Washington State somewhere and then transferred here when Robert Severns headed for the Maui resort. He's a real different personality from Bob. Bob was friendly and approachable and had the biggest repertoire of jokes you've ever heard. He knew everybody by name and would walk down to the staff rooms, into the restaurants, you name it, and chat to just about everyone. Every Christmas Bob would pick out a real nice gift for the staff on the executive floor; one you knew he'd put time and effort into. He was a great and generous boss." Clearly Richard had both liked and respected the previous director.

"And Mr. Zachary is lacking in those qualities?"

Richard Greaves looked clearly uncomfortable and checked nervously toward the glass door as if he expected to see his new director standing there. He adjusted his wide, wine-colored tie and sat up straighter in the red swivel office chair.

"I wouldn't say lacking. He's just very quiet and rather reserved. You never quite know what he's thinking or what his agenda is. Zachary's in his mid-thirties and looks Hispanic, though his name doesn't indicate Spanish blood. I suspect he was brought here because of his fluent Spanish, since 45 percent of our staff population is Mexican or from El Salvador or some other region of Latin America. I don't know anything about his family life or even if he's married for that matter, though I know some would consider him a handsome man. Keeps to himself for the most part, except at meetings and such. I really don't know him well."

Nicole sensed the nasty undertones of racism and tucked it away for further evaluation at a later time. "Do you have any photos of the people we've just mentioned? I'd like to attach some faces with these names you're giving me."

"No, but Ms. Chamberlain would have photos of all the staff. I know she attaches them each applicant's file when they come in for interviews."

"So she'd have a recent photo of Elena?"

"Yes, I'm positive she has one for everybody, including me in all my balding glory." He tried to sound jovial, but somehow didn't succeed.

"And just what is your position here exactly, Mr. Greaves?"

"I'm officially the budget manger. I oversee all financial expenditures in regards to the resort, work with the

Personnel and Business Director's, and help cut the pay-
checks every two weeks."

Nicole noted the pile of invoices on his desk and
pointed to them. "You sign for all expenses?"

"No, actually Mr. Adams does. I get them ready for
him to sign, and he just affixes his John Hancock." This time
the animosity rang loud and clear. "I simply make sure that
everything fits into the budget, write endless reports, and
obtain and keep filed quotes from various vendors. I'm more
the organizer and compiler." His bitter tone made Nicole
suspect Mr. Greaves felt the younger Scott Adams' job
should have been his.

"Were you here late last night Mr. Greaves?"

The older man flushed and nodded. "I had to work late
because I left early on the third to take my son to a Dodgers
game in LA. I'd left some accounts unbalanced for June and
I felt guilty for not completing them. Zachary's been a real
bear about making sure everything balances. Never saw
anyone more conscious about crossing his t's and dotting his
i's. He made sure that everyone was up to the mark and has
been putting in lots of extra hours himself. I had to come in."

"How late did you work?"

"Till a bit past nine. Then my eyes started acting up
and I knew I could no longer make an accurate accounting
so I gave up, stopped and got a Big Mac, and headed home."

"You saw Elena before you left?"

He nodded. "She was at the end of the hall with her
cleaning cart and I waved to her on my way out. Elena's

always very considerate, starting her vacuuming at the other end of the hall in the offices away from mine when she knows I'm working late. She's a sweet girl. Ah...*was* a sweet girl."

"There's no one to verify your whereabouts last night?"

"I did call my ex about Danny's Little League game next weekend. It's my weekend with the two boys. I suspect I probably called her around ten, but it could have been later."

"I'll have that checked out if you'll give me your home phone number." Richard recited the number and Nicole rose and extended her hand. "Thanks for your cooperation, Mr. Greaves. I'll keep in touch.

"Um, would you like me to come down to the Station?"

"That won't be necessary at the present time, but we may call you in for a further interview later."

Nicole left the obviously relieved man and proceeded back to Ms. Chamberlain's office. A few police officers milled around as the door to the men's room opened and the gurney with the still form sheathed in a large, black, zippered body bag rolled silently past her, propelled by two grim-faced deputies.

What an awful way to die thought Nicole, as she reentered the personnel office. Genny Huff glanced up from a large pile of folders on her otherwise neat desk.

"Oh, you're back now. We've found some files here that may help you." The secretary stood up and Nicole could see her belly protruding slightly under the black denim dress. Richard Greaves was right about the pregnancy. Judith Chamberlain came out of her office and beckoned Nicole to follow her.

"You seem a bit short-handed here," commented Nicole to the lovely blonde personnel director.

"Not really. We called and asked the clerk, Debbie Moore and the accountant, Liz Riley, not to come in until the afternoon. The same goes for Mr. Zachary and Mr. Adams' secretaries. We wanted to be sure that any excess staff didn't disturb the investigation or have to see the remains of that poor girl."

Judith sat down heavily at a large desk that fronted a huge window overlooking the stark desert and part of the emerald green golf course. Sprinklers sent up a fine mist over the neatly trimmed grass where a few golf carts dodged the gentle shower. The Personnel Director's office was lavish and reflected the same manicured neatness of the golf course; exquisitely done, just like the woman. Nicole could sense the woman's brilliant green eyes, only lightly touched in mascara, sizing her up. Nicole's quiet beauty spoke of preoccupation and a sense of practicality while Judith's was beautiful and exotic. A subtle hint of perfume surrounded the perfectly made-up woman. With her superb figure and manners Nicole could understand Richard Greaves' assessment a bit better. The woman was a knockout!

"I have the file on Elena Gonzalez." She handed the painfully thin folder to Nicole who opened it reluctantly, a photo of a hesitantly smiling young woman of about nine-teen stapled to the top. "She was in our employ for roughly six months. Elena previously worked at the Marriott, but left there because of transportation problems. It's on the other side of town and I know she lived in Cathedral City. There were no complaints about her work or anything unusual about her. Elena worked in relative isolation as the only housekeeper for the executive wing. Her swing shift is the lonely shift."

"Too lonely I think," agreed Nicole who leaned back in her chair with a heavy sigh. "I'm afraid I'll have to establish where you were last night Ms. Chamberlain?"

"That's perfectly alright. I had attended a Rotary func-tion at the Hilton. I believe I got home around ten o'clock. After that I just went to bed, knowing that the week after the fourth is always busy."

"You live alone?"

"Yes, just me and my houseplants, which I'm afraid couldn't provide a very credible alibi for me. I'd be happy to go down to the station and submit my fingerprints or what-ever else you need."

"I appreciate your cooperation Ms. Chamberlain, and will let you know if we require anything more from you." Nicole paused, glancing down at the information Richard Greaves had provided. "I spoke to Mr. Greaves about the other occupants of this hall. Do you have any insights re-garding your co-workers?"

"None that I think would have anything to do with Elena's death. Scott and Richard are both hard workers and often work overtime. Richard's the worst. He's at his desk until 8 p.m. nearly every evening." Judith Chamberlain asked hesitantly as if afraid to hear the answer. "When was Elena killed?"

"Sometime between midnight and four a.m." The pretty director gave a relieved sigh.

"Was Elena friendly with any of the people who work on this wing?"

"I'm not sure. I didn't even hire the girl. The housekeeping manager, Marjorie O'Toole, did. I only met Elena when she signed all the necessary paperwork, and even then, she had more interaction with my secretary Genny than me. I saw her on more than one occasion as she performed her duties, but really had no additional contact with her. I'm sorry I can't be of more help."

"That's alright Ms. Chamberlain. Any information you can give me proves to be helpful. Could we move on to the new director? His name is Justin Zachary I believe?"

Judith seemed to hesitate, an odd expression flitting across her face. "Mr. Zachary has been here less than two months and seems to be a quiet, reserved man who speaks Spanish fluently. I interacted with the old director Bob Severns much more. He was more approachable, but much less attractive if you know what I mean." Apparently, Richard Greaves had miscalculated on just who the pretty personnel director found attractive.

47

"Of course," Nicole agreed, willing the pretty personnel director to continue.

"I do remember Justin has also worked overtime more than once since his employ, but his personal assistant, as Mrs. Gaston likes to be called, says he often takes his paperwork home with him, preferring to work after hours there. All of us have our secretaries but they generally leave by five each evening, thus keeping their interaction with Elena to a minimum since she cleaned after business hours. Justin is very professional with all of us and quite fair and incredibly dedicated. I believe..." she hesitated, "that there might have been a little resentment on Scott's part when Justin got the position since he was an outsider to the resort. I did mention to Scott that he himself had been here less than 18 months and had never held a directorship before, while Justin Zachary had previous experience in Washington State as a chief executive. I unfortunately have a suspicion that Bob Severns may have made some promises he couldn't keep to Scott."

"So Scott wasn't promoted?"

"Well, actually he was. B.W. Weston, the resort owner, decided we needed a business director as well as a business manager since this resort has such a high volume of clients. Scott was promoted to that position."

"A career move Richard Greaves had perhaps hoped for?" asked Nicole carefully.

Judith Chamberlain shifted uncomfortably. "I believe that could be correct. Scott is very young and Richard has worked here for years. It seemed a bit unfair to me at the time since I had honestly believed that Richard would be the one promoted. However, I think that Richard has taken it in his good graces. He's a kind and generous man, though a true workaholic. I believe all three men are highly professional with their staff and personally think none of them could be involved with that poor girl's death. Is there anything else Detective?"

"Was it possible any of the three men were seeing Elena after hours?"

The question seemed to shock the beautiful young executive and she gasped. "Well, I'm not privy to the three men's personal lives. It could be possible of course. Richard Greaves is divorced and works way too much. Scott, well Scott likes the women and he might have I guess." The woman was clearly disconcerted by the question and Nicole tucked her flustered manner away for further evaluation.

"And Mr. Zachary?"

"I don't know if he's involved with anyone at the present time. He and Scott both, for that matter, are highly attractive and unmarried. And men, they often become involved in things we don't understand or condone. You can't believe that one of them...?" She let the question hang.

"We're not ruling anything out. Thank you Ms. Chamberlain."

"I wish I could be of more help Detective. I was thinking that perhaps a resident from the hotel could have come up last night and killed Elena?" The latter was said almost hopefully.

Nicole shrugged, "It seems unlikely since this area is always locked up after normal business hours, but of course we'll look into all the possibilities." She wasn't about to mention the reference to "the gringo," and Mr. Zachary. "Could I have the personnel files on all the workers from this floor?"

"Of course," agreed Judith, "but it will take a few minutes."

"I'll wait."

Ten minutes later, after fifteen folders had been placed before her, Nicole dug into her handbag and pulled out a business card. "If you think of anything else, please call. I'll try to return these files as soon as possible." Judith delicately took the card from Nicole's fingers with a well-manicured, pink-tipped hand and Nicole left the sweetly perfumed office, certain the attractive personnel director's scent would linger on the files for hours.

Downstairs, in the elaborate lobby, Nicole sank onto one of the soft cushions that surrounded a spectacular fountain spraying countless thin streams of water around a languid mermaid nestled amongst fragrant gardenias. The effect was cool and relaxing and Nicole took a moment before returning to the station to peruse the files. The first contained a candid shot of Richard Greaves looking overworked and camera shy. Files containing the secretarial staff followed, all women appearing efficient and not in the least menacing. Judith's photo was of model quality and Nicole smiled at the artful tilt of the personnel's director's head. Some women were just natural beauties and Nicole mentally complimented the woman on being both attractive and intelligent.

A striking blonde young man stared back at her from the next file and she studied the name with interest. So this was Scott Adams; the Budget Director who'd taken the job Richard Greaves had hoped for himself. He possessed sparkling blue-green eyes that crinkled in becoming laugh lines, a tanned straight nose, and perfect teeth. In his early thirties and blessed with a charming, open face guaranteed to drive women wild, she could see how that fact would depress a more commonplace rival like Richard Greaves.

It was the next face, however, that jolted her far more than the one of the blonde, seemingly good-natured Scott Adams. A dark arresting face, far more serious and mature than his counterpart's, hosted brown, almost black eyes and gazed unsmilingly at the camera under ebony hair styled in his long, swept back fashion. He'd taken his stern stance as if under duress during the whole photographic process and Nicole tried to assess the approachability of the man she'd met so briefly in the stairwell. She looked forward to meeting him on more neutral ground and swept the folders under her arms just as Buddy approached. It was going to be a hell of a long morning.

Chapter 4

Nicole entered the Palm Springs Police Station with an aching stomach to testify to the effect the image of the dead young woman's crumpled body had upon her. She headed straight for Dusty's cluttered desk, dropping her purse onto her adjacent office chair and depositing the resorts files next to the unfinished Monroe folder.

"Hey babe," Dusty Morant croaked, his eyes never leaving the screen of his perpetually running computer monitor.

"How'd you know it was me?" Nicole asked, affectionately regarding the heavy frame of the department's computer guru.

"No one, my dear, smells quite like you; that enticing subtle touch of gunpowder mixed with musk!" was his clever tongue-in-cheek answer and Nicole grinned. Dusty always sounded like the office Romeo, but no one was more considerate or savvy about the modern woman than he; his comments always bordering on the ridiculous, not sexual. Dusty swiveled his round head and peered at her through thick glasses, his shaggy brown hair tumbling over a heavy brow.

"Got some work for you if you're done playing your computer games for the day," chided Nicole.

"Ah, come on! Just a few more minutes and I'd have hacked my way into the City Treasurer's office and retired in style. And to think I get paid to do this!" He chuckled wickedly.

Nicole grinned and handed him the list of employees presently working on the executive floor of The Desert Sky Resort and watched him peruse it while she sat down heavily next to his desk and opened the bottom desk drawer.

"Mind if I borrow a couple of these?" she asked, shaking the small bottle of antacid at him.

"As if you'd give them back. Of course."

Nicole chewed on two of the tablets and filled the lopsided mug her friend Jesse had made for her with water. She smiled at the sudden image of his childlike face, remembering how he'd proudly presented her with the droopy mug he'd fashioned at his camp for the mentally-handicapped last year. She'd have to give him a call in a couple weeks and ask how his counselor training was going.

Under a Desert Sky

"None of these names are familiar to me in a criminal sense," pronounced Dusty. "I take it you want me to find out every little detail as usual you little peeping Tomette?"

"You've got it Dusty; astute as always. And please make careful note of all the young and handsome single men for me. I've got some irrefutable leads that the executive floor of The Desert Sky is teeming with its share of beefy, good looking men." Nicole grinned at Dusty's amused leer as he picked up the resorts files.

"Thanks for the light reading!" he commented, frowning at the fifteen or so odd folders.

"Is Jerry back?"

"Yup. You got anything juicy for him?" His beefy fingers were already flying over the keys as he typed in some information regarding the first name on her list.

"No. Is he free?"

"Nope, he's got the head honchos of The Desert Sky Resort closeted with him right now, trying to find out how anyone could gain access to the supposedly secure executive wing. Maybe you want to go in there with him and help him play good cop/bad cop. We all know it's his favorite game. So, who do you want to be today?" He smiled up at her.

"Good cop, I think. Might as well since I have on my nicest suit. Wouldn't want to sully my suave and sophisticated image. Thanks Dusty, catch you later."

"Okay love, oh and by the way, I'm certain the two executives just might be those hunky guys you were referring to earlier, already trussed up and waiting for you in Jerry's office. Maybe you should comb your hair or something."

"You swine," said Nicole good-naturedly, watching Dusty focus on his computer, and soon become lost in the figures his rapidly tapping fingers accessed. She sincerely doubted if her fiercely squinting friend had heard her last comment at all.

Nicole rose and headed for her boss' office, quietly knocking before entering upon his terse command. Jerry stood by his desk, speaking seriously to two men, one strikingly blonde and the other raven-haired. The blonde turned and gazed appreciatively at Nicole as she entered. A boyish looking man of perhaps thirty, he was perfectly tanned with a body that indicated strong physical training. His healthy, bronzed face appeared strained and unhappy, but he managed to smile at her, flashing orthodontically perfect teeth. Nicole recognized Scott Adams from his photo, noting the businesslike photograph hadn't remotely done him justice.

"I'm back Jerry, and have just given the list and files obtained from the resort to Dusty," she stated, careful not to mention that the two men standing in front of her were on that very same list.

"Thanks Detective Lewis. I'd like to introduce you to Scott Adams, the hotel's Business Director, and Justin Zachary, the Resort's Executive Director. She and her partner, Buddy Ochoa, will be spearheading this investigation. I'll expect the two of you to communicate directly with either her or Detective Ochoa during the entire time this case is open." Scott nodded in pleasure, his stunning blue eyes and perfectly sculpted face enough to make any sane woman faint-hearted. He politely took her hand and raised it to his lips, kissing the pale skin lightly just below the knuckles. Nicole remembered Richard Greaves' comment about Scott being a ladies man and mentally agreed, keeping her face straight and impassive before removing her hand immediately after the feather-light kiss. Scott Adams was dressed in a muted cream suit with an expensive blue silk shirt unbuttoned at the neck, clearly confident in his charm. Nicole smiled warily and turned to the other man, giving no indication they had met before.

Unlike Scott, Justin Zachary made no effort to be charming in the least. His lips were pursed tightly together in a thin line and he frowned at the sight of her. She once again appreciated his longish, but simply styled ebony hair that framed eyes of such a dark brown they appeared almost black. His lean clean-shaven face and the fine lines of his nose spoke of strong Native American blood. Justin Zachary's classically tailored suit of dark gray fit him perfectly and enhanced his businesslike posture without appearing overdone. Serious and practical, he was the exact foil of his gregarious counterpart, but no less compelling. Justin Zachary had been striking in the stairwell but now, with his emotions under strict control, he was simply stunning, and Nicole fought to stay calm and detached. If Scott's outgoing attractiveness disturbed him, Justin Zachary certainly hid it well. His cool dark eyes raked over her and for a brief instant the intense gaze softened and he nodded slightly, acknowledging their previous encounter.

"The gringo, he looks like one of us," echoed Rosa's words in Nicole's mind and she suddenly wondered about the resort director's ethic background. Justin Zachary gazed searchingly at her for a long moment and then briefly took her outstretched hand with strong tapered fingers, being careful not to prolong the handshake.

"I'm glad to meet you Detective Lewis," he said quietly, releasing her hand and glancing back at Captain Hernandez. "So, what would you like us to do now?" he asked simply, continuing the conversation Nicole's entrance had apparently interrupted.

"The newspapers will want to interview you and I suggest you simply defer any pointed questions directly back to us. While there's a chance that the murder is not hotel related, I'd say that's a slim chance. Until we're certain this homicide is not race-related, I want you to firmly indicate that you have no information regarding motive and will get back to them. The press can be damn persistent and I don't want a racial slant put on this case without knowing which way we're heading."

"I'm certain that I can assist Detective Lewis in this investigation and get her everything she needs," Scott inserted smoothly, eying her boldly. "I'd be happy to nominate myself as the resort liaison to the police department."

"Perhaps we should let the detectives themselves determine what information will be needed and who they'll find necessary to contact," stated Justin Zachary quietly but firmly. "We'll be available Captain Hernandez. Mr. Adams and I will be returning to the resort directly and if you need further information you can reach me either there or on my cell." He rattled off his cell number and even though Justin Zachary's voice was soft and non-aggressive, it was clear he had sent a definite message to the other executive to back off.

Jerry nodded, noting the interplay between the two men and firmly grasped their hands in a businesslike shake. "If both of you men will wait outside in the conference room, Detective Lewis and her partner will be with you in a moment to ask a few more questions pertinent to the case." Both men nodded, Scott's face lighting up as he gazed into Nicole's dark blue eyes. Nicole shook Scott's outstretched hand, noting once again he held it just a moment too long. She reached out her hand to Justin Zachary, who took it briefly in a firm grasp, unhurriedly appraising her with his smoky dark eyes. Nicole stepped aside to let the two tall men pass, her eyes memorizing the physical characteristics of both young executives. The glass door closed with a thud and Scott managed to grin at her through the window before following his superior toward the interrogation room.

"Looks like you obtained an admirer in the beach boy," stated Jerry dryly, enjoying Nicole's quick frown. "Night and day those two. Must make for an interesting working environment. Dusty checking out their files?"

"As we speak. Anything from the lab yet?" asked Nicole, refusing to rise to Jerry's comment.

"Way too soon, though we have a slight smudge of blood on the toilet handle as if our murderer flushed something away. No fingerprints though. The bathroom was cleaned thoroughly before the murder, probably by the victim herself. Unfortunately she did a fine job. I'll need you and Bud to get out to Carmen's to discover what you can about our victim after you interview our two executives. Otto should have the prints of the murder scene for you within a couple of hours. Type up your initial notes here and let Nancy compile them and check with Dusty before you go; I had him looking up everything he could find about Elena Gonzalez. See if Carmen knows anything about this Enrique character. I hope you note how I'm giving you another opportunity to practice your superb Spanish."

"Always the joker," scoffed Nicole.

Her superior smiled and glanced down at the press release upon his neat desk. "I meet the vultures in less than twenty minutes. So how do I look?"

"Grace will be proud," smiled Nicole, as Jerry fussed with his already straight tie, and left him rehearsing the speech he likely knew by heart.

———

Bud waited for her outside the conference room, jabbing at his straight white teeth with a small wooden toothpick. Nicole observed both well-dressed executives through the large one-way windowpane that fronted the rectangular interrogation room. Scott Adams paced the room nervously, his open, cream jacket flapping behind him, but Justin Zachary sat quietly near the wall with his electronic organizer placed on the oval wooden table, sedately punching in information with a slender stylus.

"You ready my sweet?" asked Bud smiling.

"Of course. You want to lead?"

"Alright, though they're both mighty cute. Sure you don't wanna take over?" he jested.

"I'd prefer to watch and listen if you don't mind."

"Leer you mean," he stated affectionately, and opened the door. Justin Zachary rose immediately and eyed the swarthy Hispanic man before him calmly. Bud held out his large paw and shook the executive's hand firmly.

"I'm Buddy Ochoa, and I believe you met my partner Nicole Lewis a few minutes ago. We'd just like to ask the two of you a few questions regarding the resort and your whereabouts last night and then give you some suggestions on how to handle the media end of this unfortunate matter."

"Of course," blurted out Scott Adams, edging closer; "whatever you need."

"Let's start with you then," stated Bud to Scott as he took a seat across from the tall sun-bleached blonde who sat down abruptly, his tanned fingers nervously drumming the table before him. Nicole remained standing in the left-hand corner of the room, slightly removed from the three men at the table. Justin Zachary glanced across at her inquiringly and then slowly seated himself again in the uncomfortable metal chair. It was obvious he'd prefer her situated at his eye level, and for that very reason Nicole chose to remain exactly where she was.

"Can you tell me your whereabouts last night?" began Bud casually. Scott turned anxiously in his chair, giving Nicole a nice view of his finely toned figure in perfect-fitting cream slacks and a blue shirt.

"I had dinner with a college friend of mine at Dino's. That's an Italian restaurant near the mall. My buddy's name is Jack Roberts and he comes up for a visit every few weeks or so. I have his number right here." He dictated the San Diego number briskly to Bud.

"The time frame?" asked Bud, as Nicole watched Scott's face carefully.

"We met at the restaurant around 6:30. At least that's the time I booked the reservation for. We had dinner, and afterwards headed to Tony Blanco's for drinks and dancing. We stayed there until at least a quarter past one. After that, he crashed at my apartment since he was in no condition to drive, and left this morning in a royal terror because he had to drive all the way back to San Diego in traffic and was going to be late."

"Where's he employed?" questioned Bud.

"At Merrill Lynch and is supposed to be at work when the market opens at 6 a.m. He's a broker. I guess you could say I'm a corrupting influence." Bud smiled pleasantly, his look disarming the tense young executive, and Scott seemed to relax.

"We'll check on your friend. You live alone?"

Scott looked across at Nicole and smiled smoothly. "Most of the time. I have visitors, but no permanent room-mates." Nicole shifted her gaze to Justin, who appeared faintly disgusted, but his dark eyes became shuttered when he noted the direction of her gaze.

"You've got neighbors?"

"Yes, of course. Muriel and Zach Ziegler live in the two-story condo to my left, but they're in Europe right now on a tour of the Greek Isles. I think my neighbors, Ted and Simon, were probably home. They're a gay couple who own that fancy salon off Palm Canyon Drive which specializes in computerized hairstyles for their clients. Their lights were still on when Jack and I returned home, but I'm not sure they could verify my whereabouts."

"We'll give then a call anyway. You'd be surprised how nosy neighbors can be."

"You've got that right." Scott then asked, "The girl who was murdered; was she shot?"

"No," qualified Bud evenly, "her throat was cut." Scott shuddered and Nicole noted every movement of his body language. He didn't appear guilty, only shocked as any nor-mal human being should be at such a gruesome crime.

"You didn't know her?"

"Only by sight. I'd wave, she'd wave...nothing more than that."

"Well that will be all then. You may wait outside if you wish," suggested Bud kindly, "while I interview Mr. Zachary. We'll call you if we need a more detailed statement." Scott Adams rose gratefully and nodded, casting a sidelong glance at Nicole who remained professionally impassive as he exited the room.

"I'd like to ask you the same question Mr. Zachary, regarding your movements last night."

"I took some work home with me around five thirty and didn't go out, remaining there alone the entire evening."

"There is no one who can verify your whereabouts?"

"None, though I called my sister and spoke at length with her last night regarding my Mother's upcoming birthday celebration. I often take papers home and it's not my habit to stay out late on work nights."

His matter of fact tone made it evident that he didn't approve of or appreciate Scott's partying the previous night. Nicole examined his dark, handsome face as the executive focused his attention on her partner. Justin's Zachary's dark hair was brushed back in a classic style, though some silky strands relented and touched the sides of his forehead, giving the man a much more casual look than she suspected he would have intended. His dark eyes probed Bud's equally opaque glance and Nicole noted Justin's full lips stretched above perfect straight teeth. His chin was rounded, not square like Scott's, giving his olive face the nearly perfect beauty that would have enabled Justin Zachary to have graced the cover of any GQ magazine. Many women would have classified him as tall, dark, and handsome, but his incredible reserve suggested that most would find him extremely difficult to know and Nicole remembered Judith and Richard's pointed comments about their new boss. This was a man of secrets, and those secrets bothered Nicole acutely, especially since she found her body tightening against his undeniable sexuality and the hidden vulnerability she'd witnessed earlier.

"You knew Ms. Gonzalez?" continued Bud, fiddling with his woefully chewed-up pencil.

"I often saw her when I had to stay late, since she worked the swing shift. We'd exchange a few pleasantries now and again. Elena appeared hardworking and diligent and I had no personal complaints about her work habits. I can see now that it was unfortunate she worked such a lonely shift, though I recognize that Richard, Judith, and myself, often put in late hours over the past few weeks as well. She was such a petite little girl to be so isolated late at night." Justin Zachary said the last words softly, but Nicole could see him visualizing the tiny housekeeper clearly in his mind. "She couldn't have held off a fly," he observed sadly. He broke eye contact with Bud, who stared intently at Justin's handsome profile for several moments.

"That'll be all Mr. Zachary. I'd like to request the phone records from your home, if possible, and you can leave all pertinent numbers with Sergeant Morant right outside this room. We'll keep in touch. My superior, Captain Hernandez, is briefing the press right now. At this point in our investigation, we feel the less the press knows the better,

65

since they had a heyday with the Rodriquez murder a couple months ago. Though I suspect this isn't race related, keep any comments to generalities and if the questioning from reporters gets too intense, refer them back to Captain Hernandez, Detective Lewis, or myself. I appreciate your cooperation in this matter."

Bud rose and shook the hand of the younger man thoughtfully. The striking executive sighed and once again glanced across at Nicole, who still leaned nonchalantly against the wall, her arms folded across her chest. He held her gaze for a long minute, studying the young police detective with eyes the shade of tantalizing chocolate mousse and Nicole struggled to appear detached and remote from that penetrating gaze, defiantly meeting his stare without flinching.

"I don't envy you your job," Justin stated finally, nodding politely as he exited the room.

Bud flipped his pencil over from tip to eraser a few times and pursed his lips. "I'd have to agree with that assessment today. Any perceptions Nikki?"

"Not yet," answered Nicole, watching the tall, dark-haired executive through the glass as he handed Dusty a business card he had written his home number on. "But I'm working on it. Interesting he stated he had no personal complaints about Elena's work habits. I wonder if there were complaints in other areas?"

She followed Bud out of the conference room as Justin Zachary glanced up. Nicole could see his jaw working in some strong emotion and he left Dusty's desk and approached her, speaking so quietly she could barely make out his words.

"Thank you once again Detective Lewis."

"There are no thanks necessary Mr. Zachary," she responded as discreetly. "Is it better now?"

He shook his head violently, turning his flashing dark eyes upon her. "It will never be any better Detective, not as long as that child's murderer walks free! Find Elena's killer," he hissed, turning abruptly, his tall frame weaving quickly through the tangle of desks cluttering the overcrowded department. Nicole shivered violently at the impact of his words and those desperate beautiful eyes.

"I'll try," she whispered.

Chapter 5

Dusty, by the time Nicole had typed up her interview notes from the morning, had loads of information regarding the deceased woman. Nicole gently massaged her neck as she peered at his glowing monitor.

Dusty rolled his chair closer and read from the lighted screen. "Elena Gonzalez came from a family of nine kids. None graduated high school. Most likely an illegal beginning, though she appeared to have a legitimate green card. She was only making sixty-five cents above minimum wage, but look at this." He tapped the screen and Nicole saw the deceased girl's bank balance.

"Whew," she gasped. Two recent deposits had been made into her account at the local bank. One for 3000 dollars had been credited only two weeks earlier. The other, for 5000 dollars, had been deposited only the past Thursday, before the long holiday weekend. "That's a fortune for a girl with nothing," she observed.

"Yep, almost an entire annual maid's salary in less than three weeks and that's not all." He pointed the curser and Nicole once again exhaled loudly. "Nice little holiday. A Hawaiian vacation on the gorgeous island of Maui during our scorching summer, complete with luxury car rental and lovely condo situated right on the beach. Aloha! Take me with you! Paid cash I see. All set to leave the day after to-morrow."

"Where would she get money like that?"

"Maybe she did some computer hacking and got to the City Treasurer before me? Or perhaps she made some very good tips!"

"Very funny. So a nineteen-year-old girl who got no further than the eighth grade obtains a wad of money like that. Those would be mighty fine tips," admonished Nicole.

"You're forgetting something very important my astute friend." Dusty leaned back in his chair and picked up the photo of Elena that Nicole had brought in with the file she'd obtained from the resort's personnel office. "She was a damn attractive girl and probably wanted all those special things any pretty girl without money wants. Who knows what she was really into? It could have been drugs or other expensive habits, or conversely, she might simply have made a bad choice in boyfriends."

Nicole nodded sadly in agreement. "And have you dug up anything on the so-called boyfriend?"

Under a Desert Sky

"Haven't discovered anything yet. So far I've come up with around forty Enrique Diazes in the Palm Springs area alone and those are just the legal ones. I suggest you send Bud down to the City to find out what he can on the streets. Elena lived in Cathedral City, right? I bet our boy's there and if he is, trust Bud to find him." Nicole had to agree. Bud Ochoa was a full-blooded Cahuilla Indian and he spoke Spanish fluently. His laid back manner, as well as his leather jacket and ponytail, didn't tag him as a police detective, and he had an exceptional ability of blending into the Latino populace of the lower desert. If anyone could find out the facts regarding Elena's final days, it was Bud.

Otto Presman wandered through the maze of cluttered desks and paused before Dusty's desk.

"Here are the photos from this morning. I suggest you refrain from eating before you examine them. I've already given Buddy his copies." Otto's pale blue eyes looked blurry. "I've gotta go," he mumbled. "Mandy's having trouble with the line-up camera and I promised her I'd look at it. See you Nicole." He hurried away, the heavy Pentax slapping against his shoulder.

"He doesn't have the stomach for this job."

"Do any of us?" asked Nicole quietly as she opened the manila envelope. The graphic photos looked surrealistic in the bright neon lights of the rest room. "At least it was quick," said Nicole before handing the top photo to Dusty, who bit his lip. "Hmm, that's interesting. She has a ring here, see?" Nicole pointed to the next photo where the tiny woman's hand was outstretched in the pool of blood.

"Nice." He grabbed his magnifying glass. "Maybe a sapphire with three, no four diamonds. Looks genuine and pretty damn expensive."

"Call Lee to take a look at these photos and follow up the ring in forensics. I doubt this was a family heirloom."

"I'll get on it right away."

Nicole returned to her desk, spreading the remaining gruesome photos across its surface. Otto was correct; one certainly lost their appetite after examining the images. "What did you know or see?" Nicole asked the dead girl, certain that this homicide was far more than just another random, senseless murder. Twenty minutes later and no closer to an answer, she replaced the glossy photos in their envelope and deposited them on Jerry's desk. Nicole once again perched on the edge of Dusty's desk to watch his plump fingers fly over the keys.

"How's the list I gave you that included the executives Zachary and Adams?" she asked lightly.

"So you got an eyeful of those two guys and want all the juicy disgusting details. Well, you'll have to wait sister, because I've decided to concentrate on Ms. Judith Chamberlain. Zowie!" He shook the photo of the smiling blonde in front of Nicole's face and grinned.

"Hmm, I see this is going to take you more time than I anticipated. Catch you later Dusty. Just remember to give *all* those names on the list equal time!" Dusty grinned evilly and opened Judith's file as he ogled over the stunning photo.

Bud waited by the copy machine, a wide grin plastered upon his broad face. "Look at this one Nicole. Ain't she a beaut?"

Nicole leaned over and smiled at the black and white copy Bud pulled from the Xerox machine.

The Harley-Davidson loomed as huge as its price tag. "You'll look like a Hell's Angel on that, Bud. What would Maggie say?"

He grinned impishly. "She'd say, move on up Daddy and make room for your Mama." He folded the copy carefully and tucked it inside his leather jacket. "I want one of those little round black helmets that look like relics from World War One. Maggie and I will be emperors of the highway. We'll glide up to my cousin Todd's in Anza and honk that hog's horn until I wake up all our ancestors on the reservation. It will be sweet!"

Nicole envisioned Bud seated on his Harley, booted feet outstretched, helmet in place, and the plump, buxom Maggie clutching him around the waist, giggling as the wind tangled her long black hair.

"Just beware of the spike on top...people might mistake you for a one-horned devil! Shall we go?" She glided out of the station, grinning at the Bud's private image of heaven.

Nicole remained quiet all the way to Cathedral City. Bud had been thorough and pinpointed the location of Carmen's boarding house, notifying the landlady they would arrive within fifteen minutes. Nicole pondered the details regarding Elena, but so far nothing made sense. The horrifying images of a young woman's life cut short on the cold tiles of the men's room shook her more than she'd imagined. Nicole was jolted from her depressing thoughts by her jovial partner giving a snort of laughter.

Bud Ochoa had the loudest laugh Nicole had ever heard. A local radio station spotlighted an upcoming Los Angeles comedian and Bud guffawed so loudly Nicole was afraid he would miss his turnoff, or at the least land the car into a sandy ditch.

"Sorry Nikki," he said at her chagrined looked and pulled his old bronze Chevy Impala in front of a dilapidated two story house in the heart of Cathedral City.

"So this is Carmen's. Not very stylish."

"But cheap & clean. Just how I like 'em!"

"Let's not talk about your love life Ochoa," Nicole retorted.

"Hee, hee, hee! I knew you had a sense of humor lurking somewhere under those stylish curls of yours, girl. You'd better let me do the talking," cautioned Bud as he readjusted his ponytail.

"So everyone keeps reminding me," grumbled Nicole, as she followed him up the wooden stairs to the old house. She consistently mixed up her Spanish pronouns and prepositions and wondered again for the hundredth time why she had taken German in school. Bud knocked loudly, but the volume from the TV drowned out his raps so he simply opened the dusty screen door and peered inside.

"Hello the house, it's Detectives Ochoa and Lewis from the Palm Springs Police Department."

Carmen's place looked run down on the outside, but inside the sturdy stylish furniture sat atop faded floorboards which were scrubbed spotlessly clean. The double-storied house was divided into two distinct parts with the wide staircase leading to the upper rooms splitting the bottom floor neatly in half. On the right, a large dining room with a huge, oval, wooden table set near swinging doors which presumably led to the kitchen. A combination sitting room and lounge dominated the left-hand side of the bottom floor and contained a large antiquated TV, several worn brown couches, and three or four comfortable chairs angled around the wide screen. A Spanish newscast blared and several members of the household sat in front of the appliance, glued to the screen. All were young women. On the screen flashed a photo of the pretty Elena, her long dark hair gleaming and beautiful. One of the young girls began to cry softly as Bud cleared his throat loudly and rapped on the wooden doorframe again. The residents turned to look at him, but didn't seem remotely startled.

Bud spoke rapid, fluent Spanish and a thin skimpily dressed girl with heavy eye makeup responded.

"Oh, si. I get Carmen." She disappeared around the massive staircase through the swish of swinging kitchen doors. Bud and Nicole watched the screen focus on The

Desert Sky's marquee where Elena's body had been discovered. The slight girl returned with a large graying woman who wore a soiled apron she wiped her broad hands upon. Carmen Salvador's large black eyes were red and swollen, the lines of grief evident in her face. Nancy had offered to call Carmen that morning to break the news and Nicole had passed on her least favorite job to her attractive co-worker gratefully. Seeing the distressed woman was bad enough and Nicole for once was thankful she didn't understand the rapid Spanish very well. Bud spoke gently to the older woman, introducing Nicole after presenting his badge. Carmen Salvador replied in soft guttural tones bespeaking sincere gentleness and concern.

"She says we can look at Elena's room. Apparently Elena didn't get along much with her mother, so she generally remained here on the weekends."

"Did she go home at all recently?" asked Nicole and Bud translated. Carmen shook her head and said something sharply in Spanish.

"She had a boyfriend, but Carmen wouldn't let him in the house, so Elena made herself scarce the last month." Nicole and Bud followed the slow-moving woman up the stairs and peered down the long hallway that ran the length of the building. Several doors opened onto the hall from each side. Two bathrooms decorated with brightly painted boards with *Hombres* and *Senoritas* written upon them were situated midway between the bedrooms. Thick walls painted a soft yellow and decorated with large framed photographs depicted desert scenes. Carmen opened the second door on the left and allowed the officers to precede her.

The tiny room, barely big enough for the double bed and worn five-drawer dresser, was warmer than the rest of the house, the window air conditioner switched off. A bright red bedspread livened up the room and a well-used guitar leaned against the far wall. A suffering Jesus gazed down upon the empty bed adorned with a small-fringed yellow pillow with embroidered ducks. Everything was painfully neat and tidy. A battered writing table hugged the left corner of the room with a couple of photographs resting upon its scarred surface. The first depicted a matronly looking woman sternly holding a small boy of about three years of age. Carmen spoke behind her.

"She says that's Elena's grand Madre." The woman looked partially Mayan with proud dark eyes and strong square shoulders. The second photo was of a short-haired laughing young man with small dark eyes and a worn brown leather jacket standing in front of a trim motorcycle polished to a high gloss.

Nicole pointed to the photo, "Is this Enrique?" The older woman nodded grimly and issued a harsh guttural sentence that clearly revealed her sentiments regarding the undesirable boyfriend. Nicole sighed and placed the framed photo into the heavy-duty black bag Bud handed her. Carmen gestured to indicate Nicole could go through the deceased woman's drawers and pulled Bud out of the tiny room, speaking to him in low fast tones.

Nicole proceeded to examine the battered chest of drawers. Inside the top drawer were a few toiletry items: nail polish, a comb and brush, a small cosmetic kit, feminine products and some face cream lay upon carefully placed paper towels. A worn Bible in Spanish and several Latino comic books with fearsome covers of dripping-mouthed monsters and suggestively dressed women were nestled next to the toiletry items. Nicole whistled under her breath, speculating at Elena's choice of reading material, and finally concluded they must belong to the boyfriend, Enrique. Several fashion magazines with slim, dark-eyed beauties gracing the covers were also there, and Nicole remembered the pretty photo of the young Elena that Judith Chamberlain had in her files. She wondered if Elena had entertained aspirations in the fashion industry.

Nicole quickly went through the next three drawers of the dresser, which held only clothing that seemed more provocative than serviceable. She removed a sleek little red tube dress and held it up to herself for a minute.

"Definitely not me!" Nicole winced and refolded the stretch dress. The bottom drawer proved nearly impossible to pull out and Nicole yanked and strained for nearly a minute before she had any success. After one last incredible tug it banged open, spilling Nicole directly on her backside. Rubbing her bottom gingerly, she peeked inside. A large sketchbook lay on the top. Underneath, several envelopes of photos were strewn haphazardly across the bottom of the dusty wooden drawer. The first few envelopes revealed only pictures of apparent friends and family, but her eyes narrowed in shock at the last. Nicole swallowed and quickly shoved the envelope into the black bag as evidence.

"Dusty will definitely want to take a look at these," she said, half in disgust.

The sketchbook itself revealed yet another side to the pretty Elena. Pencil and charcoal drawings covered page after page of the thick book. Many were of the desert and mountains surrounding the Palm Springs area and all were signed with the initials MCM. A few were of desert animals, including an incredible sketch of a coyote whose large eyes and narrow frame dominated a cactus-filled landscape.

The final three drawings were more human in nature. One, Nicole quickly concluded, could only be Enrique, appearing cool and dangerous with his tiny mustache and greased hair. He leaned upon the handlebars of an oversized motorcycle. Another was of a gnarled old man missing several teeth. His hands rested upon a smooth, twisted walking stick; his face holding that supreme mixture of knowledge and peace that only comes to the very old at the end of their lives. Nicole felt her heart jerk at the subject of the last sketch. Justin Zachary appeared relaxed and confident with a little half-smile tugging at his lips. He looked younger and more approachable, clearly at ease with the artist and himself. Nicole took a deep breath and quickly removed all three drawings, as well as two of the desert drawings, folding and placing them beside the photos in the plastic bag.

Bud's voice behind her caused her to whirl guiltily.

"Carmen has given me a couple of numbers she believes might help. One is for El Cajon, so chances are it's the Mama. The other is for 29 Palms. My guess is that's our boy Enrique."

"Good job Bud, I'm finished here. Let's go." It seemed suddenly important to get out of that claustrophobically neat room. She pushed past Bud and headed down the staircase. At the foot of the stairs Carmen waited and handed a small sheet of paper to Bud. Nicole glanced over his shoulder. Two numbers, both long distance, were written upon the page.

"Find the man," said Carmen clearly in English and Nicole understood the raw emotion behind the terse command. This had been one of Carmen's protected girls who had somehow slipped between the cracks.

Nicole solemnly shook hands with the now wet-eyed Carmen and followed the silent Bud out the door. A silver Lexus pulled up alongside the curb and a jacketless Justin Zachary got out, standing for a moment in the bright sunlight as he gazed intently at her and Bud.

"I can see you don't waste any time," he said mildly, removing his attractive sunglasses.

"Just keeping busy on a boring Monday morning," answered Bud jauntily. "We've been to Elena's room and checked out her personal belongings."

"Here's the search warrant." Nicole flipped it out, but Justin instead focused on her suddenly suspicious eyes. "And just what's *your* reason for being here, Mr. Zachary?"

80

asked Nicole carefully. "Aren't you supposed to be back at the hotel waiting for us to call and briefing your employees?"

"One of my housekeeping staff is dead, Ms. Lewis, and I need to find out the reason why."

"I'd suggest you leave that to the police, Mr. Zachary, and it's *Detective* Lewis."

"I'm sure the police will do all they can. But you see *Detective* Lewis, it happened in my hotel and some of the responsibility falls onto my shoulders since a young innocent woman was murdered only a few feet from my office. The least I can do is find out what I can about her. Maybe I might even prove to be of some assistance to the illustrious Palm Springs Police Department."

Nicole knew when she was being mocked. "Then go right on in," Nicole said tightly. "I'm sure you've *never* been here before."

Justin Zachary paused, shooting her a measured look, but instead of retorting simply nodded politely to Bud Ochoa before pushing his way past Nicole. The rusty squeak of the screen door opened and shut, his quiet voice greeting Carmen.

Chapter 6

"Interesting," Bud commented as they buckled up and pulled away from the curb.

"Yes, *very* interesting," repeated Nicole, leaning back against the worn seat. "Pull over there under that group of palms," she ordered after her partner had driven for several minutes. She removed the sketches and placed them on his lap. Bud studied them carefully.

"Well I'll be," he said after viewing Justin's portrait. "I can understand your comment back at Carmen's a bit better now. He's a damn fine looking man. Strange Elena would have sketched a picture of a man who indicated he only knew her on a "hello" basis. Mighty interesting indeed."

"And that's not all," indicated Nicole. "Look at these." She handed him the photos one by one. Buddy shook his head grimly, his lips tightening.

"What tangled webs we weave," he quoted. "Captain Jerry needs to see this right away."

Nicole carefully replaced the revealing photos back into the evidence bag. Both detectives rode in thoughtful silence the rest of the way back to the station, Nicole leaning her head back against the worn headrest as Bud turned on an oldies station that sang an old-fashioned love song. The powerful image of the lean and handsome Justin Zachary kept intruding, his dark eyes mocking, his quiet voice challenging anyone to know the real man. She contrasted him to the attractive Scott Adams and shook her head bemusedly before closing her eyes against the headrest, wishing she could deny her attraction to the raven-haired executive. Against her will she had drifted off, the stress of the morning and the intense heat finally taking their toll.

Nicole awoke as Bud pulled into the station, her stomach growling hungrily. She glanced at her watch. At nearly 12:30, the sun blazed hot and furious above them, the temperature already soaring past 110 degrees. Both she and Bud bought sandwiches out of the vending machine and Nicole added a diet soda from the staff refrigerator. Dusty, still active at his computer, mouthed a jaunty hello as Nicole placed the sketchbook and photos on his desk next to an enormous double cheeseburger and large order of fries. Dusty stopped punching his keyboard to examine the sketches and shook his shaggy head.

"Some major talent here. Who's the artist?"

Under a Desert Sky

"Our lately deceased Elena Gonzalez. And check out the last sketch." Dusty flipped the pages and shot a pointed glance at Nicole.

"Why that's Justin Zachary. Now ain't *that* a coincidence?"

"That's right," verified Nicole and then handed him the tawdry photos. "And these are even more interesting."

Dusty gave a long whistle. "Man, oh man. That's our sweet dead girl?"

"Not so sweet," qualified Bud, going over to his desk and sitting down heavily. He proceeded to take his sandwich apart and applied a lethal dose of hot sauce, which he'd removed from his bottom desk drawer. Nicole winced and wondered if Dusty had any more antacid tablets.

"Well, let me show ya what I've got." Dusty positioned the monitor for Nicole and Bud's benefit and pulled up files on each of the people working on the executive management floor. For the most part it was mundane stuff, but she noted the vitals regarding Scott Adams and smiled, truly impressed. His file looked like some sort of an elite class resume; the stuff of any girl's dream.

"Graduated with honors," she read aloud for Bud's benefit, "as an undergrad from UC Berkeley before transferring to UCLA for his MBA." She whistled silently. "Wow, a real hotshot, unmarried, with golden boy looks. I'll have to show Nancy these stats, I know she likes blondes." She moved the cursor while Dusty bit into his double cheeseburger, a pained expression crossing his face. The screen indicated that Scott had worked for The Desert Sky in Palm Springs for seventeen months, after a two-year position at a similar resort in Florida. Before his time spent at UCLA and Berkeley, he had served four years in the military as an MP. Nicole scratched her chin absently, deep in thought. She moved the cursor once again and gasped aloud at his salary. Money wasn't a problem here.

Dusty mumbled over his cheeseburger. "We're in the wrong line of business."

"You can say that again," added Bud, frowning in disgust at his own half-eaten sandwich. "Where did you get that burger?"

"Marko's. That vending machine stuff will kill you." Bud looked ready to snatch the partially eaten burger from Dusty's pudgy fingers.

Nicole moved the cursor to the overworked Mr. Greaves. His file was not nearly so impressive, but Nicole noted he had worked seven years for the hotel chain, slowly climbing the career ladder. Divorced and the father of two boys aged ten and twelve, he earned slightly more than half of Scott's generous salary.

"Judith Chamberlain mentioned Richard Greaves often worked late. Either the man is maneuvering himself into an early grave or he is desperately trying to move up in the organization."

"Nothing wrong with wanting a promotion," stated Bud, absently scratching his protruding belly.

"Yeah, but at what cost?" Nicole scanned the screen carefully again and then moved on. Judith Chamberlain's file was almost as impressive as Scott Adams's.

"She's got an undergraduate degree from Penn State and an MBA from NYU. Been an office manager for two separate hotels on the east coast before coming to The Desert Sky a couple of years ago. She's 34 and unmarried."

"And look at this," said Dusty as he scrolled down to a photo of her taken with members of a prominent rock group. "She was the main squeeze for a couple of years with the lead guitarist. What a knockout." He whistled long and sharp.

"Hey, that's one of my favorite groups," gasped Bud, clearly impressed.

Nicole smiled. "Poor Mr. Greaves. Maybe if he got an earring?"

"Wonder if she likes ponytails?" quipped Bud, and Nicole threw one of Dusty's french fries at him.

"Here's the bio on the current director. Only took control around six weeks ago."

Justin Zachary's file, though brief, was impressive as well. "A graduate of the University of Washington," read Nicole, "with ten years experience in hotel management. Hmm, attended U of W on a full scholarship."

"Hey," declared Bud, "he's a brother! It says he's over sixty percent Sioux. The scholarship was from the Native American Scholarship Fund. That's the same fund that enabled me to attend college." He smiled happily and Nicole remembered how important Bud felt educational opportunities were. He called the bestowing of the scholarship his ticket to paradise. Apparently Justin had shared the same ticket.

"His birth date, November 30, 1971," Nicole continued, peering more closely at the illuminated screen. "Transferred from Puget Sound Resort. Unmarried. Dad passed away a few years ago. Hey, look at this," both Dusty and Bud huddled around the computer as she pointed. "His father also worked for B.W. Weston, the owner of The Desert Sky. Looks like Zachary Sr. was employed at the Vancouver branch, the Las Vegas Sun Casino, and the San Francisco Weston, all as managers. "

Dusty counted on his fingers until he ran out of fingers. "Nearly eighteen years of service."

"Like Father, like son," commented Bud, rising. "I'm going to deliver these photos and sketches to the Captain. He hasn't choked over his coffee in at least 15 minutes."

"Justin also has an older married sister whose husband is an importer up north. His only other living relative is his retired mother who lives near her." continued Nicole. "He indicated he'd called her last night during our interrogation this morning. It's his only alibi so we'll have to check the phone records."

"Oh give me something hard to do for a change. If he called her from his digs in Palm Desert I'll have it verified within a couple minutes. Piece of cake," declared Dusty resolutely. He glanced up over his glasses; his expression altering. Nicole followed his stare. Nancy Williams had returned to the station along with her older partner Lee Gianotti. Even in this heat, she looked fresh and perky in her crisp blue uniform, her blonde hair pulled back in a tidy French braid.

"Hi guys," she said pausing by Dusty's messy desk. "Anything new?"

"Uh, well, we were just reading the profiles of the possible suspects. Do you want to check it out with us?" Nicole could swear a slight stammer altered Dusty's normally confident voice.

"That's okay," answered Nancy. "Lee and I are going to grab a bite to eat before heading over to the lab and coroner's to see if they've come up with anything. We'll get those results to you as soon as possible. Nolan, from the coroner's, has already indicated our killer is tall, probably over six feet, and right-handed."

"I could have told you that," said Lee condescendingly. Her throat was slashed top to bottom, shearing off some of her chin. That would only happen with a tall man."

Nancy smiled placidly. "Thanks Lee. I placed my statements from Rosa Lopez, Scott Adams, and Justin Zachary on your desk, Nicole. I also interviewed all the secretaries regarding their whereabouts last night though it's clear a man did our little girl in. Here are the phone records for Adams, Zachary, and Greaves up until eight this morning you asked for, Dusty. I printed them out for you too Bud;

thought you'd love cross-checking 'em." Bud frowned. He hated paperwork even more than Nicole.

"I'd like to check out your printouts on the execs when you're finished Dusty. Thanks." She walked briskly away, her shapely hips swaying slightly and Lee gave an exaggerated grin to Nicole and a poke at Dusty as he trailed his attractive partner, smiling as he adjusted his police blues.

"With a partner like Nancy, I almost don't have to work at all. Wouldn't you agree Dusty?" He bent and whispered loudly enough for all three to hear. "You're out of your league computer boy." He grinned and grabbed his sunglasses off the spotless desk, whistling as he sauntered away.

Nicole turned and noted her heavy friend flushed a bright pink.

"Looks like you don't even have to track down those numbers. Man, Nancy's efficient. You wanna talk about it?" grinned Bud, his dark eyes flashing.

"No comment," returned Dusty. He threw the rest of his uneaten burger down on his disorganized desk and frowned. "I hate that Lee, always so smug and insinuating! Just because he's been here the longest he's always rubbing our noses in his 'experience.' Everyone knows he's just a burnt out has-been. Without Nancy to cover for him he'd be sitting at a phone praying for retirement. Ah damn, I need to go wash my hands!" He moved awkwardly from his over-burdened desk and meandered through the maze of desks toward the bathroom.

Under a Desert Sky

"Gonna finish that burger?" asked Bud, oblivious to Dusty's distress and swooped up the messy sandwich at Dusty's denial with glee. With sandwich in one hand and photos in the other, her pony-tailed partner headed resolutely toward Jerry's office.

Nicole felt a wave of sympathy for the portly Dusty, but knew nothing she could do or say would lessen his infatuation with Nancy or make Lee's flippant comments any more tolerable. She leaned over and opened the top file on Dusty's desk. Justin Zachary's serious face stared sexily up at her and she once again felt that terrific jolt in her midsection. Nicole shook her head, trying once again to deny the strong attraction and gathered up the heavy pile of files. She returned to her over-laden desk to which Nancy's neat folders had been added. "Jeez," said Nicole to herself disgustedly, "the paperwork will kill you."

Chapter 7

Two hours later Jerry Hernandez summoned her and Bud into his small office. He pointed to the risqué photos of Elena. "Things, as usual, are taking their own sweet time to unfold and these photos only complicate the few facts we have. Nancy just called from the lab. There were no clean prints from the scene. And the sapphire the dead girl was sporting was nearly a carat. Worth what she'd make in a year as a cleaner."

"I'm not surprised," declared Nicole wearily.

"I've sent Nancy and Lee to try and chase down this Enrique fellow, but we've got a couple other problems to consider on top of everything else. It seems that The Desert Sky resort is missing a whole lot of money."

"A whole lot, like in embezzlement?" asked Nicole, tearing her eyes away from Elena's photos to meet her partner's surprised glance.

"That's exactly what I mean. I placed a call to B.W. Weston at his office in Orlando. Apparently, he's enlisted the Florida police to help pursue information regarding some major undocumented loss of funds over the last few months. They've traced the transactions here to The Desert Sky. The embezzlement originates here in Palm Springs."

"So, on top of the murder, we're now dealing with a little in-house siphoning," said Bud. "I can deal with that."

Bud viewed any new added dimension of every case they investigated as some sort of a chase or game. Nicole was thoroughly convinced that all the male officers she worked with managed their stress levels in this often horrifying job by viewing each case like some sort of video game to stay detached. Nicole wished she had perfected the skill.

"No, we're dealing exclusively with the murder. I just wanted you to keep the embezzlement piece of the puzzle in that mousetrap mind of yours Nicole."

"How much money are we talking about?" she asked.

"More than a little siphoning. Around two million total at last count. The last money went missing about two weeks ago. That was only a sweet six hundred thousand. I'm not convinced the two incidents are connected, but B.W. Weston is flying out here in a couple days to see how things are progressing. I want you to zoom back to the hotel and see Adams and Zachary again. Indicate that you know about the missing money and study their reactions. Bud, I have a list here from Dusty of all the Enrique Diazes in the area, since our scan of the photo didn't pull anything up in our national police records and Lee's sources came up dry. Our boy could be an illegal or just without a record. Start calling."

"Ah boss, let me go with Nicole. I hate sitting at my desk and phoning. I'm sure Lee or Nancy would much rather do it."

Jerry chuckled wickedly. "Now any other time you might have convinced me, but we really wouldn't want to spoil Nicole's fun. Your presence could ruin Nicole's budding and developing relationship with one very handsome beach boy."

"Very funny Jerry H!" retorted Nicole. Both men laughed heartily as Nicole stifled the urge to punch the two of them.

Rising, she steadfastly ignored their amused faces. "Maybe I'll do just that. Who knows, perhaps I'll get a free dinner out of it. I could use something a little more substantial after our gourmet lunch today." She glanced at her watch. "It's close to three now. I'll probably head home after I meet with the two executives. If there's anything earth shattering I'll give you a call Jerry. Oh and Bud . . . better get cracking on those numbers."

Bud stopped laughing and glanced helplessly at the captain. He received no sympathy there.

The little white Corolla jerked and protested against the heat that had peaked to a sizzling 115 degrees in the shade. The inside of the car remained unbearable and appeared to be getting hotter not cooler and Nicole placed her sweaty palm in front of the fan. Only scorching hot air blew out no matter how much she fiddled with the controls. Great, now the air conditioner was busted! By the time she arrived at the resort, Nicole was sweaty and red-faced. The back of her tan suit clung to her damp back and her bangs hung limply around her forehead. She blew her fringe up off her forehead with pursed lips and decided this was a great time to investigate the layout of the resort and try to cool off. Nicole automatically locked her car out of habit, and at the telltale beep mentally encouraged anyone who wished to steal the ten-year-old car to do so today.

The front lobby of The Desert Sky resort reminded one of the huge sparkling casinos in Las Vegas. The floor, a cool gray marble interlaced with huge squares of tile representing the desert and the mountains beyond, appeared cool and inviting. A giant flower vase set directly in the middle of the lobby entrance on an ebony table was loaded with birds of paradise, gladiolas, daffodils and many other flowers Nicole couldn't name. Under the huge glass arch of ceiling in the middle of the impressive lobby, the dripping mermaid knelt in the pool of knee-deep water beside the bench Nicole had used to check out the photos from Judith Chamberlain. The hotel looked cool, inviting, and spacious and Nicole savored the cold air from the expensive air-conditioning system which revived her overheated skin. To her right, the smooth, long, marble counter of the check-in and reservations desk bustled with people. Several attendants clad in mauve uniforms helped the many customers even though it was a late Monday afternoon.

Directly to her left the concierge's desk and public restrooms were clearly marked. Nicole made her way to the ladies room to try and repair the damage inflicted by Palm Springs' fearsome heat. A few minutes later, after splashing her face and hands with cold water, she felt revived though her cheeks still appeared overheated. With a vigorous overhaul of her hair and powder added to her flushed cheeks, she admitted her appearance was vaguely more passable; something like a wilted flower instead of a grease spot.

Gazing into the gold-gilded mirror Nicole realized she'd finally have to break down and take money from her savings to repair the non-functional air conditioner or buck up and put a down payment on a new car. Air conditioning was a luxury anyone living in the desert during the summer could personally not afford to do without. Returning to the large lobby, she purchased an iced tea from the vending machine and returned to the mermaid pond to analyze the hotel's layout, trying to figure out how Elena's murderer had escaped detection.

The large elevators before her gleamed, their steel and brass doors highly polished. The executive floor, located on the second floor, could only be approached by the stairs off to the right or by the elevators. The third through sixth floors housed the two parallel halls of the hotel room. Both stairs and lifts led to the second floor executive office whose double glass doors were securely locked after hours. Nicole entered the elevator, quickly noting that while punching the round silver button she could only access floors three to six; an entry card was required for entrance to the executive floor. The red-clad elevator boy wearing a jaunty hat noted her interest.

"What floor, miss?"

"The executive floor please," she said, flashing her badge. The uniformed youth inserted his passkey and Nicole enjoyed the swift jerk of the elevator's well-oiled gears. The nearly silent doors opened to the executive offices and the elevator boy pointed to the locked doors. An intercom, complete with keypad, encouraged anyone who wished to enter to punch in the code of whomever they wished to visit. Security appeared good and Nicole couldn't imagine that Elena had been sloppy and left these doors open. It had to have been someone she knew or an employee with a passkey.

Nicole peered at the list of names and slowly punched in the corresponding number for Scott Adams' office. A pleasant female voice, presumably his secretary, answered.

"It's Detective Lewis of the PSPD, here to see Mr. Adams on official business." The door buzzed and Nicole pushed the heavy glass door open, noting the stainless steel locking mechanism.

Scott Adams' secretary stood waiting for her in the wide hall.

"Hi, my name is Pamela Duvill, Mr. Adams' secretary. He unfortunately has left to go to the bank and then took the rest of the day off. Would you like me to call him on his cell?"

"No, that won't be necessary. I'll give him a call this evening."

Pam smiled and gave her Scott's business card. A middle-aged woman with graying dark hair exited from Scott Adams' office and grudgingly gave her a stiff half-smile.

"Detective Lewis, this is Marjorie O'Toole, our housekeeping manager here at the resort. We were just speaking about Elena, trying to find out if there had been any dispute between her and the rest of the staff."

Nicole briefly shook hands with the older woman. Mrs. O'Toole, of medium height, had short brown hair shot through with gray. Dressed in a matronly navy blue uniform, a large circle of keys dangled from a leather belt at her waist. Her black shoes were flat and sensible, entirely suitable for her line of work. Mrs. O'Toole's expression was neither unpleasant nor overly friendly underneath her wire-rimmed glasses, but Nicole's sensed immediately that the woman disliked her. Whether it was because of her profession or something else, Nicole had no idea.

"I was just telling Ms. Duvill that the girl seemed to get along with the rest of the workers, but had to be reprimanded twice because of overly long phone calls outside of her designated break. Other than that she was conscientious and always showed up on time. That's more than I can say about many of the other Hispanic girls here."

Nicole immediately bristled at the racial slur, but kept her face a mask.

"How long has Elena worked the swing shift?"

"Oh, about nine weeks or so. She started cleaning rooms, but the only opening I had there entailed either the early morning or mid-morning shift. Elena said she had a second job and needed to be free during the day."

Nicole remembered the sexy photos and nodded. "Did Elena have another locker? I believe Officer Williams searched one late this morning, but found it empty."

The graying woman shook her head and produced a plastic sack, which she handed to Nicole. "No, only the one, but I took the liberty of emptying it out this morning. I wanted to help."

Nicole felt a wave of annoyance. It was the police's job to empty out the locker, not Elena's employers! She took the bag and peered inside. More of the glossy magazines like the ones found in Elena's chest of drawers, an empty cola container, a paper bag holding some chips and a candy wrapper, and a worn fuzzy pink sweater filled the sack. At the bottom lay a clear zipped pouch with three dollars, some mascara, a bright red lipstick, and small fluted bottle of what appeared to be very expensive perfume. Nicole sniffed the container and remembered savoring that scent at one of the big department stores, before sadly replacing the bottle on the shelf because of its exorbitant price. How had Elena managed to purchase perfume like this on her salary? The answer was as evident as the oversized ring found on the corpse and Nicole slipped the bottle back into the cosmetic pouch.

Under a Desert Sky

"Thank you Mrs. O'Toole. I'll need to take this down to the station. It will be released to Elena's family later. You're staying in town this evening?"

"Of course," said the housekeeping manager stiffly. "You know officer, so many of those people south of the border are involved in gangs. Elena had a tattoo on her hand between the thumb and pointer finger. Some sort of initials I believe. Probably belonged to one of those horrible gangs that tracked her here on some sort of drug-related vendetta."

Nicole jotted the information down in her notebook though she was certain that the coroner's report would list the tattoo. Apparently Mrs. O'Toole wasn't finished.

"You know I would hate for this hotel's reputation to be sullied because of all the Mexicans we're forced to hire. Lots of them are legal, but many aren't and have counterfeit green cards. Elena had one, but you never know just how she obtained it. All these aliens, taking jobs from hard working Americans." Pam dropped her red head, clearly embarrassed by the track Mrs. O'Toole's comments had taken.

"So you believe Elena was illegal, Mrs. O'Toole?"

Marjorie O'Toole snorted. "More than likely. Most of them are. Anyway, I'll leave you to your job and it's back to mine." She adjusted her large black handbag and turned to go.

"One further question Mrs. O'Toole. Did you ever meet any of Elena's boyfriends?"

A startled Mrs. O'Toole threw a quick glance at Pam.

"I saw one of them, yes. A greasy sort of little man on a big motorcycle. I remember the racket when she zoomed off with him. He had a crew cut and large snake tattoo on his arm. I thought at the time he was trouble."

"Just one last question. Did Elena ever work overtime? We've noticed some extra funds in her bank account and wondered how she obtained it."

"That girl work overtime?" Mrs. O'Toole gave a snort and straightened her already rigid back. "She always clocked out the minute her shift ended. Overtime, indeed. That's the problem. These people don't have a work ethic. When I was her age, I worked double shifts to make ends meet. I guess I was raised with different standards." She whirled, purse clutched tightly, and headed out the door without a backward glance.

Pam grimaced. "She's rather opinionated, but no one runs a better housekeeping department than Mrs. O'Toole."

Pam flushed and Nicole shot her a knowing glance. "If Mr. Adams returns within the next few minutes, I'll be meeting with Mr. Zachary and would appreciate if you'd ask him to wait for me."

"No problem. Um, Mr. Zachary's office is just next door."

"I'll find it. Thanks again Ms. Duvill. I'll check back later," she added and headed past the pleasant secretary and out the glass door. Once in the wide hall she flicked open her cell phone.

Under a Desert Sky

"Dusty, this is Nicole. Any word on Adams' friend Roberts who works for Merrill Lynch down in San Diego? Uh huh. He did then. You also spoke to the manager?" Nicole listened for a moment as Bud indicated Jack Roberts had indeed given Scott Adams his alibi, plus the manager had noted Jack was late to work and personally indicated he had stayed out too late the previous night with a friend in Palm Springs."

That's good to know then." Scott seemed in the clear, which only left Richard Greaves and Justin Zachary, both of whom were well over six feet tall. She braced herself and trudged slowly toward the resort director's door.

Chapter 8

Justin Zachary's secretary, a plump middle-aged woman with a no-nonsense attitude, was called Mrs. Leslie Gaston, according to the plain wooden nameplate standing upon her organized desk. Upon learning Nicole's identity she spoke briefly into the intercom.

"He'll see you now." Mrs. Gaston pushed down her half rims and gave Nicole a penetrating stare as she gestured toward the heavy wooden door just beyond her desk.

Justin Zachary's office was huge and hosted incredible floor-to-ceiling windows framing the purple tinted San Jacinto Mountains in the distance. Unlike Judith Chamberlain's office, which looked out upon the expansive golf course, Justin's windows delivered an unobstructed view of the pristine desert. He rose upon her entry and held out a ringless hand. She shook it quickly, once again noting the strength of those dark fingers.

Nicole sat down across from a mahogany desk covered by several open folders, their papers spilling out in disarray across the polished service. His computer screen hummed and a half-consumed iced tea sat on a fancy coaster next to the phone. Justin Zachary eased back down in his black leather chair, his dark gray suit jacket hanging open to reveal a beautiful lavender silk tie in delicate designs resting against a snowy white dress shirt.

"Yes Detective Lewis?" Mr. Zachary asked softly.

"I'm here because a couple items have surfaced regarding this case that are highly unusual," began Nicole as the quietly handsome man sat patiently in front of her, his fingers interlaced as he observed her with dark, unwavering eyes. "Elena Gonzalez had two deposits totaling 8000 dollars recorded in her checking account over the past three weeks. Considering her salary, those deposits need some explanation."

"Were the payments made by the resort?" he asked simply, suddenly alert.

"Mr. Adams apparently has gone to the bank, so I must transfer that question to you."

Justin Zachary wasted no time and picked up the phone. "Richard, this is Justin. Check the records regarding all of Elena Gonzalez's salary payments during her time with us. I need it ASAP." He waited, his lean fingers drumming the tabletop. "Good." He hung up. "I should have the figures within a few minutes, if you'd like to wait,"

Nicole appreciated his prompt response. It was time for the second revelation and she watched his olive face carefully.

"We have just gotten feedback from your sister resort in Orlando, Florida. Apparently, a sum of roughly two million dollars has been embezzled from this hotel chain over the past two months. Were you aware of this fact by any chance?"

"Yes," he answered quietly.

"Is there a reason why you left out that vital piece of information earlier this morning?"

"I couldn't, at the time, see how it had any bearing on the case, Detective. Elena Gonzalez was a housekeeper not an accountant." His dark brown eyes were nearly opaque and almost impossible to read.

"Perhaps no connection. Still, it's a bit odd, isn't it, how the two crimes coincide? I'm often surprised at the strange connections two apparently unrelated crimes can hold. Your boss, Mr. Weston, will be stopping by our station personally in the next couple days to be updated on the situation."

"Mr. Weston is in Florida," stated Justin, leaning forward in his chair, and Nicole sensed intense interest on his part.

"He obviously felt that what just happened here was important enough to warrant a visit. Wouldn't you agree Mr. Zachary?"

Justin eased back into the expensive desk chair and threaded his fingers back together calmly. "But of course. So that simply leaves the question of what do you expect from me until his arrival?" The challenge was evident in his quiet voice.

"Just the assurance of your total cooperation, as well as the complete freedom to interview and interrogate anyone at the hotel who might have a bearing on this case. I also need a guarantee you'll relate *anything* even slightly unusual, whether or not you might personally believe it could have a connection to this homicide investigation."

"I can guarantee that."

"I appreciate it. This morning Ms. Chamberlain gave us the files on everyone who works in this wing. I'd also like a complete update on the entire housekeeping staff as well as their manager, Mrs. O'Toole. I'll also need the client guest list of all visiting the resort this past holiday weekend."

"I'll see to it personally. Stop by first thing tomorrow and I'll arrange that information for you from the personnel and business offices. Anything else Detective Lewis?"

Nicole hesitated and decided to ask him. "Did you discover anything at Carmen's boarding house this morning?"

He hesitated for only a moment before quietly answering. "Yes. I discovered that grief is highly contagious."

Nicole stopped scribbling on her note pad at his succinct comment and glanced up at the well-groomed executive, noticing the tightness around his mouth.

"And did you discover anything else?" she asked softly, once again moved by the understated comments of this reserved man.

"Carmen gave me Elena's mother's number and I phoned her this afternoon. She and a couple of Elena's siblings arrive tonight to arrange the funeral and collect the body after the autopsy. I also ran into Rosa Lopez, who originally found Elena's body. She point blank resigned, saying the resort isn't a safe place for her to work since we can't protect our employees and that I'm directly responsible for Elena's death."

Nicole sighed. "While I can't blame her, it's a shame, since I'm sure she needed the job, though who's really responsible for her friend's death remains a mystery. I appreciate you taking the time to contact Ms. Gonzalez' mother; I'm sure that meant a great deal to her. I believe that Captain Hernandez also phoned this morning. He speaks fluent Spanish, as I suspect you do, and gave them what details we know about the case." Nicole paused before asking nonchalantly, "Did you know Elena Gonzalez personally?" She meant it to sound simply like a casual question, but instead it came out like an accusation.

His dark chocolate eyes surveyed her features surrounded by the limp curls and lack of make-up and asked instead, "Are you feeling well Detective Lewis? You appear a little pale."

"The air conditioning is shot in my car. And while it is not great for my ego, Mr. Zachary, that you noticed, it still doesn't get you off the hook in regards to my question."

"I'm sorry Detective Lewis, I didn't mean to be rude."

"No offense taken. Now can you answer the question?"

Justin broke her gaze and seemed to be contemplating his response before raising his eyes to her again. "I met her on occasion when I worked late. She was a conscientious worker and very, very young."

"Too young perhaps?"

"She didn't have the years of experience and wisdom necessary to back up some of the decisions she made."

"And just what are some of the decisions you're referring to?"

"Her choice of boyfriend for one. I met him one evening while working late."

"You weren't impressed?"

"That would be an understatement. Enrique was arrogant and foul-mouthed and seemed totally in control of Elena, who up until that moment hadn't appeared meek or subservient at all. I didn't approve of his presence on the executive floor after hours and Enrique took offense to my suggestion that he vacate the premises."

"I see. And just what was Elena's reaction to all this?"

Justin Zachary smiled, the simple act transforming his normally stern face into something nearly breathtaking and Nicole almost dropped her pencil. Nicole glanced down in an effort to control her startled response.

"She told me he wouldn't ever be on the floor again. I later heard him shouting at her in Spanish, indicating she had no right to tell her boss where he would or wouldn't be. He seemed to think that his rank of corporal justified his arrogant behavior. She was in over her head."

"Corporal?" asked Nicole excitedly. "He's in the military?"

"Yes, I believe Elena mentioned he was stationed out in 29 Palms."

"And the bit about being in over her head, do you believe that might have led to her death?"

"It's crossed my mind more than once. Do you have any more questions Detective Lewis?"

"Nothing except asking once again where you were last night Mr. Zachary?"

He hesitated only a moment before answering. "As I said earlier, I was home alone. After a shrimp salad for dinner I watched the news, worked on some resort paperwork, called my sister, and watched a video until about 11 p.m. I, unfortunately, have no one to verify my movements last night, though the phone call to my sister around 8:30 could certainly be authenticated."

"So you didn't go out at all?"

"I said that I didn't. Is there another reason you're asking me Detective?"

The air suddenly felt too close and Justin Zachary's eyes too hot. "No, of course not."

Justin put his chin in his hand and gazed intently at her. "I just thought that you maybe wanted to discover if I was married or not."

"I know you're not married," she countered smoothly. "It's in the file."

"Then maybe you want to know if I have a girlfriend?"

"Do you?" Nicole refused to be bullied even though her heart was doing somersaults. She managed to meet his intent gaze.

"I don't, though I'm in the market."

"That's too bad because there's no one to give you an airtight alibi except for your sister and that late night phone call."

"Maybe you'll just have to take it on faith, Detective, that I was really home and alone last night."

Nicole concentrated on writing down the fact about a girlfriend and tried to pretend she wasn't acutely aware of Justin's persistent stare.

"Is there anything else you'd like to ask me Detective?"

"Not for the present Mr. Zachary, though I will probably like to follow up on what you believe were rash decisions on Elena's part at a later time. I'll give my captain the heads up regarding Enrique's military status. Until then, you'll remain where I can reach you?" Justin nodded and Nicole picked up her handbag, rising stiffly. Justin followed suit, eyeing her slim form.

"You may have picked the wrong place to live Ms. Lewis. People of your complexion do better in cooler climates. Try Bob's garage off of Indian and Tamarisk for your air conditioner; they're reasonable and seem honest." Justin preceded her to the door and held it open for her politely. A faint hint of vanilla lingered about him and she wondered at his choice of cologne.

"Thanks for the tip Mr. Zachary. I'm positive a little sunscreen and a working air conditioner is all I need to once again rejoin the ranks of the living," she answered sweetly.

His lips curled in that devastating smile once again. "Stay in touch, Detective," he said quietly as she passed in front of him, his handsome face looking thoughtful.

"It's part of the job description Mr. Zachary, especially when there's a murderer still loose."

His dark brown eyes, so nearly black, were penetrating, but he chose to ignore her suggestion that he was high on her suspect list and asked instead. "And are *you* married Detective Lewis?"

Unwittingly a blush stained her cheeks and she averted her eyes in a vain effort to escape his disturbing stare. Nicole finally swallowed, gazing up into his dark face, childishly determined not to let his offhand question rattle her.

"No, I'm not," she answered as calmly as possible.

"That's wonderful," he said so softly Nicole could scarcely hear him, "though bewildering."

Nicole shouldered her bag and once again met those dark eyes, which now held the faintest trace of a smile, and her heart suddenly pounded.

"I'm not able... what I mean to say is..." she stammered, suddenly struck dumb by his sensual roving eyes.

"I know," he stated gently and brushed a wayward strand of tawny hair from her eyes before she flinched and moved away. Justin followed her to the outer office and paused by his secretary's desk, watching Nicole make a hurried escape down the wide corridor.

"Mrs. Gaston, would you be good enough to call Brian for me and ask him for any information he can obtain regarding a Detective Nicole Lewis and her partner, Mr. Buddy Ochoa of the PSPD. Buddy may not be his real name, but that's all I have to go on."

His sharp-eyed secretary immediately picked up the phone, watching his lingering gaze follow the rapidly departing detective.

"Everything, Mr. Zachary?" she asked, already knowing the answer.

"I need to know what I'm up against." was his only response. He turned away from his all-seeing secretary who muttered angrily under her breath as her boss retreated into his office.

"This is not good. Not good at all."

Chapter 9

The next day a thoroughly fatigued Nicole stopped by the hotel to pick up the paperwork Justin Zachary had organized for her. She'd had difficulty going to sleep the previous night as the image of the slain girl intermingled with the handsome face of Justin Zachary. Her overactive mind hadn't settled down until nearly three in the morning and she awakened with a pounding headache while her persistent alarm clock shrilled. Today's newscast, as she gulped her nonfat yogurt topped with strawberries, predicated a particularly beastly hot day, so she finally relented and called Bob's Auto Repair shop, agonizing over the small amount left in her checkbook and wondering if she'd have to dip into her savings account once again. Explaining her predicament, the friendly office assistant agreed to fit her in at 9 a.m. as well as shuttle her to and from the police station.

But first she'd have to stop by the hotel and Nicole dreaded the thought of running into the handsome resort director again. At 8:30 it was already 95 degrees as she pulled into the hotel parking lot. She hurried through the main lobby and this time took the stairs. Judith Chamberlain's secretary immediately buzzed her through.

"I'm sorry Detective, Ms. Chamberlain's not here. She's in an executive meeting and asked me to give you these."

The first of the two was a large manila envelope made bulky by the number of files within and the other was a small plain envelope with her name on it. Nicole smiled and thanked the secretary, wondering what the second envelope could be.

"Oh, and Mr. Zachary said to make sure you received this today," the pretty secretary added. "He indicated it might pertain to the case." A much thinner manila envelope with her name printed boldly across the front was added to the others. Nicole staunchly refused to open the envelopes until she arrived at the repair shop. As she pulled onto Indian Boulevard in the sweltering heat, she had no doubt as to what the top item on their agenda would be.

"It should be ready by 3 p.m.," promised the sweaty mechanic in the oil-stained uniform. We'll give you a call as soon as it's finished." Unfortunately, she had to sit in the waiting room for thirty minutes before the shuttle was available to take her to the station and she took the opportunity to examine the contents of the three envelopes. The first envelope from

Under a Desert Sky

Judith Chamberlain contained roughly twenty thin files of women who may have had contact with Elena. The last file was thicker and contained the records of Marjorie O'Toole, listed as being in her early fifties and employed by The Desert Sky Resort for nearly twenty years.

Nicole raised her head and tried to envision someone working at the same place in that kind of position for almost twenty years. Her first thirteen had been spent as a house-keeper until Marjorie had moved up to assistant manager seven years ago, and finally in 2000, had been promoted to housekeeping manager. She had little education, not even possessing a high school diploma, but was a diligent and hardworking employee according to evaluation letters from three different supervisors. The file listed her as divorced and indicated she contributed several hundred dollars each month in excess of the resort's normal pension fund. Nicole noted Mrs. O'Toole lived in a modest neighborhood on the outskirts of Palm Springs.

The second envelope proved to be from Scott Adams and contained copies of all of Elena's pay stubs for the past six months. He'd attached a small post-it with the simple words, 'Dinner sometime?' stuck on the front. Nicole frowned and replaced the pay stubs, suddenly feeling annoyed at Scott's blatant suggestion, but just as quickly realizing she wouldn't have responded remotely the same way if the note had come from Justin.

The last envelope proved difficult to tear open and nestled inside was a thin magazine entitled, 'Just Skin.' A yellow

117

post-it on the cover stated briefly, '*This might help you find out more about Elena's decisions.*' Signed only with a simple *J,* Nicole cautiously lifted the cover and grimaced, quickly glancing around in hopes that no one had glimpsed the contents of the risqué magazine. A paperclip marked a page halfway through the circular and near the top right-hand corner a woman wearing a flimsy, nearly transparent red negligee was circled in red marker. The caption below the glossy photo promised '*Sexy Lena will entice you with her South of the Border secrets,*' and was accompanied by a Palm Springs number. Nicole leaned her head back and sighed sadly. Justin Zachary had been right. Elena had made some mighty bad choices, but just how Justin Zachary had known about those bad choices was the real question.

"Hey, hey! You won't believe what I've got." Dusty pranced like a young colt around the office after she arrived. A container of plain nonfat yogurt and a half-eaten banana set on his desk. Dusty was a burger and fries man--the more cholesterol the better, and her eyes widened at him in disbelief.

"Turning over a new leaf Dusty?"

Lee Gianotti strolled over chanting, "Dusty's got a girlfriend." Dusty reached out to swat him, but the lithe, balding Lee moved easily out of his reach.

"Why don't you go and catch a crook you big blabbermouth."

Lee chuckled and picked up a file. "Not until you show her these."

"What's that Lee?" Nicole took the file and peeked inside.

"The things they pay me to look at during working hours." Lee pointed to a photo near the top of the flesh magazine. "Look familiar?"

"It's Elena," acknowledged Nicole, already knowing what she would find.

"That's right. Want to know where we got these?" asked Lee boastfully.

"Stun me with your method," answered Nicole, pretending interest. Nancy's partner was often arrogant and overbearing, but had been a top-notch investigator in his day.

"In the trash bin outside the housekeeping staff's locker room. Seems like someone dumped these in hopes we wouldn't find out about Elena's separate and apparently lucrative 'modeling' career happening on the side."

"I called the magazine," added Dusty. "Elena's been working for them for over five months. They of course identified themselves as a publication of the highest caliber."

"Right," sniffed Nicole and threw down a similar issue onto the table. "Too bad I'm way ahead of you. Justin Zachary forwarded this to me this morning." Dusty appeared puzzled and picked up the magazine, instantly turning to the young Hispanic girl's page marked by the paperclip.

"How would *he* know she worked there? Somehow I doubt she wrote that on her original job application," asked

Dusty, looking relatively disgusted by the provocative photos covering the page.

"That's what I would like to know," indicated Nicole, running a hand through her now limp hair.

"Maybe a customer?" commented Lee musingly. He stopped and sat upright, looking almost alarmed. His eyes widened and he pointed a finger at the portly Dusty who removed a carrot from a small plastic bag and began to munch dejectedly. Nicole cocked a questioning glance at Lee who in turn grinned broadly back at her and winked.

"So I guess that explains the extra money?" continued Lee, watching Dusty dubiously while replacing the copy of the glossy magazine on the desk as he kept an eye on his suddenly health-conscious office mate.

Dusty, oblivious to Lee's interest, stretched and grinned. "Nope, that's the beauty of it. She only got about three hundred dollars posing for those shots."

Nicole tapped the page with her slim hand. "The number here reeks of prostitution to me."

"Nope," verified Dusty again. "The client can phone and talk to the girls and they're billed for every minute. But it's a strictly hands off organization. Check out the last paragraph."

Both Nicole and Lee stared at the bottom of the page. It indicated that girls designated with a star would 'converse' with gentlemen in Spanish. Sure enough, Elena had a star by her phone number.

Confused Nicole asked, "Well what then?"

Under a Desert Sky

"Elena only got about a hundred dollars a week for her 'conversations'," stated Lee. "So guess where she obtained the extra cash?"

Lee grinned at Nicole, obviously already knowing the answer. "Well, where then?" she asked, exasperated with the two of them.

"The money came from a Desert Sky account for...." Dusty paused for effect, "overtime."

"Overtime? I personally checked with accounting and have a copy of her pay stubs right here. Elena didn't do overtime. If she was to be paid for additional hours someone had to submit overtime amounts."

"You're right," broke in Lee, "and that someone was the hotel housekeeping manager."

"Mrs. O'Toole? I met her yesterday and she adamantly stressed Elena never worked any extra shifts. In fact she insisted Elena didn't have the tenacity to even try for overtime. Plus the pay records I received from personnel yesterday afternoon indicated no additional time had been clocked for her, ever. I don't get it."

"Neither did we," said Dusty. "So Nancy and I burned the midnight oil after Richard Greaves called the station around 7 p.m. last night in hopes we'd achieve some enlightenment. Our Richard seemed very eager to share this unusual tidbit of information with the local law enforcement." Dusty looked smug, but whether or not it was because of the tip from Richard Greaves or the fact he spent the previous evening with Nancy, Nicole wasn't sure.

Loren Lockner

A neat and pressed Nancy pulled up by Dusty's desk and smiled at Nicole and Lee before turning to Dusty.

"Here's what you asked for Charles." She handed a computer printout to Dusty.

"Charles?" mouthed Nicole.

"That's my name you know!" retorted Dusty. Lee motioned behind Nancy's and Dusty's backs, pointing to the young blonde woman and Dusty. Nancy and Dusty? The mind boggled.

"Hey look at this. It's just as you relayed to us last night Nicole. Our boy Enrique's stationed in 29 Palms as a US marine. The numbers don't lie!"

The printout clearly showed the number dialed from Carmen's boarding house was to one Enrique Diaz, 29 Palms.

"The miracles of modern technology at our fingertips!" Dusty flexed his fingers and cracked his knuckles. Nancy beamed as Nicole and Lee backed away.

"Is today going to be one of those days?" asked Nicole of Nancy's older partner.

"Yup," said Lee, grinning at the sight of Dusty pulling out a chair for Nancy as she sat down beside him. "It certainly looks like it."

Nicole worked all day at her desk, crosschecking the files and searching for any detail that could possibly have any relevance to the case. Lee and Nancy departed a few minutes after Dusty's yogurt and carrot brunch, heading for 29 Palms, where Enrique Diaz was stationed, in an unmarked tan sedan. Until they reported back, things seemed at a standstill. The coroner's report had been fairly straightforward, indicating that Elena had been a healthy nineteen-year-old female who had run into the wrong end of a knife. The only interesting fact to surface was the initials found on her hand with the letters ECD and a small rose trailing after the D. To Nicole's mind the letters weren't gang related, but simply spelled out Enrique's initials. Around two she checked again with Dusty, who'd been making strange excited noises at his desk for the past half hour after hanging up the phone.

"Now we're getting somewhere!" he chortled. "Here's an interesting one. You remember when you first brought me Justin Zachary's name and I looked him up? On the surface he's real clean, but it seems that he was asked to leave the resort in Puget Sound for undisclosed reasons. Another interesting fact is that he didn't arrive in Palm Springs on May 19 as the resort's records indicate. Justin Zachary was in residence for almost six weeks before that, according to Pam, Mr. Adams' secretary. He left his job in Puget Sound on April first. And...." he leaned forward with a look of relish on his face, "he had a pretty little Hispanic girl staying with him at his new digs in Palm Desert."

"How'd you find that out?" asked Nicole, impressed at Dusty's expertise, but sickened by the implications.

"Bud just called and told me. Haven't you missed your partner all day? He's been interviewing people who know some of the managers at the resort and came up with that interesting fact from a next-door neighbor of Mr. Zachary's.

Judith Chamberlain faxed us the records regarding Zachary's transfer and I just verified it now.

She sensed someone behind her and turned to see Jerry Hernandez, jacketless, with his blue shirtsleeves rolled up. He threw a sheet of paper with dozens of columned figures printed across it onto her desk.

"Marvin at InfoTech Specs was on the horn just a few minutes ago," Jerry stated. "Another 200,000 grand has just been tracked to the Cayman Islands. That's a total of seven separate deposits all traced back to this hotel. We're up to 2.2 million and still counting."

"But I thought the embezzlement originated in Orlando?" asked Nicole, confused. "What's this Dusty?"

"The money seemed to disappear from Orlando, but actually can be traced back to this hotel. Every transaction leaves a footprint and seven different computers at The Desert Sky initiated the payouts." Dusty pointed a stubby finger at the paper. "See the number here. That's the individual computer number followed by the resort number. Whoever's doing this is mighty clever, never using the same computer twice. But, all computers are either located at The Desert Sky or its sister Golf Resort next door."

Nicole glanced up at Jerry's lined face. He scratched his graying head and sighed.

"I don't like the feel of this thing. A housekeeper murdered on the executive floor, yet mixed up in some sort of girlie answering service. Money embezzled and a new director secretly down here earlier than records previously indicated. Nicole, give this Zachary character another visit. Find out just how he knew about Elena and what game he was pulling in the spring." He handed her the sketches from the previous day. "You can also ask him about these."

"Yes, sir," replied Nicole. Ten minutes later, thoroughly frustrated, she tapped on Jerry's door.

"Yeah," he grunted, not looking up from his paperwork.

"Mr. Zachary's out and his secretary doesn't know when he's coming back."

"Why don't you head out to the Resort and try to locate him?"

Nicole paused. ""I'd love to, but . . ."

Jerry looked up. "But . . .?"

"My Toyota's in the shop. They're supposed to call around three so I can be taxied out there to pick up my car."

"Okay. When they call I'll have someone run down and retrieve it for you. I don't want you to wait. Just take one of the cruisers."

Nicole hated driving the squad cars because they were too official and obtrusive. She preferred behind the scenes work where she could discreetly sink back into the shadows and observe unnoticed. Perhaps that's why she'd applied for and transferred to the detective squad. Or, more likely, it was the memory of her father shot down by a motorist while patrolling the Pacific Highway. The driver he'd stopped to check for a broken headlight had killed both him and his partner after they had questioned him about the vehicle registration. The SUV had been hijacked and the two officers hadn't stood a chance at such point blank range. Nicole had been new to the Santa Barbara station, an idealist rookie driven by her father's sterling reputation. His senseless death had driven all that idealism straight out of her. No longer did she trust people at face value. Things that took other officers years to learn had sunk in within a few short months. Her mother's haunted face, her brother's shocked eyes; all had been images of a reality too ghastly to absorb. From that moment Nicole reevaluated her entire life and future.

Her mother had tried to encourage Nicole to switch careers and find a peripheral job to law enforcement. Be a lawyer, anything, Linda Lewis had argued, but Nicole had insisted she needed to remain in police work. The only alterations had been to transfer to the investigative end of law enforcement and out of the Santa Barbara region. Her mother had at least seen her daughter more content and focused before she had died, settled in a job where the risk factor seemed to be minimal. Thinking about her lost parents always formed a heavy stone in the pit of her stomach as the overwhelming grief of their loss resurfaced. They should have been relaxing in one of these luxury condos fringing an emerald green golf course while bouncing their granddaughter on their knee. Instead they pushed up headstones outside the church they'd married in thirty-five years ago, and that very memory made Nicole vow to track down every man or woman who snuffed out another's life before his or her time; a life just like the petite Elena's.

Under a Desert Sky

"You're still here Lewis? Get going."

"Yes sir," saluted Nicole, turning.

"And Nicole, don't bash the cruiser."

"I'm not Bud, Jerry. I *know* it isn't a Harley!" she said, and his laughter followed her out.

Chapter 10

Justin Zachary's intelligent-faced secretary informed her that Mr. Zachary had left for the day. Nicole glanced at her digital wristwatch. It wasn't even 3:30.

"Please give me directions to his house," she demanded. Justin's secretary, Mrs. Gaston, hesitated and then reached for the phone. A few moments later she spoke quietly into the receiver.

"Mr. Zachary will speak to you now."

Nicole picked up the phone and used her most professional tone. "It's imperative I see you Mr. Zachary regarding official business. I have some questions that need answers immediately and something in my possession that might prove interesting to you."

"Then by all means come by my house. Mrs. Gaston will give you directions." Nicole handed the phone back to his efficient secretary. Justin was definitely a man of few words. The woman answered in the affirmative a few times before hanging up the phone.

Five minutes later, with a carefully drawn map to Palm Desert, Nicole was back on the road. She called the station, but Bud had not returned from his travels. She urged the dispatcher to have Bud contact her on her cell phone and then headed toward the exclusive neighborhoods which turned greener and greener, their sprinkler systems energetically watering the heavy lawns that were ridiculous given Palm Springs' intensely hot and dry climate. Checking the address, she pulled up before a large stone gate.

"2689 Jasper. This is it." Rolling down her window she picked up the intercom phone located on a small stand by the cobbled driveway. A light flashed and Justin Zachary's carefully modulated voice came through sounding tinny and impatient.

"It's Detective Lewis," she announced, and the iron gate rolled open immediately. While the grounds were more modest than she expected, they were nicely landscaped. A real effort to blend in the indigenous plants of the region among attractive water features worked perfectly. An average sized pool shaped like a lima bean, complete with small waterfall tumbling into it, fronted the white-washed house; a two-storied adobe and river rock affair that complimented the desert climate and terrain. A large covered patio leading out to the pool shaded the front of the house and offered an exquisite view of the San Jacinto Mountains towering above Palm Springs.

Nicole parked the cruiser near the long patio and grabbed the sketches, hurrying up the front pathway amidst blooming oleanders and healthy geraniums. Several small palm trees in brightly colored Navajo pots livened up the indigenous rock garden. Before she could knock upon the heavy oak door, it opened soundlessly.

Justin Zachary was dressed casually, in an adobe red short-sleeved shirt tucked into faded blue jeans that hugged his lean body. The artificial cool of the house's interior fanned her cheeks.

"Come in," he said formally and Nicole stepped onto the cool pavers of the entry hall. A wooden staircase carpeted in pale cream stood directly opposite her and a small fountain adorned with well-kept houseplants lined the left-hand side of the hall. The drip of the water sounded cool and refreshing. Justin waited patiently before her, and Nicole noticed his tanned feet were bare.

"In here," Justin beckoned and Nicole followed him into a sitting room to the left of the stairs. Once again, the gurgle of water and fresh green of the houseplants exuded a cool and inviting atmosphere. White and bamboo furniture with dark muted-colored cushions appeared comfortable and inviting.

"May I get you something to drink?" Justin asked politely.

"An iced tea or anything with ice in it would be lovely," Nicole replied as she sank onto the soft cushions and watched him disappear through swinging bamboo doors. A few moments later Justin returned with a wicker tray carrying a pitcher of amber liquid that swirled lazily. In each glass a tangy wedge of lemon nestled among cubes of ice. As he poured, Nicole tried not to focus on his red shirt, where two buttons lay undone at the neck. His chest was smooth, revealing the light brown coloring of the Native American.

"Thank you," said Nicole taking a sip of cool tea. She was surprised at the minty flavor and glanced up at him in pleasure.

"It's sun tea and my mother's favorite concoction. I find it quite refreshing on a hot day like this. You're looking better if you don't mind me saying so. I take it your new choice of automobile is air-conditioned while yours is being repaired?" Justin's tone implied his mild amusement at the ostentatious police cruiser parked in the circular drive.

"I'm forced to drive a cruiser while mine is in the shop, but at least the air conditioner works. I couldn't survive July in Palm Springs without one. Thanks for the information about a reputable repair shop. They were very accommodating and shuttled me to work."

Nicole made a pretense of examining the lovely lines of the simply designed house. Justin followed her gaze, Nicole once again was struck at how classically beautiful he was though a strange remoteness, almost sadness, marred his perfect features.

"I have a few questions for you," said Nicole, finally replacing her half-empty glass on the wooden tray and reaching for her notepad.

"I figured this wasn't a social visit." Justin set down his frosty glass and waited, bare feet spread before him on the cool tiles, his lightly clasped hands hanging between his jeans-clad legs.

"How did you know about Elena's 'other job'?"

"She told me."

"So you knew her well enough to be privy to that rather delicate information?"

"Yes, I knew her well enough." He didn't seem to want to elaborate but Nicole pressed him.

"You were perhaps a client?"

Justin's head jerked upright, his lips meeting in a tight proud line. "I was never a client!" he retorted forcefully.

"Then how did you know her?"

Justin swallowed painfully, sadness clearly evident upon his face. "She was the niece of a friend. When I transferred here from Puget Sound, he asked me to look her up. Elena was estranged from her mother who was bitter that one of her children hadn't become either a priest or nun. Jose suggested I see what she was up to. It took awhile for Elena to trust me enough to share confidences, but when I finally realized she was in bigger trouble than I originally guessed, it was too late. Elena stayed with me for about three weeks until she found an opening at Carmen's. She'd been living off and on with Enrique in one of his army friend's flats and he had rather brutal ways of showing his affection."

"Why didn't you relate this information to us before?"

"I guess I was trying to protect her. But after the shock wore off, I realized you would eventually find out everything about her anyway so I might as well volunteer what information I knew."

"Why do you think she was listed in that magazine, answering calls from men she didn't know?"

"The money I suspect. She'd done some modeling and had high hopes of being picked up by some high-powered ad agency. When nothing materialized she took that off-hours job with the magazine. Lena worked the two a.m. to six a.m. shift. She made three times what the resort paid her by whispering to dirty old men."

"Our computer tech mentioned that she only earned around a hundred dollars a week from the magazine."

"That was just their official, taxable amount. On top of that Elena took in fifty to seventy bucks every night she worked."

"That still wouldn't account for the 8000 dollars in deposits made to her account over the past three weeks. Do you have any idea where those funds might have come from?"

"Not a clue. I got the sense that Elena was moving farther and farther away from me. I even suspected she was seeing someone besides Enrique, and knowing his violent history I became concerned about what might happen if he found out."

"Were in the habit of taking her home to Carmen's? You'd been there before?"

"Yes, several times. Often, I'd give her a lift after the late shift since I knew that transport was difficult. I even offered to lend Elena some money so she could quit the modeling and phone job but she refused. Elena was inordinately stubborn and determined to find her own way in this world without someone telling her what to do, just like her parents and uncles had always done before. Lena wanted everything she couldn't afford. Her first goal was to purchase a car. I actually called around to find her a secondhand model the week before she was murdered. When I told her I'd located a good-conditioned compact, she told me she wasn't interested and to mind my own business. She was going to have a car like Scott's or mine! None of us could have guessed the final cost of those desires."

"So you were like her big brother?" Justin nodded, but Nicole felt it would be difficult for any woman in her right mind to view Justin Zachary as the protective older brother sort.

Nicole dug the sketches out of her handbag and handed them to Justin. He closed his eyes momentarily at the desert scene.

"She had so much talent," Justin said softly, and Nicole watched pain flicker across his normally passive face.

"I'd agree with you though I'm no art expert. The sketch of the old man on the next page is incredible."

"That's her great-grandfather, the patron of his village. He's 90-years-old here. She copied it from a photograph taken right before he died. I told her she had the ability to do so much with her life; just move slowly and seek different avenues. But Lena wanted everything so fast. She was so impatient and so stubborn! If any authority figure cautioned her about an action, she went right ahead and did it anyway. There was nothing I could do to stop her."

His hands moved to the last sketch and he released his breath in a long sigh. "I didn't know she'd done this one."

"Perhaps she was in love with you?" questioned Nicole, watching his face intently.

His eyes stayed fathomless. "Maybe, though I doubt it since I never told her anything she really wanted to hear. I myself have always hoped that someone in love with me would listen to my advice and not throw it back in my face."

"Were you in love with her?" queried Nicole softly.

"Not in the way you suggest," he retorted angrily. "She was just a child, only nineteen. I'm a man of thirty-four and don't have a taste for children, especially the relatives of friends who trust me! However, I must admit that how I loved her felt a bit too *parental* for Elena's taste and she protested against it. She always said I sounded just like one of her uncles, nagging and telling her what to do. Lena knew I felt she was still a child, just playing at being a woman. Unfortunately she'd discovered how a woman with looks can get what they want from a man without half trying and I'm afraid she might have gotten involved with a man far more experienced than her." He sounded bitter and Nicole sensed the helplessness that must have gnawed at his guts. She once again remembered his stricken face in the stairwell and understood. No matter what he did, Justin hadn't been able to stop Elena's appointment with death.

"Let's not forget that Elena was old enough to pose nearly nude for magazines and take sexual phone calls from men she didn't know," mentioned Nicole, hoping to ease Justin's overactive conscience.

"Who are you to judge?" he retorted angrily. "Elena had nothing and wanted everything. We've been given the benefit of a good education and choices in our life. Elena could see everything that men like me have and wanted it as well. She only had to look into the mirror twice to figure out how to obtain it."

Nicole continued quietly. "Do you believe her boyfriend Enrique had anything to do with her death?"

Justin shook his dark head and leaned back, cupping his hands over his face.

"I've gone over every possible scenario in my mind and nothing makes the least bit of sense. I've met Enrique only twice, the once at the resort and a few weeks later when I dropped her at Carmen's. I can't envision him as a killer. A punk perhaps, full of bravado and that macho swagger he had perfected to a T. But Elena's killer? I just don't think so. I actually believe he cared for her in his own way, though he was brutal about it."

"So why did Elena stay with him?"

"He had money and a good-looking bike and the arrogance to match. Lena felt like something special with him. I also have the feeling she distinctly picked someone she absolutely knew her family would hate, and when she found out I disliked him, Lena flaunted him in my face. Told me to tell her uncle Jose about her 'legal' boyfriend."

"Did Enrique believe that perhaps you and Elena were more than friends?"

Justin moved uncomfortably in his chair and then shrugged reluctantly. "It wouldn't surprise me if she even told him that, though it wasn't remotely true."

Nicole sensed it was time to move on and cleared her throat. "Mr. Zachary..."

"Justin."

"Justin, you arrived here in Palm Springs a full six weeks before your official duties began. Can you tell me why?"

He studied her a long time before answering and Nicole shifted nervously in the beautiful bamboo chair. She'd dressed casually in trim yellow pants and a white sleeveless top with pearl buttons down the front. A pale cream short-sleeved linen jacket topped off the simple outfit. Comfortable, low-heeled sandals adorned her feet and she'd pulled her golden brown hair back from her face with a simple beaded clip to fight the heat. She wore no jewelry or perfume. Exotic and beautiful was one thing she wasn't. She didn't resemble him in the least.

Under a Desert Sky

"You guys don't miss a thing do you?" he stated mildly, a strand of silky black hair blowing across his brow in the artificial breeze of the air-conditioning system. "I came early to the desert to check on Elena and begin a probe regarding the truant resort funds. Weston himself wanted me here early to discreetly nose about before I took control."

"I see. And just what's your spin on the missing funds? Apparently all transactions were made on various resort computers at both the hotel and the golf resort across the street. I'm certain you're aware of that?"

"Just what are you investigating here Officer? Murder or embezzlement?"

"I'm not quite sure. Perhaps you can tell me?"

Justin straightened in the lovely wicker chair, appearing more like a disapproving parent than a suspect under interrogation, his dark face suddenly stern and unyielding. "I think you should stick to the murder investigation and leave the problems of the hotel to its management."

"Whatever you say Mr. Zachary."

"My name's Justin, as I stated before. Do you have some problem with that?"

She shook her tawny head in denial. "Only a similar one to you calling me Detective."

"Touché."

"So let's just keep it professional then. Why are you home at such an early hour the day after a murder in your hotel?

"Maybe I'm in mourning?" he said sarcastically. "Alright... I've had trouble sleeping and came home in hopes of catching a nap. I also didn't find the mood at the hotel conducive to getting any substantial work done."

Nicole stood up abruptly, recognizing Justin had run out of patience with the interrogation.

"I think that's all the information I need for now. Thanks for your hospitality Mr. Zachary; the tea was delicious." He frowned at the use of his last name once again, but rose with her, his beltless jeans sagging low upon his slim hips. She caught a glimpse of his taunt abdomen before the red shirt settled over the top of the worn jeans.

"I'm sure Elena's death has caused more than one person to lose sleep."

"I have to take it more personally than that, Detective. Her uncle specifically requested that I keep an eye on her and now's she's dead. I don't look forward to facing him or her family again."

Nicole studied the quiet, serious man and realized what he said was probably true. In his mind he'd failed Elena's family in the worst way possible. Even though high on her suspect list, Nicole found herself admiring Justin Zachary for the role of protector he'd so easily adopted. Justin had cared about this poor lost girl and couldn't sleep because of it. Somehow she suspected Richard Greaves and Scott Adams had not looked deeply enough into Justin Zachary's quiet standoffishness to recognize he'd cared as much, if not more, about his employees than the previous director. He might not have been the backslapping, "join me for a cup of coffee" type boss, but Nicole recognized his empathy ran much deeper than that. She discovered, to her dismay, she admired Justin Zachary way too much for her own good.

"I'll keep in touch Mr. Zachary."

"That's what you say Ms. Lewis," he returned softly.

Justin Zachary's dark eyes shifted from challenging to sensual and Nicole fought a rising blush. She opened her mouth to retort but instead shut it firmly, realizing he expected that sort of response. Instead she gazed steadfastly at him for a full fifteen seconds and then simply smiled. Startled, his lips curved in an answering grin for a long moment before preceding her to the front door, which he held open.

"Until we meet again then, *Detective*," he said softly, his dark brown eyes full of warmth.

"Until then, *Mr. Zachary*."

He tentatively reached out and touched her cheek with a forefinger, a soft caress that shook her more than another man's kiss or embrace might have. Her chest clenched, refusing to obey the simple demands of breathing while she gazed into his smoky brown eyes. His lips curled tenderly and Nicole fought the impulse to simply forget her vocation and take him into her arms. Justin finally shook his head, as if trying to release himself from some mesmerizing spell croaked out.

"You'd better be going, Detective Lewis."

"Of course Mr. Zachary." Nicole turned, meaning to place as much space as possible between her and those seductive beckoning eyes. But instead she slowly pivoted, gazing into his strong dark face. "I want..." she stammered, not certain what she really meant to say and his arms suddenly shot out, drawing her close until her face was only a scant inch from his.

"Nicole," he breathed harshly and bent his lips downward. The kiss was surprisingly gentle and sensual considering the unrestrained fire in his brown eyes. He withdrew his mouth tentatively and peered into her eyes before lowering his lips again, this time kissing her in sweet desperation, his strong arms lifting her and securing her against his lean body. Her mouth opened and she tasted his full lips, enjoying how his tongue moved in sweet intensity over hers. Nicole's breathing became ragged and her arms tightened about his neck, suddenly aware of the hard length of him under the tightness of his jeans.

She was instantly pressed against the cool door jam and he moved his hips against hers while Nicole plucked at his lips with her teeth. Justin tangled his hands through her short curls, tugging gently as his hips jammed delightfully against her now hopelessly wrinkled trousers. *Close the door* she begged silently, urging him away from the door jam as she lifted his shirt and ran her fingers over the hot lean flesh. His hand cupped her left breast, her nipple hardening under his tantalizing touch. There was no telling how far their frenzied kissing and desperate foreplay would have progressed in that sun-drenched doorway before he suddenly froze. The butt of her service revolver, tucked into the back waistband under her light jacket, met his searching fingers and he recoiled as if some sort of viperous snake had bitten him. His stilled hands and rigid face caused Nicole to back away in sudden realization of what she'd almost done.

"Oh my God," she gasped, pulling away from his stiff form and fleeing down the cobbled pathway, desperate to place needed distance between her and the mesmerizing man who made her body burn and turned her normally professional mind numb.

Nicole wheeled the large police cruiser out of the long driveway, the tires squealing upon the cobblestones, having to wait for the slow gate to open. Throwing a glance over her shoulder, the tall slim man stood framed in the living room window watching the squad car pull from his driveway as she beat a hasty retreat.

He leaned against the window paneling, shaken to the core by Detective Nicole Lewis and breathed in deeply, tasting once again her lips and visualizing her steady, inquisitive eyes and earnest face surrounded by silky golden-brown hair. Unashamedly he admitted he'd finally met his match as well as the woman of his dreams. Just why in the hell did she have to pack a gun?

Chapter 11

"I don't know nothing about no murder. I'm telling you she was alive the last time I saw her."

Enrique Diaz, a short wirily man with a crew cut and a small narrow scar on his cheek, glared at the team. Lee and Nancy had brought him in around 6 p.m. on Tuesday evening and he'd been in a holding pen ever since. Now, on this already stifling Wednesday morning, the department had less than 12 hours to either charge him or let him go. The military had sent a brisk, African American lawyer with disconcerting green eyes to counsel him. Amazingly, she was very supportive and helpful; particularly after Lee showed her the photo of the dead girl lying in a pool of her own blood.

"Any solid evidence?" she asked, frowning at the photo before laying it upon the wide table of the interrogation room.

"Not yet," qualified, Lee turning his focus back to the defiant Enrique. "We have a witness named Rosa Leon who indicated that Enrique often got physical with his girlfriend, as well as the statement from the resort's director indicating he knew Enrique batted her around."

Enrique remained defiant. "The women, they get so full of themselves. Always telling a man what to do. I don't like that, no *real* man likes that." His menacing glare made cold chills run down Nicole's spine even though protected and anonymous behind the one-way window.

"So you hit her?" continued Lee, frowning at Enrique.

"Only sometimes, when she needed it. I think she actually like it. Most women do. I got witnesses that say I was at the base in my own bed when she got done in. You hafta let me go."

"He's right," said his lawyer, shuffling her paperwork disgustedly. "Unless you have some solid evidence against him you're required to release him by 6 p.m. tonight." Enrique leaned back in his chair and smirked defiantly at Lee and his lawyer. Lee glowered toward the interrogation window at the hidden observers while Lieutenant Henry, Enrique's counselor, packed up her briefcase.

Both Bud and Nicole remained in the shadows as Enrique was led away.

"Sorry," apologized Lee, running a hand through his graying hair. "We just don't have anything solid to pin on him. It's so clear he's guilty as hell."

Under a Desert Sky

"But," Lieutenant Henry said in a quiet aside to Bud once she joined them, "you've got another nine hours. Maybe you should keep him until then."

Nicole was surprised by the lawyer's attitude. She smiled while shaking hands with the counselor. Who knows, maybe the attractive lawyer had been a victim of male violence herself.

Bud and Lee grinned broadly at each other and Bud nodded briskly, his lips widening across his broad face. "My pleasure Counselor."

He slapped Enrique's file across Lee's chest as they departed down the hall.

"Can I get you a cup of really bad coffee Lieutenant Henry?"

"That would be lovely, "said the pretty lawyer, and Nicole led the way.

"Men like that give me the creeps. Why would Elena hang out with him in the first place?" asked Nancy later as the four officers sat in the conference room comparing notes. She looked tired and overworked and for once her usually perfect uniform begged for a pressing.

"Maybe that's why she's dead. Elena decided he wasn't worth it and Enrique got angry and did her. We can't let that guy back on the streets and I'm gonna do something about it!" Lee grabbed Enrique's file and headed toward Jerry's office.

"Wonder what he's up to?" asked Nancy, taking a sip of her diet soda.

147

Bud smiled. "Maybe Lee can work some magic with the Captain that would allow us to extend our noted hospitality past six." The three grinned and got back to checking Enrique's phone records.

By 11 a.m. Nicole felt tired and discouraged and it didn't help that the disconcerting encounter with Justin Zachary yesterday had cost her another night's sleep. She couldn't decide what the hell she felt; as she kept visualizing those dark dusty eyes and the way his jeans had slipped down upon his lean waist and . . . she slammed the personnel folders down upon her desk in disgust. She was nothing better than a love struck teenager who couldn't stop fantasizing about a man who was one of the primary suspects in Elena Gonzalez's murder case. Why did he have to be so damn beautiful?

The day passed too slowly; time spent on the phone and computer, reaching countless dead-ends, and verifying each and every one of the suspect's alibis. Rosa phoned around 11:30; politely informing Nicole she'd quit her position at The Desert Sky and could be reached at Carmen's.

The phone on her desk shrilled once again and Nicole raised the receiver to her ear as her eyes scanned the list of jewelry stores selling oversized sapphires.

"Scott Adams here. I wondered if any of those hunger pangs have hit you yet Detective?"

"I'm afraid I'm not in the mood for steak, but..." she paused, thinking rapidly. "I do have a couple more questions regarding the case and might be able to squeeze in lunch at the local diner."

"I'm game," agreed Scott easily. "Give me the location and I'll meet you there in 30 minutes."

The diner was crowded and noisy as usual and Scott seemed a bit out of place in its casual decor. He beamed at her anyway as he slipped into the red vinyl booth and took the offered menu.

"They have some pretty good specials. I eat here a great deal."

"Sounds good," Scott pointed to the salad special of the day with a well-manicured finger.

Once the harassed waitress left their table, Nicole said, "I need to know about the power switchover at The Desert Sky."

"Whew, you don't waste any time do you? Alright." He straightened his beautiful powder blue silk tie and threw a casual arm across the back of the booth. Today he'd chosen an expensive navy blue suit with faint pin-striping probably surpassing Nicole's entire clothing budget for the year.

"I have to admit I don't care much for Justin Zachary though I respect him. I miss my old boss. Bob Severns was as good as they get; a people person, always out and about and having lunch with the employees, able to chat with them about sports and whatnot. He knew everyone by name and made it his goal to help the staff better themselves. He's the one that elevated Mrs. O'Toole to housekeeping manager after realizing she'd worked as a maid for over 13 years. Let's face it; she wouldn't have risen to that position anywhere else. He also listened to Judith's report about raising the entry-level salaries for all employees. Talk about a morale booster among the lesser paid in the resort!"

"So why did he leave?"

"I think he was just plan sick and tired of the desert. He'd also gone through a nasty divorce about 18 months ago and from what I heard his wife took him for just about everything he had. I can imagine Maui made an appealing offer that ensured a much needed change of scenery."

Nicole smiled in agreement, "I can see why he'd take the offer. I'd consider that kind of relocation myself!"

"Zachary's just a different kind of fellow though," continued Scott, following his original train of thought. "He's polite and dignified, but incredibly hard to get to know. He puts in long hours and seems conscientious, but I'm never quite sure what his agenda really is. I always get the feeling he's judging me and finding me wanting. He's good-looking but aloof, if you enjoy that kind of exotic mix. And our Judith is really drawn to that mysterious persona of his."

Nicole shifted uncomfortably and took a sip of her iced tea, which tasted bland compared to the mint tea Justin had offered her the day before. Justin and Judith? She glanced away acutely aware of the painful tightening within her stomach.

Under a Desert Sky

"So they're seeing one another," she managed nonchalantly.

"That's the gossip. And of course it just drives poor Richard mad. He's had a thing for Judith since she joined the resort chain. But once Zachary walked in the door, Judith did one double take and started needing a whole lot of private meetings with the boss, if you catch my drift."

"And what about Mr. Zachary's relationship with Elena?"

"I didn't know he had one. But who knows? Justin's good looking and a girl in her position might have pondered what he could offer her."

"And you? Did she glance your way?"

Scott moved uncomfortably. "I . . . I admit she was very pretty. But if you want to know if I partook of the offered goods, I didn't, and a lot of that had to do with Zachary. He caught me talking to her one evening after hours and pulled me into his office the next morning warning me to keep my hands off the help. He suggested I look elsewhere. Who knows, maybe he'd already staked a claim himself."

"Maybe," she agreed.

Their meal arrived and Nicole noted he had ordered a large green salad with spicy grilled chicken on top. "I like to eat healthy. Glad to see you do as well."

Nicole smiled and dug into her fruit and cottage cheese and they munched companionably for a few minutes.

"So, do you like your job?" he asked.

"Of course. I've always worked and it really helps pay for the furnishings." She grinned and he chuckled.

"And you always wanted to be a police officer?"

"No," said Nicole truthfully. "I wanted to be a ballerina, but one has to be realistic."

He laughed." I like a girl with both beauty and brains."

Nicole could see his comment warranted a positive response so she murmured a polite thank you.

"Of course, any girl hooked up with me wouldn't have to work."

"Oh really?" said Nicole nonchalantly, remembering vividly his salary figures from the computer printout.

"Yeah, I think it's great when a woman doesn't have to work. She can shop and stay home with the kids and not worry."

"It does sound ideal."

"I wish my dad could have given that to my mom but she had to work her whole life through. They divorced when I was fifteen and after that she never seemed to have enough time or money."

"She must be very proud of you."

"That she is. Mom worked overtime to help support me through college. I had a partial academic scholarship to Berkeley but had to wait on tables at the Hilton to help make ends meet and that's when I decided I liked the hotel industry. So I graduated with a degree in business. Things have looked up ever since. I've sworn that my wife will be well taken care of and have some leisure time; not having to work her fingers to the bone like my mom."

"You must have great plans then for your own career?" replied Nicole, realizing that Scott wasn't asking her opinion.

"You bet, my goal is to someday own a group of resorts like The Desert Sky. Of course that may take a while. I need to obtain all the experience I can and make the right sort of connections. I'm saving all my extra money and investing it. Hopefully in four or five years I'll be able to buy into a small hotel chain."

"I admire your tenacity," said Nicole honestly. "And I hope you achieve your goals. Do the other members of your executive floor share similar goals?"

"Ah, back to the case I see?"

"Just trying to stay focused," she responded mildly. "What about Richard Greaves?"

"Richard Greaves would die for the opportunity to move up in the organization. Unfortunately, he's not a man of vision. He's a nice guy and all, but I'm not certain he has what it takes to be an upper-level executive. I'm afraid you have to be a bit ruthless. Richard's too nice for his own good and often tentative in his decisions. He's got to learn that when you want something you have to go out there and take it. That may sound heartless, but you can bet your bottom dollar B.W. Weston is looking for just that kind of go-getter. Richard could use a little more creative thinking skills."

"Yet one probably wouldn't want to be too creative as an accountant would they?"

Scott laughed. "That's for certain, and I'm probably miles off when it comes to Richard. I just kinda feel sorry for the guy. And then there's Judith. Now there's one woman nothing's going to stop. She's headed for the stars with the brains, beauty and personality to match. I fully expect she'll have moved into the very top circle of the resort chain within ten years. Apparently, B.W. Weston nearly made her the executive director, but decided on Zachary instead because she didn't have quite enough experience. She'll make it though."

"You admire her?"

"Yeah, I do. And if you are wondering if I'm attracted to her, I am and I'm not. She's too ambitious for me. I can't imagine her settling down and raising a family or having much time for a love interest."

"Perhaps she's too much competition for you."

"Ooh, do I hear a little venom there?"

"Of course not," said Nicole disarmingly. "You stated yourself you didn't want a working wife. She'd be striving as hard as you to make it to the top and having two workaholics in the family could be more than a marriage could handle."

"You're right. I want someone waiting for me when I get home, not facing me off in the board room." Memories of a similar conversation with her ex-boyfriend Mark Leone rang in her ears. At least Scott was honest and Nicole couldn't fault him for that. Any woman who became involved with him would know from the start where he stood on the marriage and career issue. "I just wish Richard would take more warning with Judith," he continued. "He's already been burned once by his ex-wife."

"And Justin Zachary?" Nicole asked casually.

"Ah, the boss. He's an enigma, that one, coolly professional, but distant. No one's allowed to know him well unless he wants them to. Justin's well-educated and efficient, but in my opinion not charismatic enough. Guess his father used to work for B.W. Weston years ago and that's probably how he obtained this position." It was clear Scott didn't believe Justin's abilities warranted his promotion.

"He didn't deserve the job?"

"I'm not saying that. I just somehow get the feeling he won't be around here very long. He seems to have made no personal friends, except for Judith perhaps, and doesn't appear to want to. I've invited him out on several occasions for a beer or coffee and he's only accepted my invitation once. I've seen him on the golf course a couple of times, but he's no golfer."

"Do you know what his interests are?"

"He's a bit of a movie buff because Judith mentioned his collecting classic films or something. I also think he's a runner. Judith indicated he's training for a half-marathon and works out early every morning. I tell you, I'll take the gym over running any day. Besides, the scenery's a lot more attractive."

Nicole had to grin. She knew precisely the scenery Scott referred to.

"Does he have any money problems?"

"Not that I know of and he makes a mighty fine salary. I should know, I sign his checks. He owns the Lexus and I believe rents his house in Palm Desert, but one never knows what other expenses or "hobbies," might eat up his spare cash. I'm not sure about much in regards to Zachary. I know that Judith is doing well, and Richard... well he gives most of his away to his wife. I guess all of us could do with more money. Still, I just don't see any of our team having financial problems big enough to cause them to embezzle from the company. Aren't you going to write this down?"

Nicole pointed to her head.

"Ah, a brain like a mouse trap." Nicole grinned and nodded. "And just what do you really want?" asked Scott, leaning a bit closer. "Since we're talking about everyone else's ambitions."

"I want to solve this case."

He reached out and touched her hand, running his thumb over the pale surface.

"Do you have the number of Bob Severns?" asked Nicole, wiping her mouth and moving her hand away. "I'd like to contact him regarding the resort and see what insights he might have."

"No problem," grinned Scott at her withdrawal. "I'll give you the number if you promise to go out dancing with me on Friday night."

"Dancing? On Friday night? I'm afraid not."

"Why? You got another date?"

She shook her head. "No, I don't. I just don't date men involved in a current investigation." The lie stuck in her craw. If Justin beckoned, she knew she'd come running.

Scott raised his hand signaling for the check. "That's what I was afraid of. I'll have to mention that to Justin since he was quite testy when I indicated I was joining you for lunch. That might soothe his ruffled feathers. I'll take care of the bill if you don't mind; it's a male thing. See you Nicole." He slid from the booth and managed to beam not only at her but the overworked waitress. Both couldn't help grinning back.

Back at her desk Nicole fingered the lopsided ceramic piece Jesse had made for her at camp. He'd painted it in Lakers' colors and the gold and purple had bled into each other. She imagined the Lake Arrowhead Camp was beautiful this time of year and for an instant longed to see his dear simple face. Her phone buzzed.

"Lewis."

"Zachary."

"Mr. Zachary, it's ah . . . nice to hear from you."

"Have a good lunch?" he asked tersely.

"It was both filling and informative," she countered.

"I bet it was. Just wanted to let you know B.W. Weston is arriving around 5 p.m. and indicated he'll be meeting with your Captain first thing in the morning. I'm going to have dinner with him tonight to discuss the embezzlement and murder."

"Thanks for the heads up."

Justin hesitated for a long moment. "Nicole, about yesterday..."

"There's no need to apologize," she voiced quietly so Dusty couldn't hear.

"I wasn't planning too. I just wish I were having dinner with you instead." She clunked the phone down and swore viciously under her breath; so loudly that Dusty roused from his glowing screen.

"Everything okay sweetie?"

"No," said Nicole grimly. "And there's nothing I can do about it."

Her phone buzzed and Jerry's terse voice ordered her into his office.

"I've been concerned about you Nicole."

"Concerned?" She let the glass door bang shut as she approached his neat desk.

"Lee indicated you just had lunch with Scott Adams."

Nicole felt a wave of annoyance wash over her. "A business lunch Jerry."

"Really?"

"You have nothing to be concerned about. I'm not remotely attracted to him. I've never favored blondes much."

"I've read your report on your conversation with Zachary yesterday. Is there anything else you'd like to tell me about it?" His black eyes intently scrutinized her face.

She swallowed, admitting the truth to herself and her captain. "I need to be pulled from this case Jerry."

Jerry sighed and flopped down in his chair. "That's what I thought. Is Zachary harassing you?"

"No," she whispered.

"I see. So it's not harassment, but attraction. It was evident from the first moment in my office but I chose to ignore it. You feel you can't be objective?"

"I'm not sure. No, I can't be, not in regards to him."

"Are you seeing him?"

"Not exactly."

"You're strangely becoming a woman of few words Nicole. I take it that really means you've only seen him regarding department business but that could change at any moment? Damn it Nicole. You're the best I've got and now you're screwing up!"

He appeared so fierce that Nicole wanted to laugh; if only the situation wasn't so pathetic.

"I'm not going to pull you off Nicole, but I'm warning you. Only interview him with Bud in tow—do you hear? Don't see the man alone."

"Yes sir." It was like pulling teeth, but she agreed.

"And stay out of his bed until this case is closed and he's cleared. Do that for both our sakes. You'd hate yourself if he was somehow involved in this mess."

Nicole blanched. "I'll try," she whispered, acutely embarrassed as she remembered Justin's passion of yesterday.

"You will or you'll face more than a personal reprimand! Now get back to work and keep your mind on the case!"

Jerry Hernandez stared after his favorite employee's retreating back and watched Nicole sink dejectedly into her chair. He knew he could count on her to do the right thing, even if it killed her; she was that dedicated a cop. Zachary had better be as innocent and clean as the sweet backside of a baby or he'd have to deal with Jerry himself. He only hoped he was making the right decision by allowing her to remain on the case.

Chapter 12

Thursday dawned hot and clear as Nicole drank a cup of bitter, strong coffee to wake up. At least five times the previous evening she'd ventured near the quiet phone on her kitchen counter desperately wanting to call Justin. Once, she'd even idled in the doorway of her small apartment with keys and handbag in hand, set to drive to his adobe house in Palm Desert, throwing all caution to the wind. But instead, she'd lain awake half the night fantasizing about his lean features and deep voice until she fell asleep in the wee hours of the morning only to dream again of his quiet face and devastating kiss. After a shower as cold as she could bear she headed into the station. Jerry Hernandez held an impromptu meeting in his office.

"So just what are we working here Jerry?" Nancy asked. "Is it embezzlement, homicide, or even vice case?"

"Perhaps all three," he returned quietly. "Why don't you update us Nicole, so we're all on the same page."

Nicole briefly and concisely repeated all she'd learned to the team consisting of Bud, Dusty, Nancy Williams, Lee Gianotti, Jerry, and herself. She managed to keep her voice steady while talking about Justin and left out Scott's invitation to dance. The group's interest pricked up considerably when she relayed the young blonde executive's clear desire to own a hotel chain in the near future. Jerry, using a white board, kept tally in separate columns. So far, nothing really pointed to any single suspect, Enrique included, though a female perpetrator could be crossed out as well as anyone under six feet. The ring was deemed as most likely being a gift from the killer. Jerry stood with his hands on his hips and made a decision.

"Dusty, you follow up on the numbers connected to the embezzlement. My gut instinct is that Elena Gonzalez's murder is connected to the money; and Enrique, though probably not the actual killer, is likely involved. Lee, you and Nancy return to the hotel and speak with Richard Greaves. He called again just before our meeting and indicated he may have figured out how the money was transferred. Sounded pretty urgent. In fact . . . you take Dusty along in case there's some computer gibberish only he can understand. He can work on tracking the money when he returns."

The three exited, Dusty only too happy to accompany Lee and Nancy, if the glow on his face was any indicator.

Under a Desert Sky

"Nicole, you remain here and meet B.W. Weston when he arrives at nine. Maybe we can discover why this Zachary character was picked for the directorship after being let go in Washington. After that, you start hitting all the expensive jewelry stores in the area to check on any recent purchases of sapphire rings. Dusty made a color copy—one of the jewelers must remember it. Bud, head back down to the City and flash a copy of Enrique and Elena's photos around and see if anyone recognized them. Since we let Enrique go last night, it would be interesting to see where he is hangs out in his free time. And try to blend in, will you." Jerry grinned; Bud's roughneck appearance was always a joke between him and Bud.

"I'll try my best, boss," quipped Bud, who resembled a burly Mexican trucker ready for a brawl. "I'll get into my scroungy beer hall clothes. Wish I had my motorcycle."

He appeared nothing less than delighted.

"Aren't those your scroungy beer hall clothes already?" asked the Captain, pretending to be serious.

"Nah, these are my Sunday best."

"Shouldn't I accompany him?" asked Nicole.

"I'm sorry honey," said Bud flexing a muscle. "You definitely wouldn't fit in to the places I'm going to haunt." He whistled and wagged his ponytail at her before he strutted out.

"I'm gonna lose that guy to the Hell's Angels someday," said Jerry mildly before suddenly tensing. "May the fireworks begin," he mumbled, as the glass office door banged open and a burly white-haired man dressed in blue jeans and a t-shirt that said '*Jerry Garcia isn't dead or grateful*' stormed in. Nicole hadn't known what to expect regarding the owner of the Sun Resorts, but this certainly hadn't been it.

"You better be making progress on this Gonzalez case or I'm gonna have to kick your ass Hernandez!"

Jerry seemed relatively unperturbed. "A cup of thick, over-brewed coffee that's been in the pot since yesterday, Brian?"

"Coffee? Hell, I want my money back!"

"I don't have it, so why don't you sit down, Brian, and cool off. You know how I hate it when you tower over me."

"Who's this?" barked B.W., his eyes scouring Nicole's slim frame. His pale blue eyes gleamed shrewdly, warranting no nonsense.

"This is Detective Nicole Lewis. She's part of the team working on the Gonzalez murder and its possible connections to your embezzlement case."

"You mean the team that hasn't found out anything yet?"

Nicole bristled at his implication. "Actually, we have found out many interesting tidbits Mr. Weston. Elena appears to have had many 'outside' interests as well as an angry boyfriend, an expensive ring, and a hefty deposit into her checking account. These 'details' take time to track down, as well as eliminating the many suspects, of which you're included."

Under a Desert Sky

"Me a damn suspect? Good God! You lollygag around while my money up and evaporates. Six hundred thousand this past week alone! And you want me to sit back while "Suzy Q" here does her knitting and wait for another half million to waltz out the door!"

"Do you want our help or not Brian?" asked Jerry, quietly pouring two cups of coffee and placing one before the raging B.W. Weston.

"I want something done damn it! I can't keep putting off the Board about this 'cost overrun' as your yoyo counterparts in Orlando have instructed me to tell them. I need action or I'm taking matters into my own hands!"

"Do whatever you think is right," said Jerry Hernandez mildly. "But I think you ought to know that where there's one murder, another easily follows."

"I've reviewed the facts you faxed me the other day and I can't see for the life of me how this housekeeping girl's death connects at all with the embezzlement problem. It's clear her young stud's done her in!" protested the white-haired hotelier.

"Actually, according to five witnesses who will testify to his being on base at the time of the murder, it's clear that her young man did *not* do it no matter what his violent nature might suggest," bristled Nicole.

"So you've got nothing then?" Weston glowered.

"That's not *nothing*. We know at least one suspect who hasn't committed the actual crime, though we haven't erased his possible connection to the homicide. But I can guarantee," cautioned Jerry, "that if you go charging in there like the proverbial bull in the china shop, your embezzler, and maybe murderer is going to disappear faster than you can say 'get a grip.' "

Nicole watched Jerry's calmly spoken words subdue the big man somewhat. B.W. straightened his broad shoulders and threatened more quietly. "One week, that's all you're getting," and he whirled, the glass door slamming violently after him.

Jerry smiled mildly and took a sip of his coffee. He grimaced at its foul taste. "I think that went rather well, don't you? You heard the man Nicole, one week."

"What a jerk!" Nicole retorted.

"Actually his wife would say he's a real pussycat; you've just got to let him growl."

"You knew him before," she accused.

"I was in Nam with him. He's a Texas roughneck and go-getter who's as totally honest as he is impatient. Let's hope he's got enough brains and restraint to give us some space. Wish he hadn't run out before I could ask him some questions about Zachary."

Jerry's phone rang and he answered it directly, his face taking on an alarmed expression. "Are you sure? We'll be right over."

"Who was that?" asked Nicole, suddenly breathless.

Jerry grabbed his coat and pushed her toward the door. "Judith Chamberlain. Apparently Richard Greaves has locked himself in his office and refuses to speak to anyone but the police. He says he knows who killed Elena Gonzalez!"

Jerry slapped the blue light atop his vehicle and they pulled into The Desert Sky parking lot in record time. Several police cruisers flashed brightly in the palm studded lot and Nicole's heart sank. Their presence could only mean one thing. When the elevator opened Nicole observed a subdued Lee and Nancy trying to calm a weeping Judith. The door to Richard Greaves' office hung wide open.

Lee shook his head when he saw Jerry. "We were too late. He took his secrets with him."

Nicole straightened her back and followed the Captain into Richard Greaves' office. The chief accountant sat slumped at his desk, his head centering a pool of blood staining the papers scattered before him. His left hand still clenched a .22 caliber pistol reeking of powder. The bullet's entry hole was small and perfectly placed inside the left-hand side of Richard Greaves' skull.

Jerry swore under his breath, first in English and then in Spanish. A weary Lee entered, followed by the ever-diligent Otto, who requested they back away from the desk. He began snapping quick photos at every angle.

"Why," asked Jerry disgusted, "would a man so determined to speak to the police kill himself before he even got the chance?"

Lee held out a single envelope with a latex-gloved hand. "There was a note, but it doesn't say much."

Jerry took the envelope, stained red at the edges, and pulled out the single sheet carefully, with a quickly donned glove. He read aloud.

"*I'm sorry my dearest, I'm just a weak idiot who fell into the oldest trap known to man. I just couldn't bear for you to know. Tell him he's correct in his assumptions and En...*" Jerry stopped. "I can't make out the rest."

Nicole tried to decipher the last three scrawled words, but they were so distorted and smeared their meaning was lost. "This word appears to be the first two letters of Enrique's name, but I can't make out the others. Maybe 'will' or 'wild,' who knows. The blood is smearing the letters, plus the writing is so strange."

"Very interesting. Almost as if..." Jerry paused, lost in thought. "And tell who?" he queried to no one in particular. "Check the prints on the gun and make sure he didn't have any help. This all reeks of bad timing. Let me talk to the Chamberlain woman." He handed the letter to Nicole who reread it twice, trying to figure out its cryptic meaning.

Later, the blood-dampened note whisked off by the forensics department, Nicole surveyed the wide hall. Jerry stood engaged in earnest conversation with Judith Chamberlain who sobbed openly. Nancy stood at her elbow, once again looking calm and collected. But where was Justin Zachary? Nicole quickly moved down the corridor and opened the director's glass door. His secretary, Mrs. Gaston, was vacant from her desk so she tapped on his office door.

"Mr. Zachary? Mr. Zachary, are you in there?"

No answer forthcoming, she eased open the wooden door. The spacious office was completely deserted; only a half-eaten apple sat upon the desk next to a resort notepad. Nicole was amazed to see her own name and home phone number scribbled across the white piece of paper, as well as bold letters spelling out the name Lindsey. Scooping up the top sheet, Nicole left the office suddenly feeling apprehensive.

The rest of the day was mayhem. Judith Chamberlain, totally beside herself, didn't calm down enough for anyone to get a coherent statement out of her for nearly an hour. As the facts stood, Judith had heard from her secretary that Richard Greaves raged within the confines of his office, refusing to open the door for anyone, for almost 10 minutes. Judith had listened to his incoherent shouts and upon hearing him mention he knew who'd killed Elena, immediately called the police.

Less than ten minutes later and only five minutes before Nancy, Lee and Dusty had arrived, a shot had rang out. Her secretary and the other people working the wing had all agreed to Judith's recital of the events, including the now somber Scott Adams, who stood slim and handsome in a light gray double-breasted suit. He gave Nicole a despairing nod as he dictated his statement to Lee.

Nicole read and reread the file on Richard Greaves as well as a copy of the brief suicide note at her desk that afternoon. If only she could decipher the last three words. Hopefully forensics would have better luck. Dusty was assigned to Richard's computer as soon as the body was removed and the office was dusted for fingerprints. Lee called, relaying that over fifteen good prints had been removed, but Nicole was not hopeful. The amount of employees entering and leaving Richard's office each day must be substantial. She spent most of the afternoon trying to discover to who or what *Lindsey* might refer. The hotel's data banks revealed neither an employee nor client with the name of Lindsey. By four o'clock in the afternoon her tired eyes watered and her back ached.

"Nicole, get in here quick," shouted Jerry, and she hurried into his office. Jerry's small TV blared as a well-dressed female reporter interviewed a harassed looking Scott Adams.

"We've tried to contact the resort director, Mr. Justin Zachary, for comment regarding The Desert Sky's employee deaths, but he's apparently missing. No one has seen or heard from him since around 9 a.m. this morning."

The pushy female reporter thrust a microphone into Scott's handsome face. "Isn't this the second death in less than 72 hours at The Desert Sky Resort? And weren't they committed only feet from each other?"

Under a Desert Sky

"There have been two deaths, but the second was suicide. And yes. They happened on the same floor within close proximity each other."

"Is there any speculation by you or the police that Greaves may have been the murderer of the young Gonzalez woman?"

"I have no comment at the present time."

"Is the director, Justin Zachary, a suspect at this time?"

"I really have no comment. The police are handling everything and will give you a much more detailed statement later."

"Please Mr. Adams! One more question. Isn't it true more than a million dollars has been embezzled from The Desert Sky Resort in the past few weeks?"

Scott seemed to flounder but recovered quickly. "Some monies are missing, but once again the police are working on all angles of the case."

Another male reporter threw in, "Isn't it likely that the suicide may have something to do with the missing funds? Wasn't the suicide victim the Resort's chief accountant?"

"I really have no further comment," repeated a sweating Scott as he pulled back from the reporters and hurriedly folded himself into his bright red Porsche.

Jerry slammed his fist on the desk. "Zachary's missing and the embezzlement's public. So what else can go wrong? How in the hell did that happen? The secrecy of our case is as leaky as a lopsided sieve. And this is the first I've heard of Zachary being truant. Damn Adams for not notifying us.

You scurry out to Zachary's residence in Palm Desert this minute and see if he's hiding out there. Take Dusty with you as back-up since Bud's somewhere in Cathedral City playing at being a detective. And use an official vehicle for God's sake!"

Nicole heard her Captain swearing about something "hitting the fan," as she closed the door. And why not? Justin was missing, his chief accountant had killed himself, and the Resort's embezzlement had gone public. Justin had better make an appearance soon or he'd be dragged into the station in handcuffs whether she liked it or not. Her head throbbed and Nicole had the vague sensation everything she'd done in the past couple days was all for nothing.

Thirty minutes later Nicole parked the cruiser inside the wrought iron gate which now stood open, the waterfall echoing through the vacant garden. Dusty approached the big oak door and gave the brass knocker an insistent triple knock. After four tries he gave up and shrugged, obstinately trying the knob. Amazingly it turned under his sweaty fingers.

"Mr. Zachary? Mr. Zachary? It's Detective Lewis and Sergeant Morant from the PSPD; are you in here? Is there anyone home?" Dusty's voice echoed hollowly through the exquisitely decorated rooms of the large house. The pair searched the downstairs thoroughly; calling out every few minutes to be certain the residence was indeed vacant. The house hosted a beautiful modern kitchen, spotlessly clean and seemingly unused; its stainless steel appliances sleek and shiny. A small den, obviously functioning as an office, and a large music room to the rear of the downstairs lounge with a huge black Steinway nestled against the back wall remained ominously silent.

As she and Dusty searched the extensive library down the hall, a gnawing fear began to eat at the lining of her stomach. Something wasn't right here. The house was not only deserted, but seemed virtually unlived in. Not a throw pillow appeared out of place. No magazines or anything remotely personal graced the polished oak and glass furniture of the comfortable den where a giant TV screen faced the spacious room at an attractive angle. Nicole mounted the stairs quietly, Dusty behind her, service revolvers drawn and ready.

"Mr. Zachary?" Dusty bellowed.

The upstairs contained four bedrooms, two on each side of the hall. Nicole checked out the two on her left while Dusty took the right. The first bedroom, feminine and obviously unused, was stylishly designed. A beautiful cream-colored satin comforter covered the brass bed and a lovely tan and sea foam green dressing table and stool nestled into the corner near floor-to-ceiling mirrored closets. Nicole opened the sliding doors, the huge wardrobes silent and empty. She straightened up, puzzled. It was the same story in the second room, which proved to be a gigantic master suite equipped with king-sized bed and a lovely view of the pool. Masculine tones in deep browns and blacks were expressed by the expensive bedspread and papered walls. Nicole checked the huge oaken dresser and noted the drawers were completely empty. Upon opening the massive mirrored closet, she discovered no pressed suits or expensive silk ties.

Had Justin packed everything up and disappeared or had he simply chosen not to occupy the master suite in his own home? It just didn't make sense. Any why would he have rented such a large furnished house in the first place? Across the hall, another fairly large bedroom also sat empty and unused. It contained two twin beds with matching blue patchwork quilts and lovely paintings of the desert hanging above them. No toiletries rested on the gray tile countertops in the bathroom. The feel of this room echoed the master suite; empty and unused.

Dusty called from the last bedroom on the right, which proved to be much smaller and contained a neatly made double bed covered in dark browns and blues. The spread was slightly rumpled as if someone had recently sat there. Dusty indicated the open cedar closet. At last some articles of clothing hung from the padded hangers and Nicole instantly recognized the dark gray suit Justin Zachary had worn to the office the first time she'd met him, as well as many dress shirts, three stylishly tailored suits, and several pairs of expensive dress shoes. In the bathroom a toothbrush and tube of mint toothpaste rested next to some waxed dental floss on the beautiful tile counter. A pale blue towel hung neatly on the rack and when Nicole opened the top drawer she saw a used razor, some aspirin, and an assortment of allergy tablets. The next drawer caused her to grimace painfully. It contained an open box of condoms, a hairbrush, and some nail tools.

"This doesn't make sense," Dusty's words followed her into the neat bathroom. "It's a beautiful huge house. The director, who's obviously paying the equivalent of my entire year's rent each month, doesn't reside in the master suite with its incredible view. Instead, he's camped out in this smaller bedroom like he doesn't even live here."

"Dusty, I want you to call the Captain and get a team here right away. They'll need a search warrant. Don't touch anything else. I think our bird's flown and I'm afraid I know the reason why. Check out the phone and see if there's an answering machine and have Nancy track Zachary's outgoing phone messages."

"You've got it," agreed Dusty, as he bounded out of the room.

She scoured the rest of the bedroom while Dusty headed to the front patio to use his cell phone. Except for the TV/VCR combination set standing on the dresser, there was little else to see. She pressed the eject button and eyed the well-worn copy of *Casablanca*. Three other videos ranging from *Terminator* to the offbeat comedy *The Gods Must be Crazy* set next to the TV. Nicole remembered Scott's comment about Justin's penchant for classic movies. Nicole looked once again through the closets and opened the dark dresser's drawers. A couple pairs of jeans, a few folded t-shirts, and several running outfits were all the bottom drawers contained. The top right opened to reveal several pairs of dress and sport socks while the left housed only boxer briefs in solid colors.

The bedside table held two *Runner's World* magazines, a Tom Clancy novel, and a portable CD player with a recent Sting CD inside. The right-hand drawer revealed 10-12 CD's of an eclectic variety, a micro-cassette recorder, and a Palm Springs phone book. There was no suitcase or luggage of any kind in the closet, or evidence that anyone; especially a woman, had been living here. If Justin had bolted, he'd left the majority of his clothing. Nicole exited the vacant house to join Dusty in the hot cruiser, feeling disturbed and on edge.

As she and Dusty sat idly in the shade waiting for the crew with the warrant to show up, she radioed Captain Hernandez with the news.

Jerry cursed loudly. "We've been one step behind the entire week. Who knows where Zachary's gone and why he's really missing? It's getting late. As soon as the search crew relieves you, take off and try and get some rest. Was there a computer in the house?"

"Yes, in the main office," responded Nicole.

"Have Dusty bring it in with him. He can hitch a ride with the forensics team. I suspect tomorrow's going to be a long day so get some rest while you can. Does Zachary have your cell number?"

"Yes he does."

"Are you okay?"

Under a Desert Sky

"Something's terribly wrong Jerry. I can feel it in my bones."

"Me too. May I speak to Dusty?"

Nicole sat in the sweltering shade and listened to Dusty rattle on, feeling bleak. She'd never believed in premonitions, but anxiety caused her stomach to throb as mightily as when her father died. It didn't slack off after a solid dose of fizzing antacid or even her favorite reruns of *ER*; and it was after midnight before she finally dropped off to sleep.

Chapter 13

Her cell phone blared its tinny rendition of Beethoven's fifth and Nicole sat bolt upright in her bed, clutching the damp sheets tightly to her, positive she'd just closed her eyes a minute ago. The phone repeated its heavy melody and she dashed to her handbag resting on her oak chest of drawers.

"Hello," Nicole managed, sounding only half-awake. Breathing heavily; her head throbbed painfully from lack of sleep. Nicole glanced groggily at her bedside clock whose luminous dial read 4:40 a.m. "Hello," she repeated.

She had nearly hung up when she heard a thready voice say her name. Incredibly it sounded just like Justin Zachary.

"Is that you Justin?" she exclaimed.

"Nicole," gasped out the voice again. "I can't deliver..." there was a long silence and Nicole sensed the young executive was having difficulty speaking. Had he been running?

"Mr. Zachary, Mr. Zachary? Justin? Are you alright?"

"The... Lindsey file... in..." An excited gasp and the sound of a car back firing through static caused her to jump. "You... need to..." the phone echoed before going completely dead. Nicole immediately hit the caller ID button on her phone and redialed. No response. Either a cell phone's batteries had died or Justin had chosen not to answer. Another, more sinister reason assailed her and Nicole paled at the thought.

Nicole immediately called Jerry at home, suddenly feeling guilty when the sleepy voice of Grace answered. She had forgotten it wasn't even 5 a.m. yet.

"This'd better be good Nicole," he snapped. Jerry was obviously not a morning person.

"Justin Zachary called me about five minutes ago. The caller ID button gave me this number." She recited the number and then had to repeat it after Jerry barked that he didn't have any paper. Thank goodness Grace was always amiable.

"Anything else?"

"Yeah. He gasped out something about a Lindsey file... I couldn't figure out the rest of what he said."

"Lindsey file? Has to be connected to the embezzlement. Maybe he wants to come clean. And...?"

"Nothing else. His phone went dead amidst lots of background noise and static."

Under a Desert Sky

"Since I'm already up I'll meet you at the station at seven sharp. Bring the disk with the resort's database with you and we'll have Dusty check it for a possible Lindsey connection. Good work Lewis. Just next time have your boyfriends call you at a reasonable hour." He hung up abruptly.

Nicole dragged herself into the small bathroom and stood breathlessly in front of the medicine cabinet mirror, her heart pounding violently. Her mirror reflected a pale, subdued image and Nicole leaned over the sink to splash cold water upon her face. There was no returning to the warmth and comfort of her bed so Nicole dressed simply in beige pants and a yellow and white striped shirt. After consuming a meager breakfast she headed for the station, even though her steel wristwatch indicated it was only 6 a.m. Amazingly, Nancy was already at her desk, typing up information on the now released Enrique Diaz. The quiet soothed Nicole's befuddled brain as she shuffled through her tan shoulder bag and gave a snort of disgust. The disk containing the Weston Enterprises' database still lay on the breakfast bar where she had hurriedly consumed her nonfat yogurt and granola bar. She groaned. This meant an additional trip home and back, probably running into the early morning traffic. But she had no choice; Dusty needed that disk this morning.

She shouldered her bag again and stopped by Nancy's orderly desk, noting that the uniformed officer appeared tired and stressed.

"I left that blasted disk for Dusty at home, Nancy. If Jerry comes in, tell him I'll return as soon as possible and need to speak with him right away."

"You're here early, Nicole, what's the occasion? A break in the case?" Nancy glanced up hopefully.

"I'm not sure. Justin Zachary called me early this morning and mentioned something about a Lindsey file.

"The same name you found on the notepad?"

"The very same. Tell Jerry I'll fill him in when I return. If Bud comes in the next few minutes tell him to phone me on my cell."

"Sure Nicole. Hey, we've got to talk about something when you come back. Just you and me, alright? It's really important."

"Sure. Are you okay?" Nancy seemed near tears.

Her colleague swallowed deeply and continued in a more controlled tone. "Just tired. You know they put out an APB a few minutes ago on Zachary don't you?"

"No, but I'm not surprised."

"I'll give the Captain your message. Have fun in the traffic." Nancy tried to give a pert smile, her fingers once again flying over the keyboard. Nicole sulked all the way home. Normally she was a very organized person, but lack of sleep and the stark reality surrounding Justin Zachary was making her befuddled and incompetent. Vowing to focus her energies more effectively, she parked her white Toyota at the curb instead of in the shade of her carport, since it would only take a minute to retrieve the disk.

Under a Desert Sky

Nicole paused in front of her door, searching her Lakers key chain for the right key before halting abruptly. Blood smeared the brass doorknob and trailed down an inch or so beneath in one thin stream. As she looked closer, it was evident the lock had been jimmied and her eyes traveled involuntarily toward the floorboards. Several droplets of blood stained the green shag doormat. Nicole slowly removed her service revolver, holding the barrel upright and ready, and pushed the door open with her shoulder to avoid touching the blood on the knob. Her small apartment appeared silent and dark since she had drawn the blinds earlier to help keep out the scorching midday heat of Palm Springs.

Nicole scanned the petite modern kitchen before moving to the center of the living room. Nothing seemed out of place, but as her eyes searched the floor she spotted them instantly. There and there; small round droplets of blood staining the wooden parquet floor. They stenciled a crimson trail leading toward the back of the apartment, toward her bedroom, office, and bathroom. Silently and stealthily Nicole followed the expanding blood trail, her revolver raised in readiness against her breast. More and more droplets appeared as she moved further down the hall, gradually becoming larger and closer together. Nicole popped her head cautiously into the tiny office where her laptop computer set silently on the wide oak desk. The bookshelves were untouched and her CD player sat silently on the windowsill cheerily draped in yellow linen curtains.

The hall bathroom fronted the end of the hall and Nicole gently pushed open the white door, scrutinizing its interior. The guest bathroom's diamond shaped white floor tiles were clean and blood free. She scanned the hall once again, noticing the pale tan runner covering the herringbone-patterned parquet floor now revealed blood smatterings spaced only a few inches apart from each other. Pushing the door to her bedroom open she whirled, ready to fire. Nothing. No intruder waited with dripping knife and sack full of her valuables. The Navajo bedspread was smooth and untouched, but the trail of blood now shown as a glossy dark streak on the pile carpet covering her bedroom, as if a sudden gush had seeped onto the floor.

The master bathroom light illuminated the rear corner of her bedroom, its door ajar two or three inches. Heart thudding, Nicole moved soundlessly across the stained tan carpet with her gun outstretched. Using her elbow she forced the door to swing silently open upon its well-oiled hinges. The blood donor sat awkwardly positioned upon the cream tiles between the toilet and the bathtub, his dark head leaning upon the tub edge. One arm lay outstretched across the toilet while the other hugged his body, the left hand pressing tightly against a blood stained wound on the right side of his abdomen. It was Justin Zachary.

"My God!" Nicole gasped, quickly placing her revolver inside the porcelain sink. He bled profusely, the crimson flow soaking his once-white dress shirt and seeping into his dark brown trousers. Justin's face was drawn and ghastly, as

if every drop of color had been drained from it. At her exclamation he stirred and lifted his head from the tub ledge as
if it took his last ounce of strength to gaze up at her.

"Nicole," he croaked, stretching a blood-stained hand
toward her.

"I'll call the paramedics," she cried and leapt up, panic–
stricken. Her police training, for the moment, was completely forgotten in her fright.

"No!" burst feebly from his white lips. "No Nicole,
please."

"You're bleeding too badly; we've got to get you some
help!"

"I'm a dead man if you do," he managed to gasp out. His
hand jerked and violently pushed at the seeping wound. An
enormous sense of déjà vu suddenly passed over her along with
the overwhelming certainty Justin was going to die.

"I've got to get you some help," she insisted between
clenched teeth, her heart pounding at the sight of his sweaty
matted hair and agonized face.

"Don't leave me. Please, just take a look. Don't call
anyone yet. I came here because I knew you'd help me.
Please." The last came as a desperate croak.

Nicole bent down again and forcefully removed his
blood-stained hand pressed to his stomach. When lifted, a
small stream of blood spurted out from the wound, glistening crimson against the fine weave of the once-white shirt.
She quickly replaced his hand.

"Press hard," she ordered. "Was it a knife or a bullet?"

"Bullet," he whispered. "I'm going to die aren't I?"

"Not if I can help it. Let's get you away from the wall so I can take a better look at that wound." She carefully placed her arms around his back and pulled him away from the tile wall. He uttered a terrible groan, but allowed her to prop him against the tub. The cream tiles behind him revealed a huge red stain slowly trickling downward to puddle onto the floor.

"You've got another wound?" she cried.

"I think the bullet came out my back," he denied in a hoarse whisper. She quickly examined the freely bleeding small hole located an inch or so higher than the front entry wound.

"We've got to stop the bleeding!" Nicole declared and raced to the kitchen, pulling open drawers randomly to recklessly toss aside unwanted items until she saw the small pile of square dish cloths. She grabbed a handful and bolted back to the master bathroom.

Justin was leaning over the tub retching violently. She waited until he finished and then wiped his mouth, yanking his once-white shirt out of his dark slacks. He moaned as she thrust the folded towels under his shirt against the exit wound in his back. Forcefully prying his fingers away from the entry wound, she placed the folded towels squarely over the flow of blood and replaced his hand.

"Come on, I'm going to take you to my bed." She stooped and tried to lift his long frame from the slippery floor.

"I've been waiting to hear you say that," he groaned as she heaved him to his feet. Justin, though a slim man for all his height, still took every ounce of her strength to lift him. Carefully placing his arm around her shoulders and looping hers behind his wounded back, Nicole half-carried, half-dragged him to her queen-sized bed. She eased him as tenderly as possible onto the Navajo patterned spread. His body relaxed and Nicole returned to the bathroom, nearly slipping on the bloody tiles in her haste. Under the sink were her first aid supplies and she grabbed the square white metal box decorated with a bright red cross and dashed to the bed.

Eyes shut, his breathing pitifully shallow, Justin appeared as if death might be within minutes and she began to hyperventilate, her hands fluttering aimlessly as she gazed down upon the pain-racked features of a man she just might love. Nicole desperately tried to staunch the endless flow of blood, realizing she was Justin's best and only chance for survival.

Thirty minutes later she'd done all her meager skills and supplies would allow. The exit wound had totally stopped bleeding, but even with a large pressure bandage, the front wound still seeped a small amount of blood. Justin's breathing had become ragged and his body now seemed too thin for his long frame. Nicole couldn't be certain vital organs hadn't been damaged during the bullet's entry and exit and her medical skills seemed so limited and useless. She removed his blood-encrusted shirt and sponged off the excess blood, his bare, strongly muscled chest reflecting strong native blood. Justin remained unconscious throughout her ministrations and Nicole was thankful he didn't stir when her clumsy fingers hurt him.

Nicole eyed the white push-button phone on her night-stand. It was her sworn duty as a police officer to summon help, but his desperate words kept replaying themselves over and over in her mind. She picked up his now hopelessly ruined shirt and hugged it to her. Looking down at his still form, Nicole realized she couldn't let him die or be arrested. His quiet gentle nature might be mistaken by some, such as the ambitious Scott, as arrogance or aloofness, but Nicole recognized it for what it really was; shyness.

It suddenly occurred to her that with all his blood loss he needed fluid. Her mother had sworn by chamomile tea as the cure-all for every ailment and Nicole quickly brewed some in her compact kitchen, intently listening for any sound from her bedroom. She added water to cool it down and returned to her bedroom.

"Justin," she whispered. "Here's something to drink." Nicole lifted his heavy head with one hand and tried to press the tepid liquid against his lips but it only ran down his chin. Cursing in frustration she sat the cup on her nightstand and gingerly placed two pillows under his head.

"Justin," she tried again, louder this time. "It's Nicole. You've got to wake up and try to drink something."

His eyelids fluttered and his haggard eyes slowly opened. The deep brown eyes were glazed and he gazed at her without focusing, still partially unconscious.

Under a Desert Sky

"Justin," she repeated again until he groggily came to himself, blinking several times, his head lolling. "Drink," she ordered and he obediently sipped the tea, drops dribbling down his chin.

"I've got to get you some help," she insisted again. "You need antibiotics and a blood transfusion. I don't have the equipment and expertise to help you. You've got to let me phone for an ambulance."

He shook his head weakly against the white pillowcase. "Can't trust anybody. They know about the file."

"What file?" she urged, afraid he was going to lose consciousness again.

"The Lindsey file. It's... it's in my car."

"Your car? Where's your car?"

"Behind the building, near the gas station." He feebly grabbed her arm. "They may have followed me. Not safe," he gasped. "I shouldn't have dragged you into this. I'm forcing you go against your training and the regulations of your office. I'm so sorry."

She ignored his warning. "Is it the silver Lexus from the other day?"

"Yes," he whispered. "The keys are in my pocket."

She fumbled in his pants pocket and finally produced a Yosemite key ring with several keys of various sizes hanging from it. She spotted the Lexus logo on one as he clutched her arm again.

"If I die, give the disk to your Captain. I know he can be trusted. No one else. Not Weston, not anyone. I think . . .

I think someone in your unit... I'm not sure, but..." His voice faded, blurry brown eyes closing and leaving Nicole to try and assimilate the significance of his last conscious words.

Chapter 14

Someone on the force? Justin actually believed someone at the police station sought to murder him? With that astounding thought she rose to gaze down at his limp form. His breathing was shallow and a deathly pallor had removed any remnants of healthy color from his drawn features.

Quickly moving through her small apartment she grabbed a blue hand towel on her way out. Glancing down, Nicole realized that both her yellow striped top and light pants were stained with his blood. Returning to the closet she removed her clothing, slipping quickly into a clean pair of tan Capri trousers and a peach button-down shirt while throwing a glance over her shoulder to see if Justin roused. She needn't have worried; Justin remained deeply unconscious. From the amount of blood he'd lost, she suspected his car was probably covered in it. She returned to the first aid box and removed the pair of thin surgical gloves provided with the kit before grabbing a beige hand towel off the bathroom rack and thrusting it and the blue dish towel into a black plastic sack.

Deciding it wouldn't do for her neighbor, Margie, to observe any bloodstains around the door, Nicole took several minutes to wipe down the knob and the wall where a few drops had splattered. The rough service mat proved hopelessly stained so she simply turned it over.

Trotting in the relative cool of the morning, Nicole discovered Justin's silver Lexus parked only minutes from her flat. Unlocking the car she surveyed the interior of the luxury vehicle. Sure enough, the blood had pooled on the leather seat and spotted the gray floor mats; only just beginning to dry. No one at the gas station even glanced her way, and snapping on the thin latex gloves she vigorously scrubbed the seat bottom and backrest, finally reaching down to wipe any excess blood off the carpet mat. Finally satisfied, Nicole slid behind the wheel after dropping the towel onto the passenger seat. It was intensely hot and stifling inside the vehicle even at this early hour. She placed the key in the ignition, determined to stash the silver luxury car farther away from her apartment. Nicole turned the air conditioner on full blast while the radio belted out Los Lobos' rendition of "La Bamba." She ruthlessly flipped the radio off and drove for ten minutes, finally parking the car in a large supermarket lot as far from the store entrance as she could, in the shade of a small crape myrtle tree.

Under a Desert Sky

Using the tan hand towel, Nicole methodically wiped down the seat and the window once again. She then carefully ran the towel over the steering wheel and radio dials, as well as the gearshift. A plastic shopping bag was tucked into the side panel of the driver's seat and she placed the hopelessly soiled hand towel within. Nicole tucked the computer disk she found in the dash safely into her shirt pocket. Depressing the auto lock button, she loped down the street and deposited the plastic bag with the towel and surgical gloves into a bin near a 24-hour liquor store and progressed to the nearest bus stop. After thirty minutes the large blue and white metro bus disgorged her within a block of her apartment and she raced up the stairs, grim anticipation accompanying her.

Fortunately, Justin lay exactly as before, so deeply unconscious he didn't even stir when she pulled him further up on the bed and covered him with an old red-striped blanket her mother had knitted for her twenty years before on her birthday. He slept like that for nearly three hours while she scoured the bathroom floors and walls, wiped down the parquet floor, and fretted over his too-still form. At 8:30 her captain called.

"Where the hell are you Nicole? Dusty has downloaded a copy of the resort's database with the permission of Scott Adams but needs your help. Get your lazy butt in here!" The same message was repeated on her cell, which resolutely remained unanswered upon the kitchen counter.

He called again at nine and then forty minutes later, now sounding more concerned and less angry. At 10:20 a.m.

the phone rang again and Nicole listened to the disjointed voice of Bud.

"Nicole, just checking to see if you're at home. Dusty hasn't been able to locate any Lindsey file, but we've talked to Elena's mother. She says Elena was seeing some sort of businessman at the hotel, but couldn't tell us anymore than that. Jerry is starting to get worried, but I told him you probably heard from Zachary and will update us soon. I'm sure I'll catch you at the station. Jeez, can't believe I'm talking to a damn machine! Call me Nikki, we're getting worried." The line abruptly disconnected as Justin stirred and moved painfully upon the bed.

"Nicole?" he whispered.

"I'm right here."

"You got the disk?"

"Yes. I cleaned up your car as best as I could and parked it a distant parking lot. I don't think it can be traced back to my apartment."

He nodded slightly before stopping as if pain suddenly overwhelmed him.

"They may have followed me," he managed to gasp out, his normally well-modulated voice weak as a kitten's.

"I doubt it," said Nicole bravely. "You have to make an effort to drink some more tea."

He managed a few small swallows and then gave her a bleak smile. "Tea always makes me run to the bathroom."

Nicole smiled back. "I'll just have to carry you or provide you with a bottle." He grinned and then groaned. His cheeks were slightly flushed and she placed a hand to his warm face. He went completely still and she jerked her hand away.

"You're hot," she said self-consciously and tucked the blanket more closely about him.

"More tea?" he asked finally and Nicole gave him another sip, his head sinking back weakly onto the pillow when the phone rang again. The answering machine played its recorded message and then there was a long silence before a definite click.

Justin's eyes flew wide open and he struggled to sit up.

"Don't!" cried Nicole, "You'll break open your wound." She pushed him down against the bedspread, surprised he had any strength at all.

"They know I'm here," he insisted weakly. "I'm certain they followed me. I couldn't drive very well after being shot and couldn't evade them."

"That's ridiculous."

"I've put you in danger. I have to leave." He tried to swing his long legs over the side of the bed, but fell back weakly upon the dark geometric comforter.

The phone rang again and they both froze, Justin breathing raggedly, as they listened once again to the long silence and final telltale click.

Justin tried to worm off the bed, only managing a couple of inches before he gave up, a frightened Nicole instantly at his side.

"Okay, okay. I believe you!" Nicole sputtered. "I have to get you out of here. You rest while I gather a few things. Lay still for God's sake!"

He ceased struggling and determinedly shut his dark brown eyes. Nicole grabbed her blue gym bag from the top of the closet and quickly packed it with the first aid box, several towels, and a bottle of aspirin and antibiotic cream. She ripped open her dresser drawers and haphazardly threw in several pairs of underwear, a couple pairs of jeans and shorts, and several t-shirts, as well as an unopened pack of sports socks. Nicole thrust her feet into her running shoes and rushed to the kitchen where she poured the rest of the tea into a large silver thermos. Opening the pantry she spotted a couple cans of soup, a package of crackers, and a bag of oranges. All of these joined the clothing and first aid kit, as well as a few basic necessities from the bathroom.

If Justin was correct then they, whoever they were, would be looking for her car as well. Hesitantly she stepped in front of her neighbor Margie's apartment and knocked loudly. The plump Margie appeared wearing a large pink bathrobe and matching slippers even at this time of day.

"Hi Margie," said Nicole, trying to appear nonchalant. "I have a real favor to ask you. My brother David wants me to pick up a few things at his house in San Diego and I don't have enough room in my car. I know you let me use your minivan a few weeks ago when I took all those things to the community center and I wondered if I could borrow it again for a few hours?"

Under a Desert Sky

Margie smiled. She rarely drove and had only purchased the van because her car salesman boyfriend had given her a good deal.

"No problem Honey. Do you know how long you'll need it?" Her white toy poodle Tiffy sniffed at Nicole's track shoes.

"Only until later this evening, until about eight or so," lied Nicole. "I'll leave you my car keys in case you need to run to the market or something." She knew full well that was unlikely, since Margie's doting boyfriend did all her shopping.

"Oh, all right then Honey," said her middle-aged neighbor amiably. She shuffled back into her bright apartment and returned with a key chain that stated 'I love my poodle' on a silver and red metal heart, and the women exchanged car keys. "Here you go Sweetie. Your Corolla's in your space?"

"Actually it's at the curb."

"Well mine's in the carport like always. Gotta go Honey, it's my favorite soap." She gently slammed the door and Nicole vowed to buy the friendly woman a gift certificate to a taping of *The Young and the Restless*. She retrieved the sports bag and dashed down the stairs two at a time. The van was parked exactly where Margie said it would be. While dusty and needing a good wash, the powerful engine purred like a kitten. Nicole turned the air conditioner on full blast and backed out of the parking lot, pulling up beside her white Corolla.

Nicole left the engine running and returned to Justin's side. His bare chest rose in erratic breaths. Nicole grabbed an oversized t-shirt she normally used to sleep in and touched him gently. As he stirred Nicole helped lift him up, slipping the gray Colorado Rockies t-shirt over his shoulders and replacing his stained leisure shoes. Within a couple of minutes she had managed to propel him to the kitchen door.

He panted like he had just run a marathon and both of them sweated profusely. Nicole left him leaning over the breakfast counter while she shouldered her purse, checking if she'd replaced her pistol and cell phone. Upon second thought she removed her department cell and placed it on the counter. Hurriedly she retrieved her old mobile phone whose range wasn't as good as the other but was safer since she rarely used it and few knew her number.

Returning to Justin's side, she placed his arm over her shoulders and supported him outside, pausing for a moment to lock her front door.

"Please God, don't let any of the neighbors come out," she prayed and began the long descent down the steep stairs. Justin struggled to keep his balance, clutching her and the side railing for dear life while groaning uncontrollably. Nicole had left the sliding door of the van open and eased Justin down on the floorboard between the two rows of seats where she had spread double the large green blanket Margie kept for insulating items she hauled in Palm Springs' incredible heat.

Under a Desert Sky

"I'd put you on the seats, Justin, but I'm afraid you'll fall off."

He nodded and gritted his teeth. "Whatever you say."

"Wait here," ordered Nicole needlessly as she rushed back to her apartment. She returned with two pillows and the striped blanket. Slipping one under his head, she placed the other pillow behind him, trying to make him more comfortable. The red-striped blanket had barely covered him and Nicole was slamming the heavy sliding door shut when the mailman walked by, whistling in the hot sun. He raised a tanned hand in greeting before turning up the walkway into her complex.

Nonchalantly she hauled herself in and glanced back at the injured resort director. "So I've got you," said Nicole out loud, "but what am I going to do with you?"

She turned onto Indian Boulevard, constantly checking her rearview mirror to see if anyone followed. Several times a car or van hung behind her for what seemed way too long, but always eventually turned or pulled off before she had to take evasive action. After nearly a half hour of cruising aimlessly around Palm Springs, first heading down Ramon Road, then back up Sunrise Way, and finally circling as she backtracked on Tahquitz Canyon Road, Nicole eventually felt certain she was not being followed. In exasperation at her senseless route she eventually headed up Vista Chino on the 111 until she turned onto Date Palm realizing she now headed straight for the 10 Freeway. The brown sandy desert flew by and heat waves boiled up from the hot asphalt as a thought formulated in her mind that just might work.

Pulling out her old cell and praying the battery was still charged, Nicole punched in the number of her accountant who was also a personal friend of hers from the Palm Springs hiking club.

"Hi Sherri, how's business?" she asked calmly. They chatted for a few moments about Sherri's hectic life and current love interest.

"Sherri, I need to ask you a favor. Promise me you won't tell anyone I've called."

Sherri became instantly alert. She knew Nicole's line of work.

"Police business?" was all she asked.

"Yes," affirmed Nicole.

"Whatever you want, you've got."

"Remember last Thanksgiving when you booked that place in Idyllwild as a retreat for a bunch of us girls in the hiking club?"

"Yeah, it was great."

"I'd like you to phone the vacation rental place and ask them if they have a cabin you can rent for a week. I need it for tonight."

"I can do that."

"Make sure it's not located where we were last time. Remember how the rental agency placed the key and a map in the wooden box outside their office door if you indicated you were arriving in town after business hours?"

"I remember."

"Tell them you're rolling in after five. Put the cabin on your credit card so no one can trace it back to me. I'll pay you back later," insisted Nicole.

"I never doubted you would. Is this your cell?"

"My old one." She recited the number carefully. "Don't tell anyone you know where I am."

"Not even Bud?"

"Particularly not Bud," Nicole admonished firmly.

"I'll call you back as soon as I can." Her friend paused heavily. "Are you in danger?"

"Yes," Nicole relayed simply. There was a click as Sherri hung up and Nicole drove at a controlled 55 miles per hour until she neared the city of Banning. Right before the old stagecoach town there was a rest stop and Nicole pulled off, trying to find some shade. Justin lay prone, his breathing labored, twitching hands damp. His cheeks appeared flushed and Nicole felt his forehead and discovered he burned with fever. She spied a vending machine and quickly purchased two bottles of ice-cold water. Using a washcloth from the sports bag she tried to cool him down, wiping his hot face before placing the towel across his feverish forehead.

"Justin, it's time to drink again," she ordered and he obediently opened his eyes and unclenched his teeth as she squirted the sports bottle into his mouth. He swallowed twice and eased back down.

"I want you to take some of this aspirin; it may help with the pain and fever."

He nearly gagged on the white tablets but forced them down, only to sink back down between the seats while Nicole readjusted his pillows. His natural olive skin had taken on an unhealthy pallor and his breathing was labored. Nicole peeled an orange and tried to feed a segment to Justin, who chewed on the sweet pulp obediently before swallowing. She finished the rest of the orange just as the cell phone rang. Nicole snatched it up before the second ring.

"You're set. I booked a small two-bedroom cabin in Pine Cove that's fairly remote. I told them I was having a romantic getaway with my boyfriend. The keys will be outside the vacation rental office. They close at 4:30."

Nicole looked at her watch. It was only 1:37 now; she still had lots of time to kill before getting Justin anyplace he could rest.

"Thanks Sherri, I owe you one."

"What are friends for? Take care," came Sherri's soft response and Nicole knew Sherri would not contact her again unless it was an emergency.

Nicole stayed at the rest spot for another 25 minutes until the heat became unbearable.

She twice cooled the cloth on Justin's forehead and then prepared for the long haul up Highway 243. She hoped Justin would survive the arduous climb.

The road from Banning up to Idyllwild was twisty and fairly deserted for a Thursday. As a child, Nicole remembered watching the film, *It's a Mad, Mad, Mad, Mad World* and laughing hysterically at the wild drive Jimmy Durante

202

had made down this very same road. She couldn't laugh now as she climbed up the 243. Justin made small painful noises and was talking incoherently, now firmly imprisoned in the grips of fever. If only she had some antibiotics to give him or could safely take him to a hospital!

She tried driving slowly up that winding, treacherous road, but Justin still rolled and groaned painfully at every corner. Nicole was near tears by the time she had reached Lake Fulmor, about ten miles north of Idyllwild, and pulled into the lot across from the lake. She once again moistened the small towel and pushed it against his burning forehead.

"Nicole," he said desperately. "I've got to tell Nicole."

"Shh," she soothed, trying to hush his fevered voice. "It's going to be alright." The lake shimmered quietly and saw only one other car, a bronze minivan, probably the vehicle of some fishermen trying their luck at the small stocked lake in hopes of catching a fine-sized rainbow trout.

After a few minutes in the shaded parking lot Nicole administered another dose of the cool bottled water and Justin seemed to calm somewhat. She pulled the large blue van back onto Highway 243 and continued to climb. The drive, considered a California Scenic Route, was designated by the orange poppy sign every three or four miles, but to Nicole it seemed like the proverbial Highway from Hell. The tiny town of Pine Cove finally emerged through the thick pines with its one gas station and grocery store, but she continued along the narrow twisty road until she reached the larger city of Idyllwild. Near the wooden fort, off North

Circle Drive, she turned and headed for Humber State Park, where the sheer granite sides of Lily Rock could be seen towering above the tree line.

The state park, beneath the trail, had a large parking lot where avid rock climbers left their cars before attempting to scale Tahquitz and Lily Rock. She herself had hiked the Ernie Maxwell Trail and enjoyed the views of Little Tahquitz creek, Marion Mountain, and the ominous Suicide Rock. Those had been happier times and she quickly sought a shady, cool spot under the Jeffrey and Ponderosa pines where they could wait until 4:30.

Being a Thursday, Idyllwild was fairly deserted and its two-lane road blessedly empty. Nicole parked under a large cedar tree and rolled down the windows. Mercifully cool, a nice breeze blew through the open windows. A strand of manzanita with shiny scaling bark hosted a couple of noisy gray and white nuthatches that jumped from branch to branch. Justin muttered incoherently under his breath and Nicole slipped to the rear of the van to lift his head and force him to drink some cool water.

He seemed to doze and Nicole rummaged through the car, hoping Margie had left something useful. A well-stocked toolbox sat near the rear of the vehicle with flash-lights, a pocketknife, and various tools including screwdrivers and wrenches filling the black case. Nothing was located under the seats except an outdated map of San Diego and an empty candy wrapper so she stepped over Justin and opened the dash. A Palm Springs map, some receipts, and a small white paper bag were stuffed into the small space. Withdrawing the white bag she peered inside and let out an incredulous laugh.

"I can't believe it!" Inside, an antibiotic prescription with a large bottle of pills prescribed for Margie's pampered poodle, Tiffy, stared back at her. Nicole carefully examined the dosage. "One capsule each evening and morning," she read, and glanced back at Justin. He wasn't a dog, but weren't antibiotics pretty much the same for humans as animals? She did a swift mental calculation. If Tiffy weighed roughly 25 pounds and Justin around 175, wouldn't that equal seven capsules? Make it six, she thought, and returned to Justin's side.

"Wake up Justin, it's time for your medicine," she announced, shaking him gently.

He stared up foggily at her, his dark hair matted against his forehead. "Medicine?"

"Yeah, the good Lord is on your side and has provided us with antibiotics. Do you think you can swallow a half-dozen of these?"

Justin nodded and she carefully lifted his head. Nearly gagging, the sick man swallowed all six over the next five minutes. Forty-two tablets remained. If she dosed him three times a day, she'd have enough for tonight and the next two days. Nicole bathed him again, smoothing back his dark straight hair and once again noting his almost perfect face with its straight nose and slightly stubbled chin. Dragging her eyes away from his still face, she checked his wounds and noted they'd mercifully stopped seeping. Nicole covered him in the striped blanket once again after testing his hot forehead and noticing how tight his skin stretched over his flushed face. Worried and fretful she settled down in the passenger seat to wait, leaning her tired face against the headrest.

Nicole awoke abruptly; amazed she'd fallen asleep at all. A Steller's jay, beautiful with its gray tufted head and bright blue plumage complained from a rough barked Coulter pine near the car. Justin still slept, his breathing shallow, but even. His lean limp body still felt hot to the touch and Nicole checked her watch nervously. It was nearly five! She and Justin had dozed for almost two hours.

Within ten minutes Nicole reached the rustic office of the vacation rental place. True to their word, an envelope with Sherri's name was placed in the green wooden box nailed to the side of the office door. Nicole snatched the envelope and jumped off the wide redwood deck, dashing back into the van before some late worker at the rental agency spied her. Two minutes down the road Nicole pulled over and unfolded the map, studying the concise directions before heading back toward Pine Cove, a tiny hamlet of less than 800 permanent residents. She'd read somewhere that more than sixty percent of the homes in the Idyllwild area are vacation rentals and blessed the fact that the majority were either empty or housing tenants who didn't know one guest from the next.

Under a Desert Sky

Nicole drove steadily for ten minutes, constantly referring to the map provided by the vacation rental agency. The cabin was remote all right, and located on a narrow dirt road that climbed steadily upwards for roughly a quarter of a mile. At the top, on a reasonably level plot of land, stood a small pine cabin whose shutters and window boxes were painted a bright forest green. Nicole mounted the steps, frightening a tiny lodge-pole chipmunk that scurried madly away from her, its small tail held rigidly upright. A downy woodpecker with its telltale bright red head jumped up the side of a huge cedar near the deck, but there appeared to be no other signs of life.

Inserting the key, Nicole constantly scanned the Jeffery pine forest around her that smelled so strongly of vanilla tinged with butterscotch. The compact cabin seemed ideal. Clean and efficient, a beautiful river rock fireplace dominated the pleasant sitting room of the 1000 square foot cabin. The house was fully equipped with a large bathroom separating two medium-sized bedrooms. Nicole pulled back the blue patchwork quilt and bedclothes in the first bedroom on the left for Justin and returned to the quaint front room, hurrying out of the open door toward the now idle van.

Justin was a limp, dead weight who offered no assistance as she maneuvered him between the back seats, removing the now damp red-striped blanket from his prostrate form. Staggering and sweating, Nicole hauled the taller man up the three porch steps and rested with him against the open door, trying to catch her breath. His long arms dangled over her shoulders while his head lolled limply against her damp shoulder. Nicole blessed the fact that she regularly worked out and was in peak physical condition.

"Please Justin, you've got to help me," she begged and he stirred slightly, straightening his agonized body and coming partially to himself. Heaving the barely conscious man through the door, Nicole summoned all her remaining strength and half-dragged, half-carried Justin though the front room into the small bedroom beyond. She was out of breath and the back of her cotton shirt wringing wet by the time she dumped him as gently as possible onto the double bed. Removing the gray t-shirt from Justin's hot body, Nicole noted his wound seeped again and hurried outside to retrieve the blue sports bag and first aid kit.

Within ten minutes Nicole had changed his dressing and safely tucked him away in bed, using soft flannel sheets to cover his bare chest and burning body. He appeared so ill and white, his teeth clenched tightly in pain even though he was unconscious, that she wanted to cry. After scrutinizing their meager supplies, Nicole realized she'd have to make a visit to the local market and pharmacy located on Circle Drive. Her wallet contained nearly two hundred dollars and some change. Thank goodness she'd stopped at the ATM only the previous day. Justin was without wallet or identification so the two hundred would have to last. Taking one last glance at the prone man, she dashed to the minivan, hopeful the small shopping center in Idyllwild remained open.

Under a Desert Sky

Thirty minutes later and a hundred dollars poorer, Nicole arrived back at the secluded cabin and rushed up the wooden stairs into the house, throwing her keys and purse on the counter. She'd bought several bags of ice for it was evident Justin was in dire need of a cool down. Burning with fever, he tossed and muttered, the sheet tangled at his feet. Justin's long arms flung about him as she tried to soothe him with gentle words. Nicole moistened towels and packed ice around him. For the next eight hours she continued to bathe him and change the ice, occasionally forcing tea and water between his tight lips. She crushed the bitter aspirin tablets, mixing the pills in the tea in hopes of enabling him to combat the pain.

Nicole learned a great deal about herself and that suffering man in the hours that followed. She learned he didn't swear in his delirium and twice called out for his mother. He often appeared lost and asked for the way, and once begged his father not to die. His plea was so poignant that it brought back memories of her own two parent's deaths and she cried along with him, shedding unrestrained tears for the ones they'd both lost too young.

"Nicole," he cried out more than once, "where's Nicole?" She tried to comfort him while Justin clutched at her hand, and marveled any strength remained in his hot tight grip. At one in the morning his fever finally broke; beads of sweat clinging to his upper lip, his breath suddenly less ragged. Within minutes the flannel sheets were sodden; his bare smooth chest glistening with perspiration. At that dark cool hour she allowed herself to break down and cry from the strain, sitting at his bedside and weeping helplessly as he finally calmed. Eighteen hours had passed since he'd collapsed upon the cold tiles of her bathroom. Justin slept limply; the exhausted sleep of those who have fought with death and won. Nicole dragged herself into the opposite bedroom and pulled the quaint patchwork quilt over her fatigued body to finally sleep, too exhausted to even check if she'd locked the front door.

Chapter 15

The scolding of a California gray squirrel right outside her window awakened Nicole from a coma-like sleep as she groggily opened her eyes and tried to remember where she was. She peeked at the clear face of her steel watch and jerked. It was nearly noon! The ordeal of the night before suddenly hit her and Nicole leapt from the bed and skidded into Justin's room. Her patient still slept, but now some color brightened the pale cheeks where his long dark lashes rested against the tight skin of his high cheekbones. Justin's breathing remained deep and even, the covers sliding off his bare chest to expose the tight layers of white bandage. Nicole felt once again the now familiar stirring inside her breast and gently touched his relaxed face. Justin's dark brown eyes slowly opened and this time were not blurred and ill, only incredibly tired. He had slept eleven hours straight.

"Hello beautiful," he whispered and Nicole felt herself blush. Instead of glancing away she continued to gaze at him, taking in the beard-roughened cheeks, straight nose, and full lips that now sported some color instead of the deathly pallor of twelve hours ago.

"Glad you've rejoined the living," she quipped, awed at his living warmth. "Are you hungry?"

"Just thirsty. Don't go!" he reached out his lean hand as she turned, clutching her arm. "It'll wait."

No, it won't," asserted Nicole determinedly. "You need the liquid and it's time for more medicine." She edged through the open door, unwilling to turn her back on him.

He successfully took the tablets as well as three aspirin for the pain and Nicole heated some thin chicken soup, which she spooned between his lips. He managed half a cup before lying back exhausted.

"Thank you," he said quietly and Nicole knew he was thanking her for more than the soup.

"It was my pleasure." He remained restless; his hand kept straying to the bandage covering his abdomen.

"What day is it?" he asked.

"It's Friday around noon," she responded, studying his lean face still pinched with pain and desperately wanted to distract him.

"Do you know the legend of Tahquitz?" she asked gently, willing his pain-darkened eyes to return to her face.

"The legend of what?" he whispered.

Under a Desert Sky

"The legend of Tahquitz. You can't see it from here, but when you're better I'll take you to the kitchen window where you can view Tahquitz rock, sometimes known as Lily Rock, right from this cabin." She pulled the sheet up over his chest and continued. "Many years ago there was a chief whose name was Tauquitch who ruled over all the Indians of the San Jacinto Valley. We would call those native people the Cahuilla today. My partner Bud is a full-blooded Desert Cahuilla. You're part Sioux aren't you?"

"More than half," he murmured and Nicole noticed Justin's tired brown eyes were focused on hers in interest.

"Well, Tauquitch was a good chief; tall and handsome, and ruled his people well. But after a while, he became full of himself and arbitrary in his decisions and his people became afraid of him. One day, the beautiful daughter of one of the other chiefs disappeared. She was the first of many to vanish and soon many of the lovely daughters of the tribe were unaccounted for."

"I can see why you like this story, *detective*," croaked Justin weakly and Nicole smiled

"Shh. Let me continue the tale, sir. The men searched and searched and sadly and horribly their suspicions were confirmed; Tauquitch had done away with the poor maidens."

"So even then they had serial killers?" commented Justin.

"Unfortunately, man hasn't changed much. The handsome vain chief was condemned, the tribe determining he should die by fire. Just as they were about to burn him in the pyre, a huge sparking flame burst forward and Tauquitch leapt into the air in the form of smoke and flame and they knew he was really a demon. He fled into the innards of the mountain and his rumblings can be heard even today." Justin eyes blurred and Nicole made her voice as monotonous as she could.

"Unfortunately, the daughters of the tribe continued to disappear and finally, only when the son of Chief Algoot was killed by the demon did the now-reigning chief of the Cahuilla people seek to permanently destroy the evil demon. The battle waged for many days down in the area off the hill known as Lakeview. The two powerful chiefs hurtled boulders at one another and you can still see the piled up granite throughout San Jacinto and Moreno Valley. They even fought in what we call today Lake Elsinore, and it was here that Tauquitch lost the battle. The evil demon, disguised as a serpent, lashed out with his mighty tail and cut a river-like gash through the lake by mistake and all the water drained out. Without water, the evil demon could be captured."

"Captured," repeated the drowsy Justin.

"Yes, but once again the demon managed to escape for when he was laid on the flames again, the naive people used green wood which enabled the spirit of Tauquitch to escape inside the smoke back to his loathsome cave deep within the San Jacinto Mountains. He can still be heard to this day, though his powers are weak and he is harmless except for the fearsome noise he makes."

Under a Desert Sky

Justin's eyes finally shut, his breathing deep and even. Nicole stayed with him for a few minutes and touched his gaunt face gently, awed by the feelings stealing over her before returning to the kitchen to eat some dinner herself. It had been a long time since a meal and Nicole defrosted a frozen turkey dinner in the microwave while munching on an apple as it rotated and hissed. The cabin had a TV and Nicole turned it on, flicking through the channels past senseless cartoons and soap operas. Had they both really slept that long? The caption for the Friday midday news flashed on the screen and she listened in horror as she peeled the plastic wrap off the now bubbling turkey dinner.

"And in a story that gets increasingly complicated, a fire has destroyed the second story apartment of police detective Nicole Lewis who was investigating the murder and apparent suicide of two employees at The Desert Sky Resort here in Palm Springs."

Nicole gasped. Her apartment building flashed on the small screen as yellow-suited firefighters struggled to contain the blaze that threatened to spread to the other flats in the building.

"Detective Lewis's body has not yet been found in the building, though it is almost certain she was home at the time, though her neighbor, Margie Howell believes she might have already left the building. Her vehicle was found parked in front of the apartment complex."

A hysterical Margie Howell, clutching her beloved poodle, stood in front of the camera as her apartment building smoldered.

"The poor girl came to ask me to borrow my van, but it was in the shop for repairs.

"Merciful God, I'm afraid she's still in there." Nicole sat stunned. Margie knew she'd taken the van but had lied. Could the dear woman have somehow realized Nicole was in danger?

The screen returned to the perfectly coiffured newscaster who added, "The Desert Sky's Director, Justin Zachary, remains missing and is being sought for questioning."

Nicole shuddered. Justin had been right. Whoever was after him would stop at nothing. Her cell phone rang shrilly and Nicole hesitantly pushed the receive button.

"Nicole, is that you?" Sherri's frightened voice was breaking up because of the static caused by the mountains.

"I'm fine. Just stay away from my apartment and don't talk to anyone."

"Okay, Okay. Your apartment . . . I saw it on the news. Should I contact the department?"

"No! Don't speak to anyone. You don't know where I am! You haven't heard from me in days! Not a word, not even to my brother! It's a matter of life and death. You gotta promise me that Sherri!" Her subdued friend promised and Nicole continued. "Hang up Sherri. Remember, not a word." The phone obediently went dead in her hand.

Under a Desert Sky

Nicole let Justin sleep several more hours, awakening him at 5 p.m. to take another dose of the medicine. She also managed to feed him half a piece of dry toast and more of the soup. He looked better, but after finishing the sparse meal turned his face away, his cheeks burning.

"I have to use the toilet," he mumbled.

Nicole smiled to herself. "I'll help you then." She eased his long legs off the side of the bed, waiting a second for his breathing to steady and then supported his weight to the large, rustic bathroom.

"Can you manage from here?" she asked, alarmed at his white, sweat-glistened face.

"Yes," he answered stiffly, clearly embarrassed. Nicole waited for several minutes until she heard the telltale flush. The door slowly opened and she was alarmed to see a spot of new blood on his bandage.

Nicole cursed profusely and transferred him back to the bed, changing the stained bandage and wrapping a fresh one carefully around him. Luckily the rough, puckered edges of the wound appeared to be healing and immediately stopped bleeding.

"Do you always curse so eloquently?" Justin asked, a half grin upon his face.

"Only when people I have personally patched up break open their wounds because of stupid pride. Next time ask for a bottle." Nicole eased the flannel sheet back over him and gazed into his exhausted face. "My apartment was torched," she said without emotion.

"Torched?" he repeated hollowly. He swallowed and stiffened, moving restlessly on the pillow. "My gut instinct was that they had followed me. I'm sure they had a make on my car. I'm so sorry Nicole." He obviously meant it and she patted his sweaty shoulder.

"So am I, and the important thing is that we weren't there when everything I owned went up in smoke. So I think that makes it about time for you to explain how you got into this condition."

Justin leaned back against the sheets, the unreadable mask she'd witnessed before closing down over his face. "I'm the chief suspect aren't I?"

"You're a suspect alright, but so is everyone who knew Elena and the unfortunate Mr. Greaves. I just want the whole truth for once. I don't believe for a minute you've been totally forthcoming with me."

"I only wanted to protect you and Elena."

"That's a bunch of stupid nonsense! I'm a police detective and my entire life's work is dedicated to trying to figure out the hows and whys of crime. Spare me your skirting around the issue. It's me here, hiding away in the mountains with a seriously wounded man, and an apartment I loved reduced to ashes. I've violated every rule in my department and may end up receiving a reprimand or demotion at the very least and a dismissal if I'm truly unfortunate. I deserve an explanation. You owe me an explanation Mister!"

He visibly paled, his brown eyes darkening. "All right then. B.W. Weston sent me down here about three months

218

ago to try and find out why the hotel was losing money. Even six months prior to my arrival it became evident that someone was funneling off resort funds. The first indications pointed to the beachfront resort outside Orlando. Then, it appeared that Weston Enterprises was also being compromised down in Cancun where the latest hotel building project is about sixty percent complete. B.W. kept everything quiet, but put a special security system into all the linked computer systems so he could track down from where the siphoning originated."

"The numbers on the computer that enabled Dusty to see what he called the footprint," she observed, now finally understanding her portly friend's comment.

"That's right. Only it became more complicated than that. Either this guy was in ten places at the same time or he had figured out a system to forward masking garbage to confuse the trail and hide his tracks."

"When did Mr. Weston figure out it originated at The Desert Sky in Palm Springs?"

"Around three months ago. The current director requested a transfer to Maui and for a while all suspicion pointed to him."

"Robert Severns, that all around likeable guy you so poorly replaced."

Justin flushed. "I'm not a false back-slapper if that's what you mean?"

"I meant nothing by it; I was just repeating what both Richard Greaves and Scott Adams voiced."

Justin's face clouded at the mention of Richard's name. "Poor Richard. I wouldn't have taken him for a suicide candidate."

"When you finish explaining what happened, I'll share the details of his suicide note."

Justin nodded and continued. "I had made a short list of those who had access to secure financial computer records and basically kept tabs on them."

"Care to share those names?"

"Richard Greaves, Scott Adams, Judith Chamberlain, the old director, Robert Severns, and the secretaries, Genny, Pam, and my own, Mrs. Gaston."

"That's similar to our black list. Except you have a very prominent position near the top."

He frowned. "I'm sure that wasn't the only list I was top of." His slim fingers touched his bandage and Nicole understood.

"And Elena?"

"I can't figure out how she fits in."

"Rosa, a friend of hers in housekeeping, indicated Elena was seeing two separate men. She referred to the boss man, one she referred to as the 'gringo.' That's you, I take it, since you could pass as Hispanic. Your darkness comes from your Native American blood. You said you were half Sioux?"

"My mother was three quarters and my father over a third, so I guess that makes me about 60 percent."

"So you're the gringo then?"

He nodded grimly. "That was probably me. Only Elena's and my relationship remained totally platonic. There was never a hint of anything else."

"You stated she'd stayed with you in your house in Palm Desert?"

"Just for a couple weeks until she moved into Carmen's and then occasionally thereafter. I'd promised her uncle I'd keep an eye on her since he suspected she was heading down the wrong avenue. What better place than with me?"

Nicole laced her arms around her jeans-clad leg and narrowed her eyes. "From what you indicate about your relationship with Elena, I'm not sure she could be referring to you when she mentioned the *other* man to Rosa. Do you believe it's conceivable Elena was seeing someone else at the hotel?"

"Such as?"

"Scott Adams for one."

"He likes the women," said Justin mildly and Nicole let the slight question in his voice pass. "But in hindsight, recognizing the stubbornness and ambition driving that poor girl, I'd say anything was possible. However, I'm sure Scott's mother wouldn't have approved. She has goals for her boy." The last few words came out roughly and Nicole handed him the glass.

"More water," ordered Nicole firmly and made him sip another cupful before continuing. "His mother?"

"Marjorie O'Toole." He smiled at her flabbergasted look. "Guess you didn't know that?"

She shook her head. Scott's comments about his mother working extra hours to put him through college suddenly made sense. "Guess that got past Dusty. Anyway, we're digressing from the events relating to you."

"Right. Yesterday morning. No, it was the day before; I got an urgent call from Richard indicating he'd stumbled on some information I needed to see regarding the Lindsey file. He agreed to meet me downstairs in the Oasis Lounge to discuss his findings."

"And never showed up," guessed Nicole.

"That's right. Pretty soon the police arrived in swarms and I feared the worst. A couple of them I recognized from when I visited the station on Monday. I was just about to bolt upstairs when my secretary, Mrs. Gaston, hurried out of the elevator. She stopped and spoke to a uniformed police officer for a couple of minutes. The way she conversed with him made me suspicious. It wasn't in an informative or directional manner, it was more..." He hesitated, searching for the right word.

"Familiar?" Nicole answered for him.

"Yes." Justin tried to stretch, but winced. "She then rushed out of the revolving doors and I made up my mind to follow her. Just as I was about to leave, the receptionist at the check-in counter called me over and handed me a manila folder from Richard. In it was the disk. I barely had time to say a polite thank you, certain I was about to lose Mrs. Gaston, and positive she was up to no good. She never really adjusted to me taking over from Bob Severns and was rather verbal about my shortcomings."

"Boy, Robert Severns must have had pretty big shoes to fill. No one seemed to want to give you a chance," commented Nicole, and she watched Justin nod grimly in agreement. "So, where'd your unhappy secretary go?" asked Nicole, recalling that both Justin and his secretary were missing at the time of the suicide, and now for the first time, understanding why.

"She hopped into a white Cadillac Seville. I know for certain Mrs. Gaston drives a blue Honda Accord."

"So you followed them? Jeez Zachary, you picked the wrong line of work, that's my department."

"Yeah, and I'm darn good at it too." He glanced down dejectedly at his bandaged middle. "Anyway, I followed the Caddy for about twenty minutes as it left the Palm Springs city limit, merged onto the interstate, and headed for Indio. She must have zigzagged through a dozen streets before pulling up in front of this seedy Mexican bar called Lupe's. Leslie left the car and entered through the front so I pulled around the rear. The place was smoky and dark like all good dives are and I spotted her at the bar talking to a short Hispanic man with a military crew cut. I'm sure you've met him."

"Enrique. Well, well. He was out of our custody by then."

"I didn't dare move in any closer so I watched them arguing from a distance until another bigger and older man joined him. Leslie Gaston became quite agitated, actually creating quite a noisy scene, so Elena's boyfriend bolted from the joint. The older man, who might have been part Indian, forcefully took her out the front. I suspect he was probably a bouncer. By the time I skirted the building I saw the Caddy pulling away."

"Then what?"

"I lost them." His self-disgust was evident. "A bunch of kids were playing in the street and by the time I managed to speed up again the white Caddy was gone." He rubbed his bandage absently. "I found a coffee shop and sat for a couple of hours thinking about everything I knew and was just about to call your department when I heard on the news that Richard was dead. I made up my mind that matters were getting too complicated and it was time to talk personally to your Captain. However, just as I left the restaurant I saw the Caddy parked down the street."

"You followed it again?" said Nicole excitedly, amazed at his luck.

"No! It followed me! I pulled out, for all intents and purposes planning to tail it when it damn near ran me off the road. I'd obviously gotten too close. We played cat and mouse for nearly two hours until I finally ended up just northeast of Cathedral City near the railroad tracks. I found an old tin garage close by and pulled in there to hide. I picked up my cell phone to call the police department and you know what?"

"The battery was dead," guessed Nicole, smiling. She "tsked–tsked" under her tongue and Justin glared fiercely at her, Nicole pleased to see some healthy color in his cheeks.

"I spent the night in the Lexus parked in that hot smelly garage without any food or water. Just after 4:30 a.m. I edged away from the railway while it was still dark, searching for a pay phone and finally finding one near Century Park. I dialed your number and was just starting to relate what I knew about the file when the Caddy pulled up and started shooting. I slammed down that phone and bolted, not even suspecting I was hit. I just dove into my car and drove like I was competing in the Indy 500. A burning sensation gripped my chest and when I glanced down blood was leaking everywhere. No longer sure whom I could trust, especially after remembering Mrs. Gaston talking to the uniformed officer, I headed toward your apartment instinctively knowing I could trust you."

"And I wasn't there," Nicole stated flatly. "And when you called that morning, I tried to convince myself that your cell phone had just died and those shot-like sounds were just an engine backfiring.

He nodded. "I couldn't believe it. Here I could barely stand without my head whirling at light speed and it wasn't even 7 a.m. and you were gone." He flashed a quick glance and Nicole felt sure he wanted to ask her something. Instead he said, "I took my army knife and messed with the door knob. For a police officer you sure have lousy locks."

"And subsequently you bled all over my house," Nicole reprimanded him, smiling bleakly.

"Doesn't matter now I guess," he said darkly.

"Sleep some more," ordered Nicole. "I'm going to fix myself something to eat and try to digest all this information. We'll talk later." She rose and frowned down at him, her mind already racing to make some sort of sense out of the entire mess.

"And where were you Nicole?"

His belated question took her completely off guard. "I drove into the station early since I couldn't get back to sleep after your strange call. You probably only missed me by a few minutes. Where did you think I was?"

He frowned and comprehension dawned. "Scott's a good looking man don't you think?" he stated mildly as if it didn't matter.

Nicole paused and studied his drawn face for a long moment before tucking the covers firmly around him. "I've always preferred dark-haired men to blondes, even though blondes are rumored to have more fun."

He smiled up at her suddenly and a warm glow coursed through her entire being. "I don't have a blonde bone in my entire body."

"And look where it got you mister," she breathed, and touched the front of the bed sheet lightly over his wound. "You just work on getting your strength back. I'll wake you in a couple hours for dinner and zap some more antibiotics into you."

"Where'd you get those anyway?" he asked sleepily, not bothering to muffle his wide yawn.

Under a Desert Sky

"They're doggie pills."

"What?" he exclaimed startled, suddenly awake.

"My neighbor's dog has an ear infection and Margie inadvertently left the pills in her dash. You're one lucky mutt." And with that she left him to his own thoughts.

Three hours later Nicole had made up a mental flow chart to record the events at The Desert Sky while she stood on the expansive redwood deck that boasted a spectacular view of the ridge and watched the sun go down, tinting the steep angles of Lily Rock a glowing pink. Too many loose ends existed and the appearance of the white Cadillac disturbed Nicole. The murder, the suicide, the embezzlement, and finally Justin's nearly fatal shooting that eventually led to her apartment being torched indicated much more was at stake here than just a simple crime of passion. And connecting them all was the mysterious Lindsey file. One thing remained certain; Corporal Diaz, Elena's violent boyfriend, was not as innocent as she'd first surmised. Nicole heard a squeak of disturbed bedsprings and directed her attention toward the back bedroom. Justin appeared in the doorway, his hand pressing against the tight bandage as his tall frame leaned against the pine door jam.

"Nature calls again I take it," she stated wryly and he smiled in response. Using the wall for support, he made it to the bathroom all by himself. Nicole was impressed. Justin Zachary certainly didn't give up. He reappeared outside the

227

bathroom door within a couple of minutes and ran a hand through his disheveled hair.

"I'm hungry," he said, looking surprised.

"You get back into bed and I'll fix you something. How about some tenderloin steak, stuffed mushrooms, a salad with goat cheese, and some cherries jubilee for dessert?" Justin grinned broadly and shuffled back into the bedroom. Fifteen minutes later he wolfed down a grilled cheese sandwich before taking a hearty swig of full cream milk.

"This is the best tenderloin steak I've ever eaten," he commented, his face reflecting the humor of the moment and the undisguised enjoyment of the first substantial meal he'd consumed in three days. "You're a great cook!" He laughed and Nicole marveled at the beautiful sound.

"Yeah right, it takes Betty Crocker to make a grilled cheese sandwich." But she relished the fact that he was eating and his lean dark face appeared less drawn. His long raven hair needed a good brushing and his chin a shave, but he was still the best looking man she'd ever met.

Nicole handed Justin a washcloth to wipe his hands and he suddenly gazed so long and seriously at her that she moved uncomfortably under his penetrating stare. "Thank you Nicole," he said finally. "You saved my life."

"It was no problem," answered Nicole, suddenly shy and uncomfortable at his scrutiny.

"You know the Sioux have a belief that if you save someone's life, they owe you their life until they save yours and the debt is repaid." His dark eyes narrowed in an almost sexual challenge and Nicole met those warm brown eyes without flinching.

"Hopefully you'll never have to return that particular favor sir," she said softy, and broke eye contact. Finally, resolved, she glanced up and decided to ask. "Justin, I have a couple questions that need answered for my own peace of mind."

"Sure." He lifted a piece of cut apple from his plate and munched, not appearing in the least nervous.

"You knew that I went out with Scott Adams didn't you?"

A mask closed down over his lean face. "Yes," he answered tersely.

"How did you know? I didn't tell anyone; not even Bud, even though later I was seen at lunch with him by one of my co-workers."

"Scott told me."

"Scott?"

Justin dark eyes were hard. "He seemed very eager to share that tidbit of news with me even though we couldn't be remotely considered close friends when he stopped by my office for a little chat after your luncheon date."

"He said you disapproved."

"And so I did. He'd made some comments about you after our first trip to the station and indicated he suspected the two of you were mutually interested. He intonated you asked him a lot of questions about the staff and in particular me, and said that as a *friend* he wanted to warn me I ranked high on your suspect list."

"I was hungry." Nicole defended herself.

"And that's all?" He glanced away as if not wanting to hear her answer.

"No. I did pump him for information regarding all employees on that list of yours. When you called my cell phone that morning I was in my own apartment not his."

He seemed to visibly relax, but still wouldn't meet her eyes.

"Justin... Sergeant Morant and I searched your house in Palm Desert. It seemed... well peculiar; almost as if you were a guest in your own home?"

The question hung between them and Justin smiled suddenly, as if amused and relieved.

"Guest would be an appropriate term. The house belongs to B.W. Weston, not me. He asked me to stay there while I tried to find out the details regarding the embezzlement. Said he didn't want me wasting time finding a place to live and whatnot, that I had more important things to do. It was convenient and..." he grinned, "free."

"Scott mentioned he didn't feel you were going to stay around long. He was right wasn't he?"

"Yes, I was originally slated to head the operation in Cancun since my Spanish is fluent and I'd proven myself as a director in Puget Sound. B.W. was going to promote Scott Adams and Richard Greaves to the top posts. I guess Richard is never going to get the promotion he so longed for after all."

"No," agreed Nicole sadly, suddenly wanting to change the subject for the moment at the dejected expression darkening Justin's face.

"I know you're Native American and a mixture of something else?" asked Nicole softly, really wanting to know.

"My mother was three-quarters Sioux and my Dad more than one-third as I said before. They met at a huge Pow-Wow held in South Dakota about thirty-eight years ago. My father was looking for his Native American roots and decided to attend at the insistence of my uncle. Dad set eyes on my mother and the 'proverbial' story was over. She had a French-Canadian and Sioux father and a full-blooded Sioux mother."

"And you're also Scottish; at least your last name sounds like it?"

"The name might be Scottish, but I'm actually English, Scottish, and Spanish, and of course French and Sioux. My dad was quite a mixture and sometimes referred to our family as the 'all-American mutt house', which was his take on the all-American nut house."

"It's a nice combination," said Nicole sincerely, appreciating his darkly handsome looks.

"And you?"

"A true diluted all-American girl. I believe there's some German, French, Italian, English and Finnish all mixed up to who knows what proportions. Who knows what other strains of ethnic diversity hovers in my family?"

"You're very beautiful," stated Justin tenderly, gazing into her dark blue eyes.

"No I'm not," insisted Nicole uncomfortably. "My mother said I'm appealing and can be fairly pretty when I dress up for the occasion, but never beautiful."

His face said she was a liar and Nicole felt that searing heat jolt through her mid-section again.

"I have one last question Justin, if you don't mind."

"I don't mind," he repeated softly.

"Why did you ask me if I was married?"

He paused significantly and finally met her eyes, his own crinkling in warmth. "That should be fairly obvious. I really wanted to know why a woman like you hadn't married. I couldn't see evidence of a ring, but was wise enough to know a boyfriend or lover could have been lurking about somewhere. I also wanted you to realize that it wasn't only Scott Adams who found you 'appealing.'"

"Oh!" The startled exclamation stood between them and Justin reached out and took her smaller hand, caressing its lightly freckled back with his dark, lean one. "Since I was a teenager I dreamed of finding a certain woman. I fantasized her to be strong-willed and capable, with a fresh face and sometimes over-confident eyes. So many times I thought I'd found her, but after only a short while the illusion would fade. I'd almost given up on ever really meeting my dream girl until you walked into that stairwell, so quietly compassionate, so willing to allow yourself to view me as a human being first, not just a man you had to interrogate in regards to a dreadful murder. Then, when I met you in Captain Hernandez's office again you appeared so distant and as perfectly capable of rebuffing Scott's overt attentions as to ignoring me."

Nicole had gone incredibly still, her heart in her throat. The memories of her own hopeful fantasies flooded over her and she trembled. This dark-eyed, silken-haired man was the kind women saw in **GQ** magazines and summer box office hits, their long dark hair streaming behind them as they raced high-powered cars and motorcycles on missions to save the world. They were featured beside exotically dressed women, who talked exquisitely and exuded mystery. They were not like her at all. Nicole shook her head violently, striving to convince him that she wasn't in the least what he wanted or should dream about.

"When I first observed you in Captain Hernandez's office I recognized you instantly as a woman of integrity and strength. It didn't help that you viewed me as a potential murder suspect." His voice was self-mocking. "And then during the interrogation, you just stood there and let Bud do all the talking. To someone like Scott, you fit his image of the quiet submissive woman. I realized in that moment Scott was way out of his league."

"I'm not like that at all," she protested. "I'm really just an ordinary woman in an often-difficult job."

"Ordinary," he denied. "Never. Come over here." His voice an insistent whisper, his lean fingers reached out to gently grasp her arms and pull her toward him; toward that beautiful whisker-stubbled face with its dark, dark eyes.

His mouth opened slightly to reveal straight white teeth as he drew her to his kiss, lips warm and gentle. Nicole's mouth opened and his kiss so deepened that she had to lean over him. Her hands found his smooth chest and strayed to the taunt muscles there, moving in gentle circles over the light olive-toned flesh. Justin's one hand found her hair and moved sensually through it, gently tugging and massaging, while the other caressed her straining back. Nicole couldn't breathe and couldn't think. Only the knowledge that she desperately wanted him more than she had ever wanted anything or anyone in her entire life enabled her to move from her frozen state.

The kiss ended and he simply gazed at her, moving his warm hand to her cheek and touching it in that gentle light caress he had used once before.

"Sweet Nicole," Justin breathed, and kissed her again, using his teeth to suck at her bottom lip before sliding his tongue across her teeth. Tenderness and the indescribable feeling of finally coming home overwhelmed Nicole as she placed her hands on either side of him to move closer, to get nearer to his warm, beckoning flesh. He gasped suddenly, jerking involuntarily away from her. It was not the fulfilling gasp of pleasure, but one of pain, instantly causing shame and remorse to wash over her.

Under a Desert Sky

"I'm sorry, so sorry!" Nicole exclaimed, moving away from him regretfully.

Justin's breathing remained ragged and she noticed his bare chest trembled in pain. "*You're* sorry?" Justin exaggerated, his face mirroring exactly her deep regret. "Make me well sweet Nicole, so I can love you just like I do in my dreams."

"I will," Nicole promised; and instead of moving away from him which would have been the sensible thing to do, slid carefully over his prone body and sank down upon his opposite side. Laying her arm gently across his chest, she kissed his rough cheek. "Sleep now my darling." They remained in that tender embrace until moonlight flowed through the window and sleep eventually conquered them.

Justin awoke to find that early dawn had already tinged the sky pink between the towering pine trees. Nicole's breathing remained deep and regular as he turned his head and gazed at her tenderly for a long moment, his fingers seeking the softness of her tawny curls. Careful not to wake her, he gingerly lifted himself off the mattress, determined to be an invalid no longer. The noise of the shower awoke Nicole from a wonderful dream about lounging on the deck of a streamlined sailboat with the wind in her face as Justin flawlessly steered the sleek craft.

The shower! Justin lay no longer beside her, only the imprint from his body still exuding warmth where she extended her searching hand. Nicole jumped from the tousled bed and bolted into the bathroom. She swung open the pine door and spied him in the shower, his lean body only a blur against the shower door's fogginess. His discarded bandage lay unraveled in a heap outside the sliding door next to his hopelessly bloodstained pants. Nicole pulled open the door to reveal Justin leaning against the tile wall, shaving his lean chin with one of the disposable razors she'd bought at the pharmacy.

"What on earth do you think you're doing?" she squeaked, thrilled to see him upright and moving of his own volition, but also skeptical about his strength. She forced herself to keep her eyes on his face, uncomfortably aware of his nakedness.

"Getting clean," was his mild response. "Care to join me?"

He looked so much better. His dark brown eyes sparkled with a playful challenge Nicole had never witnessed before. So she did what any woman in her right mind would do and shed her clothes on the spot.

Justin gasped and nicked himself.

"Steady sailor," she warned, closing the glass door behind her. They stood for a long moment under the warm spray just regarding each other's over-heated faces until finally Justin's gaze edged downwards. A slow appraisal, it slid from her flushed face down to the pale full breasts swelling over a flat belly. Justin casually focused his eyes farther down to the dark joining at her thighs. His hot gaze

236

lingered there for a moment and then slid past her shapely legs down to her feet. Justin swallowed painfully and his dark eyes returned to Nicole's face where her blue eyes shone in undisguised want.

"Beautiful," he repeated as before, and Nicole now believed his reverent endearment.

She took the time to slowly appraise him. Justin's sculptured face was smooth and brown, his long hair damply clinging to now clean-shaven cheeks. His long and beautiful neck perfectly gave way to a smooth hairless chest. A narrow waist tapered to long, lightly-roughened legs, proclaiming a long distance runner. The angry wound in his abdomen puckered in an ugly red color though its ragged sides were clearly healing and knitting together at the edges, and Nicole drew in a shaky breath.

"It's alright," he reassured her, and willed her to look lower where the evidence of his desperate want was so apparent. "Kiss me," he demanded and she did, leaning against that smooth soapy chest and wrapping her arms around his neck. His tongue probed and worshipped, finally leaving her mouth to trail down her neck and over her round breasts. He suckled the taunt nipples and she gasped as his hands moved in small circles over the curve of her back. She slid her hand down to his wet hardness and caressed his strong arousal.

"Let's get out of here," he hissed suddenly, never indicating any possible weakness, just suggesting a better alternative. She obeyed him without a murmur, pulling the door open as he shut off the shower and stepped damply onto the small woven rug outside the tub. He wrapped a white towel around his lean waist and she followed suit. As he preceded her she could see the encrusted bullet hole in his back and trembled again. What if he had died?

Justin sat down slowly on the bed, patiently waiting as Nicole took a fresh set of clean dressings and wrapped his upper abdomen. It was no small accomplishment since he kept bestowing soft butterfly kisses on her neck the entire time. As Nicole tied the bandage tightly around his lean waist his fingers lifted to take away the obscuring towel, but her hand stopped him. A glass of water and six tablets set upon her outstretched hand. Justin pretended to pout, but took the antibiotics.

"Now?" he asked, his voice husky after swallowing the tablets.

"Now," she responded, and removed her towel. He sucked in his breath abruptly and Nicole gently pushed him back down onto the sheets.

"I think that for this once you will need to take a more dominant role," he teased softly.

"I agree with you wholeheartedly sir," agreed Nicole, deftly removing his towel and straddling him.

"So, so ready," he voiced, his perfect fingers cupping her full breasts as Nicole lowered herself onto him, gasping at the incredible pleasure of his hard length.

She wasn't prepared for the absolute tenderness with which he touched her or the uncontrollable passion that seared her body. He gazed up at her with round pleasure-darkened eyes and she ran her fingertips along the hot smoothness of his chest, marveling at his strength and beauty. Nicole tried to be gentle, so afraid of hurting him, seeking desperately to avoid the bandage protecting his healing wound, but Justin's hands firmly grasped her hips and increased his desperate thrusts. Nicole tangled her hands in his hair and bent down to suck at his full lips, hearing her name whispered over and over again. Nicole tightened and gasped and saw her incredible pleasure mirrored upon his taunt face. Within moments he joined her, his body tensing and lifting at his release.

Later, as she cradled his fatigued body, he spoke with the deepest sincerity. "I was correct, you *are* that woman from my dreams." He fell asleep with his lips gently nuzzling her throat, his breath warm and sweet. Nicole held him for a long time, listening to the cackle of the Stellar jays arguing outside over the murmuring sway of the wind through the pines until sleep finally conquered her as well.

Chapter 16

The blue cell phone's shrillness caused Nicole to jerk in panic among the tumbled covers of their bed. Justin still slept, one arm bent awkwardly above his dark head while the other still enfolded her closely to him during sleep's embrace. The blue patchwork quilt angled at such a provocative angle that Nicole's heart swelled. His silky dark hair was tousled, his smooth muscled chest bare, and he didn't stir a muscle at the phone's insistent ring. Nicole removed Justin's arm as gently as possible, and grabbing the white bath towel provided by the rental company, wrapped it about her as she scurried to the kitchen, glad the cabin was so remote. The lit indicator button identified her caller as Bud. She raised the turquoise blue phone to her ear and activated the line.

"Nicole? Nicole?" rasped Bud's voice loudly.

"Yes Bud, I'm here," answered Nicole calmly; glad her partner could not see her scanty attire.

"Thank God. We just got word you weren't found among the rubble of your apartment. I knew it was a long shot, but I thought I'd call your old cell number and see if you responded and bingo."

"I didn't want you to worry, but I couldn't take any chances at this stage of the game."

"Where are you?" His voice rasped insistently in his concern.

"Safe Bud, that's all I can say," she responded evasively.

"You know Zachary's still missing?" Bud stated.

"Ah well, you see Bud, he's actually not really missing. Someone shot him the day before yesterday and it's been touch and go for awhile up here."

"Zachary's with you!" Bud sounded amazed. "And shot?"

"That's right. We managed to vacate my apartment just before it was torched. Justin had been wounded and some-how managed to drag himself, literally half-dead, to my apartment. I'm not much of a nurse, but I'm confident he'll pull through. I don't want to tell you where I am because we suspect there's a leak at the department."

Bud snorted his disbelief. "You've got to be kidding! A leak? Is Zachary feeding you that crap?"

"He was only inches from death's door and I don't feel had any reason to lie. Justin followed his secretary, Mrs. Gaston, from the hotel a couple days ago. She met with none other than Enrique Diaz at some seedy bar named Lupe's in the City. Find out what her story is Bud. Don't take no for an answer—but promise me you'll go stag on this one! You've got to promise me that Bud!"

"Alright, alright!" he agreed grumpily. "So you're going to hide out for a while?"

"I've got to. Justin's the only real lead we have. And listen Bud, I've located the Lindsey file, but haven't had the opportunity to examine it yet. I want you to tell the Captain I'm fine but plan to continue laying low for the present. I'm not sure if someone's after me or Justin Zachary, but right now I can't take any chances."

"May I give the Captain your number at least? He's been crazy with worry about you." Nicole's heart went out to her tough-looking Captain who deep down inside was the most compassionate and caring man she'd ever known. That was until now.

"No," she insisted. "Why don't you give me a safe number instead where I can call you without someone listening in? If someone on the team is corrupt we can't be too careful."

"You really believe that?" protested Bud.

"At this point in time, nothing makes a bit of sense to me except that Justin Zachary very nearly pushed up a headstone. After Elena and Richard's deaths, I can't take his safety for granted. It seems inconceivable to suspect Lee, Nancy, or anyone at the station, but facts are facts. My apartment's gone, two people are dead, and Justin just escaped with his life. Justin would be furious if he knew I was talking to you; he distrusts everyone now, but fortunately he's asleep and what he doesn't know won't hurt him."

"You just may be right," stated Bud reluctantly. "We've received an anonymous tip from a woman at the resort who says that's Richard Greaves' death was no suicide. We're investigating that possibility as we speak. Just hang low and wait to hear from me."

"Could you give me the number where I can reach you?" Nicole wrote down the seven-digit number, her fingers sweating.

"Take care Nikki," he said, using her pet name. "You know Maggie and I love you."

"I know," she whispered, and rang off feeling like an ungrateful traitor. Nicole returned to the dim bedroom and watched Justin sleep. He'd turned slightly on his side, his bare arm stretched over the spot she had occupied only minutes ago. Gazing at his dark beautiful face Nicole felt an incredible wave of protective love and knew she'd fight until the death to guarantee his safety. As she returned to the warm bed, Justin automatically replaced his arm over her right where it belonged.

An hour later Justin awoke feeling refreshed and complained how ravenously hungry he was.

"Alright, alright," said Nicole, pretending to grumble and rose slowly, reaching down to tousle his already disheveled hair. He grinned back at her and stretched, reluctant to leave the warm bed. Moving to the kitchen she prepared a nourishing pot of spaghetti, adding some cut-up mushrooms and browned meat as well as a half cup of red wine. Justin managed, forty minutes later, to hobble slowly to the kitchen table unsupported, and sat down gingerly across from her as she served up the steaming pasta and slices of garlic bread.

"I see you succeeded in dressing yourself," she teased, eyeing the hopelessly stained trousers topped by one of her old t-shirt's depicting a loafer wolf howling at the moon. The shirt was way too short and revealed the white bandage at his waist.

"I can only depend on you to remove my clothes, not replace them," he said mischievously, and Nicole glowed.

"Well then, I see it's time to purchase you some new clothes," decided Nicole halfway through the delicious meal which Justin devoured happily. "Yours are hopelessly stained. And, I have to find some place where I can examine that file."

"No laptop?" he stated.

"No. I actually did have one, but it was in my apartment. Guess we'll see if my insurance policy is worth its salt," she said lightly.

He frowned deeply and took a long drink of water. "So what should we do first?"

"We?" asked Nicole skeptically. "*I'm* going to head down into town and make a couple purchases and hopefully find a place to download that file."

"Not without me!" Justin insisted, his dark eyes flashing.

"It's not up for discussion." Nicole issued firmly, ignoring his glare and tucking a wayward strand of golden brown hair behind her ear. "The only problem is that unless I find a great sale, we're not going to have enough money to buy you much more than a t-shirt."

"I have money," volunteered Justin.

"We can't use a credit card or ATM; it's too easy to trace. Besides, you don't have a wallet."

"Checking out the goods while I was helpless, were you? The brazen women these days!" Justin smiled smugly as he reached into his back buttoned-pocket and pulled out a thin ragged envelope. "What do you think about this Sherlock?"

Nicole wiped her hands on a dishrag and opened the torn envelope. Five one-hundred dollar bills winked back at her.

"I guess when I frisked you I got so distracted I didn't check your pockets thoroughly enough. I *suppose* this will do." She ducked as he threw his napkin at her. "How'd you get this anyway?"

"I'd withdrawn the money for Elena, but she refused it the last time I spoke with her, saying she would be damned to accept anything from me. I placed it in the dash of my car, nearly forgetting about it until I rediscovered the cash while searching for something to eat when stuck in that stinky shed near the railroad tracks a couple days ago. After the shooting stopped I retrieved the envelope but plain forget the disk I'd placed in the CD compartment. My wallet and organizer were stashed in my briefcase in the trunk and it seemed beyond my capabilities at the time to retrieve them. Thought the money might come in handy somehow." Nicole was impressed that anyone so desperately wounded would have had the presence of mind to grab the envelope while slowly bleeding to death.

"I hope no one gets hold of your wallet or credit cards."

"Doesn't matter. It's actually better this way. I only had about fifty or so in my billfold and if it's found along with my car, I hope the speculation is that I've joined the ranks of the deceased." He smiled that gentle, sexy smile of his again and Nicole knew if she didn't leave in the next five minutes she was headed for big trouble.

Amidst his protests and warnings and her staunch orders to stay reclined while she was gone, Nicole drove the dusty blue minivan away. He stood at the kitchen window with a worried expression on his drawn face. Nicole waved and Justin lifted a hand in response as the van skidded down the steep incline.

Idyllwild hummed with people and cars this sunny Saturday morning. A favorite among Southern California natives who often visited the San Jacinto Mountains to escape the summer heat, Nicole had difficulty finding parking and finally left the car in a rear parking lot of the large wooden fort off North Circle Drive. Trying to ignore the delicious smells of freshly baked pies, Nicole discovered a trendy clothing shop at the top of the stairs. She quickly purchased two large t-shirts, one bearing the Idyllwild logo and the other a graphic of Lily Rock. Near the back of the store stood a lone rack of canvas shorts and trousers. Nicole held the trousers up next to her legs and decided that since they were roughly an additional five inches longer than ones she would pick for herself, they'd probably fit the lanky Justin. After counting out an inordinate amount of money, she headed for the local grocery store again. A half-gallon of cold milk, a couple steaks, some fresh green beans, and two roasting potatoes, along with a packet of sport socks quickly ate up an additional twenty dollars. Across the street she spotted a small computer store advertising internet access and cheap rates.

The smiling young clerk motioned her to a computer and within minutes she sat at the PC typing in the simple commands to open the disk drive. Several file names popped up on the screen, but Nicole clicked on the file clearly labeled 'Lindsey'. She gazed at the monitor for several minutes trying to understand what was so significant about the jumbled figures and miscellaneous paragraphs. Maybe Justin would be able to decipher this, but it was beyond her capacity since she was not familiar with the inner workings of an organization the size of The Desert Sky. Where was Dusty when you needed him? Feeling hopeless, Nicole pressed Print and waited for the printer symbol to disappear from the bottom of the screen before closing the file.

Under a Desert Sky

"Here you go madam," said the round-faced shop-keeper who was dressed in a loud Hawaiian shirt and bright orange shorts. "That will be thirteen dollars."

Nicole reluctantly paid the smiling man, certain she was in the wrong business as he handed her the three pages. Nicole folded the papers neatly and tucked away the hopeful evidence in her purse along with the disk. Another car had parked very close to the dusty blue minivan and she had difficulty opening the driver's door. So intent was Nicole on not scratching the gray sedan that she never noticed the tan Imperial that had pulled out of the nearby gas station and idled quietly, waiting for her to make a move. The large vehicle followed at a discreet distance down Highway 243 and watched her turn right, just after the Pine Cove city limits sign. It waited until she had begun the ascent up the steep dirt road before pulling off into the shade of a large sugar pine. The heavyset man inside made a single phone call and was told to wait for instructions.

Justin lay stretched out on the comfortable brown-striped couch in the pine-scented living room; the TV switched to a familiar rerun of *M.A.S.H.*

"Hey sleeping beauty, I'm home," called out Nicole gently, smiling at his long-legged form. She would bet that he had not planned to fall asleep after stretching out on the rental couch, but his healing body had overruled his best intentions.

Justin's tired brown eyes opened and he blinked a couple times, raising a hand to rub his foggy eyes as a look of relief passed over his handsome face. He took her hand tenderly and pulled her down beside him. "I was worried," he said simply.

"Worried and snoring," she quipped. "Look." Nicole opened the brown paper bag and pulled out her purchases. "Everything the modern man needs to be clean and in style." Justin's hands fingered the clothes and whistled as he checked the price tags. "Would any clean underwear be lurking somewhere among all these wonderful purchases by chance?"

Nicole's face dropped. "Oops!" She said apologetically. "But I can remedy that. Go back into the bedroom and wrap that slightly damp towel around your middle and I'll wash 'em.'"

He gave her a long measuring grin. "Okay. At least I know you're not used to having a male hanging around." He carefully lifted his long frame off the couch and disappeared through the pine doorway. Within a minute, muted blue boxer briefs discolored by bloodstains sailed past her ear.

"Very funny," she snorted and collected up her own discarded clothing from the night before and started the washer, using the complimentary soap left for tenants.

"Nicole," came an urgent cry from the bedroom and she slammed down the washer lid in alarm.

Grabbing the .38 from her handbag she rushed through the bedroom door, ready for anything, her shoulders braced, revolver raised at eye level. Justin lay outstretched on the bed, not a stitch on except for the binding bandage.

Under a Desert Sky

"Why you thoughtless SOB! I could have easily shot you in your altogether!" she shouted; half-amused, half-furious.

"Just thought we could make good use of our time while waiting for the washer to finish," Justin said innocently, the white bandage contrasting greatly with the deep olive of his body.

Nicole tossed the gun on the top of the chest of drawers and approached his prone body. Justin's hands remained tucked under his head as he slowly watched her remove every article of her clothing and drop them onto the floor beside the poster bed. She straddled the now grinning man and placed a hand on either side of him, gazing down into his beloved face. Nicole bent forward to taste his lips, suckling their fullness and warmth.

"Um," he murmured, sliding his hands over her naked back. "I'm feeling much better Detective and positive I'm on the road to a complete recovery. However, I could use your expert opinion."

Nicole pretended to ponder his tall, prone frame for a moment and then smiled. "I believe you are progressing nicely, but should probably be getting a bit more exercise." She moved herself deliciously over him and he moaned.

"So you think so? I hope you find it in your heart to help me return to a more regular and regimented exercise program."

"I can do that," said Nicole, gasping at their intimate contact. She watched him close his dark eyes in contentment. "And you are right Sir; it *will* help pass the time."

He moaned in pure contentment as she slipped a slender finger into his half-open mouth. Justin's eyes opened wide at the seductive intrusion and he sucked on the slim tip before grasping her straining thighs and stilling her for a moment.

"Slow down love," he begged, his chest heaving.

"I can't with you, I want you so," she denied.

Suddenly and unexpectedly Justin flipped Nicole upon her back and before continuing his passionate plunder of her, whispered Nicole's name under his gasping breath.

"Justin," she cried, suddenly afraid that he would hurt himself in his passionate ardor, but there was no stopping him. He obviously didn't want to take the passive role any longer so she wrapped her slim legs tightly around his back and urged him on, grasping his straining shoulders and pulling his mouth to her lips, unable to stop the delicious burning between her legs or the intense man who passionately claimed the woman he loved.

They both had no way of guessing that the watcher was at that very minute on his cell phone, confirming their precise whereabouts in the secluded cabin in Pine Cove; no longer remotely safe or secure as they lost themselves in their urgent embrace.

Chapter 17

It was coming on 1 p.m. before the dryer cycle finished and Justin was finally outfitted in his new clothes.

"Everything fits perfectly," he said, sinking wearily down at the kitchen table to peruse the pages Nicole had taken out of her purse.

"I can't make heads or tails out of it myself," admitted Nicole as she scrubbed the roasting potatoes at the small sink.

Justin frowned and examined the first page. "This looks like some sort of accounts payable to a building firm called Lindsey. I wonder?"

"You wonder what?"

"Weston Enterprises is in the process of building two new resorts. One of them is located in Cancun, the other outside Miami, where B.W. already has two hotels. The resort in Florida is more of a time-share. You know, those trendy two and three bedroom condos right on the beach where people can buy and reserve their own personal dates in lieu of paying those outrageous prices for beach property."

"So?" said Nicole, punching holes in the potatoes with a fork and placing them into the microwave.

"I personally hired the contractors for that project; Jeff Lindsey and Sons."

"Why would you have had any jurisdiction over a project taking place in Florida?"

"B.W. had had some trouble with the local contractor in Miami and asked my opinion. Weston and my father went way back and I had known him personally for years. Brian gave me a break on the job in Puget Sound and remained a close family friend even after my dad's death. He'd always trusted my father's judgment and wanted to pursue a similar relationship with me so I've been working closely with him for over three years. The hotel in Puget Sound had used Jeff Lindsey Sr. and we were very pleased with the quality of his work and the fact that he finished on schedule."

"That's got to be a rarity," noted Nicole, beginning to snap the green beans and toss them into a ceramic bowl.

"Believe me, it is. Cost overruns because of time overrides can inflate final construction costs to the tune of millions of dollars."

"But Puget Sound is clear on the other side of the country from Florida," said Nicole, trying to understand.

"Wouldn't he be more expensive in the long run after paying for Mr. Lindsey and his crew to relocate to Florida?"

"No, that was the lucky part. It just so happened that one of the 'sons' parts of the business had an office in Orlando. Lindsey had two boys and the youngest was starting another branch of the business down in central Florida near his grandparents. Therefore we were able to work out a deal with the Lindsey's, insuring that Jeff Lindsey oversaw the project personally but used his son's crew."

"So, what's the significance?" asked Nicole, dumping the beans into a sauce pan and adding a pinch of salt before adjusting the gas burner to low. She joined Justin at the circular table and picked up the first page of the printout.

"I don't know." Justin rechecked the last two pages and shook his head dejectedly.

"Obviously Richard found something out regarding these figures, but for the life of me I can't see what it is."

"Let it sit for a while," stated Nicole firmly. "Sometimes the brain needs off-line time to catch up. I'll put on the steaks. How do you like yours?"

From his sensual appraisal of her snug jeans and lavender t-shirt, she knew he was thinking about something other than steaks.

"Be careful Zachary, or you're going to have a relapse! I'm surprised you can talk, much less walk after our last encounter." Justin grinned smugly and Nicole laughed. "I'll take that to mean you like your steaks' medium."

Nicole bustled about the compact pine kitchen, throwing the two steaks on a low heat and putting the garlic bread into the oven to heat. She stirred the green beans, suddenly feeling happier than ever before in her life. Nicole could almost imagine the two of them sitting in her apartment discussing the trials of their day before wondering what to fix for dinner. She could only hope he was a more inventive cook than her. The memory of her small flat engulfed in flames brought her back to reality as Justin returned to the striped brown couch and began channel surfing, finally settling on a Classic Movie Station to watch John Wayne single-handedly save an entire squadron of desperate soldiers. It must not have been exciting enough because Justin's head quickly sagged onto his arm and he was sound asleep within five minutes. Nicole let him rest until she served up the simple dinner thirty minutes later, spooning mushroom sauce over the steaks and removing the loaf of garlic bread from the oven.

Justin sat across from her and tore into his steak and potato as if he hadn't eaten in years, complimenting the mushroom sauce and green beans. When she couldn't complete her large t-bone, Justin promptly dished it onto his empty plate and consumed it as well.

"I hear steak is very nutritious for the blood, but you might want to leave that bone since it's probably a bit difficult to digest," suggested Nicole, and Justin grinned sheepishly.

'I just can't seem to get enough to eat," he responded.

Under a Desert Sky

"Why don't you go lie down while I wash up the dishes? Don't expect to get off kitchen duty after you're completely healed. Oh, and don't forget your pills, Tiffy!" Justin grimaced as Nicole handed him the last of the doggie antibiotics, but took them without a murmur, finally excusing himself to stretch out on the double bed.

She let him sleep and washed up the few dishes, observing a pair of Anna's hummingbirds darting between the peeling manzanita branches while making their high pitched twill. A chipmunk, with tail held straight aloft, crept slowly across the balcony searching for seeds below the empty bird feeder. Nicole wished she had thought to buy some wild birdseed in town and then mentally slapped herself. What did she think this was, a holiday?

The sun climbed to its zenith, but the cabin remained cool inside. Nicole watched the news for updates on the fire and watched amazed as Jerry's emotionless face materialized on the screen.

"At the present time, we have no further clues into the disappearance of Detective Nicole Lewis, other than to say her body wasn't in the wreckage of her Palm Springs' apartment."

"Is it true her car was found parked outside the complex?" asked an African American newswoman.

"Yes, that's correct."

"And Justin Zachary, director of The Desert Sky Resort is coming under increased scrutiny is he not, regarding the embezzlement of over two million dollars?"

257

"He is a prime suspect at the present time," confirmed Jerry.

"And still remains missing," broke in another slender reporter, who Nicole recognized from the interview with her neighbor. "But isn't it true that Zachary's vehicle was discovered in a supermarket parking lot with excessive amounts of blood evident as well as many of his personal belongings, including his wallet and briefcase, found locked in the trunk?"

"While I am not certain where you obtained your information, a sedan matching the description of Mr. Zachary's Lexus was located in a local parking lot, but we're not willing at the present time to disclose any additional details regarding the condition of the car or items found within the vehicle."

"But the possibility now exists that Justin Zachary has joined Elena Gonzalez and Richard Greaves in death and that the death toll surrounding The Desert Sky Resort may go even higher if Detective Lewis is not found?"

"No comment," asserted Jerry, obviously becoming irritated at the persistent reporter's questions and amateur analysis.

"Just one more question. Isn't it true the 29 Palms Military Police force have direct concerns in this case and wish to take over since the Palm Springs Police Department's investigation is apparently at a standstill now that the chief investigator in the case is missing?"

"I have *no* idea where you get your information. And, as I mentioned earlier, we are exploring all connections between

Under a Desert Sky

Elena Gonzalez's death and the unfortunate suicide of the Budget Manager. Whether or not the Military will conduct their own investigation is privileged information, and as to Detective Lewis's current whereabouts, we are keeping an open mind." Jerry held up his hand to ward off any more questions and for a split second gazed straight into the camera and Nicole realized, without a shadow of a doubt, that he knew full well she was alive. Jerry could play the game with the best of them and Nicole was certain that Grace must be very proud of her slim husband.

For the next couple of hours Nicole examined the Lindsey document and made a clue map. No matter how many times she went over the details she felt certain that Elena's death was no mere coincidence. Somehow her murder, Richard's suicide, and Justin's shooting were all connected. But how? What vital piece had she missed? Her father had always instructed her to recheck the obvious, so Nicole scanned the list of suspects again.

Scott Adams' alibi seemed airtight. His friend, Jack Roberts had indeed arrived at the brokerage late the morning of the murder according to his supervisor and with a nasty headache to boot. Bud had stated the man was affectionately bitter regarding Scott's insistence that they head for the disco bar on a Sunday night and the bartender had verified the two men's presence acknowledging the two partiers had left a whopping tip.

Judith Chamberlain also checked out. She'd attended a Rotary Club dinner that evening with two friends and fulfilled her job as treasurer, giving the monthly report on the Club's finances and charitable donations. While that function had lasted only until 10:30, Nicole was certain from the forensics reports that Elena's killer had been nearly a full foot taller than the petite maid, and Judith only topped the deceased girl by a mere five inches. That would also exclude Marjorie O'Toole and the entire staff of secretaries on the executive floor. Though Nicole personally disliked Mrs. O'Toole's racial slurs, the woman was petite herself, only reaching a full sixty-two inches in her stocking feet. Her alibi, as well as all the other women's, was legitimate, though Nicole had difficulty fitting in Justin's recital of his own secretary's erratic behavior. Somehow she believed Mrs. Gaston played a key role in the whole affair. If Mrs. Gaston was somehow involved in the housekeeper's murder, what was her connection with Enrique? Nicole leaned back and rubbed her eyes dejectedly. At a standstill she continued down the list.

Enrique seemed the likely suspect, but at only 5'9", didn't fit the physical profile and had the added roadblock of being left-handed. His bunkmate at the base had verified Enrique's whereabouts, indicating the pair had been engaged in a game of poker the night of the murder until well past midnight. So why had Mrs. Gaston met the military corporal unless her business with Elena's boyfriend had some other significance?

A faint noise issued from behind her, causing Nicole to swivel in her seat. Justin ran a hand through his charcoal-colored hair, admittedly looking much better. He yawned widely and placed his lean hands on her shoulders, giving them a squeeze before sitting down stiffly across from her.

"Found any answers yet Detective?"

"Well I've given up trying to decipher those figures from the Lindsey file. I'd need Dusty or possibly even Nancy for that. Both are far superior at decoding anything regarding computer gibberish. I'm now going though all the possible suspects regarding Elena's murder. We know the killer was a man over six feet tall and right-handed from the downward slice at her throat. That excuses the women, who all had legitimate alibis anyway. Enrique, who seems the most likely suspect, is left-handed, well under six feet, and was present at the base during the murder's time frame, which the coroner gave as being between midnight and 2 a.m. Elena, therefore, was killed right before the end of her shift. Your secretary, Mrs. Gaston, has the substantiated alibi of babysitting her grandchildren, but was seen talking to Enrique in that atmospheric bar you called Lupe's less than 48 hours later." Justin smiled at her description but leaned forward attentively.

"Well, you're broadening the list of who didn't do it. So who does that leave?"

"Let's work out the men Elena knew who were over six feet tall."

Justin nodded. "I'm top of the list."

"You're right here." Nicole tapped the paper. "All six-foot of you."

"Make that 6'2"," grinned Justin vaguely, trying to lighten the impact of heading Elena's suspected murderer list.

Nicole smiled at him, her expression clearly indicating that while on the list, he wasn't a suspect in her eyes. She continued lightly, "But there's also Scott Adams and Richard Greaves. I'm inclined to excuse Scott because his alibi seems airtight. Bud checked out the description of his friend Jack Roberts, who, by the way is several inches under six feet. That leaves Richard Greaves, who admitted that he worked until well after 9 p.m. that night. He asserted he went home alone after having a quick dinner at McDonald's."

"What a life," stated Justin sadly.

"We've verified he made a call to his ex-wife around 10 p.m. regarding his son's baseball game that upcoming Saturday. After that, who knows where he was?"

"So Richard *could* have committed the murder?"

"There's nothing to say he didn't, plus we have the suicide note depicting guilt of some kind. However, I'm inclined to believe that Richard wasn't talking about murder in his letter. He asks for forgiveness from his "darling." His plea sounds more like one from misdemeanor guilt, not murder." Justin smiled at her phraseology.

"Like he was caught... cheating?" he suggested.

A sudden thought struck Nicole. "What if that note was actually addressed to Judith Chamberlain? I got the sense he was quite enamored of her and jealous of both you and

Scott. She was awfully torn up by his death, though who wouldn't be under the circumstances? Richard worked late on more than one occasion. What if he'd started something with Elena and embarrassment or threat of exposure drove him to suicide?"

"Enrique!" cried Justin, his eyes blazing. "What if Enrique discovered Richard was messing around with Elena? Wouldn't Richard have had the ability to 'donate' money into Elena's account for services rendered? If Enrique had found out, wouldn't the budget manager seem like a sure-fire pay horse?"

"Bingo!" exclaimed Nicole; pleased with the way their reasoning headed. "Unfortunately, that doesn't explain Mrs. Gaston's involvement."

"Maybe she was simply doing a favor for Richard as courier, if we're correct about Enrique blackmailing poor Richard. They'd been friends for years and Leslie was quite verbal regarding Richard's being used by his ex-wife financially. Maybe she was just trying to help him out. Who knows, maybe she was sweet on him herself?"

"Possibly," sighed Nicole, still not convinced. Nicole's cell phone rang on the counter and Justin twisted his dark head toward the sound.

"It's probably Sherri," she observed, not liking the tautness of Justin's jaw muscles as he stared at the phone.

"Hello," Nicole said tentatively. There was static and a click and then nothing. A sense of déjà vu washed over her as she remembered the telltale click on her home phone minutes before they had bolted from Palm Springs. Her apartment had been torched only hours later.

"Who was it?" asked Justin watching her face intently.

"I don't know," she said breathlessly and replaced the phone carefully onto the pine countertop. Nicole tried to walk as casually as she could to the bedroom to retrieve her service revolver, which she'd playfully dropped prior to their lovemaking. When Nicole returned to the front room Justin rose rather unsteadily on his feet, listening intently. He pointed silently toward the front door and Nicole felt her heart accelerate.

Inching the door open slowly she peered cautiously through the opening. A pair of masked eyes stared back, gave a loud startled squawk and bolted up the large sugar pine tree, the mammal's tiny feet dislodging bark as it ascended the tree trunk rising from a hole sawn through the redwood deck.

"Raccoon," she declared shakily and began to laugh. Nicole ceased chuckling when Justin didn't join her.

"We're getting out of here," he demanded. "Whoever was on the other end of that phone line is headed this way and our cabin is a dead-end at the top of the hill."

"I don't believe anyone could know we are here. I covered our tracks too well."

"Who has the number to that phone?" He pointed at the silent blue cell phone.

"Sherri... and Buddy."

"Bud Ochoa, your partner?"

"Yes, my partner. He called while you were asleep earlier. I'd trust him with my life."

"I trusted a bunch of people once. My secretary, my boss, the people who worked everyday with me at The Desert Sky and all I have to show for it is someone tried to kill me and didn't care if they took you out at the same time. We're leaving."

By the stubborn set to his chin, Nicole knew there'd be no arguing with him. Silently she followed him into the bedroom and picked up the blue sports bag, deliberately packing the now clean clothing and remains of the first aid kit. Justin sank on the bed and tried to put on one of the new pairs of sports socks since he'd been padding around the cabin barefoot. He managed to get the right sock on, but sat up gasping after stuffing his left foot into the too-tight sock.

"I won't do this for you forever so don't get spoiled," said Nicole lightly, as she knelt before him. She eased his feet into his Rockport's, noticing the dark stains splattered over them, and carefully tied the laces. Justin's hands slid over her slim shoulders and pulled her close.

"I want you safe, no matter what the cost. Is that your only weapon?"

She nodded.

"Well then, I guess we'll stick together."

Five minutes later they were out of the cabin. Justin painfully strapped himself in and began to munch on one of the sandwiches Nicole had swiftly thrown together. Amidst a cloud of dust she turned left and headed again for the center of Idyllwild. Keeping a safe distance, the tan Imperial pulled out from the driveway of a vacant holiday cabin and followed her discreetly as she passed through town and headed down toward Mountain Center. As they neared the tiny hamlet she asked Justin to choose.

"Garner Valley or Hemet?"

"Garner Valley heads back toward Palm Springs via Highway 74, is that correct?"

"It does. You can follow the back route down to Palm Springs and come out near the tramway. Or we can take a right up here after a few miles at the service station and head through Anza. We'll end up near San Diego that way. If we drive down through Hemet we have lots of choices. We can double back through Lamb's Canyon, exiting at Beaumont before heading toward Palm Springs, or take the freeway in the opposite direction to Riverside. It's your call."

"Garner Valley," chose Justin. "It's the shortest way back to Palm Springs."

"Are you crazy?" exclaimed Nicole, throwing a glance at Justin's serious face.

"Look Nicole. I'd love nothing better than to find another hidey-hole and stay there for the next two weeks making love to you. But the answers we need are back in the desert. Certainly there must be someplace we can stay where no one will recognize us and still enable you and me to snoop around."

"That's doubtful," sighed Nicole, steering carefully around a particularly tight curve. The local newscast flashed both our faces all over the screen. So much for being an undercover detective."

"It's a lousy career anyway," Justin muttered, and Nicole shot him a quick and startled look.

"What's that supposed to mean?" she exclaimed. "And it's my career you're talking about; the career I chose for myself from among countless options. You don't hear me telling you that your choices are lousy. And I thought Scott held some pretty archaic views!"

"I just don't like the idea of you being in danger, that's all. Is that so wrong, to dislike the fact the woman you're involved with is in constant danger?" retorted Justin, his knuckles white from the death grip he held on the door handle, his teeth clenched in anger.

"I'm rarely in danger. In fact, being with you is the single most dangerous thing I've ever done. I've never shot anyone; I've never even frisked a suspect. I've never given the Miranda... I'd have to read it to recite it correctly. My job is basically spent at my desk going through mountains of research and enabling the blue suits to do their job. If you've got a problem with that maybe you should have picked another dream girl." The words had a nasty ring but obtained the desired effect. Justin went completely still and turned his handsome face from her, shutting her out. In fact, he didn't speak again at all for the next ten miles.

Garner Valley was beautiful at sunset as the pines gave way to beautiful flat grassland dotted by horse ranches, but Nicole doubted Justin even noticed. They flew by the location where the opening scene of the old TV series *Bonanza* had been filmed. Angrily, Justin leaned back in the cloth seat and closed his dark eyes. Nicole wasn't sure whether he slept or not, but the quiet gave her time to think. She was now convinced the only rational thing to do was stash Justin somewhere to give him time to heal and enable her to return to the station and continue the investigation. She'd needed to transfer the disk with the Lindsey file to Dusty and get his insights. Nicole made up her mind she was not going to share Justin's whereabouts to anyone at the station, not even Bud or Dusty, as much as that pained her. If Justin was correct in his assumptions regarding someone in the department having a hand in his shooting, then she had no choice but to protect him. But where to hide?

Suddenly, a grin settled over her features as Nicole thought of the perfect place. Justin finally spoke on the downside of the mountain as they headed toward the evening heat of Palm Springs.

"I have no right to criticize you regarding your career. It was wrong of me and I spoke out of turn."

Nicole had expected Justin to eventually speak up, but never guessed that's what he'd say. She shot him a quick glance. His face remained rigid, the muscles in his jaw working.

Under a Desert Sky

"I appreciate that Justin, and thank you for saying it. Look, we're both tired and stressed out, so let's just drop the subject okay?" His expression didn't alter so she continued gently, "I think I've figured out a safe place for you to hide. I don't know why it didn't occur to me before. There's a bowling alley just ten minutes away from the station. At the rear is a small caretaker's apartment where Jesse, a guy our squad room has sponsored for the past couple years, lives."

"Jesse?" Justin asked quietly. "You want me to stay with a guy named Jesse? Wouldn't that be dangerous and compromise my whereabouts?"

"No," she answered patiently. "That's the beauty of it. Jesse isn't home right now. He's at a special camp for mentally handicapped young people up near Arrowhead. Jesse's twenty, but has the mental capacity of an eight-year-old. A few years back he was involved in a custody dispute between his father and aunt, both just wanting state funds to supposedly take care of him. The court, after an amazing speech by my Captain, declared Jesse competent to support himself and Jerry helped him get a job cleaning and maintaining the bowling alley. It turned out the owner of the bowling alley has a niece who's also mentally handicapped and felt compelled to help Jesse. The perfect thing is that a small apartment had been built at the site for the previous caretaker. Jesse has a place to live and a steady income. Every year we have a raffle and use the proceeds to send Jesse to camp. This summer he's going to be trained as a counselor which is a big step up for him. Meanwhile, his flat is empty and I've got a key since I water his plants and feed his goldfish."

"You're amazing," said Justin sincerely. "And when's your friend Jesse returning home?"

"In about three weeks' time. You might find his decor a little, well, different, but I can guarantee that no one would think to look for you there."

"Do I have to bowl?" asked Justin mischievously, his face twitching slightly. He placed a warm hand on her denim-clad leg and Nicole folded her fingers over his.

"Wise guy," laughed Nicole, relieved that the tension had eased between them and slowed down as she pulled into the outer limits of Palm Springs.

Chapter 18

The summer heat in the desert, even at night, hits one with a mighty blast. Nicole instantly missed the cool breezes of Idyllwild, but resolutely maneuvered the now incredibly dusty minivan down Indian Boulevard. She turned up a couple side streets and pulled into a deserted alleyway. A small house stood at the back of a large parking lot, shaded by one huge palm tree and fronted by a large assortment of desert cactus. The lights of the bowling alley shown brightly; and from all the music and activity milling outside, business sounded good.

"Wait here," Nicole cautioned, stepping from the dirty van and walking up the short path to Jesse's apartment. Peering through the blinds, she quickly ascertained the small flat was deserted and gestured to Justin to hurry. Justin moved

271

fairly quickly for an injured, exhausted man and pushed past her. She closed the door and flicked on the light.

"You have got to be kidding!" Justin gasped in disbelief, his dark eyes widening.

Elvis was everywhere. From his early film days to his pudgy white-suited finale, Jesse had tacked up every inch of his wall space with Elvis memorabilia.

"Maybe you should have sent him to Graceland instead of camp," suggested Justin, slowly strolling about the cluttered front room and switching on a table lamp adorned with a gaudy Elvis shade.

"We've thought about it," stated Nicole straight-faced. "But weren't sure his heart could take it."

A tape player rested on a cheap entertainment stand.

"Let me guess?" sighed Justin. Nicole smiled as Justin lifted cassette after cassette of Elvis songs.

"This is even better," grinned Nicole, as she handed several videotapes to Justin, all from Elvis' early days as a singing movie star. "I'll get the sports bag," laughed Nicole, as she delighted in the disbelieving expression upon Justin's face as he turned over the tapes and began to read the back covers.

She returned to the van, glancing cautiously about her before retrieving their small hoard of goods. She made two trips carrying in the leftover food. Twenty minutes later she reluctantly braced herself to leave. Justin had eased onto the droopy couch after making a short tour of the tiny house that consisted of one square bedroom, a small bathroom, a compact kitchen, and the front living room dedicated to Elvis. Justin bent over the twenty-gallon fish tank and tapped his finger upon the lid, watching Jesse's three goldfish rise to the surface anticipating a meal.

"Yeah, and feed the fish, they've got to be hungry. I'll call you only from pay phones. Everybody knows that Jesse's at camp, but to be on the safe side, let the phone ring eight times before you answer it. Anyone else would hang up knowing how small this place is."

"Alright," Justin agreed, resigned to the fact she was going to leave him, and leaned back on the beige couch wearily.

"And, if you're a really good boy, I'll try to bring you some new videos and different music. That is, if you get tired of the King."

"Well, I like the King, but some Stones, Eagles, or even U2 might be nice as well."

"I'll work on it," grinned Nicole slowly, gazing at the man she had come to love and respect so much. "Get well Justin." Her tone changed from teasing to tender and he rose slowly and enfolded her in his arms.

"You stay safe," he begged, kissing her gently.

"It's a given," she promised, her eyes stinging, unable to push aside the uncomfortable feeling she shouldn't leave him. Nicole started the engine and reluctantly left him alone in the temple of Elvis.

Nicole drove around for nearly 45 minutes before she settled on a hotel to stay in, located nearly fifteen minutes from the station in the opposite direction from Justin. Resigned, she pulled into the Sleepy Owl Hotel and booked a room with a kitchenette. The place, though spartan and basic and painted in a drab combination of pale yellow and green, was at least clean. One hour later she'd returned from the market, filled the van up with gas, and taken a long cool shower. Now, at 8 p.m., she resisted the urge to call Justin. Instead, she picked up the phone and dialed Bud's cell number.

Maggie answered after only two rings. In the background, Nicole could hear Bud's two boys arguing above the TV's incessant drone.

"Hello Maggie," she said quietly. "It's Nicole."

"Nicole," screamed Maggie. "Are you okay? I saw the news about your apartment and was so worried."

Nicole basked in the warm concern issuing from Maggie and quickly sought to reassure the woman. "I'm fine, just fine. May I speak with Bud?"

Bud's booming voice filled the phone line less than a minute later. "Nikki, is that you?"

"You bet your sweet life it is. Didn't think you could get rid of me that easily did ya?"

"I wasn't sure what to think anymore. Where are you?"

"I've booked a room in an old hotel about ten minutes from you in a room that reminds me of a scene from *The Terminator*. I've stashed Justin safely away and he's doing a lot better. I'm ready to talk to the Captain now that he's safe."

Under a Desert Sky

Bud's voice sounded strained and urgent. "There's something you need to know. Richard's Greaves death was no accident. From the angle of the bullet and the lack of cordite on his hands we know someone else pulled the trigger."

"You're positive Bud? People were in his office within a matter of minutes after the shooting at most. It's not like he had a back door."

"You wouldn't believe how it was done. Richard had been shot at least fifteen minutes or so before Judith Chamberlain and Scott Adams heard the shot. The murder was done with a silencer after which a tape recorder, issuing loud nonsense from Richard, played for over fifteen minutes after the fatal shot had been fired. We found the recorder in the closet, but never put two and two together. Because it appeared like a suicide, the murderer walked casually away with no one even noticing."

Nicole swore under her breath, a habit her mother had always said was most unbecoming for a lady even if she was a police officer. Nicole generally whispered her curses, obeying her dead mother's wishes. "Maybe the murderer didn't have far to walk."

"That's always a possibility. B.W. Weston was in the station yesterday, cursing up a blue streak and blaming the Captain for everything from the murders and embezzlement to overdue parking tickets. It was a royal scene."

"Sorry I missed it," stated Nicole sincerely. "What did the Captain do?"

"Told him to take a Valium in his usual sweet tones. Your apartment was totally destroyed Nikki. The arsonist simply poured a lot of gasoline around the apartment and lit a match."

"Everything's gone?"

"I'm afraid so. Three apartments went up in smoke in all; yours, the next door neighbor Margie's, who you probably saw on the news, and a vacant flat. Margie's the one who had us convinced you were in there. Boy, were we glad she was wrong. The other apartment was being renovated and luckily was empty. Margie came down to the station, swearing that her car had been stolen until we managed to weasel the truth out of her. When you weren't found in the ashes, we'd already concluded you had managed to get away with Justin in the van, though it might have helped if she'd leveled with us at the start. Lee was livid. Thought he'd burst a blood vessel!"

"That's Margie, bless her heart. She lent me the van even though my initial story was pretty lame. For all her fluffy pink slippers and soap opera addictions, she's one savvy lady, sensing she needed to keep the truth from the media and the police. Justin and I may very well be alive because of her caution. Bud, just a thought? While Margie was at the station spilling her guts, was B.W. Weston there?"

A long silence ensued until Bud finally answered. "I think he might have been."

"So he very well could have known I'd escaped with Justin in the Dodge minivan?"

"Yes," Bud conceded. "You don't think...?"

"I'm not sure what to think. All I know is that someone called on my old cell phone and hung up while we hid in Pine Cove. We high-tailed it out of the mountains right afterwards, but for the life of me I'm not sure how we were traced. I have the readout for the Lindsey disk for Dusty to analyze. Can Dusty meet us at your house to take a look at it?"

"You mean right now?"

"Right now partner," reiterated Nicole.

"Call me back in ten minutes and I'll see what I can do."

Nicole gave him fifteen, drying her hair in the process, and thinking about poor Richard Greaves. That made two murders and a near-miss with Justin. Nicole was certain beyond a shadow of doubt that Elena's murder directly related to the embezzlement and Richard's apparent suicide. It was imperative that Dusty got the Lindsey file, and fast.

"Is it set up?" asked Nicole abruptly at Bud's barking hello.

"There will be some of Maggie's homemade tamales if you want 'em," he promised. "Just get your pretty rear over here." It was the best offer Nicole had heard all day.

Dusty waited at Bud's middle class house in South Palm Springs with his laptop in hand and a huge grin on his chubby face. He enveloped Nicole in a bear hug and she was touched to see tears in his eyes.

"We thought you were a goner."

"I'm too ornery to kill, Mr. Bug Byte," she teased, but left her arm locked in his. Maggie came in with a steaming plate of tamales and a warm embrace for Nicole as they seated themselves at the huge oval table. Both Nicole and Bud each grabbed a tamale, and as Nicole carefully peeled the steaming cornhusk off the hot center, Dusty glanced away uncomfortably.

"Have some," insisted Nicole, passing him the over-flowing platter.

"Already ate," he voiced sadly and spread the computer pages in front of him. Bud and Nicole glanced at each other and Bud mouthed the single word, 'Nancy.'

"Was Zachary able to link any of these figures to something in his organization?" asked Dusty, taking a sip of iced water, not noticing their keen stares.

"Justin indicated Lindsey was a contractor who'd worked on a resort in Puget Sound for him and was later hired to complete two resorts down in Florida. These pages are for the accounts payable. He studied them for a long time but couldn't come up with any noticeable discrepancies."

Dusty glanced at the three pages and shook his head. Bud snagged another tamale and carefully peeled it, slather-ing sour cream and guacamole all over the steaming concoc-tion before biting off a huge piece with gusto. Dusty swallowed in pain and took another huge gulp of unsatisfying water.

"You still have the disk?" he asked.

"Yeah, right here." Nicole dug into her handbag and laid the black floppy before him. He powered up his laptop and inserted the disk while Nicole finished her tamale.

"These are great Maggie," she complimented.

"You take some with you sweetie," Maggie said generously. "The Captain called while you were driving over here. He wants you to call."

"Okay," said Nicole, wiping her mouth. A ten-year-old zoomed past her as she walked to the phone and Nicole noticed his new kneepads and helmet.

"Rudy's got a new hobby?" asked Nicole, as she picked up the receiver.

"A hobby that will kill him," snorted Maggie indignantly. "Jumping those skateboards! Just on Wednesday a student from summer school broke his arm at the park, but Rudy's overly generous father thinks it's a great sport that builds dexterity. I say it puts a kid in traction!"

"A boy's got to have some thrills, sweet Maggie," Bud countered from the table. "Just like a man and a motorcycle."

Maggie made a disparaging sound deep in her throat.

"I'm wearing her down Nikki!" insisted Bud, ducking as Maggie threw a wooden spoon at him.

Nicole dialed the Captain and waited, wondering if she would ever be married with a fulfilling domestic life like the one Bud so obviously thrived upon; a life filled with the noisy blur of energetic children and the sweet, spicy smells of home. A yearning feeling washed over her as she imagined Justin sitting at the dinner table and sassing her just like Bud did his Maggie. Nicole started as Grace, the Captain's sweet and loving wife, answered the phone. When Nicole announced her identity, the tender woman burst into tears. A few seconds later, Jerry came on the line.

"Nicole, is that you?"

"Yes sir," she affirmed seriously.

"Blast it! What am I going to do with you? You totally violated police regulations and left us all in the lurch regarding your whereabouts."

"I was afraid for both Justin Zachary's and my security. I don't think I was far wrong since I now seem to be homeless."

Jerry paused. "Well," he finally said, "just don't let it happen again."

"Justin thinks there might be a squirrel at the station. I swear, someone knew what we were doing every step of the way."

"Point noted," came Jerry's terse reply.

"Where's Zachary now?"

"Safe for now in a sweet hidey hole. He's still recuperating from a bullet he took from someone in a white Caddy who'd followed him out near the railroad tracks. We're fortunate he's alive to tell his tale and produce the Lindsey file for us." Her Captain sputtered and Nicole continued.

"And don't ask me where he is. No one's going to know. I even forgot where I put him myself."

"Smart aleck huh?"

"I hope so Captain. He's nearly been killed once. I think I owe it to him to try and keep him alive."

Jerry digested that and seemed to accept her answer. "Nicole... about you and Justin?"

"There's nothing I need to relate to you about that at the present time."

The ensuing pause was too long, and wrought with emotion. Jerry cleared his throat and continued. "So after this whole fiasco, please say you've got something for us."

"Dusty's studying the Lindsey file as we speak. I'll let you know if we're any closer to answers as soon as I can. I'll be in the office first thing tomorrow."

"I'm glad," said Captain Hernandez. "It would be a shame to dock your pay."

Two hours later and stuffed to overflowing with Maggie's tamales and feeling very relaxed because of a couple of glasses of sweet California red wine, Nicole allowed her mind to drift back to Justin and his tender caresses. She could hardly wait to see him again and hoped he was getting some needed rest. Maggie noted the bemused expression covering her face and smiled. Nicole had almost forgotten about Dusty in her wonderful daydream. Her portly companion sipped wine and played with the computers, downloading all the files and meticulously reading every one. Finally he whistled loudly. Nicole and Bud were instantly at his side.

"Check this out," he explained, pointing to a series of spreadsheet entries. "These denote payments made to Brock Enterprises, Lindsey & Sons, and Blue Whale Properties. Here they're balanced out with entries to the Cancun building fund. They appear to balance, but it's a false entry."

"We know what Lindsey refers to, but what are Brock Enterprises and Blue Whale Properties?"

"We're about to find out," chortled Dusty as he logged onto the Internet.

Ten minutes later Nicole clutched herself mentally, trying to comprehend the enormity of Dusty's discovery.

"Blue Whale Properties belongs to Justin Zachary's family?"

"Yup," said Dusty. "And Brock Enterprises is his brother-in-law's import firm. I think the Captain's really gonna want to see this.

"How much are the monetary transfers for?" asked Bud, munching a crisp red apple and noting Nicole's stricken face.

"A cool two million dollars."

"I think the Captain might want to bring in Mr. Zachary for questioning," stated Bud as Nicole's heart sank.

Under a Desert Sky

Justin turned restlessly on the narrow twin bed covered by a bright red Elvis bedspread. Something had awakened him out of a light sleep and he became aware of his wound itching, which he considered a good sign. He froze and listened again. Sure enough, the noise originated from the front and only door. Justin rose silently and crept to the tiny kitchen, pulling out drawers randomly in search of a defensive weapon. The third drawer revealed a nasty looking butcher knife, and clutching it he moved to the door just as it swung open. The overhead ceiling light burst the room into false day as Justin tensed.

A young man in his early twenties, but possessing the ageless face of the mentally handicapped, froze in terror. "Ohhh!" he yelled and dropped his suitcase on the floor.

"Wait, wait!" cried Justin. "Are you Jesse?"

The slightly overweight caretaker was hyperventilating and Justin quickly laid the knife down, patting the boy gently upon his shoulder.

"Who are you?" stuttered the flustered Jesse, appearing near tears.

"I'm a friend of Nicole Lewis," responded Justin, certain her name was guaranteed to soothe the agitated young man more than his unknown one.

"Nicole?" The boy repeated, his shoulders relaxing a tiny bit while his hands plucked at a striped Padres t-shirt hanging loosely over a pair of bright red shorts.

"Yes, Nicole. She said she was a really good friend of yours and because I needed a place to stay and she thought

283

you were at camp, she let me stay here. I'm sorry if I frightened you, but I wasn't expecting you to come home."

"Nicole is my friend," Jesse stated, and smiled the lovely, no-holds-barred smile of the uninhibited and trusting. His face indicated he wholeheartedly accepted Justin's intrusion of his home this late simply because Justin was a friend of Nicole's.

"My name's Justin, Justin Zachary, and I'm honored to make your acquaintance. Nicole told me you won a medal in the Special Olympics."

"Oh, yes, yes. Wanna see?"

"I'd love to," sighed Justin, feeling near collapse as the proud boy ran to an overloaded bookshelf and took down a small trophy. He handed it reverently to Justin, who studied it carefully.

"Wow, third place in the mile run. You must be very proud."

"I am," answered the boy, beaming. "You look sick," he added.

"I've been unwell and if you don't mind I like to sit back down on your couch, that is, if it's okay with you?"

Jesse smiled and bobbed his head as Justin sank gratefully onto the lumpy couch. Jesse returned the trophy to the top shelf and looked around his small home, beaming in contentment.

"I thought you were at camp," continued Justin.

"I was, but this weekend, Angie, that's a counselor at the camp, had to come back to see her mom, who's sick, and

I thought I'd like to come home. I love my home." Jesse stated in flat tones.

"It's very nice," agreed Justin gently, watching Jesse gaze at his Elvis memorabilia with a look akin to reverence. "You've got lots of cool Elvis things here."

"Elvis is the King," said Jesse simply. "I'll make you some soup. That's what my mama would always make me when I felt sick."

"I'd appreciate it," said Justin, watching the self-sufficient young man return to the small kitchen and search the cupboards. He beamed, finally securing a can of chicken noodle soup. He opened it slowly with a crank can opener and poured it into a pan. How many people would write off this kind young man simply because of his handicap, wondered Justin as he watched Jesse stir the warming mixture with a wooden spoon.

"You've known Nicole for a long time?" he asked, watching the gentle young man fiddle over the steaming pan.

"I think three years. She helped me when I needed to leave home." A wave of sadness overcame Jesse for a minute as Justin watched helplessly. "Nicole and Bud come here every week. Sometimes we go bowling. I'm a pretty good bowler. Do you bowl?"

"No," said Justin. "I bowled a couple times when I was a kid, but certainly not in recent years."

"I can get you a pass. Bud's a great bowler, but sometimes Nicole only hits the alley," he explained frankly, stirring the soup with gusto.

Justin grinned at the image of Nicole's wild bowling habits. "I'd love to play sometime with you and Nicole."

Jesse looked up and a broad smile flooded his face. "You Nicole's boyfriend?" he giggled.

"Yes I am," stated Justin without hesitation. It felt wonderful to declare it out loud.

"Good. She needs a boyfriend and I'm too young for her."

Justin smiled again. "Jesse, would you mind if I stay here? I can sleep on the couch. But for right now, I'm not able to find anyplace else to stay."

Jesse stopped and thought hard. "Are you in trouble?"

Justin decided to tell him the truth. "Yes, I am. But I feel like I could be safe here."

"You can stay here then and I won't tell no one. Except, maybe Nicole." He poured the steaming liquid into a chipped bowl and set it proudly upon a bright Elvis placemat.

"That would be great," expressed Justin, sitting down at the counter to share a bowl of warm soup with the wonderful Jesse.

The husky man in the tan Imperial squirmed. Everything had been going just fine until that kid showed up. His intention had been to take Zachary out quietly, so no one would have the slightest indication; but now it looked like a change in plans was in order. He reluctantly picked up the mobile phone and his boss answered impatiently. Silence ensued as he explained the predicament.

Under a Desert Sky

"You want me to take him out?" voiced the strong man.

"Let's wait a bit. Maybe we'll get lucky and the boy will leave. I don't want any foul-ups on this one. Too much is at stake and everything's out of control right now."

The hired man murmured a polite affirmative and hung up the phone. He would wait. He was actually very good at waiting and as he figured it, waiting was mostly what he got paid for. Flipping the dials of the radio, he removed a thick ham sandwich on Russian rye from its wrapper and settled down to enjoy his late night supper while listening to some bluesy jazz. It was going to be a long night.

Chapter 19

Nicole didn't sleep well that night after too many tamales and the negative news regarding Justin. It was difficult to remain objective and just analyze the facts. Even if Justin had somehow been behind the embezzlement; who had shot him and what were his secretary and Enrique's connection? On the other hand, what if Justin had been the one in Richard's office before the unfortunate business manager's death? He stated he'd never made it upstairs, but who was to verify his story? But while the police side of her nature suspected him, her heart and soul adamantly rejected the notion that Justin was somehow responsible for Richard's death or anyone else's for that matter. Justin was too gentle and empathetic to commit a heinous crime like murder. Yet, how could she possibly be objective since she'd witnessed him in pain and had lain in his arms as a lover?

So she tossed and turned, finally dozing off sometime after midnight, in a sleep triggered by pure exhaustion and final certainty that whoever had killed Elena and Richard was also trying to frame Justin for the murder. It was the only scenario that made the least bit of sense. Nicole rose again at 3 a.m. with a bad case of indigestion and swallowed some antacid tablets. Next time she'd try to limit herself to four tamales instead of seven.

She'd gotten what she deserved.

Nicole rose early and was cruising around Palm Springs by 7:30 a.m. Her path meandered in hopes of shaking off anyone following her. A full forty minutes later she pulled into the back parking lot of the deserted bowling alley and parked in front of Jesse's tiny house under the towering palm tree. Nearing the front door she could hear Elvis singing "Suspicious Minds," accompanied by Jesse at the top of his lungs. *Jesse?* Nicole rapped on the door loudly, sincerely doubting she'd be heard over the loud music, but the door swung wide revealing a relieved Justin appearing tanned and well. A huge smile spread over his handsome face and once again Nicole felt that charged chemical reaction burst between them. Muffling her intense feelings, she voiced grumpily, "You shouldn't open the door unless you know who it is."

Under a Desert Sky

"I was looking out the through the drapes, Ms. By-the-Book, so I knew it was you. Why don't you come in out of the heat?"

Nicole entered the cool darkness of Jesse's living room and spied the plump young man browsing through some large photo albums on the floor while singing full tilt.

"Nicole!" he yelled, leaping up to engulf her in a tremendous embrace.

"Hi Jesse," she managed to squeak, and he released her with a contagious grin on his round face.

"I'm helping out your friend," said Jesse, and raised his pointer finger to his lips, indicating his cooperative secrecy.

"Thanks so much Jesse, but aren't you supposed to be at camp?"

"Tomorrow," he said simply, and pulling at her arm dragged her to the couch beside him. "Look Nicole." Jesse had carefully placed many photos of his camp in the large binder. Justin sat down stiffly on the other side of Jesse and smiled over the boy's bent head. Nicole felt such a wave of love and contentment wash over her she was rendered speechless and could only watch mutely as Jesse mentioned various campers names and what area of California they'd originated from. Elvis switched to singing "Love Me Tender" in the background.

Nicole spent the next ten minutes paging through countless photos narrated by a rapt Jesse. The camp had proven to be a great experience for the young man and Nicole reminded herself to mention that fact to the entire department, since they'd all taken so great an interest in the future of this kind young man. Justin watched her tenderly as she glanced up from the photos. He appeared rested and almost fully recovered though still too thin.

"Let's go to the kitchen and talk," he said quietly, and Nicole followed him into the small kitchen noting he'd donned a pair of Jesse's long navy shorts and a t-shirt depicting a smiling UCLA Bruin on the front.

"Look's sporty," she said, tapping his shirtfront.

"Needed to expand my wardrobe. You ought to see my Elvis underwear. So what's the plan Detective?"

"You seem well taken care of here."

"Yeah, Jesse and I are getting along like a house afire. Thank goodness I like Elvis." He glanced over at Jesse whose brown head was buried in yet another photo album.

"It might be hard to survive here else wise. I haven't told anyone your location, just that you're safe. We might move you on Monday. Is there anything you need?"

"Just you," he said softly, and Nicole shivered at the love and longing sparking from his dark eyes.

She gazed for a long moment at him. He'd shaved and his long hair hung casually around his face. Nicole cleared her throat and Justin grinned, correctly interpreting her thoughts. He reached for her hand and placed it over his chest, enabling her to feel the steady heartbeat under the Bruin t-shirt.

"Do you like what you see?" he queried softly.

"Almost too much." She remembered his suffering face from only three days ago and thanked God he'd survived.

Under a Desert Sky

Nicole wished to relate to him all they'd discovered regarding Richard and the money, but felt her throat go dry.

"Is something wrong?"

"No," she lied. "Not at all. I'll stop by again this evening and give you a full update on what's happening." She let him pull her into his arms and kissed him tenderly.

"Jesse will return to camp tonight," he whispered, caressing her now perspiring back.

"'Til then," she acknowledged, and backed away reluctantly. Jesse had a huge smile plastered over his round face.

"You like him," he declared, pointing a knowing finger at the couple.

"You bet!" laughed Justin, and Jesse joined in delightedly. The two men, so different in stature, but similar in genuine emotions, walked Nicole to the door and watched her drive off.

"She's a peach," declared Jesse.

"Yup," answered Justin.

"Want to play a game of Yahtzee?"

"You're on partner," said Justin, closing the door, never once noticing the Imperial parked under the shade of some low palms a few hundred yards away.

B. W. Weston was in a dramatic rage. He pranced and growled in the confines of Jerry's office for nearly thirty minutes while Nicole and Bud watched the passive face of their Captain never twitch or betray his thoughts for a moment. He simply murmured words of encouragement and suggested the entire matter was quite under control.

After Captain Hernandez's last round of assurances, B.W. flamed even redder and shouted, "And what about Zachary? Just where is he? I'm sure he'd have a great deal to say about your lack of results."

"He's safe and accounted for," reassured Jerry.

"Safe! Accounted for! You wouldn't know how to keep a longhorn safe from lightning on a cloudless day!"

"He's safe and will be questioned as to why certain transfers of money have a direct connection to his brother-in-law's export company."

"He damn straight better have an explanation or I'll wring his rotten neck! Things ain't getting any clearer at all, just murkier and murkier!" Nicole enjoyed listening to B.W. butcher the language, but admitted to herself she sure wouldn't like to set B.W. loose on Justin just yet. Not until she had a little chat with him herself.

"Like I said, we've stashed Mr. Zachary in a safe house until we find out more regarding Richard Greaves and Elena Gonzalez's murders."

"Murders?" stressed B.W. Weston. "I thought Greaves was a suicide?"

"Evidence points to someone else pulling the trigger."

"Well Hernandez, you were right about one thing. You said that where there was one murder, they'd likely be another. I just hope to God that Zachary ain't the third. You'd better start turning up something more than dead bodies, and pronto!" And with that, the aging Texan stormed through the door, slamming the glass frame so hard that Nicole was surprised it didn't shatter into a thousand pieces.

"You heard the man," said Jerry softly. "No more corpses."

"Yes Sir," answered Nicole and Bud in unison.

"Call Blue Whale Industries and let's get Zachary's brother-in-law on the line and see what we can ascertain. Zachary's safe?"

"Yes. You want to see him?"

"Tonight, I'll let you know when and where. Get to work you two. It's going to be a long day."

Justin slept most of the afternoon away and awoke at 3:30 feeling more rested and alert than he had in days. Jesse hummed "Blue Suede Shoes" in the kitchen while making a peanut butter and jelly sandwich.

"You want a sandwich Justin?" he called, as Justin awkwardly stretched his long frame from the cramped position he'd assumed after falling asleep on the couch.

"Sounds great!" stated Justin, though a medium rare steak smothered in onions and mushrooms sounded a whole lot better.

Jesse proudly deposited a cut sandwich oozing peanut butter and grape jelly in front of Justin. "I like lots of jelly on mine. Do you Justin?"

"Yup, that's just how I like it." They both sat compatibly in the tiny living room enjoying their sandwiches and a diet soda when Justin heard a thump.

"What was that?" he asked, suddenly alert.

"Sounds like the wind. It can really blow around here. Maybe we're gonna get a thunder and lightning storm. They're really neat to watch!" Jesse bounded off the sofa, a smear of jelly marking his mouth.

He had just reached the door when it burst open. Jesse was thrown aside, the barrel of a lethal Glock starring down at Justin behind the florid face of a red-haired man.

"Come quietly or the kid's going to get hurt," Red said. Jesse whimpered against the kitchen counter, rubbing his shoulder.

"Justin, Justin! It's the bad guys."

"It's all right Jesse. Everything's going to be okay. Just don't hurt the boy. I'll come along quietly."

Jesse began to cry brokenly and Justin stopped and squeezed his shoulder before preceding the burly man in the too-tight suit.

"The boy comes too," ordered the copper-haired man, as Justin helped the boy up.

"I got to go back to camp tonight," protested Jesse.

"No camp tonight," laughed the intruder, swinging the muzzle of his gun between the two men.

"Nice decorations," he growled, as he shoved Jesse through the door into the hot afternoon.

Nicole arrived at Jesse's at a quarter past four. Her stomach twisted at the prospect of seeing Justin again and having to present some delicate questions to which she was afraid of the answer. She immediately sensed something wrong as the door to Jesse's small house creaked unassisted in the light afternoon breeze. Pulling out her revolver, she hurtled through the entrance of the tiny apartment. The place, deceptively cool from the air conditioning, seemed innocent enough while Elvis crooned about a "Heartbreak Hotel" in the background. An overturned bar stool, a scrunched up floor rug, and two half-eaten sandwiches resting upon the untidy counter were the only indications something was amiss. Nicole raced to the small bedroom and peeked into the closet-sized bathroom, revealing neither of the two men she so loved. Nicole's blue sports bag lay unzipped upon the floor, spilling the first aid kit and a pair of sports socks. Justin's new Idyllwild pants hung neatly over the couch and she resisted the urge to weep uncontrollably. She remained motionless for a full five minutes in the cool emptiness of the tiny house before regaining enough strength to call the Captain. She wanted to die.

Nicole sat with her hands between her knees as the milling officers attended to their various duties of dusting for prints, checking the perimeter, and taking solemn notes. Jerry purposely avoided her stricken eyes and even the ever-cheerful Nancy seemed subdued. Bud finally crouched before her, his shadow casting a cool respite from the searing heat, and searched her face.

"You okay Pard?" he asked quietly.

"I put him in the safest place I knew, and now both he and Jesse are missing or worse," she whispered huskily. "I let them down and dragged an innocent boy into a web of murder and kidnapping. What could I have been thinking?"

Bud lowered himself beside her upon the hard concrete steps that lead into the small house and studied his broad brown hands for a moment. "Sometimes our best laid plans don't pan out Nikki. And when they don't, I find the best thing to do is to take some sort of action, whether it be right or wrong, to achieve a sense of balance again. I'm a man of action and the sitting and thinking about what you should have done just eats you alive."

Nicole peered into his stoic face and responded help-lessly. "So what should we do?"

"We move on the leads and facts before us. And the first fact glaring us in the face is that Justin's secretary acted out of character and we need to question her. Second, we know that Enrique Diaz is no innocent and is somehow involved in Elena's death no matter what his alibi suggests. So, I say, let's go find them so that we can at least feel we're doing something." She nodded and he stretched out one strong brown hand to haul her to her feet.

In the neat interior of Captain Hernandez's small office Bud paced like a caged animal. Nicole sat perfectly still, her face frozen into a remote impenetrable mask, unable to describe how she felt to her superior. Jerry listened to their entire recital of events, his normally impassive face twitching as he faced Nicole with worried dark eyes.

"So B.W. was right after all," he stated softly, and Nicole jerked as if with a physical blow. "Zachary was always in extreme danger."

"So what do we do now?" asked Bud, watching Nicole's face and again wondering at its desperate expression. He had some rather pointed questions for her later.

Their Captain cleared his throat. "It's back to square one and the only real lead we have. Leslie Gaston is missing, or worse, so that leaves only our sweet Enrique. Pull him in. I don't care whose palm you have to grease or what shady deals you have to offer that bastard, but find our Jesse. If we don't make some headway now... more than just millions will be lost."

His voice quavered on the last word and Nicole glanced toward the beautifully framed photo situated on the shelf above the Captain's desk. It displayed a proud Hispanic man applauding a tired but ecstatic Jesse crossing the finish line in the Special Olympics two summers ago.

Nicole felt desolate and sick inside. She'd put Jesse in danger, as well as the man she loved. She nodded curtly, refusing to divulge her feelings to either of the two grim men before her.

"I messed this one up and I'll clean it up. Let's go find this Enrique jerk."

Jerry's voice growled in a hushed whisper for Bud's ears alone, as the Captain held the door for the stout Native

American. "Take care of her; this has gotten personal." Bud grimly gestured a thumbs up and followed his too-silent partner.

Palm Springs cools down somewhat at night during the hot summer months, but the coldness of the air conditioner still felt wonderful to Nicole's overheated skin. She sat tightly in the old Chevy's worn front seat, rigid as a statue, oblivious of her clenched hands and tense spine and what they indicated to Bud.

"Want to talk about it?" asked Bud, perfectly negotiating a particularly tight corner in the big car.

"Jesse could be dead."

"I know, but that wasn't what I was talking about. I was referring to Justin Zachary."

Her only response was a long, pent-up sigh.

"You were lovers?" he questioned, already knowing the answer.

"Yes," responded Nicole dejectedly.

"Well that changes everything," pronounced Bud, as he tapped his fingers impatiently on the steering wheel of the old brown Chevy. Nicole wiped a quick tear away as Bud tried to ignore her distress. "He's innocent of any wrongdoing isn't he Nikki?"

"I'm sure of it."

"Then it's a given. So that means someone's trying to frame him, and if that doesn't work, kill him. Why don't we go over what we already know?" he stated, hoping to distract her.

"Okay."

"Alright, fact number one," said the burly Bud, tugging at his long ponytail. "The only person we're certain was in the station when Margie gave the information about you taking the minivan was B.W. Weston."

"That's right," affirmed Nicole, relieved to talk about something other than Justin.

"Fact number two: we know that Richard Greaves' suicide was no accident. Someone helped him pull that trigger and my gut instinct says that someone was Enrique Diaz. If, as you have suggested, Enrique was involved in some sort of blackmail attempt, he may have inadvertently caused his girlfriend's death, which in my opinion is tantamount to murder. Enrique is currently AWOL which leads me to believe that we need to make a quick stopover at my house to enable us to ferret out our worm who is obviously in hiding."

Nicole was past caring and scarcely listened to Bud's ramblings, instead sitting dejectedly within the old Chevy as she alternated between kicking herself for trusting her choice of safe house and inwardly crying for the two men who might very well be dead because of her ineptitude. Within ten minutes Bud pulled up the long driveway and parked in front of his cluttered garage as his wife Maggie opened the door with a surprised expression upon her face.

"What are you doing here?" she asked. "I thought you were called out?"

"Jesse is missing," said Bud softly, and Maggie blanched. She loved that boy as much as anyone.

"Missing?" she repeated. "What do you mean missing?"

"Looks like he has been kidnapped along with the head of the resort, Justin Zachary. Nicole and I need to make a little trip into the city to apprehend a possible suspect. You still got that box Maggie?"

Maggie glanced at Nicole's tight face and nodded. "This way," she answered, as the pair followed her into a side den used as a sewing room and storage area. Maggie slid open the closet door and pulled out a huge, TV-sized box.

"What are you up to Bud?" Maggie asked, her arms folded defiantly across her plump chest.

"Now, not to worry my love," reassured Bud, straightening up and tweaking her ear. "I, um, think I hear one of the boys calling you from the living room."

"I don't hear nothing," growled Maggie, but she obediently vacated the room.

"You are lucky to find someone who puts up with you Bud," pronounced Nicole, driven out of her lethargy by the sight of a bright pink boa dangling over the edge of the box.

"Hmm," mused Bud, picking up the feathery wrap and draping it about her shoulders. "I don't think this is going to do at all. Let's see what else we have?"

Under a Desert Sky

Ten minutes later an exasperated Nicole stood with her hands on her hips gasping at Bud. "You can't expect me to wear *that*!" she exclaimed.

"If you wanna fit the part, you gotta dress the part." Spread over the top of Maggie's sewing table a skimpy, skintight leather dress with a low v-cut neck mocked her.

"If Jerry Hernandez catches me in this I could be fired," she moaned, knowing it wasn't remotely true, but horrified by her appearance.

"Or obtain yourself a hefty raise! Besides, who says he's going to see you?" rationalized Bud, as he picked up his outfit, which consisted of a black leather vest with accompanying heavy gold necklace, a bright blue-checked bandana, and tight shiny leather pants.

"Are you going to be able to fit into that?" asked Nicole, analyzing Bud's protruding belly. Upon recognizing the direction of her gaze, he sucked in his gut.

"You just let me worry about that. Let's see if you can fit into yours."

A few minutes later Nicole stood in front of the full-length oval mirror situated at the side of the sewing room, unable to recognize the woman before her. The skirt was indecently short and boasted a side slit that revealed more of her thigh than she cared for. A long silver link chain glinted over the front of the skirt, and the accompanying top wasn't any less revealing, sporting a low v-neck that emphasized her rounded breasts and exposed belly button.

"You have nice legs," commented Bud matter-of-factly. "So you don't need to worry about wearing nylons or anything. Let's see; I wonder if these would fit you?" He hoisted a dark pair of high boots with insanely spiked heels.

"I'd fall off those," insisted Nicole, pushing the monstrosities away.

Bud thrust them back at her. "Do you want to get Enrique or not?" She grabbed the despicable boots, unable to tear her stunned eyes away from the man standing before her. Her partner has transformed himself into a burly Motorcycle thug within a matter of minutes. Bud's anchor tattoo from his old navy days bulged on his bicep as he flexed an arm for her. His protruding belly draped over the top of the tight leather pants and he had donned sharp, wicked-looking, silver-tipped boots. The blue-checked bandana tied around his head, complemented by his ponytail, made him appear like a cross between a Hell's Angel and a Cahuilla Indian on the rampage.

"So are you going to put those boots on," demanded Bud of his reluctant partner, "or am I going to have to do it for you?"

Nicole reluctantly sank onto the worn couch in the sewing room and pulled on the boots, zipping up the sides to just below her knees. As Nicole rose shakily she could barely keep on her feet.

"Wow," she gasped at her startling image. "Thank God my mother can't see me now!"

Under a Desert Sky

"But your hair! Your hair is *all* wrong," pronounced Bud. "So what can we do? Maggie," he called loudly. "Could you come in here for a moment?"

After Maggie arrived in the room she stopped dead, flabbergasted at the image Nicole presented.

"What on earth?" she declared, and began talking rapidly to Bud in Spanish.

"Now, now, Maggie it's alright, but you have to do something with her hair. She's got to look like a biker's babe, and right now she just looks like, well, an undercover police detective."

"Which is what I am," hissed Nicole between clenched teeth.

Maggie analyzed her for a moment, then said, "Wait here sweetie, I'll be right back." Maggie returned with a blue tube of hair gel and pulled Nicole's hair back into a wild ponytail after applying some gel and spiking up her bangs. Side strands of her golden brown hair escaped from the ponytail, making her appear tough and sexily disheveled.

"Hmm, that will do," Maggie commented. "It looks like you just put back your hair to ride a motorcycle. What else can I do? Ah ha!" She removed some dark eye make-up from her cosmetic bag and dabbed olive green eye shadow above Nicole's lids. Maggie then applied a lethal amount of rouge to her cheeks and caked heavy powder over the top. Her final touch was to add some dark eyeliner and mascara, as well as a lethal dose of bright red lipstick. Where before Nicole had looked simply like a cheap date in Bud's suggested getup she now, after Maggie's finishing touches, resembled a low-class prostitute.

"That will do just fine," declared Bud, throwing her an approving glance. "Now to make a quick call." He bounded from the room, his ponytail bouncing over the back of the leather vest.

"Are you alright Nicole?"

"Do I look alright?" returned Nicole grimly, staring at her altered image in the mirror.

"That's not what I meant. You don't seem yourself."

"I have to live with the fact that I let both Justin Zachary and Jesse down. If we don't find Enrique Diaz it might be too late for them."

"And there's nothing else?"

"Nothing except that I'm in love with Justin Zachary, which violates every principle of the department since he's a major suspect in both the murder and embezzlement."

"Do you believe he's guilty?"

"My head might be confused but my heart is not."

"Then go with your heart. I always have. My head so many times notices all of Bud's rough edges, but my heart loves the kind, strong man within. And my heart is not wrong Nicole, as I'm sure yours isn't. Trust to your heart and your love."

"He and Jesse may well be dead because of me."

Maggie sighed deeply. "You don't know that for certain. So you just straighten those shoulders girl and go out and do your job. That's all you can do. Tonight, I'll light a candle for you and Jesse and that man of yours."

Under a Desert Sky

Nicole's eyes shone with unshed tears. She had always been so fortunate in her friends and colleagues. The sight of Maggie's steady and loving eyes bolstered her spirits as she smoothed the too-short skirt. "I will."

"Well then," said Maggie decidedly. "This Halloween outfit may well be justified after all. I have a feeling Bud is leading you down a dangerous road. Am I correct?"

Nicole nodded. "Hopefully this getup will gain us access to Justin and Jesse." Maggie's eyes were pained so Nicole added quickly, "Don't worry, I'll bring your Bud back to you safe and sound."

"It isn't Bud I'm worried about," was all Maggie responded.

Chapter 20

It was dusk when Bud pulled his old Chevy behind the automobile holding pen of the Palm Springs Police Department. A slender wiry man with tight curly hair opened the gate and handed him a set of keys.

"I just knew you'd figure out a way to score a test run of the hog," Gray Peters asserted.

"The hog?" asked Nicole skeptically and then laughed at their transportation as it sat in all its chromed glory, the large front wheel of the Harley-Davidson angled toward the two detectives.

"Your carriage awaits, my princess," bowed Bud, and he motioned to the back of the motorcycle.

"You really expect me to ride on that?" protested Nicole, eying the huge bike.

"How else are we going to show up at Lupe's, the biggest biker hangout in the entire city and the last place Justin saw Enrique Diaz?"

"But what about Mrs. Gaston?" asked Nicole, edging closer to the shiny motorcycle.

"I called her yesterday, but only got an answering machine. We sent a squad car but it seems our bird has flown the coop. So that only leaves our Enrique. So stop procrastinating and get on the blasted bike."

Nicole found it incredibly difficult to mount the bike with the miniskirt, but eventually managed to teeter precariously, though immodestly, behind Bud.

"Put your arms around my waist," Bud demanded, as he gunned the engine, twisting the handles on the Harley until the motor gave a mighty roar. "Ain't she sweet," he cooed and glided through the gate.

Gray, the wiry mechanic for the police department, raised a hand and gave a low wolf whistle as they zoomed around the corner. Less than thirty minutes later, at the edge of a less than respectable neighborhood, Bud pulled up among other motorcycles parked in front of the bar that flashed out in red gaudy florescent lights, 'Lupe's.'

There was quite a crowd tonight Nicole guessed from the twenty or so motorcycles leaning at an angle in front of the bar's front entrance. She suspected no cover charge was necessary in this low-class dive.

"No matter what," insisted Bud, "let me do the talking."

Under a Desert Sky

"That's a given," said Nicole between clenched teeth. Not only was her Spanish appalling, but it would take all of her fortitude and effort just to keep the miniskirt from creeping up and exposing her rear end.

"Stay behind me," instructed Bud, "as if I'm your man and you're slightly afraid of me. If anyone talks to you, cast your eyes downward and look nervously at me. I'll indicate you're my property. Anyone who tries to talk to you is going to have to deal with me is the message I want to send. You got it?"

Nicole nodded, and followed her so-called biker boyfriend into the dark smoky interior of the bar. Lupe's was deceptively large and spread out, boasting four or five pool tables, a cluster of back booths in dark brown vinyl, and a huge horseshoe-shaped bar behind which three large and mean looking bartenders waited on the often rowdy crowd. The bar was so smoky that Nicole tried valiantly not to cough. While all the pool tables were busy, one billiard table to the left seemed to be attracting vast attention. A thin wiry Hispanic man positioned at the end of the pool table chalked his cue while inordinate amounts of money were thrown down upon the table. Fifteen or so vested and tattooed bikers, along with their heavily made up girlfriends, surrounded the felt table. Nicole realized instantly she and Bud fit right in since no one gave them more than a cursory glance.

Bud strolled to the bar and leaned close to the nearest bartender. "Hey, I am looking for a friend of mine," he said in Spanish. "His name is Enrique and I have the money I owe him. You seen him?"

The bartender shook his broad flat face stupidly and moved away from Bud, wiping the counter with a white cloth. Bud motioned to another shorter and thinner bartender, asking him the same question. The bartender shrugged. It was clear the men behind the bar did nothing more than serve their customers, which was probably the safest thing to do in a place like this. Bud gave up and ordered two beers.

"Maybe you'll have better luck at that pool table over there, it looks like they have quite a game going," suggested Nicole quietly.

The short wiry man who'd been chalking his pool stick earlier deftly angled the last ball into the right-hand pocket as the crowd whooped and began slapping him on the back. He reached over and picked up the pile of money amounting to several hundred dollars. After pocketing his winnings he spoke loudly above the din of the pool hall, in Spanish that even Nicole could understand.

"Is there anyone fit enough to challenge me?" The majority of the crowd shook their heads until finally Bud moved forward and pointed a large thumb at his chest.

"I'll take you on," he said in Spanish as the crowd studied him.

"I'm afraid I don't know you," lisped the wiry Hispanic man dressed in a turquoise silk shirt and black leather pants. He wore a gold stud earring in his left ear and a red-checked bandana, from which a greasy ponytail peeked.

"My name is Eduardo Fernandez and I challenge you to a match; that is if you're game?" barked Bud.

The thin man smiled, and flashing a gold front tooth answered smoothly, "My name is Jose Gomez, and I'd be happy to take your money."

Bud leaned over to Nicole as more money was slapped down on the green felt pool table and pointed to a barstool not far from where he stood.

"Why don't you sit there and keep an eye and ear out for you know who." He then kissed her hard on the mouth and tugged at her hair as if she were his possession. Nicole managed to gaze demurely back at him, batting her mascara-laden eyelashes. The responding twinkle in Bud's eye clearly reveled in her new role and costume, and she had to smile. At least the play-acting took her mind off the fates of Jesse and Justin for a few minutes. After ten minutes of intense argument and frenzied betting with more money slapped on the table, the balls were once again set up inside the plastic triangle. Nicole watched the game for a while as Jose broke the balls and the men traded shots. Nicole allowed her eyes to casually slide over the customers frequenting Lupe's, but saw no one resembling the crew-cut Enrique.

Well into the game Jose scowled and aimed at the six-ball. Nicole sauntered up to Bud indicating she had to go to the bathroom and he whispered for her to be careful. Nicole headed back toward the rear of the bar, stiffening as she observed a dark-haired couple locked in a passionate embrace in a shadowy back booth. Suddenly the woman pushed herself away from her partner's chest and slapped her lover smartly across the face. The heavily perfumed woman rose and stomped hotly away, brushing angrily past Nicole as she headed toward the womens room. Nicole, her eyes smarting from the thick tobacco smoke, realized the rejected lover was none other than the arrogant Enrique. He'd changed from his military clothes, but his crew cut distinguished him from the other patrons though attired in black leather pants and an open crimson shirt. Enrique certainly hadn't grieved long for his departed Elena and Nicole seethed inside.

Enrique's black eyes discovered her and gave her a once-over, pulling his lips back in a wolfish leer. Nicole straightened abruptly, expecting him to recognize her from that day at the station. Her mind fought back to that morning, remembering she'd been standing outside the interrogation room, concealed from the young suspect by the one-way mirror, and she relaxed. She tossed her head and strutted away, but not before smiling suggestively back, making sure she swung her hips provocatively. Hopefully he'd remain in the back booth long enough for her to warn Bud.

Bud's back was to her as he bent over the table, drawing back the long cue stick and aiming at a bright orange ball. The crowd remained respectfully silent as he pulled the cue back and slammed the white ball at a sharp angle into the waiting ball. It careened off the side and landed squarely inside the middle pocket. A whoop rose from the pack and more money joined the already large hoard of cash. The irritated Jose motioned for the bills to be removed and eyed Bud shrewdly, realizing the Native American was a more formidable opponent than he'd expected. Nicole sidled up to Bud and whispered in his ear, pretending to nibble on his earlobe.

"Enrique's in the back booth."

Bud stiffened, his dark eyes widening. If he managed to pocket the last ball he'd win the game and then there was no telling when they could safely leave the bar and approach Enrique. If he lost, he would be free to pursue the suspect, though he knew in his gut he could win. Bud shook his head sadly, pretending to analyze the position of the ball. He strolled around the table a couple of time before finally returning and spitting on his hands.

Leaning over, he positioned the cue stick against the white ball.

Crack went the slam of the stick as the white ball collided with the eight ball directly mid-center. It banked against the right-hand corner and nearly deposited itself in the left-hand middle pocket. A collective groan issued from the crowd. Jose grabbed up his stick and moved into position. He pulled the stick back, and with a whish the eight ball landed squarely in the left-hand side pocket.

Condolences were given to Bud in loud back slaps as the grinning Jose licked his thumb and began to count his winnings. Bud grabbed Nicole's arm and ordered her to be ready. Earlier, Nicole had placed her .38 in the small beaded handbag at her shoulder and tapped it to indicate to Bud she was set. Both moved to the rear of the pool hall toward the secluded back booth where Enrique still sulked, waiting in vain for his disgruntled girlfriend to return. His eyes widened at the sight of Nicole accompanied by the big frowning biker.

"Hey man," said Bud belligerently, "I don't like what you said to my lady."

"What?" issued the startled word from Enrique's tight lips. "I don't know you man and I never touched her!"

"But I know you," stated Bud, suddenly reaching into his vest pocket and pulling out his badge. Nicole, standing directly behind Bud, discreetly removed her .38 from the beaded handbag. She now held it against her chest, the firearm barely discernable to anyone who might glance at her through the smoky darkness of the pool hall. Enrique moved in an explosion of speed, grabbing his half-empty beer glass and flinging it at Bud before springing over the table.

"Stop!" shouted Bud in both English and Spanish, but Enrique didn't obey the curt order. He careened into a side table before dashing down the hallway where his girlfriend had disappeared earlier. Bud followed, moving quickly for such large man, and Nicole, trusting the expertise of her partner, whirled and headed out the front exit, the crowd parting like the sea before Moses as she pulled out her badge and flashed it to the shocked mob.

"Out of my way," she said in her poor Spanish and then repeated herself in English. No one sought to delay her in the least. "Damn these spiky heels," Nicole gasped, as she teetered through the door and headed around the side of the building where she thought the rear exit might be located. Sure enough, Enrique burst out of the darkness and Nicole aimed her .38 directly at his nose.

"Not a move scumbag or I'll blow your brains out," Nicole cried, not realizing what a sight she made standing there with her legs braced wide apart in the leather miniskirt and low plunging top. She looked like some biker goddess from a tacky comic book. She must have appeared formidable enough to Enrique because he threw up his arms in surprised surrender before whirling and lunging down a narrow garbage-strewn alleyway. He hadn't gone ten feet before Bud materialized, reaching out a large paw to throw him against the stained bricks of the back alley wall.

"And just where do you think you're going?" shouted Bud. Nicole edged closer, raising her gun to eye level and flashing her badge. "We have a couple of questions for you," thundered Bud and Enrique began to tremble, not certain whether these two were crazy enough to shoot.

"You're really cops?" sputtered Enrique, still skeptical about whom he was dealing with.

"That's right, and last time you were in the station, I really didn't like any of the answers you gave my colleagues, so I'm going to ask you again. What you know about Elena Gonzalez's death?"

"Elena?" asked Enrique, throwing a frightened glance toward Nicole whose steady hands didn't waver. She moved the eye of the .38 directly to the center of his forehead.

"Yeah, you know Elena," whispered Nicole slowly and deliberately. "Your girlfriend; the one who was found dead with her throat slit on the floor of the men's room at The Desert Sky Resort just a week ago."

"Yeah," said Bud, "the girl you don't seem so cut up about losing right now."

"I told them I don't know anything about that," spat Enrique. "I think some guy do her in. She was two-timing me anyway."

"Oh really?" crooned Bud, tightening his grip on the front of Enrique's shirt. "It would take one to know one wouldn't it?"

"What's your association with Mrs. Leslie Gaston?" asked Nicole, moving closer, the gun still held high.

"Mrs. Gaston? I don't know any Mrs. Gaston."

"I say you do," countered Bud, lifting his revolver and placing it against Enrique's forehead.

"This ain't right. Police officers ain't supposed to do this. I didn't do nothing to the girl. I told her she was in way over her head, but no, the bitch wouldn't listen to me."

"And you're full of good advice," spat Bud, pulling the smaller man closer to him so their faces were only inches apart. "And just what wouldn't she listen to you about?"

"About messing with those other men. I didn't care about her in them girlie photos or phone calls; shoot it made us a whole lot of extra money. But when she started seeing that accountant fellow and he was afraid his girlfriend would find out, I knew he'd pay up."

"You're talking about Richard Greaves?" asked Bud, and Enrique nodded, a little dribble of saliva trickling down the corner of his mouth.

"He was very frightened," Enrique managed to gasp out.

"You were blackmailing him?"

"We just needed a little extra cash, that's all."

"We?" asked Nicole, "Did Elena really know anything about it?"

Enrique shrugged his slight shoulders before cocking his head to one side, "She wouldn't have liked it. She always said he was kind of a sweet guy, but then her other boyfriend found out about it and said Richard had to go."

"Did he also say your girlfriend had to go?"

"I had nothing to do with that. I didn't care if she saw other men. Shoot it was nothing to me."

"That's not what you said two minutes ago," accused Nicole.

"Hey watch where you're pointing that!" sputtered Enrique, jerking away from the muzzle of her gun, which had suddenly moved much closer to his head. "I didn't do the girl, I loved her."

"Yeah right!" snorted Bud, lowering his gun a fraction. "Who was she seeing other than Greaves?"

"Honest! I don't know, but heard her talking on the phone once when she thought I didn't hear. I think she called him Barry or Bobby or something like that. I can't be sure."

"You can't be sure?" whispered Nicole, raising her gun again, the eye aimed directly at Enrique's unintelligent face. "Bud, why don't you revisit your game inside the bar? I want to make sure Mr. Diaz and I have some quiet time to continue our enlightening conversation."

Bud dropped his arm and replaced his revolver in his leather pants. "See you later Pard."

"Don't leave me with her, she's loco!" shouted Enrique at the retreating back of Bud, but Bud simply raised a hand and headed off to where his motorcycle was parked in front of Lupe's.

"Now I am going to ask you one more time," began Nicole dangerously, "and if you don't provide me with answers I like, there's going to be one less two-timing pachuco in this town. You see, I'm still a little confused about the information you've given me about Richard Greaves and Elena. You say that he was seeing her?"

"Yes, yes, he was one of her fellows on the side! She made extra money sleeping with him and he was afraid his girlfriend, I think her name was Judith, was going to find out."

Nicole straightened. It was just as she feared. "And what happened? Did he decide not to pay up one last time so you killed him?"

Enrique looked frightened, his eyes narrowing as he tried to back away from her, but she moved closer, the blue-black of the revolver aimed right at the tiny space between his eyes.

"I'm only going to ask you one more time, what happened to Richard Greaves?"

"I . . ." muttered Enrique. "I had to do what he said. If I didn't he'd kill me."

"Who would kill you?" asked Nicole.

"Elena's gringo lover. He contacted me by phone and said Richard Greaves had become a problem and if I didn't do him I'd be gazing up at the lid of a coffin. He had it all set up. All I had to do was go in and place the tape recorder on the desk that morning before work. I had a passkey from Elena. Greaves wasn't even there, I swear it!"

"And what about Mrs. Gaston? What's her role in this?"

"That gringo lady, Mrs. Gaston, said she knew I was up to no good. She said she was gonna tell the cops she knew I was blackmailing Richard Greaves and this was the last time he was gonna pay up. She always delivered the extra money." He sneered. "She was sweet on him herself. Anyone could tell. We had him deposit some cash to Elena's account, but I got nervous and told him he had to deliver the rest in person. I didn't even know he was dead until later when I heard it on the news. I think her boss set me up to take the fall. I swear I didn't kill him! I know that gringo killed the accountant after I left. He wanted it to look like a suicide. I didn't kill nobody!"

"Just like you didn't help kill Elena but enabled it?" snorted Nicole, suddenly wanting to lock this vile little man away for the rest of his natural life. "And just how much money did Richard pay you?"

"Eight thousand in her account and ten grand in cash. I..." Before Enrique had a chance to say anything else a gunshot rang out. Enrique stiffened before slumping against the grimy bricks of the wall behind Lupe's. He gazed down at the widening red circle in the center of his chest in mesmerized amazement before slipping to the littered ground.

A commotion followed by the sound of running feet caused Nicole to whirl; and sensing a bodiless shadow at the other end of the alley she took off in pursuit as fast as her high heels would allow. She caught a glimpse of a tall silver-haired man who disappeared around the corner before her foot lodged in a small pothole and her ankle twisted. She landed in an undignified heap on all fours, scraping both of her unprotected knees.

"Nikki! Nikki!" shouted Bud's desperate voice as he stood over the too-still body of Enrique.

"Over here Bud," she called, propelling him to sprint toward her, his gun poised and ready.

"He got away!" yelled Nicole, as she pointed around the corner. Bud dashed to the end of the alley, his booted feet echoing through the darkness as a few onlookers ventured from the seedy bar's interior to gather a distance from Enrique's body. Nicole managed to rise and limp toward Enrique's bloody form. She dug in her purse, and pulling out her cell, punched in a familiar number to summon backup. Within five minutes sirens sounded and a disgruntled and breathless Bud loped back toward the spot where she stood vigil over Enrique's body.

"I lost him Nikki." His eyes drifted downward toward the bloody surfaces of her knees and he cursed heartily in Spanish.

"I figured as much. He had too much of a head start. The perpetrator was a tall gray-haired man who shot Enrique just as he relayed information about money Richard was paying to cover up his affair with Elena."

"Well at least we know what happened to Richard," sighed Bud sadly. "Sounds like our backup just arrived. What a blasted mess and just when we were getting somewhere!"

Ninety minutes later, as Nicole sat in the Palm Springs Police Department's combination lunch and storage room dabbing antiseptic on her knees, Jerry Hernandez paced before her, scowling.

"Things have taken an unfortunate turn," he hissed in gross understatement. Bud leaned against the wall, his burly arms folded across the leather vest. While his outfit appeared menacing with his belly protruding over the tight black leather pants, Bud looked anything but dangerous, only frustrated and dejected.

"So Enrique was blackmailing Richard Greaves and Mrs. Gaston was simply a courier. Of course now she's nowhere to be found, which just adds to our problems! You say Enrique referred to someone called Barry or Bobby? Something like that?"

"Yes," said Nicole, wincing as the antiseptic seeped into the open gashes on her knees. "Enrique stated he had heard Elena speaking on the phone to her gringo boyfriend."

"Wait a minute," uttered Jerry, a strange look passing over his face. He tapped the formica surface of the counter. "What if . . .? My friends, I think we've been barking up the wrong tree the whole time. You know what the previous director's name was; the one I golfed with?"

Bud glanced first at Nicole and then back at his Captain and then jerked. "Robert Severns, like in *Bob* Severns?" Bud slapped his leather pants and shook his head disgustedly. It now seemed so simple.

"That's right," verified Jerry. "Bob Severns, or Bobby Severns, as a couple of girls at the golf course used to call him when we would tee off together. It was there right in front of my nose the entire time and I didn't even make the connection. But maybe someone else did! I need to make a quick call," cried Jerry, sprinting from the office.

"That's it!" said Nicole excitedly, straightening up as much as the miniskirt would allow. Who else would have access to The Desert Sky Resort after hours and have struck up a friendship with Elena before Justin Zachary even arrived? And didn't Elena have a holiday to *Hawaii* all planned? It was there before us all the time!"

Under a Desert Sky

"Bingo!" snorted Bud. "He would know all the ins and outs of the resort's computers as well as everyone's schedules. Didn't you say that Justin Zachary mentioned Robert Severns had been under suspicion by B.W. Weston a few months earlier?"

"That's right," answered Nicole, as she stood up stiffly, straightening the too-short miniskirt. Suddenly a horrible feeling of dread washed over her. "Bud, the man who shot Enrique and then dashed down the alleyway, he was tall and silver-haired right?"

"Yup, that would fit the description of Robert Severns alright, though I think he was slightly balding as well."

"If he was the one who kidnapped Jesse and Justin and then trailed Enrique to the bar, we can only conclude one thing. He's getting rid of all the witnesses or anyone who might have connected him to the murder."

"You're probably right," agreed Bud sadly.

"Which means he's probably already killed them," Nicole stated helplessly, looking down at her violently shaking hands. Buddy pulled her close, resting his chin on the top of the tawny curls which were still spiked from the gel Maggie had applied only a couple of hours previously.

"We don't know anything of the sort yet," comforted Bud. "Don't give up hope Nikki; hope is all we have left."

Jerry suddenly appeared in the doorway of the coffee room, gazing at Nicole and Bud in a half-angry, half-relieved manner. "You won't believe it if I told you! I need both of you to come with me right now!"

Loren Lockner

Chapter 21

Jerry's personal car was a newer model Oldsmobile sedan and Nicole sat in the comfortable backseat and leaned her head against the creamy leather interior. Jerry drove intently through the hot desert night and pulled up at the Radisson Hotel, parking in a visitor's spot near the entrance. Nicole self-consciously followed her Captain, who as usual was well dressed in an attractive pair of sports pants and short-sleeved polo shirt even though it was after working hours. She and Buddy looked like something he'd pulled off the streets and Nicole grinned at the shocked glances following them from the high-class patrons. Jerry wasted no time and approached the front desk.

"I'd like Brian Weston's room," he demanded, as the blonde attendant shook her head.

"I'm sorry Sir. I've been instructed not to disturb Mr. Weston."

Jerry flipped open his Captain's badge and the girl gulped, picking up the phone.

"There is an officer to see you in the lobby Sir," she said into the phone and Jerry grabbed the receiver from her.

"I'm coming up Brian and you'd better have some answers for me! You might as well start practicing now!" He hung up the receiver with a bang. "Which room is it?"

The girl's blue eyes widened and she sputtered out, "213," watching Jerry take off followed by his two unsavory employees.

"What's going on boss?" asked Bud in the elevator. Jerry only shook his head, cursing vehemently in Spanish.

"I should have known! I should have guessed all along he would try to pull something like this. Mr. Impatient! Mr. Fix-it-myself-and-the-rest-of-you-be-damned!" A silver-haired woman distanced herself as far away from Bud, Nicole, and their ranting Captain as she could. Nicole smiled sweetly at her and Bud grinned as the woman bolted out of the elevator onto the second floor. Jerry followed the wary woman, striding rapidly down the hall, his long slender legs making it difficult for Nicole to keep up. He pounded on a hotel room door and it opened reluctantly, revealing B.W. Weston in a red polo shirt, worn blue jeans and cowboy boots. Brian stood blinking at him with innocent blue eyes.

"Out of my way," ordered Jerry, pushing past him. "Where are they? I want to know where they are right this instant!"

Under a Desert Sky

"I told you on the phone I didn't know what you're talking about!" drawled Weston. A room service dinner lay spread out beside the large king-sized bed near the beautiful wide windows revealing a panoramic view of the lights of downtown Palm Springs. Nicole felt her stomach growl as she observed the barbe-cued ribs and tossed green salad adorning the tastefully decorated tray. It had been hours since she'd eaten.

"I told you before I don't want any games. Enrique Diaz has been shot and we're pretty certain it's your old Executive Director, Robert Severns, who's done the killing. Now I want to know where Justin Zachary and Jesse Burns are this instant!"

A rap sounded on the connecting door between the two hotel rooms and Brian threw his napkin down onto the tray and moved to open the door. A husky redheaded man stood before the trio and smiled pointedly at Nicole.

"Not bad," commented the burly bodyguard, his eyes widening at Nicole's skimpy apparel. "Do you need any help boss?"

"No Charlie, believe it or not, it's all under control." Brian Weston shrugged and sighed and then pointed to the other room. "You might as well go in," he said, as he led the way to the connecting suite where, outstretched on one of the two double beds, Justin lay sound asleep. One arm, flung above his head, rested above features looking pained and fatigued. Jesse sat in front of the television watching a Kung Fu movie, and upon seeing Nicole bounded to his feet and threw himself into her arms, sobbing.

"Nicole, Nicole they took us away! I was so frightened."

Justin suddenly stirred and sat up slowly on the bed, his dark eyes focusing first on Brian, Bud, and Captain Hernandez before finally resting on Nicole, who stood gazing helplessly at him, so relieved she felt light-headed.

He gasped in astonishment at her appearance and rubbed his bleary eyes. "Nicole, is that you?"

"I cannot believe the implications of what you've done," shouted Jerry angrily at Brian Weston, who had the grace to look down sheepishly at the toes of his pointed cowboy boots.

"Well damn it! You weren't keeping them safe! You already got Justin shot once, so what did you want me to do? Let Severns blow his brains out? How was I going to explain *that* to his mother?"

Nicole seated herself by Justin and reaching out a shaky hand noted how tired and sick he appeared. She was positive worry and strain had caused a minor relapse.

"It's okay," he whispered and reached out a tentative arm. She collapsed upon his shoulder, fighting tears.

"I think we need to leave those two alone," Brian observed abruptly. "We'll head to the bar and talk all this malarkey out. That is, if they'll let him in." He jerked an accusing thumb at Buddy. Bud straightened and sucked in his belly, smoothing the front of his leather vest.

"I've been thrown out of finer places than this before," he drawled, and preceded the trio out of the room. Charles, the bodyguard, gestured to Jesse, but the boy didn't follow. Instead he watched Nicole clutching Justin's Bruin t-shirt; the one he'd donned in Jesse's small apartment several hours earlier.

"Is Nicole going to be alright?" he asked in his flat tones, and Justin raised a reassuring hand to the concerned boy.

"It's alright Jesse, why don't you go down with the nice gentleman. I bet they'll buy you an ice cream."

Jesse's face perked up, "You take care of Nicole, okay?"

Justin smiled, "You can bet on it Jesse Boy." Jesse followed the other men out of the room and closed the door behind him softly.

It was a long while before Nicole had regained enough control to stir from Justin's protective embrace and face him.

"It was B.W. Weston all the time who stole you and Jesse from the bowling alley?" she asked, running a shaky hand through her spiked hair.

Justin nodded and leaned back against the pillows, his body still stiff from the injuries he'd suffered the previous Thursday.

"Once Bruiser Charles hustled us away in the car, he rang up B.W. on the car phone and handed the receiver to me. Brian told me in no uncertain terms that he didn't feel the police department was doing a very adequate job of protecting me. Charles of course, being a man of few words, didn't think to tell him about all the effort you'd taken to preserve my life up in Idyllwild. Brian brought us to his hotel for safekeeping. Under his watchful eye, he said. He believed no one would think of looking for us here."

"He was right," sniffed Nicole, finally able to observe the expensive, tastefully decorated hotel room. "Nice digs."

"It's been alright," muttered Justin, "except we haven't been allowed to call anyone. I knew you'd be out of your mind with worry and tried to convince B.W. he should at least let you know. He said you'd find out soon enough. Brian was and is convinced someone in the station is leaking information to Bob Severns."

"So you know then," replied Nicole dejectedly.

"Leslie Gaston filled us in regarding Enrique's blackmail of Richard, as well as that afternoon Bob drove her to Lupe's to indicate to Enrique the game was up. Not knowing his role in the murder, she confided in him what was happening to Richard, not realizing he'd already gotten rid of him. He planned to frame Enrique for Elena's murder and me for the embezzlement. I was aware someone in the Caddy shot at me and wrongly surmised Mrs. Gaston was involved. It never occurred to me that Bob had used her just like everyone else, and dropped her off before looping back to kill me. He used her friendship, Richard's, Elena's; anyone and everyone to get what he wanted. And what he wanted was the money.

Bob is a tall man, even larger than me, but because he'd transferred to Maui, I had no idea he'd struck up a relationship with Elena and of course she never mentioned his name. It all makes sense now. Robert Severns had gone through a nasty divorce with big bills to pay, but I think it was more complicated than that. He simply enjoyed controlling and manipulating people and did it all under the guise of Mr. Nice Guy."

"And you could never live up to his reputation?" mocked Nicole.

"Thank God for that!"

"Enrique is dead," stated Nicole, peering straight into Justin's chocolate brown eyes, never getting enough of his tired olive face. "He was telling us about Richard's death when a shot rang out and I witnessed a tall silver-haired man running down the alleyway near that dive you mentioned; the one called Lupe's."

"So that explains the getup," chuckled Justin, smiling wickedly at her.

"I'm concerned about your secretary Mrs. Gaston. I think she's gotten in way over her head."

"I wouldn't worry about it," clarified Justin. "Do you really think I'm the only one B.W. stashed away to keep 'safe'? Leslie finally realized some things Bob told her didn't gel, so she went to the one man she really trusted and that was B.W. Weston. Brian managed to single-mindedly undermine most of the progress the Palm Springs Police Department had made in less than twenty-four hours. If he would just have cooperated, not interfered, this case might have been solved two days ago. He has a lot to answer for, and frankly, I hope your Captain gives him hell for it."

"He has a great deal more than that to answer for. You don't look so well," whispered Nicole.

"Charles, B.W.'s bodyguard, didn't explain the situation to us right away. I must admit I tried to get the boy away and he landed a well-placed elbow right into my wound."

"Are you alright?" gasped Nicole, touching the front of the old Bruin t-shirt gingerly.

"I am now," he said warmly, touching her cheek. Just sick and tired of this hotel and the whole horrible mess. I just want it to all be over."

"Then let's see what we can do about it," proclaimed Nicole. "Why don't we venture down and join the Captain and your boss at the bar. I'm sure Jerry has had just about enough time to cuss him out."

Justin smiled and rose stiffly from the bed, favoring his injured side. He placed an arm around her waist and drew her toward him for a shift hard hug.

"Well at least Bud is down there to break the ice because the two of us look like a cross between a beatnik and a prostitute," voiced Nicole against the warmth of his throat.

"We do move in the best crowds don't we?" agreed Justin, and he draped his arm over her shoulder while Nicole grasped him gently around the waist. "Let's go get 'em tiger."

Under a Desert Sky

The situation in the bar remained tense, but B.W. finally acquiesced enough to allow Jesse to depart into the safe custody of Buddy Ochoa.

"But Justin stays with me," he demanded.

"That's not an option," stated Jerry, "but I'm open to other suggestions."

"I've got it," said Buddy, finally snapping his fingers as he meditated over his beer.

"Why don't we stick him with that pretty Personnel Director? What's her name, Judith Chamberlain?"

B.W. opened his mouth as if to protest and then stopped himself, glancing worriedly at Nicole who simply smiled back at him from her seat where she sat quietly next to Justin. Judith was no threat to her in any way.

"That might be good," Jerry agreed. "I'm sure Robert Severns wouldn't think to look there. She has a nice condo out in Palm Desert not far from the resort. We'll place Justin under police protection as soon as I clear it with the lady, who after she discovers what really happened to her boyfriend will most likely agree."

"Not good enough!" rasped B.W. "He can only go if Charles accompanies him. The bastard already altered the computer records to make it appear Justin's the embezzler. He'll need a corpse to top it off. Justin stays under my protection. That's my final offer."

Nicole had to grin; you would think they were arguing a crucial business deal instead of finding a safe place to stash Justin.

"I believe Charles should stay with you. Bob may have figured out you know everything and try to erase his problems from the top," insisted the Captain, staring pointedly at B.W.

"Nope, Charles goes where Zachary goes. Besides, I always sleep with Smith and Wesson!"

"We have police protection for him," Jerry protested mildly.

"Police protection my eye. Look at the state of the boy! His life nearly went down the toilet while someone tried to protect him."

"Oh, I don't know," interjected Justin, looking sideways at Nicole who fiddled with her Tequila Sunrise. "I think she did a mighty fine job taking care of me. But I have to agree that Bob Severns views me as a threat and therefore I need to duck somewhere where he least suspects. Judith's place seems as good as any. If Charles has to accompany me, then I accept that decision."

"I'll get the car," was all the huge redheaded Charles said, having remained silent throughout the entire discussion. Used to all Brian Weston's finagling, he'd learned to accept without question any final verdict, since he valued his job.

Jesse set off quite happily with Bud, asking him if he could have an outfit just like Buddy's.

"It's really cool," said Jesse, his round face and small eyes admiring the leather jacket as well as Bud's anchor tattoo on his left arm. "Did the tattoo hurt?"

Under a Desert Sky

"There is no way on earth, Jesse boy, that you're getting a tattoo. We're gonna to take you to my place to stay with Maggie and my boys. Did you know that TCM is doing a special on Elvis this month?" At the younger man's delighted grin, the two trotted off.

Nicole looped her arms around Justin's neck. "You keep safe," she ordered, "and I'll stop by to see you in the morning. Jerry's putting out an all points bulletin on Robert Severns as we speak, so hopefully by the end of the day tomorrow this nightmare will be over."

Justin smiled and kissed her tenderly while Jerry and Brian glanced discreetly away. "Until I see you in the morning," he promised.

Judith Chamberlain's condo, a lovely cream and glass affair in softly muted hues, totally reflected the loveliness of the woman who lived there. Judith was just leaving for work as Nicole arrived the following morning. This time Nicole was more comfortably clad in yellow linen pants and a matching top, feeling only too happy to get out of the leather miniskirt of the night before. It had taken quite a while to scrub off the heavy make-up and wash the stiff gel out of her hair. She'd slept well that night in the cheap hotel, clutching a too-hard pillow to her breast and wishing it were Justin, but had been comforted by the knowledge both Justin and Jesse were finally safe.

"Justin's still asleep," announced Judith warmly as her beautiful eyes assessed Nicole's casual attire. "He's staying in the guest room, the poor man. Justin laid down right after he arrived last night and hasn't stirred since."

"Did Captain Hernandez speak to you regarding our suspicions surrounding your previous boss?" asked Nicole, staring at the beautiful blonde woman dressed in an exquisite silk lavender dress and matching pumps.

"He did. Your cute Captain mentioned Robert Severns might try to contact me and that I was to play innocent. Don't worry Detective Lewis, I won't let on that Justin is here. In fact, I've rehearsed a scene of uncontrollable hysterics regarding both him and Richard in the shower this morning. I believe I could have made quite an effective actress in another life."

Nicole had to smile, growing to like the beautiful but ambitious Personnel Director. Judith's eyes clouded for a moment at the memory of Richard's fate and Nicole moved to the slender woman to give her a reassuring hug. A sleepy-eyed Justin appeared in the arched doorway and yawned broadly.

"Good morning ladies," he announced. "Today must be my lucky day with such a pair of beautiful women to greet me."

"Sounds like you've been taking lessons from Scott Adams. Where's our old unapproachable Justin Zachary?" asked Judith cheekily, rubbing away a defiant tear and casting a knowing glance at Nicole. "I won't return this evening until around five, but will give you a call at noon. Bob... he won't get away will he?" The latter was addressed to Nicole as the lovely woman adjusted her handbag nervously.

"Not a chance," said Nicole evenly. "We've issued an APB on him and all the finest hotels in town are being checked. He's probably using an alias but we've faxed through a recent photograph, thanks to your files, and hopefully he'll be in our custody by the end of the day."

Judith seemed to relax. She hesitated briefly before walking out of the lovely foyer of her apartment. "I suppose that despicable bodyguard is still outside?" she asked sulkily.

Justin smiled. "Oh come on Judith, Charles kinda grows on you after a while."

"The man needs to take a long bath and stop referring to me as gal."

Nicole chuckled. "Say hi to him for me on your way out?" The blonde director smiled, the sound of her key turning in the latch echoing through the tiled room.

"Do you think I could ask you to make me some coffee while I take a shower?" Justin asked, his eyes raking her trim form and pale yellow outfit.

"Of course. And, I have what I believe will be a very welcome present for you," returned Nicole, indicating a large plastic bag sitting on the glass coffee table. "Brian sent over some of your clothes. He thought you might be tired of wearing the same thing day after day."

Justin grinned and reached out his hand for the bag, caressing her fingers before withdrawing his hand and heading for the shower. Nicole strolled happily into the lovely spotless kitchen to prepare some coffee and toast using Judith's state-of-the-art appliances.

Within thirty minutes Justin was seated across from her at the oval glass table flanking the kitchen and munching on a piece of toast with butter and apricot jam. Justin looked infinitely better after his long shower. His long dark hair glistened, combed back in the same executive style she'd noticed the first time she'd laid eyes on him and clad in a comfortable pair of khaki pants and a light blue polo shirt.

"Did Brian have you see a doctor?" asked Nicole.

"You bet. A private physician arrived at the hotel before you could say Jack Sprat and pronounced me almost fit but overtired. Honestly I'm a lot better. You're not to worry, love."

Nicole shivered at the endearment and examined him, but true to his word Justin simply appeared tired. Much of the strain from the previous week had vanished and for the first time Nicole felt she gazed at the real Justin Zachary. She folded her hands into his. He leaned over the tabletop to kiss her parted lips when her mobile rang. Nicole hesitated before activating the annoying phone. Bud was in a vile temper.

"I can see why Bob Severns needed so much money," reported Bud nastily. "He has very expensive tastes and was staying at the Hilton in their most expensive suite right under our noses. And you'll never guess whose name he gave upon registration?"

"Whose?"

"Richard Greaves. He pops off the guy and then has the nerve to use his name. Nancy faxed his photo to all the local hotels and a desk clerk identified him immediately. Anyway, she and Lee, along with another backup car, have gone over to the Hilton to apprehend him. They'll wait for us to arrive. I told Jerry you'd want to be there for the take-down considering what he did to Justin."

"Off course I want to be there," said Nicole, vaguely noticing the stern expression spreading over Justin's face. "I'll join you at the Hilton in fifteen minutes." She replaced the phone in her handbag.

"Who was that?"

"Bud. Look, I have to go," said Nicole, taking one last sip of her coffee. "Robert Severns has been located at the Hilton and we're going to move in and arrest him within the hour."

"So Bud will meet you there?" asked Justin, rising.

"Yes, in about fifteen minutes."

"Then I don't have much time," stated Justin oddly. "Please sit down by me Nicole." He motioned to a spot beside him on the beautiful cream-colored leather couch.

Nicole sank down on the couch, which was like sitting on a cloud. She involuntarily caressed the doe-soft leather.

"Kinda puts my old couch to shame," she laughed, but Justin didn't return her smile.

In that quiet moment before the storm Justin studied her face, noting the determined blue eyes below short brown hair whose bangs needed a trim.

"I'm asking you my love," he began awkwardly, knowing it was now or never, "to consider giving up detective work. I make more than enough for both of us and after all this has died down I'd like us to start over somewhere else. I'll transfer anywhere, any place, to start a new life with you. Maybe we could hatch a couple kids and watch them turn us gray-headed."

"You're asking me to marry you?" breathed Nicole, suddenly rigid upon the beautiful white leather couch Judith had spent a fortune on.

"Not the best proposal I admit, but I've never before had the opportunity of asking the woman I love to share my life with me."

"Share your life," stated Nicole softly, gazing long and earnestly at the face she loved. Justin's dark eyes burned earnestly, his handsome face intense. For a moment Nicole nearly submitted. "But what about my life?" she asked quietly, rousing herself from his mesmerizing spell.

"Our life would be together," he insisted, looking puzzled.

"No, our life would be what you chose it to be, never considering what I value or what makes me feel worthwhile as a human being. You're asking me to give up everything I've ever worked for; my career, my friends, and most of all, the chance to make a difference in this world."

"But you make a difference to me. Isn't that enough? Can't that be enough?"

"No it isn't! I haven't asked you to give up your goals. I haven't asked you to change your career or to go wherever my job leads. I wouldn't dream of requiring that from you or asking you to even consider it!"

"That's right Nicole!" he cried hotly. "You haven't asked me for *anything*. You haven't made any demands on our relationship and that in itself scares me. I want you to make demands on me as much as I want you to honor the fact that I'm afraid for you and the choices you seem hell-bent to make. I watched Elena make bad decisions and by God I won't let what befell her happen to you!" The last was spoken between clenched teeth.

"I refuse to be controlled by your fears Justin. I have a right to choose my own life, just as Elena did. Yes, she paid dearly for her choices, but Justin, they were *her* choices."

"And what if I don't like those choices you've made. What if I told you it is impossible for me to come home every night and wonder if you're really coming home or if I'll have to check a body bag to see if all your parts are there!"

"Those possibilities exist in every relationship," protested Nicole. "Every time a person steps into their car they're taking their life in their hands. Every time one boards a plane or goes for a hike unforeseen danger lurks. Life is one big risk. You can't expect me to hide behind your job or transfer to an unfulfilling career just to be safe. My father died in the line of duty and though I miss him dearly I'm proud of the career choice he made, as was my mother. I can't give up on a career that matters so much to me. That's simply not me. Can't you understand that?"

"But the life you're chosen means you're always in danger; that you're never really safe."

"I work at my desk ninety percent of the time for God's sake!" Nicole shrieked. "What do you want me to do? Sit at home and do my knitting, protected and forced into some restrictive cocoon because of your fears?"

"I want the assurance then that you'll *only* work at that desk. I want reassurances that the other ten percent of the time will never take you where there is danger; where people exist who have no regard for human life. People like Robert Severns who never really gave a damn about Elena, or anyone else for that matter. I never want you to go undercover again like you did at Lupe's. That there's never an instance you'll have to check to see if your gun's loaded. I need to be certain you're safe. I need that as much as I need you! You're the one Nicole. The one I've been waiting for my entire life and I want to share my life with you. But I can't face the possibility of losing the person I love most. And I do love you Nicole, more than life itself, and beg you to understand how much you and your safety mean to me."

"I can't do that," protested Nicole, talking slowly as if somehow he were daft and her slow precise words could reach into his closed mind. "I was trained for police work. Some of my happiest moments were at the academy where I used my mind and instincts to strive to make this world a better place. You just can't ask me to give up my life's work. I'd never ask you to do that Justin." The last sentence trailed off into a plea, but his face had, during her short recital, turned to stone.

"Well, I guess that's it then. I had this strange notion I could somehow influence you and make you love me as much as I love you."

"But I do love you Justin, I do!"

"No you don't, because if you did I'd be able to convince you just how important your safety is to me. I have no more influence over you than I did with Elena and now she's dead. I won't stand by and watch another person I care for die. I can't do that." He swallowed painfully before continuing, his voice somehow harder. "You're going then? You'll wait for backup I hope?"

"That's department policy," said Nicole tightly, wondering how the situation had suddenly gotten so far out of control. She reached an unsteady hand to touch his arm, but his body remained stiff and unyielding and she dropped her fingers away. His face had become a remote mask, his lips thin and hard and his mind clearly made up. If he couldn't have her on his terms then he wouldn't have her at all. He rose and urged her to the door.

"Then you'd better go. For my sake, stay behind Bud and..." Justin bit his lip, cutting off whatever he was about to say. It was clear to him that Nicole would live her life as she pleased; just like Elena who now laid cold and dead in a lonely grave far from home.

"I'll be careful." Nicole promised helplessly, picking up her shoulder bag and resting a hand on his too-rigid arm before leaving. "I'll..." she sputtered. "I'll talk to you later after Robert Severns is in custody." Justin shrugged indifferently as the door banged behind her, effectively shutting him out of her life.

Chapter 22

Nicole trudged outside in the stifling heat, her heart aching and her eyes smarting. For some reason she found it difficult to catch her breath and a permanent lump seemed to have settled in her stomach. She noticed Charles sitting in the tan Imperial under some palms surrounded by bright pink oleanders, his window rolled down and Louis Armstrong's distinctive voice crooning through the shimmering waves of heat. He raised a nonchalant hand to her before laying his head back against the seat. Nicole's cell phone rang insistently.

Bud cursed over the brittle line. "He got wind of us closing in somehow," she managed to decipher from his harried tone. "Just as Nancy and Lee pulled up to the Hilton, Severns raced out of the lobby through a rear exit and jumped into his other car; a big white Mercedes. Nancy and

Lee caught a glimpse of a wildly driven sedan and Nancy put two and two together. They managed to follow him and radioed us for backup. They've got him in their sights right now. He's heading down Palm Canyon Drive as we speak and I suspect is planning to cut up Gene Autry Trail toward the airport. You're not far from there are you?"

"Pretty close, I'll intercept you at the intersection Bud. You're in the Chevy?"

"Yup," echoed his terse reply. "And Nancy and Lee are in a black and white. Jerry's sending more backup. Meet me at the corner of Gene Autry and Ramon!"

Nicole drove like a demon, urging the unmarked police sedan equipped with radio and shotgun console to breakneck speeds as the dry desert scenery sped past. She'd nearly reached Mesquite Street when her cell rang again.

"There's a problem Nicole. It seems that Severns somehow slipped away from Lee and Nancy a couple of minutes ago. We're trying to trace him now."

"How could that have happened?" she cried, banging the steering wheel angrily.

"I don't know. Lee says Robert Severns suddenly turned left off Gene Autry and headed back toward Palm Desert. They followed him as he wove in and out of the traffic on Palm Canyon Drive before suddenly pulling over into a shopping center and dashing into a convenience store. When he didn't come out, Nancy headed inside the front of the shop as Lee approached the back of the store searching for a rear exit when suddenly the Mercedes tore off. Somehow he managed to slip by them. By the time Nancy got back into the cruiser, they could vaguely make him out half a mile ahead before the Mercedes disappeared somewhere near the Mall."

"That's just great. But that doesn't make a lick of sense—I was certain he'd head for the airport. So what do we do now?"

"Wait for the Captain to make a decision I guess. Meet me outside the west entrance of the Mall and we'll hook up there."

Twenty minutes later a highly frustrated Nicole fumed in the unmarked car, chewing on her lip. They'd had Bob Severns in their hands and somehow he'd slipped away. A convenience store, her eye! Never had she been witness to so many slip-ups in a case in her entire life.

Nancy sidled up to the car and held out a package of salty chips.

"Want some Nicole?"

"I don't know how you stay so slim munching on these things all the time," grumbled Nicole, knowing extra gym time had to be worked into her schedule if she indulged.

"That's what Dusty says," Nancy answered affectionately and fingered her blonde braid.

"How could he have slipped away?" asked Nicole again for the umpteenth time.

"It beats me. The guy must have hustled out the back and then gone around the side of the building while Lee watched the front entrance. Lee thinks he probably opened the back car door and entered the Mercedes without our noticing it." She seemed to take no offense at Nicole's questioning. Nicole wished she maintained a similar attitude to the laid-back Nancy. "Is Zachary safe?"

"Yeah," said Nicole, "I just hope we haven't put Judith into danger."

"Nicole, there's something I need to talk to you about sometime after all this is over."

"Of course Nancy. You sound so serious. Are you alright?"

"Yes, well no. Something's just come up and I need some advice. I think..."

Lee came to the side of the car and stole one of Nancy's salty chips. "I wonder what's keeping Bud?"

"Don't know," wondered Nicole. "But knowing Bud, he's probably on the horn to the Captain and formulating some sort of game plan."

"Well I certainly hope so. I was just thinking that if I were Severns I'd hightail it out of this valley faster than a roadrunner. With the amount of money he's got away with there's no reason for him sticking around now that we're onto him," surmised Lee.

"Still," trailed off Nicole, when a sudden thought hit her. Several inconsistencies that had fretted the back of her mind suddenly fit into place. The real reason Severns was still here in Palm Springs became clear and she looked at Lee with speculative intensity. He nonchalantly munched on another chip, appearing fairly unconcerned for a man who'd just lost his chief suspect in a triple murder and embezzlement case. Nancy had moved deeper into the shade of some white oleanders, looking anxious.

"I think I'll call the Captain and tell him to cover not only the main airport, but the helicopter strip near the main highway. Severns is a desperate man, but not stupid," Lee stated, noting Nicole's serious look. "Don't worry, we'll bring him in; it's just a matter of time."

He sauntered off to his squad car and lifted the car radio. He spoke earnestly into the phone and then hung it up. "Oh shoot, I forgot," Nicole heard him say, and he lifted the phone again and spoke for a couple of minutes. He walked swiftly back to them, excitement covering his perspiring face.

"The Captain wants us to meet him at the Palm Springs Airport ASAP! Severns has been spotted heading that direction! Come on Nancy! It's showtime!" Nancy dropped her chip bag into the bin and jumped into the hot squad car, staring pointedly at Nicole as if she wanted to say something. Instead she buckled herself up as the door slammed and the blue light began to flash.

Nicole immediately called Bud on his car phone.

"Almost there," he stated and pulled into the mall, parking his bronze Chevy under the shade of a huge date palm.

"Come on Nikki, you can ride with me," said Bud, urging her into the car. He had removed a white handkerchief from his back pocket and mopped his wide face.

"Lee just heard from the Captain and indicated Severns' Mercedes has been spotted near the airport."

"Let's get shaking then."

"You know Bud, I think I'll meet you there."

"So now you like to drive?"

"Something like that."

"What's going on girl?" demanded Bud, suddenly alert.

"Just don't rush to the airport that's all. Keep off your car radio just in case I need you. If I do, I'll call you on your cell."

"But the Captain said..."

"Lee said the Captain said," declared Nicole, and waited for his reaction.

"Okay. Let's have it."

"How many times has Robert Severns managed to slip out of our hands? You remember when Richard Greaves was killed. Who was late getting to the hotel to meet with him?"

"Nancy and Lee?"

"That's right. After which we find out that Richard had some help pulling the trigger only minutes before he could be questioned."

"And Justin mentioned he saw a policeman talking to his secretary. Justin never met Lee so he couldn't identify him. What if Lee spoke to Mrs. Gaston, informing her to go meet with Enrique, accompanied by Robert Severns?"

"Did Lee know that you had called me in Idyllwild?"

"No, no he didn't, though I think Nancy figured it out. She's pretty astute."

"Nancy? I wonder? She wanted to talk to me about something, and before all this broke loose she was in the station early and seemed preoccupied. What if she has started to suspect Lee? He walked up to us just when she started to say something. Bud? If Lee is our leak he'd know Justin is at Judith's, right? What if he's relayed that information to Bob? Justin could be in mortal danger!"

"It's so hard to believe Nicole. It just doesn't make any sense to me. What reason could Lee have?"

"If Robert Severns gets away, I can think of about a cool two million reasons."

Bud remained silent and tapped the dashboard of his Chevy fretfully.

"Lee was on the car phone to the Captain twice," continued Nicole, following her train of thoughts. "What if he was only on the phone once to the Captain and the other time to Robert Severns?"

"And the reason?"

"To warn him not to go to the airport and give him time to take care of some unfinished business."

"Unfinished business?"

"Justin Zachary. He failed the first time getting rid of the only man who could connect him to the embezzlement and Elena's murder. Justin's the key because he knew about Elena's involvement with another man who he figured out was Bob. Embezzlement would only put Bob away for fifteen to twenty years; murder a lifetime. I've got to warn Justin!" She hurled into the sedan and slammed the door, rolling the window down. "You head toward the airport just to be sure. I'm going back to check on Justin. If anybody asks, say I ran out of gas or something. Be prepared to turn around at a moment's notice!"

"Okay sweetie," said Bud disbelievingly, but he obeyed her.

It took fifteen minutes to make it back from Palm Desert to Judith's pretty condo. Nicole parked outside the grass curb where sprinklers watered the deep green lawn. Before getting out she checked her service revolver, praying her instincts were wrong.

The sidewalk was a mass of puddles and Nicole tried to sidestep them as she approached Judith's second story townhouse. It was then she noticed the sleek white 500 series Mercedes parked in front of the garage next to Judith's maroon Infinity. But where was Charles, B.W.'s diligent watchdog? Nicole dashed to the large Imperial parked in the heavy shade and winced. Charles' face was a mass of blood, but Nicole thankfully discovered a light heartbeat over the bloodstained collar of his shirt. Ducking behind the vehicle she rang Bud.

"I think Severns is here and Charles is hurt. It appears Judith has returned for some reason. Send an ambulance and

354

reinforcements! Tell Captain Hernandez that Lee may be our squirrel and that I'm positive Bob is here to kill Justin."

"Nikki! Nikki! Wait for the backup—I'll be there in ten minutes! Nikki, are you listening to me?" Nicole abruptly disconnected and headed for the steep staircase to Judith's condominium.

The rock stairs disguised any sound from her light sandals and Nicole paused briefly outside the beautiful oak door to listen intently. All seemed too silent. Nicole removed her gun and held it before her, turning the knob one centimeter at a time until finally the door swung open on silent hinges, enabling her to step inside the cool, open room. Justin sat on the long white couch, deathly still, his eyes gazing past her to where Judith perched upon a cream bar stool to his left, her face pale and pinched in the artificial light. Nicole moved another two feet into the lovely decorated room, feeling the heavy blue and rose Chinese carpet under her feet. A click sounded at the back of her head.

"How nice of you to join us," said the friendly voice of Bob Severns. "I don't think you'll be needing this."

He reached in front of her and jerked the now useless weapon out of her hand and tucked it into his belt. His other hand held a deadly-looking dark berretta aimed straight at Justin's heart.

"Perhaps you would like to join your lover on the couch. There's room enough for two."

Nicole moved slowly and seated herself by the frozen Justin, who gave her a brief dejected glance.

"I just mentioned to your boyfriend that you'd probably have it all figured out by now. I hoped that I'd have enough time to take care of my unfinished business without involving you, my dear, and have to admit that I just hate the idea of B.W. sending his spy here to try and track me down. Things were going so well until the illustrious Mr. Zachary arrived. Killing women is always such a messy business and hard on the heart, but true to my suspicions, here you are, just like the Canadian Mounted Police to the rescue!"

Justin glared at the well-dressed man, making no effort to disguise his contempt and hatred. "You killed Elena you bastard."

"I didn't want to of course, but it was just a matter of time before she spilled the proverbial 'beans' to you. You were such good friends after all, and she was quite generous with her love." The insinuation in the mocking voice was clear and Nicole felt Justin tighten like a spring beside her.

Judith squirmed in her lovely violet dress and looked despairingly at Nicole. "I'm sorry Detective Lewis. When I got to the office Genny indicated you wanted me to return home immediately because you'd discovered some important information regarding the murder. I walked right in my door and found him waiting." Robert smiled enchantingly, his silver hair making him resemble a dignified grandfather, not a callous murderer. He was such a good-looking man for his age.

"You'll be accompanying me now Judith my dear, to help me escape this hell-hole furnace you call home. I need

your car and assistance so be a good girl and come along."
He motioned to a brown briefcase sitting on the round glass
table in front of Justin and Nicole. "If you'd be good enough
Judith, I always find that cash is the best bet when you're on
the run. Wouldn't you agree detective?" His voice seemed so
pleasant and agreeable it was hard to believe he was a cold-
hearted killer.

Judith retrieved the briefcase and Bob Severns took her
slim arm forcefully, causing her to wince in pain. She
mouthed something to Nicole who shook her head slightly,
not understanding what Judith warned her about.

"If you want to see Ms. Chamberlain remain alive, I'd
suggest that you don't try and follow me. Come on my dear,
I've got a flight to catch." He shoved the reluctant Judith out
the open door.

Justin appeared ready to leap up at the mock politeness
of the ex-director.

"Justin, you really would have made a wonderful fall
guy and I thought I had the embezzlement pinned on you.
But, oh well. You were always too nosy for my taste and I
regret not finishing it fully the first time, pretty boy!" He
aimed the gun directly at Justin and Nicole screamed, pushing the suddenly still Justin forcefully out of the way. She
was a split second too late as Nicole saw a wave of blood
burst across Justin's forehead. An accompanying shot rang
out and she twisted her body around in a desperate attempt
to escape the flesh-seeking bullet, diving for the floor and
rolling for the protection afforded by the cream leather

couch. It was then she smelled the gasoline, so pungent Nicole knew the source could only be a few feet from her. That was what Judith had been trying to warn her about! She screamed again and pulled the bleeding Justin away from the telltale can standing between the couch and the side wall.

Justin stirred and fought her arm. "Come on!" shouted Nicole in his ear, her urgency rousing him enough to spur him into action and he lurched to his feet, staggering as blood streamed from his forehead and blinded him. Nicole grabbed his arm, dragging him to the open doorway as Robert Severns aimed again, this time not at the wounded Justin Zachary or her, but at the red gasoline can sitting in the middle of the ornate living room. The shot caused an instantaneous explosion that threw Nicole against the far wall. Flames shot up to the ceiling and within seconds the living area became an inferno. Through the intense heat Nicole searched desperately for Justin who had been flung to the other side of the entry hall, closer to the exit than she.

"Get out!" she screamed, and dove for the cool tiles of the foyer.

Justin propelled his tall frame through the door and grabbed her hand, dragging her onto the wide landing as flames and smoke pillowed through the door. They pulled themselves away from the door, coughing and fighting for breath as the beautiful condominium was consumed by the inferno.

A maroon Infinity backed up from the garage with a screech and Nicole saw Judith's terrified face peering through the front windshield. An elderly shorts-clad woman pulling a tiny Maltese dog on a short red leash gazed wide-eyed from her frozen spot on the walkway.

"Call the fire department!" Nicole barked before grabbing Justin's hand and plunging down the steep stairway two steps at a time. The white-haired woman broke into a run and turned into a sand-colored townhouse several doors down. Flames licked out of the open door and it would be only a matter of minutes before the entire upstairs unit collapsed. Justin and Nicole stumbled to the bottom of the stairs, chests heaving.

"Over there Nicole!' shouted Justin, as Robert Severns jerked the car into reverse. "He'll never let Judith out of this alive!" His frantic words motivated Nicole to dive for the police cruiser's door, thrusting it open and grabbing the high powered shotgun tucked into the console between the two front seats.

Well-practiced habit took over as she threw the gun to her shoulder and squeezed off a shot at the careening Infinity. The front tire exploded in a hail of rubber. The driver's seat window rolled down, the black eye of the .22 pointed directly at her. The car bucked and sputtered as Judith pummeled Robert Severns with clenched fists. His right arm jerked back and slapped her hard across the face. Her door suddenly burst open and Judith lunged from the rocking car, the ensuing struggle probably saving Nicole's life as Judith's legs desperately kicked against Robert Severn's chest as she tumbled onto the asphalt.

Justin's frantic shout of warning echoed as both she and Robert Severns fired simultaneously. Nicole tried to jerk to the left, the kick of the heavy gun helping propel her from his unerring aim. A searing pain exploded in her left upper shoulder, and as she fell she recognized her shot had shattered the front windshield of the Infinity, leaving a large gaping hole stained red around the edges and sending hairlike cracks throughout the windowpane. The sidewalk was hard and the pavement uncomfortably hot to her touch, but she couldn't seem to dislodge her burning cheek from its searing surface. Justin's muffled voice broke through the hot fog, calling her name and begging her to hold on, but finally the pain and heat won out and eased her into swirling darkness. She was never aware that her desperate lover tried to staunch the blood with his own recklessly torn-off shirt, crying for help as a mortified Judith watched everything she owned disappear completely in the matter of a few fiery minutes.

Chapter 23

Nicole had hated hospitals ever since the death of her parents, and the first thing she became aware of was the glaring lights and antiseptic smell of the operating room.

"Relax," urged a soothing male voice as a heavy mask issuing a strong sweet smell was placed over her nose and mouth. She wanted to ask about Justin and Judith and Charles, but words wouldn't cooperate so she simply closed her eyes and accepted the inevitable.

Bud lingered at her side when she awoke, holding her free hand and rubbing his thumb up and down its freckled back. Her other hand was connected to a fearsome looking IV that dripped a clear liquid, one drop every two seconds.

"Bud," she whispered, her mouth dry, her throat hurting fiercely.

"I'm here Nikki," he said, leaning over and kissing her cheek very lightly.

"I was shot," she declared, accepting the reality of Robert Severns' bullet.

"That you were my girl and only two minutes before the troops showed up. You have a wicked sense of timing Rookie. Here, take some ice." Bud always called her rookie when things went wrong.

"Judith?" Nicole asked, her voice wavering as she sucked on a cold cube.

"Looks like she'll be joining you in your quest for new living accommodations and except for a dandy of a black eye and some nasty scrapes to her right leg and arm, she's fine. That woman is a fighter. Reminds me of my Maggie. We may just want to recruit her."

"She'd be better off to stay in the personnel office. What about Charles?"

"A hairline fracture and a raise from B.W. Weston. Man's got it made." Bud chuckled.

"And Robert Severns?"

Bud looked steadily at her. "You shot him through the windshield, your bullet passing through his throat. He was killed instantly. Damn good shot for someone who only practices with paper outlines."

Nicole swallowed painfully, the realization that she had killed someone hitting her hard. Bud's hand patted and soothed. "It's going to be alright kiddo."

"And Justin?" she managed to ask.

Under a Desert Sky

"He had a nasty gash across the front of his forehead that bled a lot, but he's going to be fine. Doctor gave him a few stitches. It was his quick action that helped stop the bleeding in your shoulder."

"I guess he finally returned the favor then. We're even now," said Nicole desolately. "Is he here?"

Bud's look was evasive. "He stayed in for observation last night, but B.W. Weston picked him up this morning. Sounded like some heavy-duty Pow-Wow was about to happen. I'm sure he'll visit you later this evening. But right now you need to rest and do everything the nurses order."

"Yeah, yeah," complained Nicole, suddenly feeling very tired. She shut her eyes and drifted off again.

She awakened the second time as a portly nurse placed a large bouquet of flowers on her side table. The yellow vase was crammed with daisies, gladiolas and babies breath. The arrangement looked sunny and cheerful so why did she feel so depressed?

"Hello," Nicole began tentatively, and the nurse turned beaming.

"Why hello honey," she crooned, and Nicole read her nametag; 'Lucy Moore, R.N.' "Feeling any better?"

Nicole nodded.

"I bet you'd like your head raised a little so you can see all these lovely flowers." She rotated the crank located at the foot of her bed until Nicole said stop and then brought over a small white envelope.

Nicole found she couldn't open the blasted thing and turned helplessly to Nurse Moore. The heavy woman smiled and removed the card from the envelope. The card was brief and to the point and Nicole felt a sterile coldness wash over her as she read the brief missive.

Hope you're well soon Nicole. I'm leaving with B.W. Weston for Orlando this morning and won't be returning to the resort, but wanted to wish you the best in all of your life's endeavors. Thanks for everything. Justin.

Nicole read the note twice before dropping the card onto the floor. Now, as when she had suffered other great losses, tears evaded her. The nurse bustled around her and a meal was brought to her consisting of unappetizing strained foods of assorted colors, but she only sat motionless, misery her only focus. Three hours later she'd steeled herself to the reality of life without Justin and was ready for the Captain's visit, her face a grim mask. Suddenly, for the first time in her life, Nicole wondered if her job was more important than the tender caress of a man she knew she'd always love?

"You're looking a hell of a lot better," was Jerry's first comment as he approached her bedside. She sipped water through a straw and noted that once again he was the consummate professional in a dark blue suit and red tie.

"You should have been some business executive, not an overworked and under-appreciated police captain."

Under a Desert Sky

"Right on all accounts Nicole. I am under-appreciated but my staff loves me," he exaggerated, and Nicole forced a smile, wincing as a sharp pain shot through her left shoulder.

"How long am I going to have to endure this place?" asked Nicole, knowing she was not the best patient.

"What do I look like, a doctor?" he returned cockily. "Glad we didn't lose you Lewis." Jerry cleared his throat and appeared slightly embarrassed.

"Bud told me Judith's okay," Nicole said, switching to a less awkward subject.

"More than okay. Boy, if I weren't a married man . . ." He let the statement dangle and Nicole punched him weakly.

"How are Nancy and Lee?" Nicole asked carefully. Her superior's face became darker.

"Lee's on suspension. Nancy's taking it okay considering Lee has been her partner for over two years. She had her suspicions for a while, but still found Lee's betrayal hard to swallow. She's quite disillusioned right now and has asked for a couple weeks off to sort things out."

"Then I was right?" questioned Nicole sadly.

"When Bud relayed your suspicions I was flabbergasted. I called Internal Affairs and received the authorization to check out Lee's credit and bank accounts. Dusty discovered he was heavily in debt, even though he had more than ten grand coming in a month."

Nicole gasped. "He must be paid a lot more than me?"

"Robert Severns made sure of that. Once all the figures came in, Lee admitted he had been taking payoffs from various other sources for more than three years. Dealing with Severns was just a step up financially for him."

"Why did he need the extra money?" asked Nicole mystified.

"Remember all those weekends he talked about heading out golfing. He wasn't golfing, just betting on the horses. He even drove down to Mexico a couple times a month to gamble on the greyhounds. Lost a pile of money that way. Between the child support and bad habits, he had to come up with some extra cash. What a waste of a good man."

"And Robert Severns?"

"What a Jekell and Hyde he turned out to be. Mr. Nice Guy on the surface, while recruiting housekeepers for his girlie shows and magazines on the side. I think that deep down inside Severns believed the world owed him a living. He'd sing the sad song about how his wife had left him and took his money, but in reality, he was cheating on her, smiling that big smile of his all the time."

"So how did B.W. Weston figure it out?"

"After Weston tagged all the computers, he personally sent Zachary down here to investigate Severns. By this time Severns appeared to have transferred to Maui. What both Zachary and Weston didn't know was that Elena still fiddled with the numbers. Severns had Elena take the swing shift in the executive offices and guided her through the computer passwords using his cell phone. He was out of state with the perfect alibi, only Elena slipped up."

"Enrique," guessed Nicole.

"That's right. The housekeeper Rosa was wrong about thinking our Enrique would be angry that Elena was cheating on him. He didn't care as long as he had a cut of the pie."

"Blackmail?"

"One of the oldest games in the book; only the team of Elena and Enrique were no match for Bob Severns. He flew back to California under a different name, killed Elena and made it appear her boyfriend was the guilty party. When we started to squeeze Mr. Diaz though, it appeared that our bird was going to sing, and unfortunately he informed Severns that Zachary was nosing around. Dusty found out that the Lindsey file had been doctored to look like Justin and his family were taking payoffs. That was to be Bob's final gift to his successor."

"So the last part of the apparent suicide note from Richard was really to Justin. The part that said 'he' was right in his assumptions. But it had originally been a letter, not a suicide note, and Bob Severns just doctored it a little."

"Yeah," said Jerry, fiddling with the button on his cuff. "That's why the end of the letter trailed off. He'd been killed before he could finish his confession about his infidelity with Elena."

"How did Severns know Enrique was going to crack?" As she asked the question, Nicole suddenly knew the answer. "Lee."

"Yeah Lee. While I'm certain he didn't have any part in the actual murder of Enrique, Lee certainly sent him to his death by relaying what you had found out about the black-mail. Bob Severns couldn't afford to have Enrique talk."

"And Richard?"

"Poor Richard made the mistake of taking up Robert's offer of spending some 'time' with a couple of the girls, including Elena. Judith was seeing Richard secretly and when Richard threatened to expose what he'd discovered about the Lindsey file, Robert in turn threatened to tell Judith. You have to give the guy credit since he finally decided to confide in Justin Zachary. That sick bastard made Richard dictate that final tape under duress before he killed him and then Bob helped him along with the suicide."

"Poor Richard. I think basically he was a good man. So Scott and his mother Marjorie O'Toole had nothing to do with anything?"

"That's correct. In fact, we discovered it was Marjorie who phoned us with that anonymous tip regarding Richard's possible blackmail. Seems she was a little fond of Richard herself."

"Maybe if Richard had looked her way, she'd have possessed a sweeter disposition."

"Oh, I'm sure her disposition is about to improve. B.W. Weston's promoting her son to the hotel's directorship. I'm sure she'll also be moving up to a nice, air-conditioned office very soon."

Nicole shrugged. "Couldn't happen to a nicer gal," she mumbled and Jerry laughed. He reached over and patted her arm.

Under a Desert Sky

"You're looking a little tired. Try to get some rest." He rose and then suddenly remembered. "I forgot. I have a little present for you from an admirer." In his hand a plastic Elvis, looking about thirty, appeared; his hair slicked back and clad in tight jeans and a shiny ivory and black-striped shirt. Jerry turned the key located at the back of the music box and a boisterous rendition of "Jail-House Rock" sang out. Elvis jiggled his hips to the song and Nicole laughed.

"Bless Jesse's heart. This is definitely a keepsake to remind me of our adventures together." Jerry placed Elvis onto her portable food stand and looked measuring at her.

"I have B.W. Weston's number in Orlando if you want to call him about... um... anything?"

Nicole shook her head slowly. "No, I don't need to call him."

Captain Jerry Hernandez sighed and left her to her own thoughts as Elvis gyrated. She seemed very alone in the oversized bandages against the uncomfortable pillows. Damn this job anyhow!

Nicole endured the hospital and its overnice staff for a week before she begged Bud to enlist the Captain's aid in releasing her.

Bud and Jerry showed up with wide grins at 10 a.m. on Tuesday morning and slowly wheeled her out of the modern hospital facility. Nicole had never been happier in her life to vacate a place.

"Where we going?" she asked Bud and the Captain as they gingerly strapped her into the Captain's Bronco. She felt privileged since he only drove his pet vehicle on the weekend.

"Since you have managed to burn down your apartment," wise-cracked Bud, "as well as Judith's abode, you get the honor of staying with Maggie and me until we subsequently drive you crazy enough to force you to find a new place to live. Until then, you're our guest."

Tears welled up in Nicole's eyes as she gazed out of the Bronco's tinted window at the manicured lawns and swaying palm trees dotting every maintained corner of Palm Springs. Bud's middle-class house was the ultimate combination of noise and chaos. His two boys chased each other through the sprinklers while his pound-rescued German Shepherd barked and skirted the water, driven to a frenzy by the shouting boys.

"Welcome to paradise," grinned Bud as they pulled into the driveway. Maggie stood on the porch wearing a large red sundress and waving a damp dishtowel in her hand. She shaded her eyes as Jerry and Bud helped Nicole out of the car. Bud took Nicole's arm as Jerry removed her suitcase from the back. Nicole halted abruptly and pointed.

"What's that?"

"What?" answered Bud innocently, and Jerry whistled appreciatively.

Under a Desert Sky

A nearly new Harley-Davidson decorated with purple flames and equipped with a German WWI-style helmet resting on its padded seat sat in the driveway.

"You got the bike!" yelled Nicole, pleased to see a big smile plaster itself over Bud's wide face.

"Yes, the man was incomplete without that bike. So I relented and there it is," grinned Maggie.

"That must have cost a mint," said Jerry, shaking his dark head.

"Not when it's sold at police auction as confiscated property. I got it for a fourth of the price. Maggie said go ahead as long as I bought a matching helmet for her."

"What a bargain," chuckled Nicole, and let the two men help her into the house.

Maggie's house smelled of enchiladas and chili peppers. Nicole sipped on an iced tea with her feet up watching the Dodger ball game over the sounds of the boys splashing in the backyard pool. Maggie sang a song in Spanish and its melancholy tones sank Nicole further into depression. Between Justin and her there loomed the catch-all phrase, 'irreconcilable differences.'

"You doing okay?" came Maggie's voice from the kitchen and Nicole fought to put some life into her words.

"Just fine, Maggie. I really appreciate you guys busting me out of the hospital and putting me up."

"What are friends for?" smiled Maggie, chopping some green and red peppers. "You seem really down. Want to talk about it?"

"I'm sad about Richard and Elena and the whole mess. I keep seeing Elena's lovely sketches and wonder why she did what she did. And Lee? His decisions remain incomprehensible to me. What a waste of promising lives."

"So that's what's making you so sad?"" asked the heavy Cahuilla woman. "I thought it might have been that cute Zachary fellow?"

"I never thought of the word cute as describing him," joked Nicole.

"It's his Indian blood; makes him as sexy as hell," quipped Maggie. "You gonna call him?"

"Nope."

"Why not?"

"Because it's over. And when something is over, I let it go. I don't want to talk about it anymore, alright?" She rose stiffly as Maggie empathetic eyes followed her thoughtfully.

Ten days later Nicole started physical therapy and allowed Maggie to drive her around looking for a new place to live. After a dozen places, Nicole settled on a small two-bedroom condo located in Palm Desert. While a longer drive to the station, its lovely landscaped area interlaced with paved paths for walking and jogging was exactly what she wanted. Not that she was in any condition to jog. Physical therapy simply became new words for torture as Nicole resolutely gritted her teeth and worked the damaged shoulder. Jerry Hernandez had warned her she couldn't come back to work unless the therapist indicated she was at least 85 percent.

Moving slowly into the condominium and buying new furniture with the insurance money from the fire helped her maintain a purpose and not think about Justin Zachary too much. Her plan worked brilliantly, except at night when he intruded upon her dreams and scolded her for her pride. The condo took shape and personality, exuding a bright inviting decor with its light tan and white wicker furniture, but no matter how she rearranged the woven couch's pillows, every night the rooms echoed in empty mockery.

Jerry quietly told her one morning, over a month later, as she sat on her new couch accepting some of Grace's homemade tamales, that Justin Zachary had obtained a substantial promotion as building director for B.W. Weston's vast holdings. He was now down in Cancun finishing up the final details on the new resort scheduled to open within the month. Nicole listened politely and listlessly, but made no comment. Jerry shut his mouth tightly and wanted to curse. Nicole started back at the station amidst glowing accolades from her colleagues and Jerry Hernandez, but wanted nothing better than to crawl under her desk rather than hear their endless comments about her courage. It hadn't mattered what she did, she'd still lost the man she loved. It was Dusty who came to her rescue.

"Ever hear of the reluctant hero, guys? Cut the girl some slack." Slowly the comments died down and things seemed pretty back to normal within a few days. That is, except for Dusty and Nancy. Dusty lost a good twenty pounds and started working out at the local gym. Two weeks after Nicole had returned to work he strutted into the office and twirled around in front of her paper-laden desk, his shaggy hair cut and styled and thick glasses missing.

"Dusty," whispered Nicole. "Is that you?"

"No," said Dusty haughtily. "It's the new me. Or should I say, the me I've always wanted to be."

"Wow!" said Jerry, coming up behind Nicole. "It's amazing. You look great Dusty!"

"I know. But don't worry. I'm still the department computer guru; I'm just a good-looking one now. If Nancy calls, tell her I'll meet her for lunch as planned at the Veggie Cafe at 12:30." He scooped up a pile of papers from his desk and headed toward the Records Room.

"I think I liked him better before," suggested Jerry, scratching his head.

"I'm not sure what I think, but I'm going to withhold judgment. Looks like a wedding just might be in store."

"I'll warn Grace. She always likes an excuse to shop," Jerry said affectionately of his wife. "Three months," he bet.

"Two," countered Nicole. "Twenty bucks."

"You're on," agreed Jerry, returning to his office and the mound of paperwork stacked upon his desk.

Under a Desert Sky

Nicole picked up a missing child's folder and thirty minutes later set it down, not certain she'd made any progress. Her phone buzzed and she punched the flashing light.

"Lewis," she answered briskly.

"Zachary."

She finally made her throat work. "How are you doing Justin? I hear that congratulations are in order. That's quite a coup making Executive Building Director."

"I don't know. I just think B.W. Weston always rewards those who get shot in the line of duty with promotions." His joke fell flat as Nicole remained calmly silent. "And how are you?" he queried softly.

"Great. I'm working on a couple missing persons cases. Confined to deskwork until my shoulder is completely healed. After that I may start training Nancy Williams. She wants to start as an undercover detective in Vice. Tired of her old police blues."

"That's great," he said woodenly. Nicole became suddenly angry. Just what did he expect; that she was wasting away over their lost love, ready to trash everything she'd worked so hard for so she could ride off into the sunset with him?

"It *is* great. She's doing what she wants and her significant other is quite proud!"

The silence stretched between them until finally Justin broke the uncomfortable pause.

"I'm going to be in town the day after tomorrow to work with Scott for a couple of days. I was just wondering if you'd care to have dinner with me one night."

"Why?" asked Nicole bluntly.

"I don't know," he responded softly. "Old times sake maybe. Maybe we can talk about . . . things."

"I'm afraid I'm busy," she answered, even though it killed her.

"I see," he voiced, and she was positive he did. "Well, I wish you the best then," and the line went dead in her hand; dead like her heart.

Chapter 24

Some people might have said, 'How could you have let him go?' But Nicole wondered how could he have let her go? Whichever the truth, the outcome was bitter by all accounts. She worked diligently over the next couple months, closing several cases and opening others, always striving to keep the image of Justin's lean face from intruding at an idle moment. By the end of October she felt so restless and empty she often caught herself staring off into space at lull times during the day. Within moments she would visualize Justin's dark brown eyes and remember his lips gliding over her body and want to weep. Why couldn't she get over him?

Her new apartment was finally decorated. She, Sherri, and Judith had gone out half a dozen times to antique stores and finer-quality furniture showrooms to make the place exemplify what Nicole wanted to express. The final results were stunning. The master bedroom appeared soothing and feminine without being too frilly. She'd returned to the Native American motif, enjoying the symmetry of the geometric lines and subtleness of its muted tones. The computer room hosted a state-of-the-art computer table and new laptop, this time equipped with scanner and digital camera. She'd stenciled and wall-papered with the help of Maggie and Sherri, and in early October had a first-class housewarming. Everyone came; her co-workers, friends, and especially Jesse, Margie, and the irrepressible Sherri. All were dear friends and amidst toasts, laughter, and one nasty wine stain on the pristine Navajo carpet, the new condo was initiated.

But still the emptiness would not disappear. Filling it with work and outings with friends did nothing to erase the lonely nights or aimless weekends. At the end of October Sherri called to change all that.

"Hi girl," she said. "Do I have a recipe for relaxation for you!" Her African American friend always managed to cheer her up and today was no different as Nicole sat at her desk swamped by paperwork. Sunny and mild, it was the kind of day Palm Springs is famous for.

"A tax refund?" Nicole joked, trying to focus on what Sherri was saying.

"No... just a relaxing, got-no-business-to-attend-to kind of weekend. Are you game?"

"Maybe," said Nicole, fiddling with her pen.

Under a Desert Sky

"I rented a cabin in Idyllwild. We haven't been there for so long."

Nicole hadn't ventured to the beautiful spot since she'd hidden out with Justin Zachary in Pine Cove nearly four months ago.

"That's true," returned Nicole, not sure she wanted to return to the San Jacinto Mountains.

"It's a two-bedroom log cabin near Strawberry Creek, not far from Humber Park. It's nicely decorated and just waiting for two overworked career women."

Maybe it was the reference to 'overworked career women,' that decided Nicole. "I'd love to come."

"I'm heading up around noon tomorrow to put up groceries and stuff, but you can arrive anytime you want."

"That's great," said Nicole, "because I work until five. I'll probably make it up sometime between 6:30 and 7:00."

"Be sure to bring some warm evening clothes. It's starting to get nippy up there. If you've got a pencil, here are the directions." Within minutes all was settled.

The traffic on Friday was unusually heavy and by the time Nicole ascended the narrow road past Garner Valley, she was immensely thankful for a change to her mundane routine. Upon passing a large semi-truck bearing the logo of a major supermarket chain, she managed to pick up some speed on Highway 74. It had turned dark by the time she passed the Elementary School located in Idyllwild proper and Nicole

379

rolled down her Corolla's window, allowing the heavy vanilla smell of the Jeffrey Pines to permeate the inside of the small car. Making a right on North Circle Drive she began climbing again. Unfortunately, it was too dark to glimpse Lily Rock, but she hoped to take a hike in the morning and perhaps collect a couple of the nice sugar pine cones that could be found in abundance near Fern Valley.

She turned a hard right and then another, following a narrow paved road where the cabins were not clustered so closely together or setting right on the road. One more left turn and she turned onto a short cul-de-sac. Sherri had indicated the cabin was at the very end of the street, so she crept up slowly and let her headlights shine on the brass-plated number. This had to be the place. Even in the dark, with only a couple porch lights on, she could see the lovely lines of the log cabin with its accompanying large deck off the right-hand side. As she rolled up her car window she caught a whiff of smoke and smiled. Sherri had already started a fire.

Mounting the six steps to the deck, she noted how nicely the cabin was finished off. Two storied, the top stained glass window was pentagon shaped and a huge stone chimney broke through the rustic roof. She smiled again and opened the door, not bothering to knock.

"Hi Sherri," she called, and paused just within the cabin's entryway, noting the bright pine-scented fire in a river rock fireplace burning to her left. The perfect spacing of the logs throughout the cabin gave it a rustic, comfortable feel. Nicole swung her weekend bag off her shoulder and deposited it near the brown and red couch that hugged the fireplace corner. The kitchen was beautiful and compact with all the amenities including a curving long counter and center island. On the stove bubbled a large pot of something that smelled delicious and she could see the faint glow of the oven light indicating something baking. Bless Sherri's heart; she certainly knew how to pull out the welcome carpet!

Nicole heard a creaking sound to the right and looked up, her heart and throat suddenly paralyzed. Justin was clad comfortably in faded blue jeans and an old olive green sweatshirt. Scuffed tennis shoes and white crew socks completed the outfit, but Nicole was certain she had never seen anyone look so good.

"Hello Nicole," he said softly, descending the pine staircase.

"Hello yourself," she managed to croak out, noting his lean form and confident bearing.

"I hope you're not angry. I had to bribe Sherri with a promise of obtaining some courtside Lakers seats to get you up here. She's one tough customer."

Nicole said nothing; she couldn't. He gazed at her with those dark chocolate eyes, searching her taunt face and jeans-clad form.

"You look thin Nicole. Are you fully healed?"

"Yes, I'm perfectly alright." She studied her hiking boots; unable to voice anything that could slightly reflect the way she felt. He moved into the kitchen and stirred the bubbling pot on the stove.

"Hope you like potato soup. It's my mother's recipe for cold nights. I also made some corn bread and baked chicken." He checked in the oven and adjusted the knobs on front of the door before straightening.

"Want to help me make a salad?'

"Okay," said Nicole, trying to stay calm.

"I have something for you," he stated quietly. "It's from Brian Weston."

For a moment she looked puzzled. "B.W. Weston?"

"That's right. When he heard I was going to try and see you, he asked me to give you this." He slid a long white envelope with her name written in bold black letters across the top of the tiled kitchen counter.

Certain it was a thank you for the Gonzalez case, she broke open the seal while Justin returned to the stove, giving the soup another stir and then opening the well-stocked refrigerator. The letter was to the point and very clear in its intentions.

"He's offering me a job," she blurted out.

"I knew he was going to," said Justin, not turning around. He'd removed some bright red tomatoes and romaine lettuce and began washing them in the sink. Were his tense brown fingers really trembling?

"And you approved?"

"I told him you were the best person for the job, even putting my personal feelings aside."

"So he knew all about us?"

382

Under a Desert Sky

Justin turned slowly, a dripping tomato in his lean hand. "He asked me why I was so miserable while working on the Cancun project. I ended up telling him everything. After hearing for nearly a week what a damn fool I was for letting you go, he came up with the 'Weston Plan.'"

"The Weston Plan?"

"The plan to solve all the problems between Justin Zachary and Nicole Lewis, enabling them to talk about the really important issues between them, like love and sex and babies and marriage." He replaced the tomato on the counter and wiped his hands on a dishtowel.

"He told me that a woman as highly intelligent and totally dedicated to her work as you should be empowered to do as she wishes career-wise by the man who truly loves her. He understood my fears for your life, especially after Robert Severns shot you, but mentioned how often I fly or take taxis driven by uncouth drivers. My life is always at risk too. So… he came up with something that might prove agreeable to both of us."

"Chief Security Director of Weston Enterprises?"

"That's it. While in Cancun it became clear the hotel was already being ripped off by some of the locals because the resort did not implement inadequate security measures. B.W. is convinced that if he installs proper security measures, freedom from embezzlement, theft, and equipment and material overrides will save him millions of dollars. Weston Enterprises has thirty-eight hotels and resorts, with plans for an additional four already on the board. It behooves him and the company to ensure that his money and goods don't go walking."

"And you convinced him I would be willing to take the job?"

"I actually told him you'd probably throw the offer back in my face, but he seemed determined to make you the proposal anyway. You'd, ah..." he seemed at a loss for words. "You'd be able to travel with me while I checked and monitored the different resorts; me managing the growth and health of the resorts and you dealing with the stop/loss procedures. I just want you to know that the offer stands no matter what you decide about me. One is not contingent upon the other. But... please consider *all* of the offer."

Nicole turned her back on Justin and the delicious smelling kitchen and gazed into the fire blazing in the corner of the big room.

"I like this cabin," she said irrelevantly.

"I'm so glad. I bought it when I was down here at the end of August to see Scott Adams. Even then, I hoped that maybe, if we returned to a place we'd once been so close, you'd agree to see me. That just maybe you'd give me another chance to try and work it out." He stumbled for words; the man to who words had always come so easily.

"Do you have B.W.'s number? I believe I owe him an answer personally."

Justin swallowed deeply, his normally brown face suddenly pale. "Of course," he managed, and dug around a top drawer, finally pulling out a zippered organizer. He found the page and pointing a shaking finger at the number, gestured to the wall phone. "Be my guest."

Though it was nearly 10 p.m. on the East coast, Nicole picked up the phone and punched in eleven digits. B.W.'s gruff voice loudly answered just after the second ring.

"This'd better be good," he growled.

"As sweet as always," said Nicole, unfazed by his grouchy tone. "This is Nicole Lewis, calling from California in regards to the job offer submitted to me this evening by Justin Zachary."

"Well girl," he barked. "Are you going to be an idiot like your lovelorn counterpart Zachary, or are you going to put us all out of our misery and accept the damn job?"

"I accept the damn job."

"Well, that's great. I'll fly you out to Orlando mid next week and we'll do some paper signing. I suppose you want to know your salary?"

"Well?" she hesitated, and then gasped as he mentioned a figure in the six digits that way more than doubled her present salary. Justin had turned away from her to face the opposite kitchen wall, his back turned to her, palms pressing flat upon the counter before him. She barely heard what B.W. was saying, wanting only to touch Justin's shaking shoulders; so she cut him off.

"We'll discuss all that next week Mr. Weston. I've gotta go."

She hung up the phone slowly and walked around the open counter, finally placing her hands upon Justin's shoulders and turning him about to face her. Tears shone in his eyes.

"I love you," she whispered, and standing on tiptoe kissed him tenderly upon the mouth. His arms closed tightly around her in a bear hug and she could feel his chest heaving.

"Nicole," he sighed huskily. "I just wasn't sure. It was only a long shot."

"It was my stupid pride getting in the way. I couldn't compromise. I was so stubborn that I didn't hear the love in your voice when you said how much my job scared you. I'm so sorry Justin and because of it we've wasted so much time."

"Yes, but never again," he promised, and gave her in a long sweet kiss.

"Are there any bedrooms in this place?"

"Thee of them, all upstairs," he said, a fiery light suffusing his eyes.

She gazed for a long moment into his dark face, and taking his hand pulled him toward her.

"I think you'd better turn off the oven and stove. We'll have to come back to it later." And so they did; much, much later.

Epilogue

It was a strange assortment of characters making up those in attendance at Justin and Nicole's wedding. Of course Nicole's brother David was present with his wife, and Nicole's small niece made a lovely flower girl, dressed so prettily in violet frills and ruffles. Carrie dropped the pink rose petals carefully across the beige carpet of the Lutheran church as she daintily strutted up the aisle under the watchful eyes of her proud mother and father.

Justin's mother was there as well, resplendent in a long slender tan dress that reflected the pride of her Sioux heritage. Her thick hair, only faintly streaked with gray, was twisted into a lovely French braid that hung halfway down her back. Justin's sister and her portly jovial husband watched in disbelief as Justin stood so intent and solemn on his wedding day, since both had long ago given up on her older brother ever marrying.

But it was the opulent best man that stole the scene. Clad in a white tux, opened wide at the neck, that greatly resembled one of the last outfits ever worn by his idol, Jesse had even slicked back his hair to resemble Elvis. He'd checked and re-checked his vest pocket over a dozen times to be certain that the simple gold ring would be available at the exact moment needed.

"See," he whispered dramatically to the groom as he pointed to himself. "Elvis *is* alive." Justin smiled broadly, pleased at his choice of best man and assured that the gaudily clad youth would do a perfect job as he patiently awaited his bride-to-be. Buddy Ochoa shifted anxiously from one foot to the other, clad uncomfortably in a powder gray tuxedo whose top button kept popping open, much to the amusement of his wife. Positioned on the opposite side of Jesse, he appeared to the casual onlooker far more nervous than the groom, who waited in his perfectly fitting dark gray tuxedo, so content and expectant.

Nicole appeared at the end of the aisle on the arm of none other than Captain Hernandez, who as always was dressed impeccably; this time in a precise-fitting powder gray tux. He smiled at the lovely woman next to him who had donned a simple full white gown for the occasion and wore tiny yellow daisies in her beautifully braided chestnut hair. B.W. Weston watched as the couple glided past and growled at his gentle wife who patted him sympathetically on the arm.

Under a Desert Sky

"Nicole had to let Jerry take the place of her father dear. She barely knows you."

"Humph," mumbled Brian Weston. He had wanted that honor badly, having fallen for the straight-backed young woman who had stood up under his sharp tongue and focused scrutiny the first time he had met her in Jerry Hernandez's office. The bride turned and smiled openly at him and his discontent fell miraculously away. Justin Zachary was one lucky man. Nicole was the first woman who remotely reminded Brian of his petite wife; the one who ruled his heart and his house. Justin had been fortunate to find someone as fine as his Veronica. He glanced at the slender woman next to him and smiled conspiratorially. He and Jerry had booked a week in Hawaii to surprise their own wives to a second honeymoon. He had tried to convince Justin to join him, but the young executive had balked politely.

"My bride and I have a special affinity for the San Jacinto Mountains," was his calm reply, and Brian could not argue with a man so self-assured and confident about what would please his new wife.

After the vows were exchanged, a pause came in the solemn ceremony. Jesse cleared his throat as the background music swelled. His deep voice carried Elvis' "Love Me Tender" to a new high and the audience smiled happily. Nancy nestled close to the much slimmer Dusty, and seated by them were Grace Hernandez and Bud's beloved Maggie.

They watched Jesse sing while tears glistened in their dark eyes, moved by his clear-pitched tones.

Toward the rear, Scott Adams sat quietly besides a subdued Judith Chamberlain. He reached a hand out and took her slim one, squeezing gently. She turned her lovely blonde head to him and shook it softly, forcing him to drop her hand. The attraction between them wasn't to be enough in their lives, and thus the relationship was over before it could even begin.

Judith wished Richard could be with them to watch this simple ceremony and hear the lovely, even tones of the mentally-handicapped boy sing the glad couple onto their union. She sincerely hoped that the poor girl Elena, who'd enabled all of them to come together as a group today, had finally found some of the true peace and happiness that had eluded her all her life. She watched with batted breath as Justin slipped the eternity ring onto Nicole's slim finger and sighed. It was truly a beautiful day under the desert sky.

THE END

Printed in the United States
57187LVS00001BA/1-3